Chasing Home

A CHERRY PEAK NOVEL

HANNAH COWAN

First Edition

ISBN: 978-1-990804-40-3

Cover designed by: Mary @booksnmoods

Edited and proofed by: Sandra @oneloveediting

Interior Illustrations by: Jordan Burns @joburns.reads

STEELE RANCH
STEELE RANCH
WELCOME TO CHERRY PEAK CANADA
TOWN HALL
FIRE STATION
BEAUTIFULLY BOLD
THISTLE & THORN
SCHOOL
COFFEE SHOP
ANNA'S HOUSE
POPPY'S HOUSE
FARMER'S MARKET
PEAKSIDE
BRYCE'S HOUSE
RUSTIC RIDGE
MADE BY @JOBURNS.DESIGNS

For my real-life girl gang. Thank you for taking me in and loving me for all that I am. You've been my inspiration for the love and friendship between Bryce, Poppy, Anna, and Aurora, and I am forever grateful.

PROLOGUE

Johnny

I'm late. It's not much of a surprise, but with Bryce amongst the friends waiting for me at Peakside, I know I'll hear about my tardiness regardless. My friend's got an obsession with punctuality that borders on straight up crazy.

"Our impending doom is completely your fault," I say, glancing across the truck at Darren.

The volunteer firefighter ignores me, his mind somewhere else tonight. Most likely on the messy status of his relationship with his daughter's mother. It's tricky territory.

"How are you doing?" I ask, softening my tone.

"I'm fine."

It's the most obvious lie I've ever heard. Who's fine after watching their ex-wife drive off with the daughter they share custody of and a new man he's hardly met? He needs a drink the most out of everyone we're meeting at the bar.

"Well, I'm here if you want to talk."

He tips his chin jerkily. "Thank you. Sorry you saw all that."

"It's not a big deal. I'm glad you weren't alone."

"I'm a grown man. I can handle my own shit," he grunts.

His anger is a front for a deep feeling of hurt, so I don't take offense to it. Fuck me, I'd be pissed with everyone and everything if I were in his shoes.

"I can drop you off somewhere else if you don't want to go to Peakside," I offer.

"If I don't go, Poppy will know something's up. It's fine."

"I'm sure your sister is well and truly distracted right now. And if not, I can make sure she doesn't worry tonight. Tomorrow, I make no promises."

Darren shifts his body to look at me now. His blank expression makes my chest pang, but I keep my concern to myself.

"Leave it. This isn't the first time I've been in this position, and it won't be the fucking last either if I know Sasha."

"It still ain't right, Darren. We're all here for you. Anytime."

"I know. I appreciate it. Now, don't mention my sister being distracted again, you fucking dick. I hear enough about her and Garrison from our mother. Don't need it from you too."

I bark a laugh, offering a completely half-ass sympathetic smile. "You poor thing."

"Fuck off."

"Alright, alright. No more talking about your sister and my best friend. I'm sure they're sitting at the table lookin' pretty right now and nothing more," I say, thickening the drawl in my voice.

His hand flies toward me at lightning speed, and I jerk the wheel to avoid being smacked upside the head. Thank fuck the road is empty and no deer decided to prance into my front bumper or through my windshield.

Darren acts tough, but he likes his sister's boyfriend enough. Myself, on the other hand, I love the guy. Garrison Beckett isn't my usual type'a friend, but he's good people. You just have to push past his walls of steel to get to that ooey-gooey inside.

The rest of the drive to Peakside is spent in a comfortable silence, Darren not up for more talking about his ex or sister or much of anything. I don't mind the silence, although I much prefer filling it. Talking is my thing, as outgoing as I am. The quiet bores me.

The moment I pull up outside the bar, Darren's up and out of the truck before I've shifted it into park. He leaves me with a quick wave as he weaves around the few vehicles in the parking lot and ducks inside the building. His first stop will be at the bar. A tall glass of whiskey will be in his hand the moment I step inside.

Poor guy. He's been through the goddamn wringer this past year.

I pull my truck keys from the ignition and step into the night. Once my boots hit the pavement, I reach up to bend the brim of my baseball cap and then readjust the buckle on my belt before chasing after Darren.

It's been a scorching summer, and tonight, that June heat lingers, slipping its sweat-slicked fingers along the back of my neck. My farmer's tan is atrocious. To the point I've been considering stripping my clothes off during the day just to try and tan my bright white ass and chest.

Wade Steele would kick my ass three ways to Sunday if I walked around his ranch with my dick out, though. So it's best I keep my clothes on while I'm working unless I'm itching for punishment.

Peakside is as busy as it's ever been when I step inside. The music is loud, a handful of couples out on the makeshift dance floor two-stepping along with it. Some do a good job, while others look like they've never heard a steady country beat in their lives.

I suck back a laugh as I lock onto Poppy and Garrison. Poppy leads him through the simplest dance I've ever seen, and he manages to only stumble a few times. The stuffy, arrogant CEO who arrived in Cherry Peak two months ago now is a far cry from the guy I see today, holding his woman like he's terrified of ever letting her go again. I won't say I'm responsible for their relationship, but I'm not about to deny that I had something to do with it. Or rather, something to do with kicking his ass into gear when he needed it.

The next couple I find is Brody and Anna, the most well-known duo in this town due to Brody's country music career. Goddamn, everywhere I look, happy couples greet me. It's a kick to a romantic man's gut. I feel the tip of the boot against my ribs, the impact nearly pushing the air from my lungs.

Avoiding the dance floor, I loop around the outside of it and then stall, my head going empty in a blink. Air whooshes through my ears before everything comes flooding back, creating a pulse in my brain that should hurt but doesn't.

Her.

The woman sitting all alone at the table my friends and I always occupy is the prettiest fucking thing I've ever seen. Long, dirty-blonde hair with golden streaks, full pink lips that naturally lift on the right side, and eyes that I want on me. Stormy ocean-blue ones. The colour of rough waves beneath the helm of a ship.

They're dim, dull, despite the startling colour. Her long fingers tap on the edge of the table, over the scratched wood and years' worth of stains that just won't come off no matter how hard they're scrubbed at. She watches the couples dancing but makes no move to get up and join them. I want to know why.

The moment she looks up, as if feeling the weight of my stare on her, I'm moving. Making a beeline in her direction, my long legs eat up the space between us. A few people turn to stare at me as I sidestep out of their way, not risking looking away from the woman to watch where I'm going. One blink and I fear she'd be gone. A figment of my imagination. A dream, maybe.

My heart is racing, thumping so damn hard against my ribs that I'm scared it'll burst right through them. I don't stop walking until I'm standing in front of the table, my breaths huffed as I stare down at her in awe.

Finally, our eyes lock, and just like that, I know I need to dance with her. Need just a single moment in her presence, with her in my arms, before the moment disappears.

"Hi," I say, offering her a shaky hand. "Feel like dancing with me?"

She blinks slowly, digesting both my sudden presence and question. Her posture straightens, and I know I've come on too strong, but I don't give a shit. Now isn't the time for subtle.

"I don't know how to dance," she says, the rough rasp in her voice sounding far too natural. I feel the effect of it deep in my gut as it burns hot.

"I'm a damn good dancer, darlin'. I promise I won't let you slip up."

"Promises from a stranger don't mean much to me."

"So let's not be strangers. I'll tell you all about myself while we're dancin'."

I grin, wide and bright, knowing that both my dimples are on display and loving the way she can't help but glance at them. Some of her steel softens, and I take advantage of the change.

I lean down and slip both of her hands into mine, using them to turn her in the booth until she faces me. She shakes her head but doesn't pull away. Her soft hands stay tucked inside my loose hold.

"A woman like you deserves to dance."

She lifts her brow, staring me down. "A woman like me?"

"A woman beautiful enough to make a grown man's knees shake at the sight of you. To have him tripping over his feet just to get over to you before someone else swoops in."

"Do you even know my name?" she asks.

"'Course I do, Aurora." It rolls off my tongue far more seductively than I meant it to, but fuck does it ever sound good.

She's Anna's new employee. The new girl in town that two weeks ago stumbled in out of nowhere. Nobody knows a damn thing about her. But I want to.

I'm incredibly fucking curious about her now.

Her cheeks turn a soft pink, and those plump lips part on

words that get lost in the music around us. I tug her up and out of the booth before sweeping her into my arms and leading us into a slow, easy sway between the tables.

She's stiff, her eyes wide. I wait for her to shove me off. Instead, a beat later, her hand settles on my shoulder. I keep a hand on her round hip, ensuring my touch is respectful despite every inch of me screaming to explore the soft, curvy body so close to mine.

"You've drawn a crowd, Johnny," she whispers, tipping her head back to stare up at me.

She's tall, but the way she still has to crane her head to look at me right now has my pride tripling in size.

"You know my name."

"And I was expecting you to be wearing a cowboy hat tonight," she says.

"Disappointed?"

I spin us around, glancing over the top of her head to find Poppy and Garrison and Brody and Anna watching us without a care of how obvious they appear. Ignoring them, I give Aurora's hand a squeeze and pull her a hair closer.

"Not disappointed. Just surprised," she says.

I can't keep from smiling again as I wink. "If I had brought it, I'd have already set it on your pretty head."

"And that's a bad thing? Don't think I'd look good beneath it?"

Oh, we're flirting now, are we? I'm a downright feral beast beneath my calm exterior. Her perfume drifts up my nose, and I swallow a groan.

Dipping my head, I bring my lips to the hot shell of her ear and say, "No doubt in my mind you'd look perfect beneath it. But there's a rule when it comes to a man settin' his hat on a woman, Aurora."

Her breath hitches. "A rule?"

"Curious now?"

"You know I am," she mutters, jerking her head to the side so I'm forced to give her space again.

"I'll tell you the rule if you keep dancing with me," I barter.

"I'm already dancing with you."

"I want more time."

"I wasn't even going to come tonight. I've given you enough of my time."

Her attitude makes me stiffen in my jeans. I fight the urge to readjust myself and spin us around again, this time maneuvering so she can roll out along my extended arm without hitting a table. Her plain tan sandals scuff along the floor when I pull her back into my grasp and quicken our pace.

"I can beg if you want. I'm not above it. Just don't make me get down on the floor. It's filthy," I tease.

Her eyes aren't dull anymore. They're alive, bright, the blue nearly glittering. They light up her face like this. If I didn't know any better, I'd assume she's having fun with me right now.

She rolls her lips together before letting the corner of her mouth tug into a half-smile. "Something tells me you don't mind getting filthy."

"I sure as shit don't. But not here. I have a feeling the moment I let you go, you'll take off on me."

Her throat strains with a swallow that I nearly miss behind the curtain of her wavy hair. My fingers itch to touch the shiny strands just a single time. But I keep my hands where they are, one on her waist and the other wrapped around her fingers.

"You're smart," she replies.

"So why haven't you shoved me off yet? I'd hate it, but I'd let you go."

Her fingers splay over my shoulder, and I fight off a shiver when she lowers them to my bicep, keeping them there. The soft prick of her nails through my shirt is criminal. A threat or a promise, I'm not sure yet.

I'm out of my depth here right now. Not once in my life have

I experienced anything like this before. Love at first sight or something cheesy like that. Yeah, it's gotta be. Or close to it.

"I don't know," she answers honestly, her perfectly plucked brows scrunching together. They're thick and bold but somehow work on her features without being too much.

"Just let go, then. Let yourself have fun." *With me,* I don't say. It goes without saying.

Another song starts, this one slower than the previous ones. I almost laugh when I recognize the male voice on the track. They do this every damn time Brody's here, either to bug him or to flatter him, I'm not fucking sure. He hates it either way.

I dip my chin and chase Aurora's gaze as she attempts to keep it darting around the bar. Her expression has shifted in the past few seconds. To one of concern, fear maybe. My mind runs laps, attempting to come up with something to say to make her stay or to recall what it was exactly that could have sparked this.

She doesn't give me the chance.

As if struck by a realization of something, she drops her hand from my arm and yanks her hand from mine. I freeze, taking a gutted step backward as she twirls and grabs a long-strapped black purse from the booth and loops it over her head.

My throat is dry as I blurt out, "Don't go."

"You got your dance, but I'm not here for fun." She doesn't look at me when she adds, "Bye, Johnny."

By the time I get myself to move, she's already shoving open the door and all but leaping into the night. I stare at the door and lean back against the table behind me, hoping to fuck it will support my weight because my legs are doing a piss-poor job of it.

I should chase after her, right? *Fuck,* no, I shouldn't. In the few minutes I just spent with her, something tells me she wouldn't appreciate me following after her like a desperate fool.

No, for now, I'll let her run. But I'm far from done getting to know Aurora, and I intend on learning all I can.

Soon.

It would be a crime against the universe not to, after all.

1

Aurora

1 MONTH LATER

Will there ever come a time where I don't skip breakfast and then complain an hour into my shift about how hungry I am? Probably not.

My stomach growls as I recline in my wheely chair and spread my legs out beneath the front desk, letting my eyes drift shut. There are snacks in the back room, but I'm too dog-tired to get up and search for them.

Anna, my boss, offered to pick me up something for lunch on her way back to work, and like an utter idiot, I turned her down the way I have since she offered me a job here six weeks ago. It's only a matter of time before she stops asking altogether. The only reason she hasn't yet is that she's too nice of a person. A bit of a momma bear, honestly.

Curling my body forward, I scoot toward the desk and plonk my forehead against it. My nails are blunt and uneven from my new habit of biting them raw, and as I rub them back and forth over my knee, they scratch at my skin. A manicure would be a good choice. That or some pants instead of the same pair of denim shorts I've worn every day in this disgusting summer heat.

I must have missed the memo where Alberta's supposed to get hotter than Satan's asshole in July because I don't remember it ever being this hot in the past thirty years of my life. Yeah, it gets hot in the summer, but I feel like every summer, the top temperature climbs a few degrees. By the time I'm fifty, I'll probably be better off living in Australia.

When I packed my suitcase and booked ass to Cherry Peak, I wasn't thinking of summer. I packed with only one thing on my mind: finding answers. My lack of common sense is why I settled into my shitty rental with a suitcase full of socks, a handful of pairs of sweatpants, one single bra and pair of shorts, and too many baggy crewnecks. I clearly reached for my comfort clothes and not much else.

Go fucking figure.

A buzzing sounds from the desk, and I groan, slapping a hand over my phone before looking up at the screen.

> Mom: Good morning, Aura. Can you let me know you're alive so I don't have to keep thinking the worst?

I swipe the message away and go to set my phone down when another pops up.

> Mom: I love you, you know? Always. I'm sorry.

Dropping the phone to the desk harder than necessary, I contemplate whether or not it's acceptable to block your mother's phone number from your phone. If nobody knew that I had but me . . . no. Not yet.

Happy, high-pitched chatter sounds from outside the salon before two women swing open the door, making the bell above it chime. The first woman, the one with short brown hair that's been twisted into a bun and threaded through the back hole of an old baseball cap, is Anna, the owner of Thistle and Thorn, the only hair salon in town. She's beautiful, with a wide, comforting grin that never seems to waver, eyes the colour of hazelnuts, and a tiny nose that should look out of place on her features but fits her perfectly.

Her entire personality is the complete opposite of the woman who follows her inside. Bryce, one of her best friends, is the sharp to her smooth. The cool to her warm. While intimidating as fuck, she's also my favourite of the women I've gotten to know in Cherry Peak.

Bryce's glacial-blue eyes land on me once she's finished taking in the empty salon. She heads right for the desk before leaning two tattooed arms against the edge. They're bare, her lack of suffocating, hideous work clothes obvious as I get a full view of the piece of artwork on her left forearm.

Just like the first time I saw it, I can't help but stare, tracing my eyes over the scene and the skill that was used to create such a thing of beauty. Whoever the artist was that created the piece is insanely talented.

There's a story in the image, from the densely forested background, the cherry blossom tree that stands front and centre, to the cobra wrapped around one extended branch with its collar flared and fangs out. A leopard pokes its head around the trunk of the tree, lips curled and one thick paw set in front as if it's contemplating leaping at the viewer. The storm clouds above the trees add something to the tattoo that ties it all together in a beautiful way.

Usually, the high-collared button-up blouse that she wears for work hides nearly all of her tattoos, so it's a bit shocking to see her in a jean skirt that only reaches the middle of her thighs and a cropped band tee.

"No work today?" I ask her.

"The office is shut down for the rest of the week. A water line broke and flooded the back rooms."

"It smells like sewage all down Main Street," Anna says, scrunching her nose.

She grabs her black apron from its hook beside her station and slips it over her head before tying it at her back. It's long enough to hit just below her knees, hiding her cut-off jean shorts and the oversized rodeo tee she has tied above her waistband.

"Maybe that's the shit under your boots that's stinking. You've been fully introduced to ranch life, baby girl," Bryce says, one corner of her mouth lifted into a smirk.

She turns and leans her butt against the desk, slinging one leg in front of the other so her black cowboy boots touch at the ankle. Between her, Anna, and the third member of their group, Poppy, it's a bit disconcerting how often they wear cowboy boots. I've never worn a pair before, and I can't say I have the undying urge to either. Especially at work.

Anna's are a lot more subtle than Bryce's black ones or Poppy's hot pink pair. At least the ones she wears to work are.

Flinging a finger into the air, Anna points at Bryce. "You're rude."

"You're just figuring that out?"

"True. It's my fault for letting you hang around. But I'm not about to turn down free help. Now, get to work. The inventory sheets are on the desk," Anna says, waving a hand in my direction while she starts sorting her station.

I lift a brow at Bryce as she turns her head to look back at me and extends her hand. The stack of papers on the desk includes everything that she needs to get started on the weekly inventory check, but usually, I'm the one in charge of it. I hover my fingers over the sheets but don't hand them over to her just yet.

"Hold up. You're not trying to steal my job, are you?" I ask.

Bryce snorts. "You wish. No, I'm not into the whole salon thing."

"But you're into the whole office thing?" Anna counters, clucking her tongue.

"I'm not into either, but you're not my father, so it's easier to say no to you."

"Ah, daddy issues," I mutter.

Bryce snags the papers from the desk before I can stop her. "You sound like you have experience with that specific ailment."

"You could say that."

"Wanna elaborate?"

"Nope," I say, popping the *p*.

She nods, letting it go. "Fair enough."

With Bryce, it's always that easy. She has a big heart inside that iron shell of hers, but she knows when to use it and when to keep it tucked away. Her sense of understanding is one of the biggest reasons why I connected with her so quickly and easily.

I'm not a talker. I don't share and gush to people about my life or problems often, and being here in Cherry Peak these past six weeks hasn't changed that. Even if Anna loves to try and wiggle her way inside my brain more often than not.

I don't dislike that about her, but it's just different than Bryce's cool understanding. I'm still unsure if I fit into their group at all. Despite how willing they've all been to take me under their wing, I've just always been more of a lone wolf. This new sense of friendship with not only one woman but three terrifies me. Makes discomfort wiggle beneath my skin.

I'm grateful for the job Anna gave me after I stumbled inside the salon on my first day in town. Although I was expecting someone entirely different to greet me the moment I busted through the door. My entire trip here was counting on it. So, Anna's offer helped bank some of my disappointment.

I still haven't figured out exactly what I'm going to do now that the person I was searching for has just up and disappeared. Maybe that's played a part in why I haven't let these women into my life yet. Not deep enough for it to mean much more than a friendly conversation here and there and a casual Saturday night out when they drag me out with them.

If I'm to leave any day now, wouldn't it be cruel to grow close to them?

"Are you coming out with us Saturday night, Rory? Poppy and Garrison should be back in town," Anna says, finished with preparing her station.

It's only her in today, and with one final client left on the schedule, I know we're both itching to go home. Thistle and Thorn isn't a boring place to work by any means, but some days drag more than others.

I prop my chin on my palm and lean over the desk. "I'm not sure."

"If you're attempting to become a hermit, I should warn you that that doesn't really work here in CP," Bryce says, thumbing through the stack of papers in her hand before snagging a pen from the cup beside my arm.

"I'm not becoming a hermit."

Anna comes over to us, looking down at me with a deadpan expression. "Yes, you totally are."

"I've always preferred having time to myself."

"What do you even do in that house of yours, anyway?" Bryce asks.

"Lots of things."

Anna nods heavily. "Go on."

"Sit on the back porch. Watch TV. And I don't have to explain myself to either of you," I mutter, folding myself back in the chair to create more distance between them and me.

Bryce starts writing on the inventory papers, her script ungodly messy. "The house you're living in is one thunderstorm away from collapsing on you in your sleep. Don't blame us for not wanting to find you trapped beneath a piece of rotted wood with a squirrel eating your toes."

I scrunch my nose. "That is so grossly detailed."

"It could happen."

Anna doesn't look disturbed by her friend at all. Her expression is warm and soft as she says, "I understand if you don't want to come out. I overstep sometimes because I've been in your position and didn't know how badly I needed some genuine fun until I had it shoved beneath my nose."

I relax slightly, my walls softening. "Thank you. I'll think about it."

"It's your funeral. I'll keep an eye on your house for squirrels," Bryce says before taking her papers and heading toward the storage room.

Anna and I watch her go. I want to laugh and tell the black cat of a woman to mind her own business at the same time. In the weeks I've been here, I haven't seen a single squirrel. And yeah, the house I'm staying in is . . . lacking charm and decent water pressure and even a genuine aura of safety, but it's a roof over my head, and that's all I need. Not to mention, it was the only rental available in all of Cherry Peak, which, once I arrived and saw the size of the town, wasn't all that surprising.

"I'm sorry if we've made you feel pressured to go out with us at all. That's my fault," Anna says, nipping at the inside of her cheek with a guilt-stricken expression.

"You're not pressuring me. I'm just still getting accustomed to the place."

"I get it. Honestly, I do. The offer is still there if you're up for it. It'll always be there. We all really liked it when you came out with us the first time." She smiles, and the honesty in her words is impossible to deny.

It's why I don't tell her that she's wasting her time with me and instead flash a half-smile that I hope looks convincing enough. I don't plan on joining their crazy group of friends. Connections like that will only lead to trouble when it comes time to leave. A time that I hope is coming soon.

The only thing I plan on doing while I'm in Cherry Peak is track down Wanda Rose and learn why she up and left this town before I got here.

2

Johnny

I PULL MY COFFEE MUG CLOSER TO ME, LETTING IT HOVER ALONG THE edge of the table before grabbing a tiny pod of cream and ripping open the top. Tipping it above the mug, I watch the white liquid drip into the steaming coffee, turning it from black to a light brown colour. The sugar comes next, three pouches ripped open and hastily dumped into the beige liquid before getting a quick stir.

The coffee burns as I gulp it down, the long day having suddenly caught up to me. My energy is gone, leaving my limbs heavy and mind lagging.

Setting the cup down once it's empty, I catch the eye of my waitress and nod eagerly when she lifts the carafe of coffee in a silent question from behind the long red counter. I flash her a grin, hoping my appreciation is obvious. I've got no problem walking up and asking for more, but Kristen's a real nice girl. Too nice to make me come to her.

"If you're that thirsty, I can just bring you some water," she says once she arrives back at my table. "You drink more coffee than the old men who come in before dawn."

"I'm an old man at heart, Kristie. Don't let my smooth skin and healthy locks convince you otherwise."

She laughs while refilling my mug. "Is Daisy still meeting you?"

"Yup. Late as always, though."

With another pod of creamer and three more packets of sugar, I make my third mug of coffee the same way I have the previous two.

"How's school treating her?"

"She's grateful to be on her last year, that's for sure."

"Daisy's never loved school much. I've never understood why she'd want to go into teaching."

Kristen is one of my twin sister's oldest friends, which means she knows her pretty damn well. Knows the both of us well. You'd have to to confidently draw that conclusion about Daisy. She hated school when we were growing up, but once she went off to university, she learned how to love it in her own way. That doesn't mean she isn't about ready to graduate.

"She says learning and teaching are two entirely different things," I say.

"Do you believe her?"

"I have to. If she didn't love it, she wouldn't be doing it. You know that. Plus, Daisy's always loved kids."

Kristen nods, her thick blonde curls bobbing with the action before she tucks them behind her ears and glances at the diner door. Her parents own the joint now, but years ago, it belonged to her grandparents. Just like every other business in Cherry Peak, Rustic Ridge has been handed down from generation to generation since long before Kristen, Daisy, and I were born.

"Fair enough," she agrees.

One of the perks of a window table is being able to see out on the street, and the moment I get a view of my sister rushing down the sidewalk toward the door, I'm grinning like a fool.

Bells chime, and then Daisy's rushing to the table. Her cheeks are pink and decked out in light brown freckles that have popped from long summer days in the sun. We've both always had terrible freckles in the summer, but they fit her better than they do me. Mine are chunky and spread oddly, mainly centred on and around my nose, while hers are thin and scattered evenly.

Her deep cherry-red-coloured hair, which in the evening looks almost black, and blue eyes that border on grey make us look eerily similar. But luckily, I'm far taller than her. I'll continue to poke fun at her for it until the day I croak.

Our moms are utter saints for putting up with our shit for the past twenty-two years. Not to mention our other two sisters on top of just us.

"I fucking missed you," I say as I stand and tug my sister into a tight hug.

She returns the hug just as eagerly, even as she tells me, "I've only been gone two weeks."

"Is that supposed to matter? It's been four years of you being gone all damn year, and it ain't any easier to let you go."

"I'm only three hours away. You could come see me more often," she scolds, stepping out of the hug, brow already arched as she stares up at me.

"Yeah, yeah. Sit and tell me how you've been. Did you just get back?"

Daisy ignores me as I sit back into my booth and turns to her friend instead. "Hey, Kiki."

"Hi, Didi."

Their hug is quick but just as warm as ours was. This might be the fourth year that Daisy's gone up to Calgary for school, but she's not someone you can just let go of, especially not with the bond we have. It should be a crime for twins to be separated so often.

Once they've broken apart, Kristen moves to take the order of the man sitting behind me while Daisy slides into the booth across from mine and reaches for my coffee. Daisy drinks from the opposite side of my mug before setting it back down. Wiping her mouth with the back of her hand, she shivers.

"You're still drinking sugar instead of coffee," she states before I glance down at the mug, finding it empty.

"And you're still stealing it, knowing that it'll be ungodly sweet."

"Bad habit."

I meet her eyes across the table, a heady sense of calm filling me. "It's nice to see you."

"You too, Jonathon," she replies with a smirk.

My grin flips into a scowl. "Don't make me take it back."

She leans back against the booth and crosses her arms. It's only been two weeks since she left Cherry Peak to get set back up in her Calgary apartment, but the bags beneath her eyes are already back. The fall semester starts sooner than I'd like, and I worry like crazy about her being over there all on her own. Growing up in a house full of only women has turned me into a bit of a protective beast. I'm not ashamed of it, but I know it drives my sisters nuts.

"Tell me what I've missed in CP. Any news on your lady love?" she asks bluntly.

Kristen comes to our table and slides a tall glass of orange juice in front of my sister, along with two plates of pancakes, eggs, and hash browns, before ruffling Daisy's hair and leaving again. I reach for the strawberry syrup while she grabs the blueberry kind beside it.

"No news. She's still avoiding me," I say.

"Do you want me to pretend to be shocked?"

"Not at all. I do expect you to show me some sympathy, though. Maybe."

She drowns her stack of pancakes in deep purple syrup before glancing up at me, disbelief heavy in her gaze. "Sympathy? As if. I think a part of you loves having to chase after her for attention. Personally, I think it's good for you."

"You think it's good for me to have to pant after a woman like a dog?"

Shrugging a shoulder, she answers, "You're too used to

getting your own way all the time. Aurora is putting you through the wringer, and personally, yes, I think it's highly entertaining. But also, you need to struggle a bit from time to time. It builds character, you know?"

I choke on a startled laugh. "I have plenty of character already."

"Clearly not. Maybe she thinks you're boring."

"Me? Come on, Daisy. We both know my being boring is not the issue here."

She slices into her pancakes with her knife and fork before stabbing a piece and lifting it to her mouth, hovering it there. "Alright. Well, she could just not be into you like that."

I'm shaking my head instantly. "Nah, that's not it either."

Chewing her bite of pancake, she lifts a brow.

"You weren't there that night in Peakside. If you were, you would know that physical attraction isn't the issue."

I haven't been able to stop thinking about that night since. Four weeks is a long time to dwell on one single memory, but it's all I have. Not for lack of trying, but because Aurora has avoided me like the plague since she slipped herself out of my arms and hightailed it out of the bar without looking back.

Maybe she's forgotten all about it, but fuck, I haven't. And I plan on reminding her as soon as the time is right. I recognized something there between us. Something incredible. A spark that I haven't felt a single time in my life before then. Not with anyone.

I'm not going to let it go without at least speaking to her again.

Unfortunately, it's a bit hard to speak with her when she makes an obvious effort to be everywhere but where I am. I'm one more Saturday night without her presence away from marching my ass down to the salon to take matters into my own hands.

Surely, I didn't make the entire thing up. *No.* There was

something there, and I'll risk sounding like a complete weirdo by standing with that statement.

Daisy takes a swig of her orange juice before stabbing two pieces of pancakes with her fork. "Well, what are you going to do, then? I love you to death, but I can only take hearing the same story so many times before I want to slam my head into a wall."

"I don't talk about it that often. You asked me about her today," I say accusingly.

"Yeah, that's true. I did. I'm just not used to seeing you so knotted up. You're supposed to be the calm, easygoing one of us. I'm too stressed to pick up your slack."

I narrow my eyes, focusing on her mention of stress. "Is something going on? Outside of the usual?"

"No, you overbearing baboon. I'm just saying. If you need advice, I can give you some, but I don't have a lot of experience with stalker-like men."

I scoff, scooping a pile of pancake into my mouth while flashing her my middle finger. Once I've swallowed my mouthful, I say, "You're a brat. I'm not a damn stalker. I don't even know where she lives."

She gasps, hand to her mouth. "What? Maybe not all hope is lost after all."

"I'm going to get up and leave if you keep picking on me."

Laughing lowly, she wipes her mouth with a napkin and settles back in the booth. "I'm sorry, I'm sorry. For real, though, have you asked her friends for more info on her? Like why she took off on you and has avoided you like she's scared you'll give her a rash or something."

"No. I wanted to try and figure it out on my own first."

"And how's that been going?"

I contemplate loading the spoon beside my plate up with syrup and flicking it at her before turning the idea down. "Yeah, I get it, smartass."

She cocks her head, smirking. "Your hair is getting a bit long."

"I know."

"So, you should get it cut."

"Where is this conversation heading, Daisy?" I ask.

She huffs a breath, annoyed. "You said she works at the salon, right? So, go get your hair cut. She has to talk to you then. And if not, well, then I suggest you take the L sooner rather than later."

I jerk forward in my seat, a rush of excitement shooting through me. "You're a goddamn genius."

"Yeah, I know." She brushes invisible dust off her shoulder. "Now that that's settled, can we focus on something more serious? Like the upcoming season of *The Bachelorette*?"

I nod, too grateful for her help to put up a stink with this. "You got the list of contestants to share?"

She rolls her eyes and pulls her phone out of her pocket while I dig into my eggs. The next several minutes are spent scrolling through the men up next in our favourite reality show before I snake the bill and settle it. Daisy thanks me with a kiss to my cheek, and by the time I walk her to her car and make her promise to drive safe back to our mom's house, I'm wondering how hard it'll be to convince Anna to sneak me an appointment at Thistle and Thorn tomorrow.

3

Aurora

Mom: Good morning. This is me asking for sign of life again.

Me: I'm alive.

It's the only answer I can get myself to give her.

I tuck my phone back into my pocket immediately after hitting Send. The bottles of shampoo on the shelves in front of me have begun to blur. Labels upon labels, brands upon brands. They all do the same thing, in my opinion, but the customer up front demands one with a price tag that lets me know she's not struggling in the finance department.

I find the deep blue bottle of shampoo with a fancy label tucked behind a row of grey ones and snatch it from the shelf. Bryce finished inventory quickly yesterday, but obviously, she isn't as anal with the order of the shelves as me. I could spend hours organizing supplies until everything is perfectly laid out, whether in alphabetical order or sorted by colour. Maybe both, if I have the time to burn.

The bell above the front door chimes, and I leave the storage room quickly, hoping my lack of pep in my step hasn't sent a customer leaving without what they came here for. It's still hard for me to comprehend that Anna can make a living here in Cherry Peak with a population so small, but from what I've seen, she isn't struggling in that department. Somehow, there never comes a day where she isn't either busy with clients or chatting up a customer who's curious about something. Just yesterday, a woman came in from Edmonton, having driven five hours just for a cut and colour.

I've been tempted to ask her to fit me into her schedule for a trim, but from my inches of dry, dead ends, clearly, I haven't.

My sneakers hit the floor in quick procession as I round the corner and paste on a smile for the customer I left waiting. Only it isn't just the customer anymore. Not by a long shot.

"I'll have to give Daisy a call, Johnny. Thank you so much," the woman who asked for the shampoo coos, a hand decked out in a long-tipped french manicure sweeping over the exposed skin of his bicep.

The same half-white, half-tan, rippling-with-muscle bicep that shows only because he decided against wearing a shirt with actual sleeves today and instead wore one that's torn at both shoulders to expose a hint of his obliques, as well. A goddamn DIY tank top that's tucked into the front of his tight jeans and behind a belt buckle the size of my fist.

His hair is long, wavy, and so, so black. It's kept half hidden beneath a dark brown cowboy hat instead of a filthy baseball cap like the night we met, and suddenly, all I can think of are the words he spoke into my ear the moment I mentioned it.

"There's a rule when it comes to a man settin' his hat on a woman, Aurora."

I fight back a familiar shiver and straighten my posture before letting the bottle hang at my side as I walk past the two of them to the front desk. Ignoring the burning side-eye coming from where I know Anna's standing at her station, I walk a bit faster.

Everyone that was at Peakside the night I let Johnny pull me out of the booth and into his arms for far too many dances has clung onto the moment with steel claws, refusing to let it drop and move on. Anna and Poppy especially. I've lost track of how many times I've told them that it meant nothing until finally, they stopped bringing it up, their hopes crushed. I know that doesn't mean they believe me in the slightest, though.

It's fine with me if they don't. I know what it meant, and that's that. It meant *DANGER* in all caps with red lights flashing. It was a warning not to ever allow myself to fall into that position again because it's *not* what I came here for. Even after only a few minutes in his presence, I knew everything I needed to.

That he would be bring me nothing but utter heartbreak.

That night was my first time ever meeting the outgoing cowboy that the girls said would be in attendance at the bar, and I wasn't expecting what I found.

From the moment he appeared at the edge of the table with a giddy, confident glint in his eyes, I knew I was in trouble. It was obvious that I should have taken off. But I didn't. Johnny has an uncanny ability to yank you into his orbit without warning, and once you're there, it's nearly impossible to break free. Which is why the moment I could, I did.

And I've done everything in my power to avoid taking another trip to Johnny Land since. This sudden appearance has thrown a massive cowboy-sized wrench in my plans.

"I'll let 'er know you'll be calling. She's home for a couple weeks now before she heads off again," Johnny replies, and I can hear the grin in his voice.

Is it dimpled? Like it was that night?

Doesn't fucking matter.

I keep my eyes down and set the bottle on the desk before reaching for the debit machine and putting in the price. That tingle you get when you know someone's watching you hits me a beat later, and I know without having to glance up that it's not Anna looking at me this time.

Maybe he won't even speak to me. Who's to say he hasn't

forgotten all about our dancing? I've done a great job of keeping to myself since that night, and he seems like a smart guy. Smart enough to read and understand the signs I'm showing him.

"You get sweeter with age, handsome. I appreciate it," the customer adds.

I wish I knew her name. She probably mentioned it earlier, but I've always been terrible when it comes to remembering them.

"I have your shampoo," I blurt out, the debit machine already extended over the raised edge of the desk.

Thank God for the soft music playing throughout the salon. Without it, the silence as the woman walks to the desk and takes the machine from me would have been too much.

I lift my stare to hers and give my best customer service smile. "Was there anything else you were wanting today? To book an appointment, maybe?"

"No. I've got all I came for," she tells me kindly before turning to flash another grin at Johnny. "Thanks again. I'll see you around, I hope?"

I can't help but look at him as he grins right back at her and waves. There's nothing but a calm sincerity in his eyes.

"Sure thing. See you."

The machine beeps, and I print off her receipt before handing it to her along with the shampoo. She takes them both and strides out the door, her designer purse hung over the crook of her elbow.

Dropping my gaze again, I bend at the waist and start fidgeting with everything in the top desk drawer, waiting for Johnny to leave. I don't know what he came here for, but the sooner he walks back out the door, the better.

Anna, the little traitor, doesn't say a damn thing as I try not to run and hide. If I had to guess, I'd assume she's not even around anymore. Most likely hiding in the back room like the scheming woman she is.

I feel it in the air the moment he takes a step toward me. His boots clap on the floor with every step until a moment later, they come to a stop. I swallow, accidentally slamming the drawer shut after dumping the debit machine inside of it. Once I've reinforced my blank expression, I stand straight and meet his waiting eyes.

The soft blue shade of them reminds me of a winter morning sky. Maybe comparing them to one of my favourite things is what had me lost in them only a month ago. Refusing to go there again, I blink and divert my stare to the blotches of deep brown freckles over his face. A safer space, but one just as beautiful.

Johnny is a gorgeous man. I'd have to be blind not to recognize that. Rugged and pretty all at once, he's wrapped into a package with a bright red bow on top that begs me to tug on it and explore what's beneath with eager hands.

I focus on his chin and the small dimple in the centre of it when he speaks, avoiding looking at his naturally pouty lips.

"Good morning, darlin'," he says, all deep drawl and confidence. "Long time no see."

"Good morning," I reply stiffly, ignoring his last sentence.

"How are you?"

"Fine. How are you?"

I watch his lips curl from where I stare at his chin.

"Peachy. Got a good night's sleep and managed to push my start time at the ranch this morning just in time to make my appointment."

Right. He works at Steele Ranch, Anna's boyfriend's family ranch. That's how he knows every single person in the friend group I've found myself being welcomed into.

"Appointment?" I ask, confused.

"My hair appointment, Rory," he says cheekily.

"You're here to get your hair cut?"

"'Course I am. Did you think I came here just to see you?"

Scoffing, I roll my eyes. "No."

His grin grows at my blunt response, dimples popping. "Well, I won't lie. It was actually a bit of both."

"You weren't on the schedule."

"Were you looking for me on there?"

I huff, dropping my attention to the computer screen as I bend again and jiggle the mouse to wake it up. The schedule is already open, today's date and every appointment scheduled for today sitting right in front of me. Ten, one, and four fifteen. A quick glance at the corner of the screen tells me it's only 9:21, and there isn't anything written down to tell me he should be here.

Clicking out of the schedule, I plop my hands on my hips and stare at Johnny, keeping my mouth in a firm line. "No, I wasn't looking for you. It's my job to know when clients are coming in. You're not on the schedule."

"Do you like coffee?" he asks.

"What?"

He leans forward against the desk and levels me with an innocent stare, his fingers tapping a quick beat. His question came out of left field, but he looks content with it.

"What does coffee have to do with anything?"

His shoulder lifts. "I'm wonderin' if I should have brought you some. It seems I have quite a bit to do still to get you to warm up to me, and if you do like it, then I'll slip out and go get you some right now."

I cross my arms over my chest, needing to put more than just this desk between us. Coffee sounds really damn nice right about now. Especially if it's coming from the place down the street where I've become a regular. But I'm not about to tell him that.

"I don't need coffee. I don't need *anything*."

"Come on, sugar. Give me something here."

The nickname has me physically reeling back, revolted. He doesn't miss my reaction, and the laugh that comes out of him is deep and proud.

"Alright. No to that nickname, then," he notes.

"No to any nickname," I push out before rounding the desk

and attempting to leave him standing there all by himself. "I'll get Anna for you."

"That your coffee on the desk there?" he asks before I make it all of three steps away.

I spin on my heel. He's bent over the desk, his hand reaching for the empty clear cup beside the computer monitor with my name scrawled over the side. It's empty, has been since before I got to work because I gulped the entire thing down on the walk over. I forgot to throw it out. Figures.

"Don't touch that! God, you are relentless," I snap, rushing right back toward him.

It's already clutched in his massive hand, and his eyes are scrunched as he reads the printed white label stuck to the side of it.

"A caramel macchiato with extra caramel," he says before glancing over at me with a smirk. "You got a sweet tooth just like me."

"Don't be creepy, Johnny," Anna says, appearing on the left with her shiny black apron on and hair pulled back out of her face. "Come sit down so I can get started. How much am I taking off, anyway? You didn't mention that in your text."

Johnny whips his head to smile at her. "I'm not creepy. I'm just trying to figure out Aurora's coffee order. And like . . . a quarter of an inch?"

"Oh. I could have just told you that. It's a caramel macchiato with extra caramel," she says before patting the spinning chair in front of her station. "And a quarter of an inch? That's nothing. Definitely not emergency appointment worthy."

"I just don't want a lot off," he says, the picture of innocence.

He doesn't have hair so long that it looks shaggy or unkempt. It only hits the middle of his neck, but it's healthy and silky. If I were him, I wouldn't be cutting it at all today. There's no need to. Not even a quarter of an inch.

Anna nods and pats the chair again, careful to keep her expression neutral as she looks between him and me. Johnny doesn't bother with the same coyness. He winks at me before moving his tall body to the chair and flopping down onto it. Our eyes meet in the mirror, and I hate that I enjoy the view.

For some reason I don't know, Johnny looks at me like a man who sees something in front of him that keeps drawing him in. Something that has and will have him coming back over and over again, even if I give him nothing in return. It's the same look now as it was in Peakside. It had me running that night, and it has me running today.

Well, not running exactly. But rather, disappearing into the washroom until I know he's gone again.

4

Johnny

I'VE NEVER IN MY LIFE MET A GROUP OF MEN WHO HAVE APPEARED AS clueless when it comes to construction as the ones in front of me right now.

I knew from the moment I saw the crowd of them hunched over a high pile of untreated wooden planks when I pulled back onto the ranch that something was wrong. And as I stride toward them now, my hunch is confirmed.

The foreman, Rick, lifts his white hard hat from his head and runs his fingers through his hair, his eyes moving from the pile of ugly wood to the timber exterior of the under-construction stable only a few yards from the tall walls of the current one. My gut grows heavy when I get close enough to pick up the hushed words moving between the men.

"It wasn't supposed to be untreated, Rick. I didn't order this shit."

"It doesn't matter. It's here, isn't it? And it's my head on the line right now."

"I've got no problem returning it. Once we swap it out, we'll be good to go."

"Good to go? It'll take another week, maybe two, to get the new planks. That's gonna have us pushing back far into the fall."

I've got a cool head. Always have and always will, considering how badly I need one with the family I've got. But it's still mighty frustrating to hear that this crew has fucked up.

Steele Ranch has had a number of problems this summer. One after the other, the dominos keep falling. Wade Steele doesn't have even close to the amount of patience that I do, and every day that something's gone wrong, I've watched what's left of it get stomped further and further into the ground.

I take a look around the area for the owner of the ranch and breathe a sigh of relief when I don't find him nearby, red face and all. It's just me and the crew of fuck-ups.

Stretching out my shoulders, I take wider strides and then step into the centre of their conversation. It cuts instantly, and that's not a good look for them either.

"Hey, guys. How's it goin' today?" I ask brightly.

Rick makes eye contact with me, albeit reluctantly. If he'd ignored me, it would have looked ten times worse. He's got at least twenty years on me, but I've got four inches on him. His age doesn't mean much at all in this situation, and I know he knows it just as well. I've been telling him what to do on the ranch since the moment they stepped foot on it three weeks ago.

It took six weeks of talks between the Steeles and some hoity-toity architect firm from the city to come up with the perfect stable design plan, but it seems that may have been the easiest of the steps so far. Construction started late, and we all knew going into it that there was a good chance we were going to run it into the fall, maybe even past that. But these setbacks . . . they just keep on coming.

"Been better," Rick grunts.

I glance at the man he was speaking to and tuck my hands into my pockets. "You got a problem that needs fixing?"

Rick answers for him. "No. We're sorting our shit out."

"Like the pile of firewood beside you? Is that the shit you're planning on sortin'?"

The other man lingering around tries not to be obvious that

they're watching us. I shake my head at them, and a beat later, they disappear, suddenly busy with something else.

Rick's features harden when I bring my attention back to him and cock my head, waiting for an answer. It's only a matter of time before I have to call Wade and let him know about this, so I need all the information possible. It won't save them, but it might help.

"It was an honest mistake, Johnny," Rick says, waving a hand at the wood.

"Can you return it all?"

This time, the other man speaks before Rick can stop him. "We'll return it. I'll take it myself."

"I appreciate that. Thank you . . ."

"I'm Jimmy. Jim," he says.

"Thank you, Jim. Do you happen to know the wait on getting a new order of the proper siding?"

"Two weeks max, one week minimum. Depends on current demand," Rick says.

"If you want my advice, I say make it a week. Doesn't matter where you have to go or who you have to sweet-talk to make it happen. If you want to keep your job here, you'll keep it to a week."

Even that is too long, but if that's what we've got to settle with, then so be it.

Rick nods sharply. "Have you gotten a raise recently that I haven't heard about around here?"

I lean back on my left foot, taking another look around the ranch. "Why are you asking?"

"Forget about it," he says, brushing the comment off for one of two reasons. Either he meant it as a lowball dig and didn't want to risk angering me, or he doesn't want to compliment me by saying I deserved one.

There was no raise. I'm still just Johnny the common ranch hand, but I don't offer him that information.

"Alright. Get started on returning that wood, and I'll give

Wade a call. I'd stay away from him for a while afterward if I were you," I tell them.

Jimmy nods, his smile grateful. "You got it, John—"

"What the fuck is that pile of shit doin' in front of my stable?"

I flinch at the rough scolding, watching as Jimmy and Rick do the same. Poor Jimmy pales at the sight of a pissed-off Wade Steele storming our way.

The brutal rancher's black cowboy boots crunch over the gravel road as he crosses it, his hands balled into fists at his side. His expression is shaded by the brim of his matching black hat, but I don't need to see his face to know how spitting mad he is. I saw it coming from a mile away.

Rick, knowing his job's on the line, is quick to shake off his fear and step forward, his mouth opening quicker than I can warn him to stay quiet.

"We've got it under control, Wade."

I drop my head back, staring at the cloudless blue sky with a groan. The moment Wade reaches us, I feel the air shift, growing tight and tense.

"You've got it under control? Is that a fuckin' joke? Do I look like a fuckin' joke to you?" Wade shouts, voice thick with disdain.

I look at Rick, taking in his pale skin and wide, worried eyes. Usually, I would have offered him a sympathetic smile, but not right now. Not when Wade's watching me now with a tired rage in his eyes that cuts me to the core.

I've known this man since I was a boy. Hell, most of everyone in Cherry Peak has known him for their entire lives. He's a staple in the community despite his oftentimes brash attitude. Especially for a guy like me who found a home at his ranch. I annoyed the fuck out of the man until he agreed to take me on as a ranch hand when I was sixteen. Now, he can't get rid of me.

I don't think he wants to be rid of me either. At least not all the time.

My knowledge of him is why I know that Rick shouldn't

have said anything. He should have allowed me to speak for him.

I try now, hoping it might help smooth even a couple of Wade's feathers. "I've already talked to them about it. Got them to fix the problem as fast as they can. It'll be a week max before the siding can go up."

Jimmy's eyes dart to me, and I simply shake my head, giving him a look that tells him to get it done. Wade stares at me hard, and I smile back like a little shit until he seems annoyed enough by me to pin Rick beneath his stare instead.

"I'm not payin' you what I am for fuck-ups, Rick. Order the proper shit, and then get this the fuck done before you're out here workin' in minus fifty-degree weather with snow up to your ass crack," Wade snaps. "Or I'm kickin' you off my land and bringin' in someone else to do what you couldn't."

"Yeah, you got it," Rick says, already setting his hat back onto his head and waving at his employees left standing around, pretending to be busy. His expression turns hard as stone as he barks at his guys. "Load these planks back into the truck and get them out of here."

They all burst into movement. Jimmy ducks out of sight the first chance he gets. Rick follows quickly after, rushing into the centre of his grouped employees. Wade's forced to suffer with just my company now.

"Up for a walk?" I ask, risking a pat to his shoulder.

His eyes tighten suspiciously at the corners. "I'm not goin' to commit murder today, boy."

"Hey, I never thought that. It was an honest mistake. Just really bad timing," I tell him once we start walking away from the framed structure.

The massive expanse of Steele Ranch land is beautiful on a normal day. But during the peak of summer? It's a marvel. All green fields, budding flowers, dirt paths, and noisy animals. Horses, cattle, chickens, and, as of a couple of weeks ago, a duo of rowdy donkeys.

"It's more than shitty timing," he grunts.

"I know. Have you heard about the money yet?"

He lifts a hand to his face, fingers gripping his jaw hard enough it must hurt. "Yeah. Got a call from the officer on the case yesterday. The money hadn't even left the fucker's account yet when we caught 'im."

"Jail time?"

"Maybe. Could be up to ten years. Could be less. Most likely will be half or less that time. I'm just damn glad Eliza noticed when she did."

I nod, anger swelling in my stomach. "How's she been handlin' this?"

Wade's wife is sweeter than honey on ice cream. She's been in charge of the financial side of Steele Ranch since the two of them got married. I don't think a single other person has ever touched the ranch's finances in the past twenty years. Not until the new financial analyst they hired last month to help with the budgeting for the new stable expansion and the few other changes they've been wanting to do to the place, that is.

It only took a week for them to get burned by that decision. One bad apple plucked from a tree bursting with a million juicy ones.

The man took one look at their finances and created a plan to get rich quick. It didn't work the way he thought it would. The moment Eliza took a curious look between the lines and found that their supposed seventy-thousand-dollar stable was really only going to cost fifty-five while the guy took fifteen for himself, he was laid flat out on his ass.

"She's workin' herself to the bone. That's how." Wade scowls, his exhales harsh and short. "It's damn time she retired. I was selfishly hopin' that asshole was goin' to help with that. Maybe open her up to the idea of lettin' someone else take over soon. Now she'll be workin' the ranch's books in the grave."

"There's someone else out there, Wade. I'm sure of it. I'll help convince her any way I can. She deserves rest just as much as you do," I say pointedly.

"I'll rest when I'm dead."

"Typical bitter old man response."

"I ain't bitter, Johnny."

"No?" I look over at him, arching a brow as we get closer and closer to the house. "Fine. Not bitter. Just plain old grumpy."

"You're goin' to wind up neck-deep in cow shit today if you don't quit pissin' me off," he warns, but there's no venom there.

"Don't tease me with a good time, Wade."

His laugh is gruff and raw, speaking to a lifetime of smoking cigarettes. He slaps me on the back.

"There's a hole a foot long on the far south fence real close to the wood beam again. Fuckin' bulls won't stop taking chunks out of it. I need it fixed up as soon as possible. You got it?"

"Yeah, I've got it. Swapping the wire for steel pipe over there might be worth it at this rate. They've got a vendetta against that fence."

He twists his mouth, thinking. "Yeah. I'll think about it. For now, just get it fixed up. The last thing we need is someone hittin' a bull on a country road and flippin' their shit on me."

I tip my chin and pat my back pocket, confirming my gloves are still there. "Sounds good. Tell Eliza I'll see her at lunch."

"Yeah. And try not to make a habit of changin' your schedule so you can fit in the time to bug that poor woman in town. You'll set a precedent for the others."

I chuckle, flashing him a bashful grin. "I don't have a damn clue what you're talking about."

He huffs a breath and continues toward the main house, leaving me behind before he calls over his shoulder, "Keep it that way, boy."

If he knew that I'm still not an inch closer to winning Aurora over after this morning than I was before, he'd be even more unimpressed with me. But I'm still far from admitting defeat.

I've got a few tricks up my sleeve that are guaranteed to convince her to start giving me the time of day. *Hopefully.*

5

Aurora

The water coming from the rusty shower head above me sputters as I finish washing the conditioner out of my hair. A beat later, a brief wave of cold hits my skin, sending my body into shock before it warms again to absolutely fucking scalding.

Hissing at the burn, I frantically turn off the shower and then clench my teeth, fighting back a wave of shivers at the sudden cold. I rip back the deep green shower curtain and step onto the matching mat, letting myself drip-dry for a minute before snatching my towel from the back of the toilet.

I'm already late for work. I don't have to look at my phone again to know that. My alarm didn't go off, and I knew the moment I saw how late it was into the morning that I wasn't going to make it in on time, regardless of how fast I moved. The apologetic text I sent off to Anna before I got into the shower was met with a sweet, understanding reply that made me feel even more like shit.

I'm too old to be rushing into work late. Thirty is far too close to thirty-five to be as big of a mess as I am. It's not answers I should be chasing, but rather a real life. A family to come home to every night and a plan for our future. Marriage, RRSPs, and Crock-Pot dinners that everyone groans at the sight of. Not living off savings and small paycheques all alone in a nowhere town surrounded by strangers.

My entire life plan was laid perfectly before I took off to come here, and now . . . now, I fear I've screwed myself and that very plan with my impulse decision. Back home, my life is even more of a mess than it is here.

The job I loved, gone. My relationship with my mother, also gone. Each pill has grown harder to swallow, and now I'm positive another will choke me.

I wrap the thin towel around my body and blink back the tears that have built in my eyes, refusing to let them fall. I've self-inflicted this loneliness. But it's all I know. The only person I've ever really let in is my mom, and now, the thought of talking to her fills me with poison.

For as long as I can remember, I've been a closed-off person. There's no exact reason for it. No trauma or deep-rooted insecurity. It's just who I am. But in moments like these, where I sit and wonder what I have to show for my life, it hits me that I have nothing and no one.

It should be easy to decide to change that. To go out and make a shit ton of friends and find a position at a new job where I'll feel even half as fulfilled as the one I left behind. But it's not that easy. It's terrifying as hell. Not to mention impossible with my current plans, or lack thereof.

"Get a grip, Rory," I mutter.

With a scowl, I finish drying off and get ready. Ten minutes later, I'm rushing out the door with my wet hair twisted into a low bun and my face bare. My thick thighs eat the inner material of my denim shorts through the entire walk to the salon, and I pull them back down for the millionth time before stepping inside.

Anna's quick to turn to me as the door chimes. Her hair is down today, the caramel-brown length of it brushing the tops of her shoulders in soft waves. She smiles at me and lifts the comb in her hand.

"Morning, sunshine!"

I lift half of my mouth into a weak smile. "Morning. I'm sorry for being late."

"It happens to the best of us. Don't worry about it."

"Thanks."

"And how have you been doing, sweetie?" an older, raspier voice asks.

The woman sitting in the leather chair in front of Anna is too familiar not to recognize. I've only met Eliza Steele briefly, but she's unforgettable. If she's not at Thistle and Thorn getting her hair done, she's here to chat with Anna or around town mingling with every single person she sees. A people person in its purest form, Eliza's presence is a Cherry Peak staple.

Anna swaps the comb in her fingers with the scissors that are expertly tucked alongside it. She laughs every time I say something about the speed at which she flips between scissors and comb, but I'll never stop being in awe of it.

"I'm good," I tell Eliza.

A thin eyebrow jumps with disbelief. "I'm all ears, my love. How is an old woman supposed to stay entertained during a haircut if there's no gossip?"

I move into the small lunchroom long enough to drop my purse on the table before joining them again. Eliza catches my eye in the mirror, her gaze soft yet curious.

"Doesn't Anna have gossip for you?" I ask.

Anna snorts. "I do, but apparently, it isn't interesting enough for her."

Eliza beams, clearly enjoying their banter. "You know it is, honey. I'm just a nosey Nelly."

"Am I allowed to agree with you?" Anna teases.

"I wouldn't have said it if you weren't. You know better than to ask such silly questions."

Anna smiles, carefully snipping a small chunk of Eliza's silver hair before grabbing another between her fingers and running her comb through it. "Have I ever told you about Aurora's fancy university degree, Eliza?"

A loud gasp fills the salon. "No! Please tell me more."

I grow hot, my cheeks flushing from the sudden change in topic. I'm more shocked than embarrassed when I realize Anna really was paying attention the other day when I explained how I was so easily able to comb through the budget she left open on the main computer last week and create improvements for her in the same hour. It was easier than anything I did at my last job, but it was still a great confidence boost to know I hadn't forgotten anything.

"I'm just good with numbers," I say bluntly.

Anna shakes her head, her hair whipping back and forth. "No. You're incredible with them." Snaring Eliza's eyes in the mirror, she adds, "Not only did she create three different budgeting plans for Thistle and Thorn, but she also helped me organize the mess of receipts and invoices in my desk and curated an entire system for them. She's a lifesaver."

"It's really not a big deal. Your books are cleaner than any I've seen before. You just needed a second set of eyes."

"You're only saying that because I'm your boss. You have two college degrees, Rory. That is *so* something to brag about."

"Two? Why on earth haven't you been telling me all about them yet?" Eliza guffaws.

"They're not interesting to most people. Quite the opposite, actually. Nobody wants to hear about finance or business," I defend myself.

Eliza frowns, the lines at the corners of her mouth deep. "Well, I can assure you I won't find it boring. I've been working with finances for five decades now. Give this old woman a chance to prove you wrong, sweetheart."

I try to hide my surprise as I say, "If you're sure."

"I'm positive," she confirms.

"I have a bachelor's degree in finance, a master's in business, and spent the last six years working for one of the biggest Canadian-based auction enterprises as their corporate financial advisor."

"Oh, wow. That's incredible," Eliza says softly.

Anna shoots me a knowing look in the mirror. "See? What did I say?"

I roll my eyes. "Yeah."

"I mean this in the sweetest way, but what on earth are you doing here?" Eliza asks after a moment of silence.

My skin feels tight over my bones as their attention remains fully placed on me. I know they want to know more about me, and I should just tell them even the smallest thing. Right here, right now. I want to tell someone *something* before I find myself squashed beneath the stress I've put myself under.

"In Cherry Peak or at the salon?"

"Both."

"I've already asked this a million times, Eliza. She's a tough egg to crack," Anna says.

"No egg is too tough for me to crack."

I smile slightly at that. If there was anyone that could do it, it would be Eliza.

"I needed answers, and Cherry Peak is where I thought they'd be," I tell them before I can think twice about it.

Eliza's features grow thoughtful. "And you aren't so sure anymore?"

"No," I admit. "I'm still trying to figure things out."

"Sometimes all it takes is a bit of time."

"And some killer friends to spend said time with while you get it all sorted," Anna adds pointedly.

"Yes. Friends, and without insulting Anna here, perhaps a job that will fulfill you a bit more than this one. Do you miss working with numbers?" Eliza asks. "I can't imagine you're feeling very stimulated scheduling appointments and answering phone calls."

"I'm not insulted at all. You have a point," Anna says.

I shift on my feet, anxious to see where this is going to go.

"Yeah, I do miss working with numbers. But I'm happy here too."

Eliza tips her chin, ignoring Anna's grumble when the hair she was holding slips from her fingers and she has to grab another before snipping it.

"What would you say to coming over to Steele Ranch this weekend and having a bit of a chat with me? I may have an opportunity for you."

I dart my eyes to Anna, searching for any tell that she's annoyed with me or Eliza's offer. But there's nothing, and when she nods at me with a genuine, easygoing smile, I relax slightly.

"Um, sure. If you're okay with it. Yeah, I could do that. When?" I ramble.

"Saturday at eleven? I can whip us up a light lunch to have while we talk."

Anna does a terrible job of hiding her smugness as she listens to us talk, and I take that as another good sign. It appears that I trust her enough after these past weeks together to know that if she thought me going there was a bad idea, she'd voice that to me. Eliza might be her boyfriend's grandmother, but I don't think that would keep her quiet in this situation.

"Alright. We can do Saturday."

6

Johnny

WIRE DIGS THROUGH MY GLOVES AS I HEAVE ANOTHER HAYBALE onto the growing stack in front of me. Sweat drips down my forehead and chin and chest. The shirt I wore to work this morning lies on the ground, warming beneath the sun as I work. I sweated through it ten minutes into my task and was quick to chuck it off when it started to stick to my skin.

I'm probably burning to shit right now in the thirty-five-degree weather with no sunscreen on my bare back and shoulders, but it's better than the alternative. And it'll help even out my farmer's tan.

The horses in the field beside me watch from behind the fence, giving me pouty eyes like they think the hay I'm hauling is tastier than the grass beneath their hooves. Joker, my black-and-white polka-dotted mare, is inside the original Steele Ranch stable, munching on the exact same hay I'm hauling. Special treatment for the special girl. Maybe the other horses have a point.

Lifting another bale, I swing my torso and start a third stack beside the previous two along the stable wall. The construction crew behind me is loud, banging and drilling at the beams they're meant to finish by tomorrow. The structure will be done in the time they promised, but the siding issue is still ongoing. They've returned the wrong wood and ordered the new stuff, but it'll take eight days to get here.

I made the decision to keep that information from Wade for now. What he doesn't know won't hurt him. Not when it comes to this. A day is a day, and if he's pissed about being kept in the dark about it come eight days from now, then he can take it up with me.

"Stacking bales is one job I don't miss doing."

The familiar voice comes from behind me. I spin to grin at my friend and yank my gloves off before tucking them into my back pocket.

"You're here early today," I say, heading toward Garrison.

A few months ago, seeing him dressed in a pair of thigh huggers and a plain white tee would have taken me by surprise. But not anymore. While Garrison Beckett hasn't shed his billionaire CEO skin quite yet, he's become a pro at adapting to a more casual, rancher vibe while he's here. His time living on Steele Ranch is partially responsible for that, but I think him falling in love with Poppy had more to do with it than anything else.

"Poppy said we had to be here by eleven. Something about a show happening at the ranch? You know anything about that?" he asks.

I smooth a hand over my head before shaking it. "A show?"

Garrison shrugs, his eyes inspecting the area around us. They linger on the crew behind us, something like cold annoyance growing there before he's focusing on the main house across the road.

"Who knows. It isn't a bad thing to be here early."

"You say the sweetest things, Garry. If you wanted to spend some time with me, you could have just called or texted."

He ignores me, but I know he heard every word I said. His grumpiness is one of the things I like most about him. Well, that and his blunt humour. I love that shit.

"Where is Poppy, anyway?" I ask.

"Talking with Eliza. You know how they are."

I laugh, twisting to face the main house. "Yeah, I should have figured that one out on my own."

"You'd think they'd all been separated for months, not a week."

"It's cute, though. That they're all so close. It's like you, me, and Brody," I tease, knocking our shoulders together.

He scowls at me, shaking his arm out. "Not quite."

"Yeah, you're right. Just you and me, then."

Garrison and Brody's relationship has grown over the past few months, but they're nowhere close to the finish line. Brody working under Garrison's music label, Swift Edge Records, has kept the line between friends and colleagues nice and thick between them. Regardless of the fact both of their women are best friends, they haven't quite followed suit just yet.

"Yeah, like you and me," he admits.

My lips stretch into a smile as I nod to the house. "Should we go join the girls now?"

"Put a goddamn shirt on first, Magic Mike."

"Was that a stripper joke?" I ask while grabbing my shirt. Shaking it in the air, I clear it of dirt before slipping it on. "Poppy would flick you in the nose for making that."

"No, she wouldn't. She loves that movie."

I burst out in laughter. Garrison curses beneath his breath and shoves me enough to have me stumbling forward.

"What's wrong with you?"

"Sorry, I'm just picturing you sitting down watching *Magic Mike*," I wheeze.

"You can stay here while I go to the house, actually. Keep stacking bales. Preferably until your arms fall off," he grunts, leaving me behind.

I chase after him, laughing loud enough to grab the attention of the construction crew. They watch us until Garrison pins them with a dark look, and they busy themselves again.

"Oh, don't act all tough and mean, Garry. I'm sorry. I've watched *Magic Mike* before, and it wasn't half-bad," I say.

"It was terrible. But Poppy wanted to watch it, so I sat my ass down and kept my mouth shut."

"Good man," I tell him, reaching his side once we both cross the road.

The ranch house is exactly what you'd expect. Old but well-kept, with a large porch, screen door, and endless flowerpots outside. The windows are big, with wood shutters on either side of each one that are solely for decoration. It was the biggest house on the land until Brody and Anna built theirs last year further out, away from everyone else but still close enough to pop up every day.

Eliza, Poppy, and Anna are sitting on the porch when we get close enough to grab a view of them. The oldest woman of them all is rocking on her chair, its yellow cushions bright against the soft pink of her shirt. Poppy's dyed her hair again, this time to a deep brown a few shades darker than Anna's. It's a habit of hers that I often take bets on with Eliza. From the brown today, I know I've just won twenty bucks.

Eliza looks over at Garrison and me as we approach and smiles. "Hello, boys. You're just on time."

"For what?" I ask at the same time the sound of gravel crunching becomes audible.

"For our guest," Eliza sings.

Closer and closer, an old sedan crawls toward us. My heart gallops, excitement having me damn near bouncing on my toes when I make out the driver.

"The show makes sense now," Garrison mumbles.

Yeah, it does.

I'm the scheduled performer, and I'm not the least bit ashamed of that.

Tucking my hands in my pockets, I let my lips tug into a grin and wink when Aurora spots me, her eyes bugging out. The curse she so obviously mutters before parking in front of the house is adorable. I want her to say it again for me to hear this time.

Garrison barks a laugh, and I flip him the bird over my shoulder, not bothering to tear my eyes from Aurora to look at him.

"You did this on purpose, Eliza," I say while we wait for the ranch guest to step out of her car.

"Me? Would I do that?"

Both the girls answer for me. "Yes."

Eliza laughs her loud, warm laugh, and I take a few steps closer to the porch. Aurora opens the car door, and it creaks so damn loud she cringes, her cheeks flaming red. When she darts her stare from her door to the house and then to Garrison behind me, it's obvious she's purposefully avoiding me.

"How long has your door been creaking like that? I'm going to have Brody take a look before he heads off again. He'll get it all right as rain," Eliza says, a firm nod following her words.

Aurora stares at her, cheeks still pink. I roll my lips to hide my amusement. She doesn't know what to do with the offer, and fuck me if that doesn't make me wanna give her another one. Like an offer to help fix up that shack of a rental she's gotten herself.

It should be wrapped in caution tape and demolished. There's no way there was an inspection done prior to her moving in, and if there was, it definitely didn't pass.

After learning that that's where she's been living, I've had to fight the urge to get to work on it every time I drive by. The only thing that's kept me from doing so this far is knowing that she'd take my own hammer and hit me upside the head with it if she caught me there.

I know better than to spook her further. Not if I want to get anywhere with her in the near future. And I do. Badly.

Still, I don't know the exact reason why. The romantic in me calls it love at first sight, but the realist laughs at that reasoning. It's obvious that I'm curious about her. I felt something that night, and I want to learn more about it. Figure out why her touch sparked along my skin and her voice made my toes curl in my boots.

Aurora softly presses her door shut. "I don't need that."

"I wouldn't bother arguing. There's no stopping her now," Anna says.

Eliza nods in agreement. "Come inside, and we'll get him over right now. By the time we're done talking, that door will be as silent as a summer breeze."

Aurora still hasn't looked at me since pulling up, and I'm itching to call for her attention. She looks beautiful today, all flushed skin and loose, wavy hair. The deep, dark blue T-shirt she's wearing brings out the colour of her eyes, as if she purposefully bought it for that reason. The colour draws me in further than I already was, and now I'm more than itching for her attention. I'm desperate for it.

"Let me take care of it, Eliza. There's no need to get Brody out here when he's already working," I say, my long legs eating the space between me and Aurora's car as my pulse thumps.

My attention is laser focused on her and her alone, and I know she feels the weight of it. Her posture straightens, shoulders pushing back before she turns her head and finally meets my stare.

My jeans tighten at the crotch at the annoyance in those pretty blues. "That okay with you, Rory?"

"Does it matter?"

"'Course it does, darlin'. I won't touch it unless you give the okay."

Her tongue darts across her berry-tinted lips, and fuck me if it isn't one the world's worst distractions. I hardly notice the way her chest heaves before she replies.

"And I'm supposed to believe you? Who's to say you don't actually rip it from its hinges the minute I leave you alone out here?"

I shrug, the corner of my mouth ticking up. "Guess you'll have to give me a try. Let me prove that I'm serious."

"Do you know anything about cars?" she asks bluntly despite the slightly higher octave of her voice.

"Enough to know where the door hinges are so I can oil 'em for you."

"You're such a smartass," she blurts out before clamping her lips shut and glancing guiltily at everyone watching on the porch.

Poppy's the one to reply. "Don't look so guilty. You're not wrong. He is a smartass."

"Worse than that sometimes," Garrison adds.

I turn to him and lift my hand in a silent question. What happened to loyalty? He'll be hearing about this later.

"Is everyone joining us for the meeting?" Aurora asks suddenly, eyes trained on Eliza.

I return my gaze to her and watch as she scurries right past me toward the house, a small purse over her shoulder and sandals slapping against the soles of her feet. My smirk appears of its own accord. She has so much to learn about this group of people if she thought they'd care about her calling me such a ridiculous name.

"No, sweet girl. Just you and me. These hang-arounds just wanted to say hi," Eliza replies.

It's unclear whether Rory believes her or not, but I don't have a chance to find out before she's escaping into the group of women and giving me her back.

My moms raised me better than to let my eyes drop to her ass, regardless of how badly I want to look. Blindly ogling a woman's body isn't my specialty, but with Aurora, I've wanted to do so from the moment I saw her in Peakside.

I force myself to stay focused on the curves of her waist and the way I can see the imprint of her bra from beneath her shirt instead. It's a fucking great distraction, and that in itself is a bit alarming. It's probably creepy to get hard from staring at someone's bra strap, and I'm already halfway there.

As if sensing where my mind's wandered, Garrison slaps me on the back. The pain from the hit shakes me from my thoughts.

His laugh is low and gruff. "Fuck me. You're screwed."

"You're just learning that now?"

Aurora doesn't pay me a second glance before letting Eliza lead her inside the house. I don't let her lack of attention deter me, though. There's something there between us. A crackle of flame that I'm dead set on drowning in gasoline.

Our conversation just now has confirmed that she feels that something too. Even slightly. And whatever it is that's in the way of her exploring it, I'm prepared to tear it down.

7

Aurora

It's hard to be annoyed with Eliza when she's so damn cute. She's the type of woman that talks with her hands. Throughout the entire tour of the ranch house, she's had her hands waving in her face and out in the space between us. I follow behind her and listen as she recounts family memories and every renovation that's ever been done to the place.

Wade and Brody are her life, with this place coming right after. That much is obvious.

"What about you, my girl? Do you have any happy memories to share with me, or shall I keep yapping?" she asks once we step into the small office space.

It's painted with soft browns and full of old, aging bookshelves so full of books there are stacks of them on top of the neatly lined rows. Trinkets decorate any and all empty spots and, of course, family photos in a million types of different frames. Anna is in several of them, as if she hasn't only been here for two years but decades.

I shift away from Eliza and trail my eyes over the bookcase closest to me, taking in all the photos and the stories they tell. It's a lot. Like I'm living through Eliza's eyes for some of the most important days of her life. I look between a wedding photo that's yellowing at the edges and a dark photo with a yellow time stamp on the bottom corner, marking about a time that would make the young boy riding a rocking horse with an oversized cowboy hat on his head Brody. I smile slightly before looking at the golden frame beside it.

My heartbeat stalls.

It's a photo of a young couple at what looks to be a carnival. Simple enough, but not at all. While the young couple has to be Wade and Eliza, the one beside them . . .

"Who is this beside you?" I ask, my fingers brushing the top of the frame, tracing the grooves along the edge.

"Oh, this was a long, long time ago," she says, more to herself than me. "That's Bernice and James Rose. It's been . . . oh, at least a decade since I've seen them last."

"Did they live here?"

Eliza takes a step closer to me, her gaze burning into my cheek. "Yes. They moved up to Edmonton shortly after their son left town."

My throat is so clogged I can hardly swallow as I ask, "When did he leave town?"

"Well, I'd say shortly after he met your mother."

I snap my head to look at her before growing as still as death. "What?"

Her lips part on a soft, comforting smile. "I recognized you the moment I saw you. You're a spitting image of your mother. My memory isn't shot quite yet."

"You knew my mother?"

"Knew *of* her and saw her a handful of times," she corrects me. "Everyone here knew about Lee Rose's city girl from up in Calgary. She spent a couple of years down here with Lee before they both left. Lee came back alone a few months later. We didn't know why she didn't come back with him at the time, but maybe . . ."

"It was because of me," I say, knowing without a doubt that I'm right.

"That would make you, what? Thirty? A year older than Brody and Wanda." She nods to herself. "Yes, that would line up about right."

Hearing my half-sister's name spoken out loud right now is a shock to my system. I've heard the name several times during my time in Cherry Peak, but it hasn't hit as deep as right now. This time, it's coming from someone who knows my grandparents and more about my father than anyone else does. At least anyone who's here and willing to talk to me about him.

Fuck, that's weird to think about.

"Yeah, I'm thirty. Wanda's only a year younger than me?"

Mom didn't mention that when she told me about her. My skin crawls at the realization that Lee Rose met another woman he liked enough to have a child with so soon after being with my mom.

If I didn't already think the guy was a piece of shit for leaving my mom in the first place after she got pregnant with me, I would now.

Eliza lifts the gold photo frame with gentle fingers, bringing it closer to her. "I didn't bring you in here today for this, Aurora. You have my word about that. This photo has been here for so long that I hardly notice it anymore."

"I believe you," I say sincerely. "Would you—*could* you tell me about James and Bernice?"

She stares at the picture for a moment more before setting it back down and looking my way. Tucking a short silver curl behind her ear, she gestures past the oak desk and yellow lamp toward the two brown chairs tucked into the corner of the office.

"I'll tell you everything I know and remember. But first, I need to talk to you about why I asked you here today."

"I'm listening."

"Come sit with me."

She settles into one of the chairs, and I drop into the other. Extending her hand into the empty space between us, she offers it to me with a cautious expression. The dump of information

I've just learned has my thoughts running a million miles an hour. When I place my hand into hers, she squeezes, and I let the comfort relax me slightly.

"I need some help around here, Rory. I'm still young enough that I'm not ready to cut back my work altogether, but I can't do it on my own anymore. Not if I want to keep my sanity," she starts, the words heavy, like she's upset she has to ask for this. "It's like you were just plucked up and dropped into my lap here in Cherry Peak with that beautiful brain of yours. I want you to come work with me here. Work with all of us, if you'll take me up on my offer."

"I've never worked with a ranch before. Or the farming industry in general. I'm not sure I'm qualified," I admit.

She chuckles. "You're more than qualified. And even if you weren't, I'll be here too. Like I said, I'm not ready to step back yet. But soon. And we need the ranch ready for when that day does come."

My mouth is dry. A mix of surprise and appreciation for the offer takes flight in my mind.

"I don't want to sound like I don't want the job—because I do. God, I miss working with numbers. But are you sure, like *positive*, that you want me for this? If you posted a job listing, I'm sure you'd have dozens of resumes come in from people who know how to do this job far better than I do."

Her nod is full of conviction. There isn't a fleck of doubt in her stare as she watches me. "I'm positive, Rory. I may not know you all that well yet, but you're no stranger. You're not from Cherry Peak, but there's still some country blood in you. One of us, my dear. That's what you are."

I bite down on the inside of my lip to keep from telling her that she's wrong. If there's any country in my blood, it's more watered down than a warm stadium beer. This place doesn't call to me, and I sure as hell don't call to it. My home is in Calgary. That won't ever change. No matter how far I run or how long I ignore what I left there.

"I don't know a thing about country life, Eliza. And I won't lie to you and say that I'm interested in learning. But I'll take the job as long as you know that I'm not planning on staying."

"Well, I appreciate your honesty. And I'm perfectly alright with that."

I snort. "Some call it bluntness more so than honesty."

"Aren't they the same thing?"

"Maybe."

"Am I allowed to ask why you're here if you don't plan on staying for long?"

I fight past the immediate urge to close up and shift in my seat. "I came here to meet Wanda. And to learn about Lee—my father, I guess. I don't know if I even want to call him that. But Wanda was supposed to be here to help me figure that out."

"It seems there are gaps that have been left in the story for far more than just us in Cherry Peak, then," she says.

My laugh is angry. "That's an understatement."

She gives my hand another firm squeeze before releasing it and holding the armrest. "I don't know a lot about Lee. Only bits from when he was a young boy, long before he became the big name he is now. But his parents, I'll share all I know."

"Thank you," I say with a relieved exhale.

For the first time since arriving in town and learning Wanda's gone—my hopes of learning about my lineage lost with her—I have hope. I'm fully aware that I might not learn anything that will bring me closer to a meeting with Lee Rose, but maybe I'll be able to answer some of my burning questions.

Like why what he had in this place was more important to him than my mother. *Than me.* The life we could have had.

What made Wanda and her mother so much better than us?

Clearing my throat, I close off those thoughts. They'll do nothing but tear at my heart, and it's far too sensitive already.

"What kind of people are they? James and Bernice, I mean."

Eliza hums. "They're kind people. Bernice and I grew up here together, but James moved from Nova Scotia a couple of years before Lee was born. Some of my favourite laughs came from James's blunt jokes. He's a hard-looking man, but he's a comedian at heart. And Bernice, well, she's a bit more like you than she is her husband. She's quiet but not because she's shy, and I can't forget about her brutal honesty."

"You're a bit too observant, Eliza Steele," I mutter, feeling like I've been put under a microscope.

Her laugh is warm and kind, making it harder than usual to keep my walls high and reinforced. My gut tells me that it would be okay to let this woman in, but it's too early for my mind to agree.

"I'll take it. There are worse things to be."

I search the office for anything that will tell me more about the unknown side of my heritage, but there's nothing more than the single photo on the shelf.

"Do you still talk to them at all?" I ask, hesitant to hear both a yes and a no. I'm not sure which would be better.

"No. Time and distance have taken its toll on our friendship."

My stomach falls. Clearly, a no was worse.

Catching onto my disappointment, she's quick to add, "But I do still have their house number in my contact book. You could give it a try and see if they've changed it in the past few years or not. There isn't anyone better to tell you about your father than the two of them."

I nod, offering a half-smile in return for her offer. "What about Wanda? Do you think it's worth trying to track her down?"

"Sweet girl, Wanda's been gone for over a year on a mission to get to know Lee. She may have grown up here with him, but he was no more a father to her as he was to you."

"What?" I gape, guilt swelling in my chest.

Eliza grimaces. "Lee Rose has a lot of making up to do, Rory. With everyone. Even family."

"I thought . . ."

She reaches for my hand again, and I let her take it. "That

Wanda had the life you didn't get a chance to have. I know, honey. How could you have thought anything different with the information you had?"

"Maybe it's a good thing she isn't here. I'd have said something stupid and put my foot in my mouth."

"But you didn't. And now, you have a potential place to start on your search for answers," she soothes me.

"I do. You're right."

And I don't plan on wasting it.

8

Johnny

I TUCK MY HAIR BEHIND MY EARS AND SLIP INTO PEAKSIDE. IT'S HOT inside, the type of muggy that makes the air stick to your skin like a tight, uncomfortable knitted shirt from your grandma that you're too nice to tell her you hate.

A few people lift their fingers in waves from the tables I pass on the way to the bar, and I flash dimpled grins back. Saturday nights are for dimpled grins, laughing until your throat hurts, and empty beer bottles, which means I'm already a third of the way there.

The grumpy, sour-faced owner of the bar listens to me order a couple of beers and then makes quick work of serving them without so much as a hello. She's gotta be one of the rudest people I've ever met, but considering her daughter is Bryce's evil ex, our entire group of friends has been written off. It's no skin off my back, and I know the feeling is mutual throughout all of us.

I pay and grab the glass bottles between my fingers before heading toward the table at the back of the bar. Noticing the table isn't full yet has me whooping in victory, drawing the eyes of Bryce and Darren.

"Am I early enough for you, Brycie?" I ask while folding my body into the booth across the table from the two of them.

"Could have been earlier," she mutters before lifting her red drink to her lips and taking a sip. "I'd have been spared the alone time with Darren."

Darren rolls his eyes and lifts his beer to mine as we cheers. "Stop acting as if you don't love the time with me."

"I don't."

"I'll stop bringing you ginger beef every Tuesday night, then," he threatens.

Bryce glares at Darren, her sharp blue eyes brutal. "Don't you dare."

"You like ginger beef, right, Johnny?" Darren asks me, pretending he isn't playing with fire.

"I fuckin' love it. And I wouldn't mind a cute date with you either," I tease.

"Please. I'd never go on a date with Darren," Bryce balks.

He whips his head to look at her, eyes tightened at the corners. "Do you have to sound so disgusted at the idea?"

"As if you're not equally as disgusted."

"I am. But at least I'm not making it obvious."

"People are going to think you're into each other for real with how much you bicker," I say, my first beer pressed against my lips.

Bryce finishes off her drink before saying, "Maybe. But only those who don't know that I'm not currently in the market for a man."

Intrigued, I set my beer down and lean closer to her, folding my arms on the table. "Oh, do tell, Brycie."

"No."

Darren chokes on a laugh. "Brutal."

"I think the word you're looking for is 'bully,'" I correct him.

"I'm not a bully. You're just snoopy," Bryce counters.

I wave her off and settle back in the booth. "God forbid I want to know about your love life."

"If I wanted you to know anything, you already would, Johnny."

"Does Darren know?" I ask before snapping my gaze to him. "Do you?"

He smirks, shoulder lifting. "Maybe."

"He doesn't," Bryce says, giving Darren a rough shove. "Because there's nothing to know other than I'm not interested in Darren. Got it?"

I hold my hands up in surrender. "I've got it, sunshine."

She smiles at the pet name. "I'm going to get another drink. Let me up, you oaf."

"A please goes a long way," Darren mutters but lets her out of the booth without a fight.

"You're not my daddy."

As she walks away from the table, Darren places his hands around his mouth and yells, "I could be!"

Bryce flips him off over her shoulder before disappearing from view. I wait for Darren to settle back down before saying, "You look happier today."

"It was a good day."

"I'm glad. You've been through enough these past few weeks."

"Abbie's with me this week while Sasha's out of town, and I'm just happy to be with her. She's started wanting to make these adorable beaded bracelets, so I went and ordered three hundred dollars' worth of materials for her," he says, his voice light and more animated than I've heard it in a long damn time.

Shoving the sleeve of his shirt up his forearm, he shows off the stack of beaded bracelets on his wrist. All four of them have big, thick knots in the clear elastic and hot pink and purple beads with a few smaller gold stars and white block letters throughout. One says DADDY, and another says LUV U, while the other two have their initials.

"Those are cute, Darren."

He beams. "Aren't they? She's only five and already so good at making them. Maybe she'll be a jewelry designer one day."

"I'd buy from her."

"Everyone would."

"Ah! Are those friendship bracelets?" Poppy squeals.

Both Darren and I turn to see her and the rest of the group making a beeline for the table. Anna's got Poppy's hand in hers, and the two of them move the fastest toward us.

They stop at the side of the table and bend over the edge as Poppy grabs her brother's wrist and pulls it closer to her.

"Stop it right now, D. Did Abbie make you these?" she asks, tears in her eyes.

Garrison's behind her the moment he hears them in her voice, a stone guardian at her back. I look at him and smile, hoping it'll help him realize there's no need for the protectiveness right now.

"She did. Isn't she incredible?" Darren asks.

Anna presses her fingers to her heart and sighs dreamily. "I think my ovaries have just exploded."

"Alright, stop fawning over Darren. He'll never let it go," Brody grumbles, sidling up behind Anna and wrapping an arm around her stomach.

The girls ignore their men and continue to fiddle with Darren's bracelets. I'm rolling my lips, struggling to keep my laugh inside, when I see her. Suddenly, laughing isn't a concern for me. Breathing is.

I wasn't expecting her to come tonight. But I was hoping she would. It's been a long time since she was here last, and I'm already desperate to dance with her again. On the dance floor or in the aisle between tables again, it doesn't matter. I'd even settle for a single song out back behind the bar.

I'm quick to slide out of my seat and offer it to her while the others are still too focused on Darren to notice her arrival. Her steps slow as we get closer together, and I drag my eyes down her body a single time.

I've never enjoyed the sight of plain blue jeans and a loose-fitted band tee as much as I do right now. Not to mention the slick backed ponytail that I know is swishing along her spine as she moves toward me.

I grip the back of the booth and keep my body language loose and open, not wanting to spook her. It's like approaching a wild horse for the first time. Slow, steady, calm. No sudden movements or so much as a hint of abrasiveness in your tone.

"You better take a seat before they steal them all," I suggest.

Her eyes are wary as she looks at the empty booth and then to the crowd of people hanging over the edge of the table. I hold my breath as I wait for her answer, prepared to pull a chair over from one of the tables near us in case she says she doesn't want me to join her. But there isn't any of that.

She slides into the booth and then scoots all the way inside before looking at me again, waiting with a firm, curved brow. I laugh in slight disbelief before sitting beside her, making sure to keep my arm from brushing hers as I cross my hands on the table.

"They'll be finished drooling over Darren in a minute," I tell her.

"They don't have to be."

"Nah, they will be. It's rude to ignore someone."

"They're not ignoring me. I snuck in behind them because I didn't want it to be a big deal that I'm here."

I cock my head in her direction, holding her stare as I try and dig into those deep pools of blue, desperate to learn more about her. "It's a big deal to me that you're here."

She rolls her eyes, brushing me off. "What's your play?"

"My play?"

"Yeah. The reason for the flirting and interest. Is it a bet or something?"

"I'm not a teenager, darlin'. I don't make bets where women are involved."

"How old are you?"

I wrangle back a smirk at her interest. "Twenty-two."

Her lips part, a quick inhale following closely after. "You're a baby."

"How does the saying go? Age isn't anything but a number?"

"Yeah, and twenty-two is a very low number."

"Well, how old are you? Twenty-three?" I ask slyly, shifting the smallest bit closer to her, just enough to face her more fully.

Her cheeks pinken up at my question, and my chest lurches. "Not even close."

"It doesn't matter either way. Twenty-three or thirty-three, my interest stands where it is," I say, my voice thick with conviction.

"Well then. I'm forty-three," she bluffs.

I snort a laugh and pick up my near empty beer from where I left it on the table. "Nah, you're not. But like I said, all I hear is a number. It doesn't mean anything to me."

She shakes her head, her throat rising with a swallow as she does a damn good job of playing off how flustered I've made her. I'm not a fan of beating around the bush. Not with work, my family, or women. It's just not my style. That hasn't changed in the presence of a woman as beautiful and complicated as Aurora.

"You're right. I'm not forty-three. But I'm not twenty-two either."

"Like I said, I don't care. I'm interested in you regardless of my age or yours."

"You shouldn't be," she says rigidly.

I keep my eyes on her, categorizing her every reaction and response to my statements and questions.

"There are plenty of things I shouldn't do. Can't say I've ever heeded more than a couple warnings."

"You should heed mine. I won't give you what you want."

My mouth kicks up into a no-good grin as I push my second, untouched beer across the tabletop toward her. "You know that for a fact, huh?"

"I do," she answers, tapping a finger against the dewy bottle I've offered her.

I'd have preferred the cap be on so she knows it's safe, but nobody's touched the bottle other than the bartender when she removed it.

"And how do you know that? Because I think you're jumping the gun. You don't know a damn thing about me yet, and I don't know much about you. I want to change that," I say, putting it all out there.

"And I'm supposed to care about what you want?"

I nod. "I'd prefer that, yeah."

The corner of her mouth twitches. "It's your funeral, then, Johnny. But don't say that I didn't warn you."

It takes everything in me not to fill the bar with another obnoxious whooping noise. I settle on a wide grin instead, making sure she can see how elated I am.

"I never knew funerals could be so fucking exciting."

9

Aurora

Two hours into my Saturday night at Peakside and I have a belly full of overly frothy beer and chicken nachos. Well, more beer than nachos as Brody scarfed most of the giant plate before anyone else got a chance to have more than a couple of chips.

I didn't think that I'd feel as comfortable with such a large group of people as I do tonight. There hasn't been any awkward silence to fill or the pressure to hop into certain conversations when I don't have anything worth adding. Everyone seems genuinely happy to be in each other's company. It's nice. Relaxing.

The first time I was here with this group, I was terrified. I wasn't ready to be introduced to so many people all at once, but I agreed anyway, only to regret it the moment the table began to fill.

Anna was my new boss, and when she asked me to come, I fell into the trap of not wanting to risk my job by turning her down. I know now that that wouldn't have happened. These people are kind and real. The genuine type that are hard to find.

And like a cruel joke from the universe, they've all fallen into my lap at a time in my life where it isn't possible to keep them.

All they are to me now is a temptation I want to give in to but know I can't.

I take another gulp of my second beer and eye the group, listening intently to their conversation while pretending that I can't feel Johnny's heat seeping into my side.

We've been shoved so close together now that everyone's here, and our booth is full. I've lost track of how many times our arms have brushed and our knees have knocked. My tongue is going to have permanent teeth marks by the time the night is over.

It doesn't help that he smells really fucking good tonight. Like something deep and rich and woodsy but also the tiniest bit sweet. I want to lean into his body and bury my face in the front of his shirt just to get a stronger whiff of it, and that's fucking weird.

As if he can tell exactly what I'm thinking, Johnny glances over at me, a knowing smirk tugging at his plump lips. God, they're *really* plump. The bottom one looks almost swollen, but in a sexy way. Like it's been sucked and bitten on for hours prior to him coming out tonight.

My gut pinches at that thought, and I'm quick to extinguish the discomfort at the thought of him coming here directly after a hookup. I'm not jealous, and I'm absolutely not annoyed that he's got a sex life. But I would be put off if he's here flirting with me so soon after.

"Is beer your liquor of choice?" he asks lowly, starting up a conversation for just us.

"Usually."

"I had a feeling."

"Oh?"

"Yeah, *oh*," he teases, flicking his eyes to the almost empty bottle I have clutched in my hands. "I'm a lightweight, so it's always beer for me."

I swirl the bottle between my palms. "I'm not even close to a lightweight."

"Ooh, interesting. So how many of those would it take to have you giggling at my bad jokes?"

"More than I plan to drink tonight." I twist so my shoulder's pressed to the wall and I can look at Johnny properly. The loopy grin on his face has me blurting out, "How many will it take to have you telling me said bad jokes?"

"Oh, darlin'. I'm already halfway there."

"From two beers?"

"From two beers," he confirms.

"That's got to be a record somewhere."

"If it was, does that mean you'll give me a reward for my success?"

A laugh slips from me far too easily. I blame it on the alcohol. "What kind of reward are you hoping for?"

He taps a finger to his lips and hums for a minute before deciding. "Let me walk you home tonight."

"That seems like a waste of a reward."

His eyes snare mine, the determination in them causing an uptick in my pulse. "Not even close."

I swallow before clearing my throat, and when I still feel like I can't breathe, I bring my beer back to my lips and drink the last sip.

"I drove here, but I won't be driving home. I'll drop you off and come back so I can grab a ride from someone. All I want is to walk with you," he adds.

"Fine. But when you get bored of walking in silence, it's not my fault."

That determination I saw flares, growing into something even stronger. "Bored? I doubt it, Rory."

He purrs my name, and I set my bottle down before smoothing my sweaty hands down my thighs, careful to keep my arms to myself.

"Are you two done with your private conversation yet? I have a question for you, J," Brody says from across the table.

I blink and stare at the several sets of eyes now fixated on me and Johnny. The man beside me doesn't seem to mind the attention as he winks at Brody, but me? I want to crawl into a hole and wait for it to collapse on me.

"Go for it," he tells his friend, sounding far too casual.

Brody tips his chin and starts to speak, but I miss the entire first half of his sentence when Johnny nudges me with his elbow, the touch searing through me. It would be an accidental brush if it were anyone else, but by the mischievous twitch of his features, I know it was anything but.

"—she should be okay, but I want an extra set of eyes on 'er while we're gone. You up for it?" Brody asks.

I hide my confusion behind a blank expression, pretending that I've been paying attention when I damn well wasn't. God, I'm bound to make a fool of myself one of these days if I can't keep myself out of my head.

Johnny doesn't seem to suffer from the same lack of concentration as I do. He replies in an instant, having *not* missed half of the conversation. "Of course. You don't even have to ask."

Brody releases a sigh of relief, and the arm he has slung around Anna's shoulder relaxes some. She gazes up at him dreamily and rubs his chest in slow circles. It's a casual movement, and I latch onto it, thinking back to a time where I would have touched a man that easily just because I wanted to.

It was a long, long time ago. Back when I was a book nerd spending my days in the front row of lectures and my nights tucked in the empty corners of closed libraries. I wasn't exactly a wild one, but my ex didn't care. I think he preferred me nice and tame. It made it easier for him to control me and our life. But never again. I'm not the same person I was then.

"Was the cut deep? Wade never mentioned it earlier," Garrison states, swaying slightly to the music playing with Poppy in his lap at the edge of the table.

They pulled up a chair after disappearing for a few minutes shortly after arriving. It only took one look at them when they got back to realize why they left and what they were doing.

Unless Garrison's into wearing red lipstick smeared along his throat and staining his white button-up.

Everyone teased them, but I was content simply watching everyone's interactions.

Poppy rolls her head against her boyfriend's chest and rubs her cheek against his sternum. "It's not deep at all. Brody's being a mother hen again."

"I'm not bein' a mother hen. She's favouring her front leg, and I don't want her hurtin' herself further while I'm gone," Brody grunts, and I put the pieces together that they must be talking about an animal. His horse, maybe.

Johnny stares straight across the table at him, as serious as ever. "I'll take care of your girl, Brody. Don't worry about it."

Brody looks back at him with equal seriousness before nodding slowly. "Thank you."

"Aurora, as your friend, I think it would be in incredibly poor taste for me not to tell you that I don't think you should be living in your rental," Poppy says, focused on me now.

I push my empty beer bottle away from me and grab a napkin before tearing it up to keep my hands busy. "It's really not as bad as you all think it is."

"It might actually be worse." Anna grimaces.

Poppy points at her best friend in approval. "Exactly right. I hope you at least have a few crosses hung on the walls. Maybe I should bring you some sage to light. Just in case you're not really alone. I heard someone say once that they saw a creepy woman standing in the upstairs window."

"It's not haunted," Garrison tells her.

She leans out of his arms and stares at him deadpan. "And you know that how? Have you gone inside and asked if anyone's there?"

"Fuck no."

"Well, then you don't know that it isn't." Her brown eyes find mine again. "Have you noticed anything? Any banging at night or woken up with bruises?"

I shake my head, stifling a laugh. "No. It's not haunted. Ghosts aren't real."

Bryce gasps, setting her glass down on the table hard enough for me to feel it on the other side. "Ghosts are real. And just because you said that, they're going to haunt your ass."

"Don't start with your ghost hunter shit again, Bryce," Darren groans.

She pins him beneath a sharp glare. "I'm genuinely shocked no ghost has thrown a plate at your head yet. You certainly deserve it from time to time."

"Okay. So, Bryce is into ghosts," I mutter, desperate for everyone to drop the topic. "There aren't any in my house. We can move on now."

"She's dressed up as a Ghostbuster for the past five Halloweens in a row," Poppy says.

I blink. "Oh."

Poppy grows more alert, jerking into a proper sitting position. Garrison grips her tight around her middle as if he's worried she'll slide from his lap.

"That reminds me. We should start planning our costumes for this year. I'm thinking we can have the party at our house. Maybe invite some of the new girls from my Calgary Beautifully Bold location over too," she suggests excitedly.

"A Halloween party?" I ask, discomfort slithering up my spine.

Parties have never been my thing. I've avoided them like the plague my entire life, and I don't plan on changing that at thirty years old. Plus, isn't it a little early to be planning for Halloween? It's only August.

Suddenly, Johnny's forearm glides along mine as he reaches across the table toward the stack of napkins. I watch as he grabs one from the top of the stack and then brings his arm back, purposefully touching me again, this time lifting his eyes to look at me as he does. I grow still. He smiles gently, and then his touch is gone. When I look at what he's doing, I find him using the napkin to wipe at the already dry table.

It's not until I notice my discomfort has settled that I realize he didn't need a napkin at all. That move had been just for me.

"I'm sorry, Pop, but I'm exhausted, and I promised Rory I'd walk her home tonight. Can we talk about Halloween next time?" he asks, yawning loudly.

I don't buy it, and as the group sweeps their eyes between the two of us, it's clear they don't either. I've grown tired of caring what they think to bother adding an excuse, though. That's a problem for Monday morning when Anna will no doubt ask about it.

"Yeah. I'm tired too," I mutter.

Poppy lets it go and flashes us an easy smile. "Of course. Let us know when you're coming back so we can be ready to drop you at home."

Johnny does a two-finger salute, and then Darren's scooting out of the booth to let us out. I say goodbye quickly and follow behind Johnny as he leads us out of the bar.

The moment we step outside and the cooling evening breeze hits, I have to swallow a moan. It's silent, the street empty besides the two men leaning against a car smoking cigarettes. Johnny waves at them, and they return it before we turn our backs to them and start down the sidewalk.

My nose feels oily beneath my makeup after a long night in the hot bar, and I'm beyond ready to take it off and get in bed. It's probably half melted off my face at this point. At least it's dark so Johnny can't see the splotchiness anymore.

"For what it's worth, I don't think the house is haunted. Raggedy as fuck, yes. But not haunted," he says.

"Raggedy? That's rude."

"Rude but true. You have to know it isn't safe."

"It's safe enough," I argue stubbornly.

We keep our pace slow, easy. I can't help but look down his legs at his booted feet, curious how much he has to be stunting his large steps to keep up with such a leisurely pace. Those things are a near kilometre long.

"Safe enough isn't really all that settling, darlin'."

"I wasn't aware that I was supposed to be settling you, *sugar*."

His laugh fills the street, bouncing off the much nicer, sturdier homes we pass. It makes my pulse skitter, and I kick my toe at the sidewalk harder than usual on my next step.

"You know, I actually like that pet name. Keep it coming," he teases, glancing my way just long enough to wink.

"With all the winking you do, some would assume you constantly have something in your eyes."

"Fuck me, you like busting balls," he says, a low rumble from deep in his chest following the words.

"You should stop leaving them so open for me to abuse."

"How do you suggest I do that?"

I open my mouth to shoot back some sort of teasing dig but close it before I do. Honestly, I don't want him to change anything he's doing. This back-and-forth feels good. It's easy, and I haven't had easy in a long time.

"Did you want to walk me home tonight because you're worried about the rampant crime in Cherry Peak?" I ask, changing the subject.

The tip of a finger finds my wristbone and glides across my knuckles before disappearing again, leaving me with skin scattered with goosebumps.

"No. I wanted to walk you home because I've been trying to get time alone with you for a month now with no luck. I figured this might be my only shot, and I wasn't about to pass on it. Even a few minutes is better than nothing," he admits.

It's the confidence in his admission that affects me the most. The surety in the fact that he actually wants to spend time with me in any way he can just so he can get to know me that little bit more. It threatens to do my head in.

I'm not used to such fearless pining. Especially not from

someone I hardly know and have turned down on multiple occasions.

"You're putting a hell of a lot of eggs in one basket. How do you know you'll like what you find the further you dig?"

His shrug is adorable in the most naïve of ways. "I've got a good sense of intuition."

"I've never made a decision based off of blind faith before."

"I don't know about blind, darlin'. I've got twenty-twenty vision, and right now, it's dead focused on you."

10

Johnny

JOKER SWAYS BENEATH MY BODY, KEEPING PACE WITH WADE AND Kip. The black beast of a horse beneath my boss keeps his head up and ears alert as we follow behind the herd of cattle, bringing them toward their new home for the next few weeks.

My pup, Tracker, leads the herd, running from one side to the other with sharp yaps that force the cattle back in line when they sway a bit too far from the others. Rotation days are his favourite because he gets to mouth off without getting in shit for it. And that's a common occurrence around here.

I got him from a farmer a few towns over who offered an entire litter of Australian cattle dogs to Wade in exchange for one of our best bulls. Wade told him, in more polite terms, to kick rocks, but I took one look at the grey, black, and brown puppy with a tongue damn near the length of my forearm dripping puddles onto the grass and took him as my own.

"You should get a couple of pups for yourself," I say to Wade. "The ranch could use a few more."

"Between you and Thomas, I already got plenty of mutts around here."

"I can't tell if you're referring to us or our dogs."

He scoffs a rasped laugh. "Both."

Thomas, one of my friends from school who works with me on Steele Ranch, bought one of Tracker's sisters that same day. He doesn't spend a single day at work without her by his side. We have our obsession with our dogs in common, amongst a handful of other things.

Bandit looks similar to Tracker but has grey-blue eyes instead of brown and enough energy to put every other animal on the ranch to shame. It's hard to tell them apart unless you're face to face, so I make sure Tracker's fitted with his blue bandana before we get to work every morning to try and help.

The siblings battle back and forth with their yippy barks, as if competing to see who'll do a better herding job, until I lift my fingers to my mouth and whistle. They shut up instantly and get back into their proper positions, no longer concerned with one another.

I spy Thomas on an ATV near the front of the herd, getting closer to the pasture gate that we left open this morning. The grass there is thick and green, healthier than the one we've just left. With fall coming soon, we've got a million things on the list of to-dos, and just like I do every year, I feel like there isn't enough time to complete it all. Not even with the full team of ranch hands and Brody and Garrison here, as opposed to a few years back.

The fencing around the pasture we're moving this herd of cattle to is solid, recently checked for any holes or sharp pieces, and I can't help but think back to the fence around the bulls. The assholes are only a field over, and if they keep acting like they have been, it'll only be a manner of time before they bust through to say hello to these cows.

"Have you thought more on the fence situation?" I ask.

Wade doesn't stiffen at the question, but he also doesn't look pleased either. It's the old-fashioned stubbornness in him.

"No."

"Why not?"

"I've got a lot of things on my mind right now. A lot more important things than the bulls and their tantrums."

"You'd prefer to think about them after they've smashed their way into a herd and fucked their way through 'em all before spring hits and we're ready for it?" I ask calmly.

He jerks his head in my direction and glares viciously. "I've never had anything close to that happen here before."

"I'm trying to keep it that way with steel fencing around the bull pasture. Let me figure everything out. I'll take care of it," I offer, close to begging. "We don't gotta redo every side. Just the two facing the road and the cattle."

My gut tells me it needs to get done soon. If he doesn't take me seriously here, I'll just do it without his permission and deal with the consequences, knowing the herd is safe.

"You've never let anything happen to your cows before, Wade. Everyone knows you love 'em all. So just let me do this," I add.

There's a moment of heavy silence as we stare at each other. He keeps his glare brutal, resolve unshaken. The look threatens to have me backing up and telling him to forget I said anything. But I don't. I hold his glare and keep my features relaxed, proving that I'm sure about this.

"Fine," he mutters reluctantly. "But make a plan, and then bring it to me. I want more than a half-cocked idea before you destroy a perfectly good fence."

I grin so wide my cheeks burn. His approval is more than simply acceptance. It's him putting his trust in me and believing that I can do this.

"Will do. I'll figure it out tonight."

He jerks his chin. "You better."

Thomas revs the ATV and takes off ahead of the herd before swerving between the open gate and leading us all into the pasture. Tracker and Bandit keep the cows in line as they slip through the gate and then spread through the field.

Wade tugs on Kip's reins and leads him to the left side while

Joker and I take the right, herding the back. It moves fast after that, and by the time we ride into the field with the final cow following the others, I take my hat off my head and run a hand through my sweaty hair.

I don't know what time it is, but my stomach is growling, and my throat is parched. The heat is unforgiving today, and I know my back is slick with sweat. It's everywhere. One swipe at my upper lip, and I taste it there too.

Thomas makes a long loop and then drives the ATV back toward me, his face red and shirt sticking to his chest just as badly as mine is.

"Lunchtime?" he shouts over the engine.

I look for Wade and find him talking to his second-in-command, Renner, on the opposite side of the pasture.

"Lunchtime. I need to get out of this heat before I pass out," I reply.

Thomas nods, his ball cap flipped backward, not doing anything to protect his eyes from the sun. At least he's wearing a hat, though. His buzzed blond head would be bright red if he hadn't.

"I'll meet you there, then. I'm excited to get a first real look at the new girl."

The sly tone of voice would have riled me if I thought he actually stood a shooting chance with Aurora. If *I* hardly do, he sure as shit doesn't. Something tells me that she isn't into back-woods cowboys with chips on their shoulders and a habit of sleeping around.

"A look is all you'll get," I shoot back.

"We'll see about that, J."

I roll my eyes and slide my fingers back into my mouth before whistling for Tracker. His head lifts and whips in my direction before he takes off, his legs pumping beneath him. After turning Joker to the side, I give her a scratch on her neck and wait.

Thomas whistles for Bandit, and suddenly, the dogs are

racing, tongues flopping in the air and tails swatting. I laugh and pat Joker's side when my pup gets close enough to jump. He doesn't hesitate before leaping from the ground and jumping onto Joker. Settling into the spot behind me, he shoves his head under my arm, forcing me to lift it and tuck him in my armpit.

"Good boy, Tracker. You beat your sister like I knew you would," I coo, scratching behind his ear.

"You're a cheater. He had a head start," Thomas says.

"She wouldn't have beaten him if she had a head start, and you know it."

Thomas waves me off at the same time Bandit jumps onto the ATV and sits on the cushioned seat beside him. He revs the engine a few times before racing off, leaving the air thick with the scent of gas and exhaust.

My horse shuffles forward, wanting to follow him, and I give her the go-ahead while adjusting the reins. Tracker nuzzles into my side, and I keep him secured against my body and beneath my arm as we head back to the house.

The closer we get, the more my excitement grows. After walking Rory home Saturday night and watching her disappear behind her front door, I've been counting down the minutes till I can see her again. I didn't know that it would be this morning or that she was working for Eliza and Wade now, but fuck me, learning of her new job was great news.

Getting to see her every day while I'm working is a reward of epic proportions, even if she still hasn't actually agreed to spend more time with me than our walk the other night.

I haven't exactly asked her out yet, and I won't for a while still. Not because I'm unsure that I want to shoot my shot after everything I said to her the other night but because I'm trying to win her over first. If I did it now, I know she'd reject me. And while I'm a confident guy, I'm not a glutton for punishment.

The ranch house grows bigger and bigger the closer we get until, soon enough, I can see the number of trucks parked in front and hear the loud slap of boots on wood inside the stable.

It's silent around the second stable, so my construction crew must have taken off for lunch too.

Thomas's ATV is parked beside a brand-new lifted Chevy that Brody brought home with him last week. It's nice, really damn nice, with thick black tires and dark rims to match. My truck is a decade old now, but she runs as good as new. Once she kicks the bucket, I'll dive into my savings to find something newer, but until then, I'm happy with what I've got.

The house is loud even from outside. Laughter and shouts, even a few hissed curse words, escape the open windows and the flapping screen door. It sounds like home, and once I've tied Joker up and ordered my dog to wait for me in the shade of the porch, I'm walking inside with a smile on my face.

"It smells like heaven in here, Eliza," I say, slipping into the kitchen.

"Your heaven smells like melted cheese?" I hear from somewhere in the throng of sweaty men and cowboy hats.

It sounds like one of the older guys who spends all his time with the calves, but I'm too hungry to investigate.

Sidestepping my way toward where I know Eliza's griddle sits on the counter, I rub at my empty stomach. The first peek of silver hair behind a broad shoulder is a relief. Eliza stands at the counter with a stack of paper plates in her hands and a griddle full to the brim with tortillas full of shredded cheese beside her. The three empty pitchers next to a stack of plastic cups don't surprise me. I'm one of the last ones in today, and these fuckers have stolen all the good shit.

Noticing me, Eliza pulls me to the sink so I can wash my hands. The water is cold, and I don't give it time to warm up as I pump too much soap into my palm and scrub my skin until it's pink instead of black with dirt. Then, once I'm clean, she shoves a plate at my chest.

"Dish up, Johnny. You're always the last one in, and I'm tired of slapping greedy wrists while you're busy puttin' in more work than you need to be. Hurry up."

"You're sassy today," I tease but do as she says.

The tortillas are still hot and steaming as I grab one and toss it on my plate. A vegetable tray rests on the opposite side of the sink, and I go to reach for the carrots when Eliza pinches my inner arm.

"Don't just take the carrots. Take a bit of everything. That plate is for Aurora," she whisper hisses.

I jerk, more alert. "She hasn't eaten yet?"

"No. I couldn't get her to come out here in time before this lot showed up and scared her half to death."

Nodding, I start collecting a few of each vegetable and setting them on the plate, well enough away from the quesadillas with their gooey cheese in case she doesn't like her food touching.

When the plate is full, Eliza swaps it for a new one, and I get my lunch served up.

"Go bring it to her. She's in the office," she urges as I grip both plates.

I drift my eyes to the empty pitchers and then slowly look back at her. She scoffs and takes two cups from the stack before turning to the fridge and pulling another jug out. My thirst intensifies as I stare at what I know is Eliza's famous peach iced tea and wait for her to pour it into the cups.

"You're just as bad as Banana, you know? Pouting and hoping to get your own way," she chides, but there's no heat in the words.

"You gotta stop givin' in to them both, and maybe they'll knock it off," Wade grumbles, stomping past me toward his wife.

She flashes him a dazzling smile and pats his chest. "You know as well as I do that I can't do that."

He snorts and starts plating himself up some food. I take his entry as my cue to go, and Eliza helps slot the two drinks into my bent elbows before I leave.

I'm only jostled once, but I manage to keep all the food on the plates and the liquid in the cups. The office door is cracked open, and I nudge it further with my socked toes before stepping inside.

The clacking of a keyboard fills the room as Rory hunches over the desk and leans toward a computer screen. There's a stack of papers beside her and a pen bouncing between her middle fingers as she hums a tune low in her throat.

It almost feels wrong to interrupt her concentration right now, but she needs to eat, and I need to sit beside her for a little while.

"I brought you some food."

And company, if you'll take it.

She jumps in surprise despite how gently I speak, and I smile apologetically when she whips around to face me. Her lips are parted, chest heaving as she scowls and uncurls the fingers that must have fallen to her lap.

With her hair up and braided down her back, I can almost see the thump of her pulse in her bare throat as she asks, "What are you doing in here? And what is that?"

"This?" I lift the plate in front of me. "This is your lunch."

"I'm not hungry."

"Humour me. Eliza gets sad when people don't eat her home-cooked meals."

"It's cruel to use an old lady to get your way."

"If it means you won't spend your day hungry, then I doubt she'll mind." I risk moving closer, and when she doesn't tell me to leave, I walk the rest of the way to her. "I didn't know what you liked, so I grabbed some of everything."

She watches as I set the plate and cup of iced tea on the desk beside her computer mouse. Blue eyes scan the selection of food before skipping over the cauliflower, her nose crinkling slightly. I hyperfixate on that reaction.

"You don't like cauliflower?" I ask.

Slowly, she lifts her stare to my plate, watching as I set it beside hers. "Apparently, you don't either."

"Not in the slightest."

The second office chair—the one Wade occupies during the long nights Eliza's holed up in here working—is tucked beneath the opposite side of the L-shaped desk. I snag it by the back and drag it toward Rory. The wheels are stiff as I sit and roll closer.

"Anything else you don't like?"

She twists in her seat and looks back at the computer screen. "If you're going to eat in here with me, you'll need to be quiet."

"You don't mind if I eat in here?"

"Not as long as you aren't a gross eater."

"What makes someone a gross eater to you?" I ask, continuing to dig, knowing already that I'm not a bad eater. My mom used to threaten to glue our mouths shut if we chewed with our food showing.

Aurora sighs before turning her head to give me an up-close view of those gorgeous eyes that I can't get enough of.

She taps the fingers of her left hand over the keyboard keys. "Chewing with your mouth open. Talking with your mouth full and spitting little bits of it out all over everything. Sucking your fingers clean and making that loud smacking noise."

"Well, I don't do any of those things. I'm the politest eater you'll ever see," I declare.

"Alright."

Returning to her work, she glides the mouse over the plain black pad beneath it and clicks on something on the screen. I rest my forearms on the edge of the desk beside her and grab one of my quesadillas, the smell of the cheese making my stomach grumble.

With it raised in front of my mouth, I say, "Please eat, Aurora. I'll leave you alone once you do if that's what you want, but you need brain food."

A twitch of her brow.[SD1] "I thought nice guys weren't supposed to be demanding."

"You think I'm a nice guy?" I ask through a wide, split grin.

"You're helpless," she mutters, but I see the way the right side of her mouth tugs despite her best efforts to keep it straight.

"What kind of music do you like?"

She doesn't give a reaction to my question this time. Is she getting used to them?

"Pop. And I don't want to hear any judgment on it."

"You won't find any from me. I have three sisters and am quite a pop connoisseur. Especially if we're talking boy bands."

Her eyes grow as round as buttons as she stares at me and blurts out, "You have three sisters?"

"Yep. I have a twin and then two older sisters. Daisy and me are the youngest of the bunch."

Setting my quesadilla back on my plate, I slip a hand into the pocket of my jeans and snag my phone. Opening up my music app, I click on a pop playlist and keep the volume soft as I set my phone on the desk. The upbeat song that plays covers the upcoming sound of my chewing as I take a big bite of my food.

Aurora glances at the phone for a moment before blowing out a long breath, nearly whistling. "That's . . . that's a lot."

I swallow and nod. "Yeah. There has never been a quiet moment in our house ever. Even after my oldest two sisters, Giana and Josette, moved out."

"When was that?" she asks softly while picking up a carrot stick and swirling it in ranch before biting into it.

"Giana moved out about . . . ten years ago now. And Josette half of that. Daisy, my twin, is still at home when she's not in school, which seems to be all the damn time now."

"What's it like? Having sisters? Siblings in general?"

The question hardly sounds louder than a whisper but is sharp with something similar to sadness. It gnaws on me, making me move quickly to help dissolve whatever it is upsetting her.

"It was annoying when I was younger. With so many kids in the house, it was always loud and crowded, and I didn't get my own room until I turned thirteen. But it has its benefits. Like never being alone when you're sad and having someone that has to love you even when they hate you."

I take another bite of my lunch and make sure I chew extra softly to keep from letting her hear it above the music.

She swirls a green stick of celery into the dip. "That sounds nice."

"Yeah, I wouldn't have it any other way. Do you have any siblings, Rory?"

I fix my gaze on her features and watch as her lips turn down and the blue in her eyes grows hard and solid. She's angry, but I'm unsure if it's from my question or something else.

"I have a half-sister."

"I'm going to assume that you aren't close?"

Her next bite is ruthless, and she rips the end off the celery stick and glares at the remainder of it. "You could say that."

A laugh builds in my throat before I swallow it down. "I'm sorry you're not close. I couldn't imagine not being close with my sisters."

"We're hardly sisters," she huffs.

My brow jumps. "Wanna elaborate on that?"

"No."

I laugh at her bluntness. It's refreshing. Reminds me of Garrison.

"Alright. Well, if you ever decided that you wanted to, I'm interested in learning more."

Her nod is jerky before she lifts the quesadilla to her mouth and sinks her teeth into it. I divert my eyes while she eats and focus on eating my food. Soft music continues to play as we eat in silence, and I let it be the only noise. I don't want to force her to open up to me.

I'm happy with knowing what I've learned so far.

11

Aurora

The empty cup that once held a caramel macchiato with extra, extra caramel stares at me from my desk as I attempt to scroll through the updated expensive filing system I've been implementing into Steele Ranch the past two days.

I wasn't anticipating coming into work this morning to find my favourite coffee waiting for me. And I definitely wasn't expecting the note written on the side of the cup.

Everyone should start their day with something sweet, darlin.

I've since drank it all. Down to the very last drop and gob of caramel sauce. I've been dealing with the sugar high since.

"Is there anything I can do?" Eliza asks from behind me.

With a glance over my shoulder, I offer her an appreciative smile. "Actually, I was hoping you could answer some questions about Wanda for me. If you don't mind."

Her lips purse. "Wanda? Well, I don't know much, but I'll try my best."

Good enough. "Thank you."

I should be asking about my grandparents and father, but ever since Johnny told me about his sisters, I haven't been able to stop thinking about Wanda. If I asked any one of the people I've gotten to know here, they'd give me her number so I could speak with her myself. But I can't do that yet. I'm not ready to hear her voice or see her face, even if I came here with the intention of doing just that.

I'm not at all ready for that meeting. First, I want to know what I'm getting myself into with her. Have some sort of idea for what kind of person she is.

She's my direct line to Lee Rose, and I've realized that facing him scares the shit out of me.

Eliza sits in the same chair she did during my unofficial job interview and exhales tiredly. The wrinkles above her brows scrunch together as she readjusts her position, and then I'm up out of my chair. Compelled by the flash of pain in her eyes, I set a hand on her shoulder and try to offer support as she leans side to side, getting comfortable.

"Oh, you're sweet. I'm alright. Just old," she says with a half-smile.

"Are you sure? I don't mind getting you anything you need."

"I'm sure. My joints aren't what they used to be, is all. I grow tired much too early nowadays."

"I'm sure you've earned the extra breaks."

Her eyes twinkle despite the exhaustion in them, as if her kindness outweighs all else. "Today, you have as well. Now, come sit beside me and ask what you want to know."

I don't hesitate to sit in the opposite chair. Leaning in toward her, I cross my leg over my knee and flip through the series of questions in my mind. There are so many I want to ask and the smallest bite of worry in my side that I won't get the chance to get answers to them all.

"If she's not close to Lee, what about her mom? Are her . . . *parents* close?"

Eliza turns her head so her cheek brushes the high back of the armchair as she holds my gaze and answers, "Lee and his wife are—" She cuts herself off and twists her mouth before continuing. "I only know what I've heard. Gossip in a small town is a blessing and a curse, my sweet. There's no way to confirm the rumours unless we get answers from the mouths of the Roses, but from what I know, their marriage was not built from love. Wanda was raised by her mother, that much is true. Lee was off for long stretches and only home for the occasional holiday. Myself and everyone else can only assume—"

"That he stayed because of Wanda."

The statement sounds wrong. Gross.

Despite being cruel and selfish, I hate that he found a life somewhere else, with a woman who wasn't my mother and a daughter that wasn't me. But I'd rather my mother find a man who truly loves her than settle for one who only chose to be with her out of obligation.

"He's an asshole," I mutter.

Eliza chuckles. "He is an asshole."

"It sounds wrong when you say it."

She winks. "I've said far worse."

"Do I want to know?"

"I'll tell you another time," she promises.

I nod and fidget in the ultra-comfortable chair, uncrossing my legs only to cross them again. "What is Wanda like? Personality-wise? Anna's told me a couple things in passing, but nothing much."

Like that she doesn't know what it is she wants to do in life yet, so she's trying a million new things until she finds something that sticks. The salon, for example. It was hers before she decided on a whim to abandon it to go find our father. It was a blessing for Anna, but I'm not the type of person to leave things unfinished the way my half-sister does.

Will we even get along when we meet?

"She's to the point. Blunt and crass. Determined and fearless. She doesn't care much for the opinions of others. You have more in common with one another than you think."

"I don't know about that."

"Why not?" she asks, not a hint of judgment in her tone, just simple curiosity.

I ignore my discomfort at diving this deep into my thoughts in the presence of someone else and change the subject. "Is she open-minded? Because once she learns about this, she's going to be . . . upset."

"Or she could be happy. Isn't there a part of you that's excited to have a sister?"

I pause. "That's why I'm here."

Her smile is knowing. "I know."

"When she gets back to town, from what you know about her, do you think she'll listen to what I have to say?"

Eliza reaches across the space between chairs and grabs my hand from my lap. Her thumb rubs softly over my knuckles with a gentle reassurance.

"I think that if she knows what's good for her, she'll do more than just listen to you, Aurora."

LIFTING my hair off my neck, I step out of the house and onto the porch. The wood planks creak beneath my sneakers as I twist to let the screen door shut, but the sound of hooves clopping along the gravel road is too loud not to hear.

A black-and-white polka-dotted horse is running right for the house, its ears forward and wispy tail slashing through the air. My mouth dries when I glance up at the man atop its back, sitting snug in a massive brown saddle that nearly blends into the horse's coat.

With long legs and thick thighs that cup the horse's sides, a pair of dirty, scuffed-up brown cowboy boots tucked into the stirrups, and two gloved hands gripping a set of black reins with a sureness that stirs my belly, Johnny watches me. His smile is wide and goofy. Like he's genuinely excited to be seeing me.

"Hey!" he shouts, one arm lifted in a wave.

I press my tongue to the back of my teeth before replying. "Hi."

"Looks like I'm right on time."

"For what?"

Johnny slows the horse to a calm pace as they get closer, the horse's tail brushing the slatted railing of the porch. The hat on his head is tipped back enough that I get an unobstructed view of his handsome face while he stares at me. *There are so many freckles.* Too many to count in this lifetime and possibly the next.

"To walk you to your car." He says it like it's obvious, but it really never was.

I look from him to my car parked on the grass and then back to him. "It's parked like twenty steps from the house."

"Still gonna walk you to your car, darlin'."

"Why?"

"You ask a lot of questions," he notes, his eyes the lightest shade of blue I've ever seen.

"That's usually a good thing. I hate surprises."

Intrigue tugs at his features. "Why's that?"

"Now who's asking all the questions?" I throw back, moving quickly down the porch steps before dropping onto the grass. The horse beneath him watches me with a concerning level of concentration. Deep, dark eyes examine me, sizing me up, maybe. "What's the horse's name?"

Johnny pats the side of its neck affectionately. "Her name's Joker. Want to give her a pat?"

I shake my head and tuck my hands into the back pockets of my jeans. "I'm not much for animals."

"You're kidding."

"Not at all."

He blows out a long, weighted breath while cupping the top of his hat in his hand and lifting it. The mass of curly black waves he had hidden beneath it ripples in the warm breeze, making him look like something out of a goddamn cowboy porn magazine. I keep my expression blank and rock back on my heels, debating just making a run for my car. Something keeps my feet planted to the grass.

"Everyone is an animal person deep down," he says.

"Not me."

"I don't believe you. Maybe you just haven't met one you like before."

"I've met plenty," I argue.

From the duo of creepy raccoons that used to use our trash can as a five-star Michelin restaurant to the snappy Chihuahua my neighbour had growing up, I've met far too many animals that I didn't like.

"You have stories to tell," he notes, reading my expression with an expert gaze. "I'm a good story listener."

"And damn nosey."

His laugh travels in the wind, making it sound as though it came from right beside me instead of a few feet across the yard.

"I'm curious about you, Rory. I've been honest with you about that. It would save us both a shitload of time if you would just open up to me already."

"How do I know you don't just want me to tell you every deep, dark secret of mine because you're simply eager to learn gossip? A coffee on my desk and an offer to walk me to my car isn't going to grant you that honour, Johnny."

Some of the light fades from his eyes as his expression morphs into one far more serious than I think I've ever seen on him. It's enough to make me feel guilty, and I hate that. I've got no reason to feel guilty about what I've said. But damn him for looking like a wounded puppy all the same.

I don't expect him to swing off his horse with a speed and expertise that startles me. His breath escapes him in a low puff as his feet hit the dirt, and he twists before heading right for me. Each step he takes forward is confident, certain. He's a man on a mission.

I force my eyes not to linger on his thighs as they rub, the denim worn between them the same way mine do. He's all muscle, though. Every inch of his body has been carved from long hours spent doing physical labour in the hot sun, and I'm self-aware enough to recognize that reminding myself of that is one of the stupidest things I could have ever done.

Swallowing, I force my eyes upward only to find myself immediately snared in his gaze. No longer wounded, he looks . . . determined. My stomach threatens to fall out of my ass.

"You want more coffee? More than just a quick walk from the house to your car? Say the fuckin' word, gorgeous. I've been waiting weeks for the opportunity to give you more than that," he declares, or maybe vows. Fuck, each syllable is a promise wrapped in a pretty bow and a tag that reads *please let me woo you.*

"There are secrets in your eyes, darlin'. Ones that, yeah, I'm damn curious about. But they're not important right now. What is important is that I'm about one second away from beggin' you for a chance to tie my horse up and drive you home, knowin' that I've got a long walk back ahead of me, just so I have peace of mind that you got home safe. The extra time with you is just a bonus."

My cheeks are on fire, exposing how flattered I feel. The slight twitch at the corner of his mouth snags my attention, and I focus on it as it curls just enough to be considered a smirk.

"So? What do you say?" he asks, voice soft yet deep.

I think I black out. Because one moment, I'm preparing to duck back inside to ask Eliza for help, and then next, I'm ignoring my instincts and throwing caution to the wind.

"Get in the car, Johnny."

12

Johnny

THE INSIDE OF RORY'S CAR IS IMPECCABLE. IT'S CLEAN AND organized, with everything in a designated spot. Tiny pink garbage cans rest inside both front doors, and a thick bottle of hand sanitizer is nestled in the small storage slot below the dash.

It smells like vanilla and the cotton-candy-blue, tree-shaped car freshener swinging from the rear-view mirror. I don't remember the last time I hung an air freshener in my truck. Too long ago, that's for sure.

Aurora reaches across her body and clicks her seat belt into place before jamming the key into the ignition. The engine putters slightly before coming to life. I keep quiet and buckle my belt.

Movement at the front window of the house catches my eye, and I see Eliza peeking through the slats of the blinds before she notices I'm looking at her and the blinds slap shut again.

"How are you liking the new job?" I ask, opting out of telling Aurora that her boss was just watching us.

Aurora rolls down her window before shifting the car into reverse, and we move away from the house at a creeping pace. "It's fine. The Steeles are nice people."

"They are," I agree, waving at Joker from where she roams in the open field behind the stable, watching us. She's pissed that I locked her up outside instead of tucking her into the stable like usual, but she can take one for the team right now. "How long are you planning on working here?"

"As long as I need to."

"That's vague."

"It's the only answer I've got right now."

Turning onto the gravel road, she drives us through the ranch, past the construction crew packing up for the day, and out the open gate. It's hot enough that the air ripples above the hood of the car, and the dust kicking up behind the tires remains stagnant in the air, lingering for miles as we drive. The inside of the car isn't much better.

With a wave of my hand in front of the vents that should be blowing air-conditioned air by now, I feel nothing but heat against my palm.

"Does your AC work?" I ask, my brows knitted together as I start to fiddle with the climate-control knobs, turning it to full blast and down again.

"Sometimes," she answers gruffly.

My eyes bulge. "Sometimes? In this heat?"

She straightens in her seat. "I don't need a lecture from you, Johnny."

"I wasn't gonna lecture you, darlin'. Just wanna make sure you're taken care of is all."

Softening a bit, she rolls her pink lips before saying, "Thank you. I just haven't had a chance to get it into the shop yet. It blew on the drive down here. Maybe it was a sign from the universe that I should have just turned around and stayed."

"Nah. I don't think so."

"I haven't exactly had much luck here since I arrived. Haven't done what I set out to do either," she grumbles beneath her breath.

"Did you have big plans, then?"

Her laugh is sarcastic. "Yeah. You could say that."

"Is there anything I can help you with?" I offer.

She releases a tight breath, shaking her head. "I brought this on myself."

"That doesn't mean you have to do it by yourself. Whatever it is, I'm sure it's not that bad. And even if it is, I'm up for the challenge."

"I heard that you ride bulls."

I fold my hands in my lap and watch her with an easy stare, curious to see where she's going with this. And I damn well like that she's been listening to things about me. Maybe even asking. Either-or, it makes my confidence grow two sizes.

"Yeah, that's right. Sometimes. It's a hobby that drives my moms nutty," I answer.

She tips her chin and flicks her blinker on before turning onto the road that leads right into town and down Main Street. "Well, getting to know me isn't like riding a bull. I may attack like one, but there won't be any glory in spending the allotted time with me without injuring yourself. Because you *will* get hurt, Johnny. Maybe not the same way you would getting tossed from a bull's back, but it'll hurt all the same."

The warning is meant to be subtle but is still as obvious as if she had screamed it at me. It's a real shame her warnings don't matter much to me.

"It's only fair that I make that decision for myself, though, right? And if I decide that it's worth the pain, then that should be the end of discussion."

"If you willingly sign yourself up to get hurt, you're either stupid or reckless."

"Do I get bonus points if I'm both?" I tease.

I'm rewarded with a slight smile. "No. You don't."

"Worth a shot."

There's a pause between us as she slows the car's speed, following the limit sign at the corner of the road, and we turn off Main Street. The towering house she's staying in grows larger in size the closer we get to it, and my gut tightens. Despite the groups of nice homes that we pass, I can't drag my eyes from the total eyesore at the end of the block.

"The only person who knows why I'm here is Eliza," she admits.

"She's a good one to trust. I can see why you'd tell her."

"And you want me to trust you."

I nod. "I do."

"Tell me something about you to make us even, then. Something nobody else knows."

"Shit, that's tough." Running my palm over my mouth and jaw, I consider what to say. "I've always been an open book with everyone I know."

"You have to have at least one thing. Nobody is that open."

I chuckle, dropping my hand back to my lap. "Fair enough. Alright, when I was thirteen, I snuck onto Steele Ranch through a hole in the far-west fence and took one of the tractors for a joyride. Scared the shit out of a few cows and their calves before Brody found me and joined in. We stayed out ripping around the pasture until an hour before we knew Wade would be up, and then Brody smuggled me back out."

"What?"

The horror in her tone has me barking a laugh. "Oh yeah. Brody was a shit disturber in his young adult years."

A soft amusement fills her expression. "I can picture you driving around in a tractor and causing mayhem. I'd bet you did it often."

"As often as possible. I still try and have fun. Maybe that's why I find myself on a bucking monster's back from time to time."

"Have you ever hurt yourself riding a bull?" she asks, her teeth digging into her lip.

I keep my eyes trained on those straight white teeth, my belly growing hot. "A couple of times. Nothin' serious."

"Yet you still do it?"

"Sometimes a little pain reminds you of something you

accomplished. A goal you met despite the hardships you faced along the way. I've got a body full of scars and bruises, Rory. I love each one of 'em."

She falls silent again, so I add, "Does my admission pass inspection?"

With a fleeting glance, she meets my waiting eyes and nods. Some of the nerves in my stomach dissolve.

Her grip on the steering wheel tightens as we pull along the curb outside of her house, and the car comes to a gentle stop. After shifting into park, she drops her hand to the centre console, her long fingers decorated in a few rings that shimmer in the sunlight. Some are tucked above her knuckles, and a few are left just below them. All of the rings are silver, though. Without a single diamond in sight.

She taps a beat on the edge of the console and exhales, the weight of it staggering. "I found out the identity of my father when I was helping my mom organize the attic for a semi-annual garage sale her neighborhood always puts on. It was an accident. A massive one. I wasn't looking for anything, and I certainly wasn't interested in learning what I did. Everything, from piles upon piles of old photos and letters both unsent and returned, was inside of the box I found. There were years of time locked away inside of it. Stories I'd never heard."

Surprise clamps down on my brain. I grapple for a decent reply, something helpful or sympathetic, but a stupid question stumbles out instead.

"And what you found led you here?"

She snorts. "More like shoved me here. I dropped the box of stuff in front of my mom, and she cracked like an egg, thirty years of secrets spilling like a runny yolk. She's the one that told me to come here. Said I'd find my half-sister in Cherry Peak and she'd be able to tell me more and answer the questions that my mother either truly didn't know or didn't want to answer for me."

Before I can think twice about it, I reach for her hand on the console. She doesn't yank it away.

Her skin is cold despite the heat, and as I wrap it beneath mine, I will it to warm. I ignore the rightness that follows the simple touch and focus on what she's said instead.

"Have you found your sister?" I ask softly.

Her jaw tightens, back teeth grinding. "No. She's long gone."

"Who is it? I might be able to help. Maybe I know her."

When our eyes meet again, the dimness in hers has me squeezing her hand. I don't like it. Not at fucking all.

"Yeah, you do know her."

My stomach sours. "Who, Rory?"

"Wanda Rose," she says, her tone sharp. "It seems Lee Rose makes a habit of knocking up women and then disappearing from their lives."

My breath escapes me in a surprised gasp that fills the car. I use the hand not tightening around hers to roll down my window and suck in a large breath of the muggy air.

"Fuck, darlin'."

"Yeah, I am fucked. *Royally* fucked. Fucked worse than I've *ever* been fucked before."

"You should take home the award for the most fucked in the history of fucking," I agree.

Her frown twitches at the corners, a hint of a smile tugging at it. "Shut up."

I sober a bit, my grin faltering. All jokes aside, she's got to be torn up about this. Who wouldn't be? This isn't something that you learn about and move on from. Knowledge like this lingers forever.

"Are you okay?" I ask with a swipe of my thumb over the first bump of her knuckle.

Her throb strains with a swallow. "No. Not really."

"Can I help?"

"I've never needed help before."

"It's not a bad thing. Maybe you don't need it, but it's okay to want it."

Staring out the window at the house beside us, she wets her lips with her tongue and flips her hand beneath mine before squeezing my fingers. It's the quickest length of time someone has ever held my hand. One second, one breath, and then it's gone, the touch a phantom in the wind. But the heat lingers like a brand.

"I'll see you tomorrow, Johnny," she says, the sound of defeat heavy in her voice.

The seat belt clicks as she undoes it and makes a move to get out. I let her go, watching her push open the door and step out with my lips sealed shut and pulse racing. Wanting more and knowing that I can't have it without risking sending her skittering off like a trembling mouse keeps me in my seat for a moment longer.

She steps onto the sidewalk and glances at me over her shoulder. Arms crossed beneath her chest, she lingers, waiting for me to get out of her car so she can go inside, most likely.

I swing my body out of the car and stretch my neck while softly shutting the door. Who knows if a slam would knock it clean off the hinges.

"Thank you," she mutters.

Surprised at the words, I whip my head up to look at her and steady myself with the door. Spreading my fingers out on the top curve of it, I ignore the burn of the hot metal against my palms and flash her a soft smile.

"No need to thank me, darlin'. I meant my offer," I say.

"I know."

"And did you mean it? That you'll see me tomorrow?"

Her expression shifts just enough for me to notice. A slyness that I haven't seen before greets me, and goddamn it, I like it a whole lot.

"You do work tomorrow, don't you?"

I bark a laugh, my head dropping forward as I shake it. "Yeah, Rory. I work tomorrow."

"Then I'll see you. I suppose you'll interrupt my lunch break again."

"Only if you'll let me in to join you. No cauliflower this time, though, right?"

She drops her arms from her chest and presses her palms to the curves of her hips before patting them once. It's a fidget move, and I want to know if she's doing it because I make her as nervous as she makes me.

I doubt it.

"No cauliflower," she confirms.

"It's a date, then."

I throw the offer out and wait. Each second that ticks by without an answer is painful. The silence bites. But I don't let myself take it back. It's already out there.

And as she twists toward me, her expression open and honest, I know I made the right choice in asking. A brick to the back of my head couldn't tear my attention from her when she speaks, voice low.

"We'll see."

13

Aurora

"You know, this entire neighbourhood garage sale thing is very outdated," I grumble, ducking my head into the hole in the attic in preparation to shove myself up.

It smells like dust and mothballs in here. This house is far too old for any of us to be coming up here so often. The floor is going to collapse one of these times.

"You know how Susan is. She's ever the poster woman for a perfect community. You should have heard her at church last Sunday," Mom says from the ground beneath me.

The top two rungs of the pull-down ladder aren't all that sturdy anymore. I try to keep as still as possible while eyeing the attic and the white cloths draped over the several furniture pieces stashed up here. Half expecting the sheet to be tugged from the mirror in the corner of the room and a half-rotted face to appear in front of me, I keep my body tense and at the ready.

"Your first problem is continuing to go to that church in the first place, Mom. Susan is the nicest person there, and that says a lot."

"I've been going there since I was a little girl. No number of gossiping hags are going to chase me away," she replies stubbornly. I don't have to look down to know she has her hands planted on her hips and a scowl on her face.

"Alright," I huff out before slithering my arms up through the hole in the ceiling and pulling myself into the attic.

It's a tight fit that's only gotten tighter as the years have gone on, and I've grown from a little girl into a woman with boobs as big as two cantaloupes.

"Do you see the chair? I'm thinking of donating it this year!"

"No, I don't see the chair. I'm not even fully up yet."

"Okay, watch the attitude!"

"How about you come up here, then?"

I tune out her reply when it comes. I was in a terrible mood when I arrived this morning, and I'm in an even worse one now with my hips rubbed raw from the attic entrance and my fear of spiders flaring to life at the sight of cobwebs all around me.

Pushing to my feet, I brush my hands off on my thighs. There's so much shit up here that it feels like an impossible feat to find the armchair she's talking about. Years—no, decades—of family history are tucked away up here. A lifetime of insight that I couldn't care less about. As far as I'm concerned, my "family" doesn't extend past my mother.

"You should just sell everything up here this year. There isn't anything worth keeping," I shout.

Mom laughs tightly. "You say that because you don't have anything up there that means much to you."

"And you do?"

The stacks of boxes along the one wall are lined with dust that's collected since this time last year. Beside them stands the creepy mirror and a dresser with missing knobs. There's the typical spooky attic window on the opposite wall that faces out to the busy cul-de-sac and an old easel on its left that's never seen the light of day. It belonged to my great-great-aunt Juniper, or so I've been told. Personally, I think my mom just bought it at one of these stupid garage sales and shoved it up here when she realized she hated painting.

"You don't have to believe me, Aurora. It makes no difference," she calls back.

I roll my eyes and make my way toward the stack of boxes. My guess is this chair has been lost behind the mountain of them.

With a steep exhale, I begin moving the boxes. Dust fills the air in puffs and coats my skin and clothes as I lift and then drop each one. Some are labelled, and some aren't. There's duct tape across the tops of a few, while the others have been folded to stay shut. It's the latter ones that start to piss me off.

Cardboard flaps start popping open when I drop the boxes on the ground. More dust fills the air and my lungs as I cough and turn my head in the opposite direction. My eyes water as I blink and kick the box closest to me.

"This place is a death trap!" I shout while using the hem of my shirt to wipe at my eyes.

"What are you doing? There's glass in some of those boxes!"

"There isn't anymore!"

"Aurora Jean!"

I ignore her again. Not because I don't want to reply but because I can't. Something slimy slithers through my veins as I peer down at the contents of the open box in front of me.

Words like Cherry Peak, Return To Sender, *and* Unable To Forward *bounce in my vision. I drop to a crouch and shove my hand inside the box, feeling the stacks of thick letters and the silk texture of photographs.*

With my hand full, I yank it free and drop to sit on my ass on the filthy floor. Intrigue has me laser focused on doing nothing more than examining what I've found. The first letter in the stack I grabbed is addressed to a name that has me stiffening with uncertainty.

Lee Rose
125 1st Cherry Street
Cherry Peak, Alberta
Canada

The bold black letters stamped over the address read Return To

Sender. My brows knit together as I toss the envelope to the side and grab another. The address is the same. Everything about it is.

I grab another, and another, and another, before digging my fingernail into the next and tearing it open without a care of being tossed into jail for committing mail fraud. The messy scrawl written not only on the centre of the envelope but in the top left corner where the return address sits confirms that it was my mother who sent these letters.

My pulse pounds in my ears, the sound of it so horrendously loud that for a moment, I worry that they'll start to bleed.

With the envelope torn open at the top, I tug the letter free from inside before unfolding it. When I read the first sentence, I stop hearing my pulse. And when I get to the bottom of the page . . . I stop feeling my lungs inflate too.

SCROLLING DOWN THE COMPUTER SCREEN, I nurse my coffee and tap my foot anxiously. The clock on the top right of the screen tells me it's only been one minute since the last time I looked over my shoulder at the door to the office that I left open. I can't help but risk another peek.

There's still nobody there, and I feel like an idiot immediately for hoping otherwise. *It doesn't matter,* I remind myself. We didn't actually agree on a date. It was just a joke. A way for us to fill the silence. I roll my shoulders and collect myself with a reassuring inhale.

Opening back up the budget file for last quarter, I ignore the instant blast of alarm at the number spent and remind myself that things here work differently than I'm used to, even in the corporate world. The money going in is still four or five times the sum going out, and that's . . . well, that's incredible. Steele Ranch is a marvel in and of itself. Learning the inner workings of an organization like this is turning out to come with quite a learning curve, but I'm more than ready for the challenge.

It keeps me busy too. I enjoy the focus.

"I should have known that you were hiding away in here again."

Eliza's words are calm enough not to scare me. I spin out from the desk and toward the doorway. She's frowning at me, but I pay it no mind.

"I told you that I won't be going out there to spend my lunch break with all those loud men," I say.

She wipes her palms over the white lace of her apron that hugs her stomach. "I've warned them to be quiet when you're out there. They'll be on their best behaviour."

I cock my head, levelling her with a disbelieving stare. "Is that so?"

"Okay, fine. Maybe they'll still be a bit loud. But I don't want you in here by yourself all day. You need to eat before they leave you with the scraps."

"I assure you that I haven't been going hungry, Eliza."

She hums, a no-good smile flashing back at me. "Oh? And who has been keeping you fed, my sweet?"

"You're a shit disturber, Eliza Steele."

"And you're an expert question avoider, but I don't pick on you about that, hmm?"

I roll my eyes. "You do pick on me about it."

"It must be my old age, then. Silly me. I forget things so often," she says with a dramatic sigh.

"Maybe that's why I heard Brody asking Wade about which old folks' home he was going to stick you in before he left."

Her gasp is loud enough I wouldn't doubt the cattle in the furthest pasture could hear it. I bite the inside of my cheek to keep from laughing at her disturbed expression and remind myself that she so deserves this teeny tiny fib.

"You're lyin'," she declares, a hand to her mouth.

"Do I look like a liar?"

Squinting her eyes, she leans forward an inch as if inspecting me before saying, "Yes."

"Eliza!" I cry, mouth parted wide.

The lines beside her mouth become more prominent when she grins wide and laughs. "You started it, my dear. As if my boys would ever consider sending me to a home. If anyone is going to go to a home, it'll be Wade for how often he gives me sass for my farmers' market hauls."

"Alright, well, that sounds fair, at least. Does he know that he's tempting his fate when he does that?"

"Of course he does. Stubborn man thinks he can spend damn near a half million at an auction, but when I come home with three bags of jam, that's a problem?" She clucks her tongue as if she's annoyed, but the light in her eyes is bright, betraying her.

"What do you need three bags of jam for?"

She waves me off with a dainty hand in the air. "Oh no. Not you too. Keep teasing me and I won't tell you where your missing lunch date is."

My cheeks heat instantly. "What?"

"I wasn't born yesterday, my girl."

I have my smartass reply locked and loaded on my tongue, but she cuts me off with a laugh and a finger pointed in my direction. "Don't even think about it."

"I wasn't going to say anything."

"Well, in that case. I'll tell you that Johnny won't be back here for a couple of hours still. He's out working with a herd. Probably will be for a while if I know him as well as I think I do."

I wish I didn't feel the instant disappointment at her words. It's not like I needed the company today. I didn't.

Fuck, I wanted it, though.

"Is he always this busy?" I ask before giving myself a mental kick in the ass for bothering. *It shouldn't matter.* The busier, the better, right?

"He's one of the hardest workers on the ranch. Has been from the moment he begged Wade to hire him. Sometimes people are born for this life."

"And Johnny's one of them?"

"Damn right he is. Nobody loved it here as much as he does. Well, no one other than my husband, that is."

I nod, tucking my hair behind my ear when the breeze from the open window sends it blowing into my face. "Where is he right now?"

"Mm, I think he's in the north pasture. A group of them are working on desensitizing the calves from the spring."

"Right."

"I could take you up there if you want," she offers, her expression strained as she avoids grinning.

"I have work to do here still," I say.

"Leave it for now. What better way to learn more about the ranch than to see it with your own eyes? To feel the grass beneath your feet and smell the fresh air?"

"Are you sure it's fresh air I'll be smelling?"

Her smile breaks through. "Would you still go if I told you otherwise?"

It's alarming how easily my reply comes. "Maybe."

"Come on, then, Rory. Let's give you a proper introduction to Steele Ranch."

14

Aurora

Eliza chats with me the entire drive from the house. Brody is one of her favourite subjects, and I nod and hum along with every little tidbit of information she drops about him. It's obvious she loves him a lot. More than I think even he knows.

Wade too. I'm sure he'd grunt and scowl if he knew she told me about the time he got kicked in the ribs by a bull and was left with a crater in his chest or when they drove out to a cabin in the middle of winter and blew a tire only to not have a spare.

Every memory spilled from her lips is a reminder that all of these people I've met are a family. Regardless of someone's last name, everyone in Cherry Peak is family. A chosen one.

"I've got a million stories about Johnny too, but I'm sure his mommas would like to be the ones to share them with you," she drawls.

I roll my lips together, staring out my window at the endless green grass and wire fences. "Right, he mentioned he has two moms."

"Yep. Boy was raised by two of the best women in this town. Smart as hell and sweet as honey pie."

I shelve that important information away for later, curious

enough to ask him about it. I'm sure he'd love to tell me all about his family if given the chance.

"I've never heard of honey pie. Are you sure you didn't make that up?"

Eliza laughs softly, tipping her chin. "Oh, my dear, honey pie is a delicacy. I'll make you one of your own to try."

Under normal circumstances, I'd tell her that unlike the story my coffee preference tells, I'm not usually a fan of overly sweet things. But apparently, if my sudden—albeit *reluctant*—interest in Johnny means anything, it would seem that maybe that isn't so true anymore.

"Thank you," I say instead.

She taps her palm to the steering wheel of the truck she insisted we use for our drive. I expected it to be filthy inside due to the age of it but was pleasantly surprised to find it well-kept. The hula girl dancing on the dash is a nice touch, as are the fluffy seat belt covers.

"You know, I haven't learned much about your family yet, and I've been here yappin' about mine."

"You know a bit about my family," I argue lightly, using the half-truth as a way to avoid having to talk more about it.

Eliza doesn't care about my reluctance. "Your real family, Rory. Not Lee. What's your momma like now? She happy?"

"Yeah," I mutter, resting my elbow beneath the window and propping my chin on my palm. "She got married a few years ago to a nice man who treats her well. It's been good for her to have that."

She didn't for a long time. For the majority of my early years, it was just us. I loved the one-on-one time, but she was vulnerable on her own in a town full of judgmental piranhas. They always looked down on her for getting pregnant out of wedlock and raising me without a husband at her side.

A bunch of pigheaded assholes stuck in the fifties. I haven't missed while being here is a single one of them while I've been here.

"Good. So, you approve of him, then?"

"I love him. He's the only dad I've ever had, and I don't plan on replacing him."

Not like Lee Rose is going to want to try and fill his shoes, anyway.

I keep my eyes trained on the fields we pass, noting the obscure number of brown cows that fill each one. We pass several men on horseback and one on an ATV who blows a kiss at Eliza before turning off the gravel road in front of a tall steel shop. I've never been surrounded by so many cowboys, and it's exactly as intimidating as one would think.

Tall, muscled, rugged men with dirty jeans and tans that disappear beneath ripped shirt sleeves would intimidate most people, I'm sure. The cigarettes in their mouths and brutal glints in their eyes make them look as if they don't give a shit about much, but I doubt that's the truth. Their gentle pats to their horses' necks and softly spoken words to Eliza give me a pretty good idea of who they are beneath it all.

I remind myself of that when we pull off the road past a set of horses tied to the fence and park. Johnny's easy to spot through the two men watching him from our side of the fence. Or maybe that's because he's invaded my thoughts like an infectious disease, and I'm apparently now searching for him.

Rolling my eyes at myself, I ignore the weight of Eliza's stare on my face and hop out of the truck. The humid air sticks to my throat when I inhale and flatten my frizzy hair with my palm.

"Why are you boys out here and not in there with Johnny?" Eliza scolds, squinting out at the field, where Johnny stands in front of a single cow with a neon orange paddle in his hand.

"He told us to leave. That damn stubborn red heifer he's got there won't get in the trailer."

I look at the man who spoke, trying to remember a name before coming up blank and letting it go. He's the typical rough-and-tough rancher with a face full of scowl lines and a collection of scars on his hands that I catch when he scratches at his jaw.

It's like everyone here has a dress code they have to follow or something. Wrangler jeans, shirts that have seen better days, and boots. At least they switch it up from cowboy hats to baseball caps from time to time.

Eliza huffs and heads for the gate without giving him an answer. The two men look to me now, as if realizing for the first time that she didn't arrive alone. I stare back, keeping my expression blank so they can't tell that their presence intimidates me. It's not like I can help that fact either. They're huge, unfamiliar men who are more than likely strong enough to snap a metal rod with their bare hands.

"You must be Aurora, right?" the second one asks me, his smile infectious and kind. The soft expression should look out of place on his sharp features, buzzed head of blond hair, and dark eyes but doesn't at all. He's familiar, barely so. Almost as if I've only maybe passed by him a couple of times.

"Rory," I say, correcting him.

His grin grows, revealing the two rows of teeth and the small gap between his front two. "Rory, right. I'm Thomas, or Tommy if you're feeling like using a nickname. And this is Loren."

"Loren? You don't get a nickname too?" I ask, flicking my eyes to the other guy.

He blinks down at me from his staggering height, his short black lashes fluttering over leap-pad-coloured eyes. They're heartbreaker eyes. Too bad I'm already more than covered in that department.

"Lo is a terrible fucking nickname" is his reply.

"So, no nickname or accent, then. Interesting."

Thomas laughs and squeezes Loren's bicep. "Loren's from Manitoba. Hard to believe with the way he looks that he's the least hillbilly one around here. The most boring, though."

"Ah, fuck off, Tommy," he grunts back.

"Leave the woman alone, you behemoths," Eliza says, the jingle of the gate sounding soon after. "We're goin' to see if Johnny needs any help. Make yourselves useful and go give

Wade a hand with the sprinklers before he ends up damaging the system even worse."

"Got it," Thomas says, giving her a two-finger salute before glancing back at me. "I'm sure I'll see you around soon, yeah?"

"I work here now, so I'd assume so."

He barks a laugh. "You'll warm up to us sooner or later. I'm sure of it. But until then, it's been lovely, Aurora."

Loren keeps his eyes on me after Thomas leaves us. The corners of them crinkle as he inspects me like I'm a criminal on a courthouse stand and he's the lead prosecutor. I lift my brows in question and let him look.

"Get on your way now, Loren. Don't be lookin' at Rory like that, you damn grump!" Eliza calls.

Finally, he blinks and takes a step back. "It was a pleasure, Aurora."

Really? Was it?

"Likewise," I reply.

Thomas makes a loud clicking noise from behind me, and then Loren is heading his way. I swallow at the sight of two large horses coming around the front of the truck. Thomas is on the back of a dark brown one, and Loren doesn't hesitate to swing himself onto the other one. In a flash, they're taking off on horseback, leaving clouds of dust behind them.

"Come here, sweetheart," Eliza urges. I do as she says. "Sometimes they need tough love. They're good boys, but they're protective of one another. You know?"

"I know. That's a good thing."

"It is. As long as they aren't rude about it. If they ever are, you just let me know, and I'll beat some sense into them."

I attempt to smile. "Does everyone know that Johnny is . . ."

"Interested in you? No. I don't think they care as much about his interests as they do teasin' him from time to time. Nobody is going to force you to give him anything. That's not how we work around here. You make that boy work for your attention if you so choose to, or tell him to get lost. Either way, you've got my support."

"Thank you," I say, and I mean it.

I'm bullheaded enough not to give in to anything simply because someone wanted me to, but it's nice knowing it wouldn't upset her if I stayed true to my original decision and didn't let myself get swooped up in all that Johnny is. I quite enjoy spending time with Eliza, and I don't want to lose that before my time is over here. Even if that's a choice that could hurt me later on.

"You got it, honeybee. Now, are you ready to meet your first cow? Fair warning, this one . . . she's a stubborn thing. She's liked to do things her own way since she was a calf, and it drives Wade downright bonkers. I'm certain that's why Johnny insisted the other boys leave. He's got the patience to get her followin' the right lead," she explains.

I listen with rapt attention and follow her into the pasture. Looking down at where I step, I pay close attention to the thick patches of green grass and areas where it's a bit more mown down. There's a significant lack of weeds around, and I wish I knew more about ranch life to know if that's due to the cows eating them all or if they make sure none grow at all instead.

"Come on, sunshine, you've gotta work with me here, yeah? One hoof in front of the other. The ramp isn't gonna hurt you," Johnny coos. "Go. Get going."

My eyes jump in the direction of his voice. He's standing tall beside the open end of a long silver trailer. The ramp is down, and I focus on every calm movement of the paddle in his hand as he moves it toward the trailer and back to his side before glancing at the cow across from him.

I stay still at Eliza's side, unsure what type of movements will spook the cow. Eliza waits as well, but she's much more at ease, like she knows exactly what to do. I follow her lead.

"You two can come closer. She's just stubborn, not scared," Johnny says to us. He clicks his tongue and takes a step closer to the cow. "You're goin' to embarrass us both if you don't get up this ramp, missy."

Eliza extends a hand to me, and I take it before letting her lead us to Johnny's side. Standing beside him now, I hold my breath on instinct. Our arms are so close that a breeze would have trouble sliding between them. I keep my eyes trained on the red cow in front of us and force myself to take a breath.

"How long have you been out here alone with her?" Eliza asks him.

"Not a damn clue. The guys led the rest of the herd back a while ago."

The cow remains still, her dark eyes watching and observing us in a way that makes me think she knows exactly what she's doing by refusing to get in the trailer. Maybe she gets a kick out of driving people mad with her stubbornness.

Johnny shifts, and the space between our arms disappears. They glide together, the dark hair on his tickling my skin. I swallow and look up at him at the same time he glances down at me. A swipe of his thumb over my wristbone electrifies my blood.

"If you're here, I'm assuming I missed lunch. I'm sorry, darlin'. Real fucking sorry."

"You're busy. This is more important."

His eyes dart between mine as he strokes my wrist again. "What about you let me make it up to you?"

"I'm available for lunch every day." The words escape me quickly, racing out like they knew I would have tried to keep them in.

Eliza moves from my opposite side, but I can't tear my attention from Johnny to find out why. It's like this every damn time. No matter how hard I try to avoid falling into this trap with him, I wind up there anyway. I flounder under the weight of his gaze and, instead of fighting back, allow myself to drift there as if there's nowhere else I'd rather be.

"I was thinking we do something else. Something away from this place," he says, his first real proposition dropped at my feet.

"What did you have in mind?"

"I've been itching to fix that front porch of yours since I walked you home the other night. What about I come over this weekend with beer and takeout, and you keep me company while I fix it up?"

A tiny laugh of disbelief escapes me as I wait for him to tell me he's just kidding and offer some elaborate dinner plans instead. I wait and wait, and wait some more for it to come, but it doesn't. He doesn't so much as blink as we stare at each other, and the sincerity in his eyes grows more obvious.

"You want to come spend an evening fixing my porch with beer and soggy, lukewarm food?" I ask.

He dips his chin. "Yeah, Rory. That's exactly what I want. As long as you'll be there."

"Oh," I mutter.

"Oh . . . yes?"

I smile, just a tiny curl of my lips. "Yeah. Okay, fine."

His grin puts my smile to shame. Fuck, it's brighter than the sun. Could light up the world better than it too.

"Sounds like a plan, darlin'. Can't wait."

I roll my eyes and distance myself from him a step. "Just don't be late, or I'll lock the front door, and you can drink and eat alone."

If anything, I think my threat excites him. "I wouldn't dream of it."

"So, if you two are done, there's a cow here that needs to get loaded up and then back to her pasture," Eliza says, a teasing tone obvious in her voice.

Johnny lets his eyes linger on mine for a beat longer before placing them on the cow again. The immediate loss of his attention makes me feel cold. Alarmingly so.

"Just one time, big girl. One time up the ramp, and I'll let you go back to eatin'," he murmurs to the cow, once again using the paddle in his hand to encourage her forward. "Go on. Get going."

She doesn't move. Not in one minute or five. She just looks around the field and moves in small circles, as if doing everything in her power to annoy us all. It's working for me, but not Johnny. I watch him for longer than maybe I should, paying attention to every moment of calmness on his face where I can feel mine growing tense. He doesn't seem to mind the waiting, and that's . . . curious.

Eliza meets my gaze once we've been standing here for a while. She glances past me at the truck as if asking if I want to leave. I shake my head, content with watching how this will play out, even if I'm out here until the soles of my feet ache.

"Alright, let's try something else. Please just don't kick me in the face," Johnny says.

He moves from the spot he chose minutes ago to the cow's side and taps the paddle twice to the side of her butt. She takes a single step forward as he reaches into his jeans pocket and pulls out a green cube made of some sort of wheat before offering it to her.

Clicking his tongue, he says, "Let's go. Get moving."

Her tongue leaves her mouth and wraps around the green cube before she's chewing on it and taking another couple of steps forward. Johnny taps her again, so gently I bet she hardly feels it, and offers her another cube when she continues moving.

Finally giving up her stubborn act, she steps right up onto the ramp and strolls into the trailer with a dozen treats in her belly. Johnny gives her a pat on the head when she turns to face us from inside the trailer as we watch at the bottom of the ramp.

"Good job, Johnny. She's a greedy one. Let everyone else know that she needs treats for motivation, and it should be easier next time," Eliza says.

"Will do. She's a sweet one, though. All the stubborn ones are deep down," Johnny replies, staring right at me with a smirk that I want to give a hard flick.

He's got one thing right. I am stubborn. But I need a lot more than a handful of treats to obey anyone's orders.

15

Johnny

Sliding my belt through the last loop in my jeans, I stare at myself in the bathroom mirror and decide I hate what I've done with my hair. It's too long, and I've never liked it tied back. Daisy, on the other hand, thinks it makes me look distinguished, and apparently, that's what I need to convince Rory to give me more than one date.

I'm not sure she's right about that, but once my sister gets started, there isn't much you can do to shut her down. Even as I clamp my buckle into place and shimmy my waistband until it feels just right, she rambles on and on.

"Have you brushed your teeth yet?" she asks, picking up my sweatshirt from its place on the edge of my bed. Sniffing at the collar, she adds, "At least you washed this recently."

"Do you think I'm a slob, Daisy? Of course I brushed my teeth. Used mouthwash too. *Before* I brushed."

She beams at me, popping both of her thumbs up. "That'a boy. You do listen from time to time."

"Some things are hard not to listen to. Especially when you say them to me every single time we see each other."

She flashes me a different finger, and I return the gesture before reaching behind my head to tug out the elastic in my hair.

"It's important information, J."

I lean forward and brace my pelvis on the bathroom sink while running my fingers through my hair, trying to make it seem like the messy look was on purpose and not because it's in need of a chop. It doesn't fucking work. I just look like I haven't brushed it in a week.

"You're hopeless. Crouch down and let me help," Daisy commands, stepping into the bathroom and patting my shoulder.

Lowering myself a couple of inches, I fold my arms along the edge of the vanity and rest my chin atop them as I stare at my reflection. My cheeks are flushed, my freckles too obvious, and my bottom lip still a bit swollen from the hit it took earlier today.

I should have been paying closer attention to my surroundings, but when Aurora stepped onto the porch this afternoon with an old brown Stetson on her head . . . it was a miracle I didn't do something worse than smack face first into the stable wall. It was Eliza's—I'd recognize it anywhere—but fuck me, I wished it were mine instead.

All week, I've been searching for her everywhere I go, but I've been too busy to stop by the house to make small talk or take her lunch like I'm aching to. Eliza's probably tired of me asking if Rory's eaten every damn day.

Daisy manipulates my hair with a cool confidence, like she knows exactly how to fix what I've done. There's no point in trying to take notes on what she's doing. Hairstyling is a skill I simply don't possess. I've never had to worry about it because I wear a hat all day, every day.

"So, you have the beer in the fridge, and the food will be ready in . . ." She checks the time on her smartwatch. "Fifteen minutes. You have cologne, right? Women like men that smell good."

I lift a brow and stare at her in the mirror. "Yeah, D. I've got cologne. Plenty of it, in case you forgot how often you and Jos use cologne as an easy gift for my birthday."

She tugs on a strand of my hair. "Cologne isn't an easy gift if you're doing it right. We spend at least two hours searching for the perfect smell every time."

"Well, it might be time to find a different gift idea for this year. I don't think a guy needs seven bottles of cologne at once."

"Seven? And you still smell like shit as often as you do? Jesus."

I rest my forehead on my arm and laugh. "Fuck, aren't you supposed to be helping hype me up before I go on my date instead of tearing me down?"

"Oh, I'm not tearing you down. You know I love you damn near to death. It's my job to razz you from time to time. Besides, a bit of teasing builds character. It's a sister's job to make sure you don't turn out to be a conceited asshole. There's enough of those out there."

I narrow my eyes on her reflection when I catch her mouth droop into a slight frown. Daisy's never dated a man and has always been open about preferring women, but that doesn't mean she can't still have problems for me to take care of.

"You got somethin' to tell me?"

The droop disappears. "No, and even if I did, we wouldn't be talking about it today." Slapping my back, she straightens and says, "Voilà. While you do need a haircut soon, at least now you don't look homeless. And don't you dare put a hat on and ruin all of my work. Leave it at home for one night."

"Got it. Thank you for coming over and helping. I'm a bit on edge," I say, forcing out a laugh to try and hide how true that statement actually is. My stomach tightens as nerves play a game of bowling inside of it. "I'm going to head out now. Don't want to be late."

And I need a moment alone to puke. Preferably in a back alley with only the raccoons to see.

"I'll lock up before I leave."

"You can stay if you want. I'd rather you here than driving on the highway in the dark."

She's the worst damn driver I've ever seen. It's a miracle she passed her driver's test in high school. The tiny sedan parked outside is the third car she's had in two years.

"If I stay, you better leave me a beer in the fridge."

I'm already dipping out of the bathroom and into the kitchen to grab the six-pack I've left cooling all day. I set a glass bottle in the fridge beside the jug of half-drank orange juice—no pulp—before nudging the door closed with my hip.

"You drink, you stay, D. Promise me no driving," I say when she joins me and takes a seat at the small breakfast nook.

And by small, I mean small. There's only room for two stools, but it's only me here. The entire cabin is small, but I've done a lot to it in the year it's been mine.

The hardwood throughout the entire house is original. The only thing I did to it was give it a good wax and seal. The wooden beams in the ceiling haven't been touched, and I left the trim just how it was when the place was built. It's the walls that needed a bit of TLC. Every single one of them was coated in yellowing, apple-tree-patterned wallpaper. It took two weeks to peel it all off.

With only the master bedroom, a small office/guest room, and a single bathroom with a tub-and-shower combo that I dumped too much money into renovating, there isn't much space for guests. I've never minded that, though. All of my friends have plenty of it to offer up.

"Yes, I promise, you overbearing ape. As long as you promise not to bring Aurora back here tonight."

I bark a laugh at her crinkled nose. "That won't be happening anytime soon."

"No?" she asks, a spark of intrigue appearing in her voice.

"No. And I'm not explaining anything more about it to you. I'm leaving. Thank you for all your help."

I tug her into a hug, careful to keep the now five-pack of beer out of the way, and kiss the top of her head before heading for the door.

"Have fun, J. And make sure you listen to her. Listening is the most important thing you can do on a first date. Well, that and not being a gross pig."

I swallow nervously, feeling the back of my neck grow damp. "Yeah, I've got it."

Seeing my hat sitting on the entry table and not reaching for it is a true testament to my control. I'm much more comfortable with it on my head. It gives me some sense of confidence.

Fuck it.

I pick it up, set it on my head, and duck outside before Daisy has a chance to notice. Shaking out my shoulders, I head for my truck. Over and over again, I recite the same confident speech in my mind the entire way to the diner to grab the food I put in an order for during my lunch break.

Fifteen minutes later, I haven't puked, and the cab of my truck smells like burgers and fries. I worry the milkshakes will be melted with how long I've been here stalling. Shit, I'm nervous. More terrified than I've ever been for a date.

I want it to go well. Better than well. *Fan-fucking-tastic.* So good that she can't help but want to go on another with me. It would be too easy to mess up now, whether from stumbling over my words and saying something stupid or just straying away from my character in hopes of impressing her. I'm sure of myself, but Aurora makes me feel like a young boy with his first crush who's ready to do anything he can to impress the girl.

It's ridiculous, considering we're still just getting to know each other, but I don't think I really care.

With a swipe of my hand over the back of my neck, I sniff my pits and then turn the truck off. It's a challenge carrying everything up the sidewalk, but I make it work with a five-pack in one fist, a cardboard tray with two shakes in the other, and a takeout bag tucked beneath my arm. There's no way I'm asking her to help with something so simple.

"Drop my beer and you're going to be eating alone, Johnny."

I grin up at Rory where she stands waiting on the porch.

Arms dangling over the railing, she watches me with the tease of a smile. I try not to stumble over the cracked, uneven sidewalk, but she's so beautiful it's hard to drop my stare to watch my step.

"I don't plan on it, darlin'," I reply.

The wooden steps are rotted and falling apart, so I avoid them completely and lunge up to the porch itself. Turns out my long legs are good for something. Rory is quick to reach for the bag of food slowly slipping from beneath my arm. Once she takes it, I relax a bit.

Unrolling the top of the paper bag and looking inside, she asks, "Burgers and fries?"

"Don't forget the fifty ketchup packets I asked for or the best milkshakes known to man."

Her eyes lift, focusing on mine. "That's a high claim."

"'Cause it's the truth, and I can back it up. Do you want to eat out here or inside?"

I leave the option up to her. It was my idea for us to go to her place, and the last thing I want to do is pressure her into thinking I want to go inside for anything other than devouring this food and listening to her speak, even if I'm obviously fucking interested in having a chance for more.

There's a lot I still have to do to prove myself to her, and I have never been this interested in putting in the work to do exactly that.

Rory darts her stare to the front door and holds it there. I wait with my lips sealed shut as she contemplates what she wants. It's warm enough outside despite the gloomy day that I wouldn't mind sitting out here with her. Cherry Peak is a calm town, so we'd have peace and quiet to talk.

"The back porch is better than this one. It's nicer," she says.

"Alright. The back porch it is, then."

Her hair slips over her cheek as she nods, and I'm suddenly grateful my hands are full. If they weren't, I'd be struggling not to push it behind her ear.

She opens the door, and I glare at the hinges when they creak. Bright light streaming through the windows greets us as we step inside, and she rubs her shoes on the carpet in front of the door before moving through the house. I shut the door behind us before looking around the front room with greedy eyes, trying to take in as much of it as I can while also keeping up with her. My worry for her grows at the sight of the old wood-burning fireplace that's full of ashes, cracked walls, peeling plaster, and an old yellow plaid couch that looks like it was hauled out of my great-grandmother's basement.

Aurora's pace is hurried, and I wonder if that's so she doesn't have to show me around the place properly.

I abandon my exploration and focus on her instead. When and if she actually decides to show me around, I don't want to already know everything.

The back door is in better condition than the front, not creaking when she pushes it open. The place could use a nice screen door in addition to the heavy wooden one. Especially in the summer when a cool early evening breeze is needed to cool the muggy inside these older houses.

"I haven't put a lot of effort into the house or the backyard, so I know it looks . . ." She crosses her arms and taps her fingers against her bicep. "It's a work in progress."

I step outside after her and take a look around the back porch. She wasn't lying in saying this porch is nicer than the other, but it's not by much. The wood slats are still chipped and cracked, with what's left of the stain worn to shit. There aren't railings along the edges to block the view of deep green grass. It isn't spotty and dead like the front yard.

Only one single fabric camping chair sits on the porch beside a tiny folding table. The tall wooden fence is uneven along the top and leans onto the neighbour's property behind the tiny garden shed.

"You can have the chair," she mutters, drawing my attention right back to her. Cheeks pink, she avoids my eyes.

"No, darlin', I'm good here." I drop to my haunches and set the beer and milkshakes on the wood planks before sitting my ass on the edge of the porch. Letting my legs dangle over the grass, I feel my boots brushing the high points of it. "You always take the only chair when you're around me, okay?"

"Alright," she says, voice softer than I've ever heard it.

But instead of sitting on her chair, she takes a few steps toward me and sits on the porch, her legs swinging beside mine. My chest warms as I smile and reach for two beers, uncapping both before handing her one.

"I assume I have you to thank for the sudden air conditioning in my car?" she asks before taking a sip of her beer.

"So it works? Good. I was worried I'd have to kick some ass at the ranch tomorrow."

"How did you even get it fixed without me seeing you take it?"

"It was easy. I had the guys tow it to the shop so Brody could fix it up while you were workin'. He got it done in a blink," I explain.

She's quiet for a moment before saying, "Thank you."

"You're welcome, darlin'. I like knowing you're taken care of. Anything else happens to that car, you let me know, yeah?"

"Alright, I will."

The crinkle of a paper bag fills the night as she sets down her beer and pulls out the giant box of fries and a handful of the packets of ketchup. Brows twitching, she offers them to me, and I take them with a wink.

"I've got a thing for condiments. There's nothing worse than dry food. Give me a squirt of ketchup on damn near anything any day," I say.

"Anything?"

"To an extent."

"I knew someone in college who ate ice cream with ketchup."

I shiver in disgust. "Fuckin' nasty."

She nods, handing me a thick burger wrapped in silver foil.

"I'm assuming because this one weighs a million pounds that it's yours?"

"I haven't eaten much all day, and Wade had me chasin' bulls all day."

"I don't care what you eat or why you eat it, Johnny. I just know I'd have wasted most of it if you got it for me."

The clarification wasn't needed, but it's damn nice to know she's thinking about my feelings.

"Poppy told me you weren't a vegetarian. That's how I knew—" I jut my chin at the unwrapped burger in her hands. "There's a possibility she lied to me just to make things awkward for me, though, so if you actually are against eating meat, feel free to toss it. There's a veggie burger in the bag, too, just in case."

"You asked Poppy if I was a vegetarian?"

I shrug. "Yeah. The last thing I needed was to ruin my shot with you because I assumed you eat something you don't."

"But you still got a backup option."

I set my hands in my lap, my still-wrapped burger warming my fingers. Swiping my tongue over my lips to wet them, I try to wrangle my words together. She's already looking at me when I turn my head toward her.

"I've got manners in spades, Aurora. Spent a lot of time thinkin' about how I'd treat a woman I was this interested in. One thing you'll never have to worry about with me is being treated less than you deserve. And buying a veggie burger as a fail-safe is nowhere close to what I've got up my sleeve when it comes to you. Am I bein' clear here?"

Her throat stretches and strains with a thick swallow. Our gaze holds. "Yeah, you're crystal clear."

I take a risk and move my hand to the top of her knee, keeping my touch soft, testing. When she doesn't jerk her leg away, I give it one single squeeze before removing my touch and starting to remove the foil around my burger.

She watches me take the first bite, those deep blue eyes focused on my mouth as I chew before falling to her own food. I watch her just as seriously, curious for her every reaction to the taste of it.

And when she sinks her teeth into the thick bun and mix of all my favourite toppings before getting to the burger patty, I grow rock-solid in my Wranglers. Her moan is deep and thick. It tugs at my gut and nearly draws up one of my own.

I shove my mouth full of dry fries before I can let one loose.

16

Aurora

I WASN'T SURPRISED THAT THE DINER FOOD WAS REALLY, REALLY good. I've been there more than a few times since I've come to Cherry Peak, and it's never disappointed me. It's been so long since I've had a real home-cooked meal, though, so maybe I've just forgotten what something less greasy tastes like.

My fingers curl tighter around my Styrofoam milkshake cup before I drop it and Johnny's into the garbage can. They hit the bottom of the bag with a plop as I turn and take in a steadying breath. The ragingly loud noises outside are a reminder that Johnny is still here. My next inhale is stuttered.

I'm content with having him here. After we ate, I realized I didn't want him to leave yet. I was relieved when he went out to his truck and hauled a tool box from the bed of it before starting to demolish my porch if it meant we got some more time together.

And demolish is putting it lightly.

I go to the front window and gawk at the instant view of him balancing a crowbar in one hand and rotted wood slats in the other. Each broken piece is tossed onto the growing pile in the yard. I've only been inside for two minutes, and it's already nearly doubled in size.

He doesn't need to be doing this for me. I'd never have asked anyone for their help with this place. It's not mine to begin with, and soon enough, it'll go back to sitting on the street empty, waiting for another renter to stumble by. But it would be nice not to worry about falling through the steps on my way to work every day . . .

A fist bouncing off the front window has me flinching before refocusing on the man now staring at me. Johnny smirks knowingly and rests his hands on his narrow hips, his head cocked.

His voice carries through the screen door. "You're not allowed to hide in there all night, darlin'!"

"I'm not hiding! And it's only been two minutes."

He laughs, and intent on proving him wrong, I swing open the door and step outside. My eyes bug at the full state of the porch and the broken railings that now cover my yard. I'm grateful we decided to have dinner a bit earlier than I'd usually have it on my own. We'd have gotten a noise complaint from the neighbours if he started this at night.

"You work quick," I tell him.

"When I want to. There's a time and place for all kinds of speeds," he replies smoothly, coming to stand at the bottom of the stairs.

The sexual innuendo isn't lost on me, and I can't help but play into it a bit, enjoying knowing I can do that with him. "I haven't had a lot of experience with that, actually. Fast is usually my speed of choice."

One hand slides into his pocket as his smirk stretches wider, bordering into smile territory. "Always?"

"Most of the time."

"There's still time to open your horizons and experiment. I'm always up to share some of my insight with interested parties."

"Oh? And how many interested parties have you shared this insight with?" I ask, the question sounding just the slightest bit jealous.

He doesn't seem to mind. Not if the obvious twinkle in his

eye as he sets one foot on the bottom stair and leans closer is anything to go off.

"Give or take about . . . six."

"Six?" I squeak, my jaw hanging open. "That's it?"

He tips his head. "Yeah, darlin'. Six. That alright with you?"

"Why shouldn't it be? You can add another six tonight for all I care."

My outer shell grows thick as I retreat back a few mental steps, focusing on not flinching at my ultra-bitchy comment. He doesn't need to ask me those sorts of questions. *He shouldn't.*

My stomach sours thinking of hurting this man's feelings, but damn it all to hell, I can't do this. It's better to stop playing into it right now.

I expect Johnny to look hurt by my words or maybe even just put off. But no. I find him leaping up the steps and moving toward me with a soft yet determined expression. His gaze is gentle and calm and unexpecting as it caresses my face.

"Even if I could physically tear myself away from you long enough to go add six to my tally, I couldn't get there mentally," he says, standing so close the toes of his boots touch my sandals. My breath hitches when he takes my hand in his, the calluses on his palm scratching my skin. "Been only one woman on my mind since I saw her, and I've been tryin' to impress her tonight, but maybe I haven't done a good enough job yet."

"You have," I blurt out before lowering my voice and repeating myself. "You have. I'm just not the one for you."

"I don't believe that."

"Why should you believe otherwise? I've given you nothing."

He wets his lips and reaches up to remove his hat. His hair is wild, sticking up and parted a million different ways. Like him, I realize.

Without the hat, he doesn't appear as tall and intimidating. Even still, as he has to dip his chin to meet my eye, I don't feel like he's a million feet above me.

"I've got three sisters, two moms, and have watched more fairy tales than anyone in their right mind. Love at first sight isn't a taboo topic for me. It isn't hard to believe in. Romance doesn't scare me or intimidate me. It never has. And do you know what I felt the first time I saw you, Aurora?"

I shake my head, unable to speak. Too scared to. He moves impossibly closer and drops the hat before resting his hand on the wall behind me. I hadn't realized I'd backed up against it.

My pulse thrums in my ears as he drops his head, and I bring mine back, my throat arched.

"I felt like I'd been punched in the gut. You were sittin' at that table with your fingers tapping the way they do when you're nervous or uncomfortable, and I knew I needed to get over to you. The woman with the sad but fuckin' prettiest eyes I'd ever seen. I followed the tug I felt between us and only needed one minute with you to know that I made the right choice."

"I don't believe in love at first sight," I say on a breath.

"No? Alright. So you didn't feel anything with me that night? When I had you in my arms as we swayed between tables? Because you could have shoved me away at any time. God knows I'd have let you go without a fight if that's what you wanted. I *did* let you go."

That night was a blur of loud laughter, friendly conversation, and an undeniable discomfort that I felt the entire time sitting at that table. I didn't know the people I was with, and they intimidated me with their closeness to one another. I was an outsider that didn't know how to accept their welcome.

But then Johnny came over, and I just . . . I slipped. Suddenly, the thoughts in my mind had quieted, and I let myself get swept into the peace that he brought me during those few dances. He was comfortable and familiar in a way that had me running away the moment I pulled myself back together and realized what was happening.

It was terrifying. And every time I see him or speak with

him, I feel that fear again. Because men like Johnny don't stay in your life for a moment in time.

They stay there forever.

I was smart enough to recognize that that night, and I've reminded myself of it every day since.

Johnny exhales, the heat of his breath blanketing my nose. He traces every dip of my knuckles with his thumb and holds my fingers against his chest.

"I see all of those thoughts running through your pretty head, Rory, but I want to hear them. Tell me no—a *real* no—and I'll leave right now. I'll back up and let you find your father without me complicating anything. But if you tell me yes, I'm jumping in headfirst.

"I'll be here every night fixing up this house of yours until I deem it safe enough and bringing you food at lunch. I've got a list of things a mile long that I want to show you and teach you out at the ranch, but only if you say yes. I won't keep pushin' if you don't feel what I do. You've got my word."

"I . . ." My throat is so thick I can't even swallow properly. Heat engulfs my cheeks. "I can't tell you no. That night was a lot for me too. There's something here, I know that. But I'm not staying in Cherry Peak. I can't make you any promises. I'm here for Wanda and Lee."

I clench my teeth and look at the street over Johnny's shoulder, not wanting to see the disappointment on his face as my words settle between us.

My muscles tighten when he softly curls his finger beneath my chin and turns my head, forcing me to meet his stare. His smile is unexpected and confusing.

"Why are you smiling?" I ask.

"Everyone thinks Cherry Peak is a blip on the map for them, but oftentimes, it's never that. I'm more than ready to prove that to you, darlin'," he answers.

"And if you can't? You'll hate me for leaving." And I'll hate myself just as much for hurting him.

He strokes his finger over the ridge of my jaw before swooping it up my cheek. "I don't think it'll be possible to hate you. But if I have to watch you leave, then at least I'll be able to know that I had my time with you."

"I'm kind of a bitch, in case you haven't noticed."

The sentence escapes me too quickly to stop it. Fuck, my cheeks burn now. I shut my eyes, attempting to pretend I didn't just say that.

Johnny's quiet laugh has me peeking them open again. His forehead falls to mine, and my lips tug at the corners.

"You're not a bitch, Rory. I've never thought that."

"If we do this," I start, feeling something warm start to build in my chest. "Would you help me contact Wanda? Not as a quid pro quo or anything, but . . . I can do it on my own—it would just be nice to have someone—"

"Name anything you need, and I'm here to help you get it. You've got my word," he says instantly.

I release a breath. "Okay."

"We can start tomorrow. Tonight, I have you to myself, and I plan on taking advantage of that."

"What did you have in mind?" I ask tentatively, my eyes dropping to his mouth on instinct.

God, since when am I so horny?

His answer isn't the one I expected. "Have you ever used a crowbar before?"

17

Johnny

I'VE NEVER BEEN AFRAID OF HARD WORK.

As the only man in a house full of women, I've always taken my responsibilities seriously. My moms aren't old-fashioned in the sense of having separate tasks for both me and my sisters—quite the opposite, really—but I took it upon myself to carry that weight.

If the lawn needed mowing? I was out doing it. My sister had a boy over? I was the one standing in her bedroom doorway with my arms crossed and my glare fixed on the douche. Late-night pickups, telling off bullies, watching tutorials on how to fix leaky pipes so we didn't have to spend money on plumbers. I've made myself learn skills that I knew would be beneficial in the future.

Like when I meet the woman I decide to marry. Which isn't me saying I'm ready to propose to Aurora right now or anything. God, my moms would kick my ass for even considering that already, but the fact still stands. I want to be able to say that I know how to take care of a woman and be someone that she can depend on when that time comes.

That's what has me pushing my ass so hard to do as much as I can for Rory while I'm here, sweaty and desperate to impress her. The sun isn't glaring in my eyes anymore, which means I'm running out of time. Every nervous glance Rory shoots at the neighbouring houses has me speeding up, desperate to get as much done as I can before being forced to stop.

Maybe I should be slowing down and dragging this out. If this place wasn't such a death trap, I probably would, as selfish as that is. But I'm confident that I'll be able to capture her attention in other ways once I'm finished with this project.

"Give me just a couple more minutes to get this all cleaned off your yard, and then I'll go," I say once she's tossed another chunk of rotten wood onto the pile.

Blowing a piece of hair out of her face, she sets her hands on her waist and stretches her back before looking across the yard at me. Her lips are just the slightest bit downturned, but it's enough to have me speaking again.

"I don't want to keep your neighbours up."

"Right," she says coolly, unbothered. "It is late."

"You'll keep the beer, yeah? If I take it home, Tommy will end up finding it the next time he's over, and I'll have to house the drunk while he sleeps it off."

"You won't just drink it yourself?"

Dropping to a crouch in front of the bottom porch step, I use my gloved hands to rip the final piece of wood off. It's soft, rotted, and full of water from the last rain. The nails are rusted and dull as they stick up out of the plank like the majority of them have been.

Just like I've done with all the rusted-nail-infected planks, I toss it directly into the bed of my truck. I'd never forgive myself if she stepped on one because I left it lying on her front lawn.

Facing her again, I answer, "I'm not much of a drinker outside of Saturday nights. Alcohol doesn't mix well with bein' up at five every morning."

"Five? That sounds terrible."

I chuckle and move closer to her. "You get used to it."

"I doubt it."

"When do you get up in the morning?"

"Seven at the earliest."

I blow out a breath. "That's my Sunday sleep-in time. Even that's pushin' it. My internal clock is a sensitive little shit."

"When's the last time you slept in properly?"

"I don't actually remember. Gotta be at least before I turned sixteen and started at the ranch."

"Why did you want to work there so young?" she asks, throwing herself back into work as if that will make her question that much more casual.

I see past every attempt she makes to pretend she isn't interested.

She bends to fill her arms with the rotten wood on the lawn and then crinkles her nose in disgust when it rubs against the skin of her forearms. The sleeves of her deep blue shirt are shoved up to her elbows, but she hasn't been scratched too badly from the wood.

Her jeans are the high-waisted type. I only know because I watched her fiddle with the waistband through her shirt when she joined me in ripping apart the porch, and it was far too high to be normal. The flicker of discomfort I saw when she gave it a tug had me wanting to urge her to change into a pair of sweatpants instead, but I figured that wasn't the smartest move. Plus, I like thinking that she wore the painted-on denim just for me. That in itself was enough to have me keeping my mouth shut.

Her steps are confident as she carries the armful to the truck and dumps it all onto the open tailgate before beginning to toss each piece into the bed. Unable to help myself, I join her.

"I always wanted to work on Steele Ranch," I say, keeping an eye on her bare fingers as she grips each piece of wood. Every haphazard toss has my muscles tensing. "You should wear gloves. You're going to get a sliver—"

"Fuck!" she shouts while yanking her hand to her chest and then holding it up to her face. Her eyes slide toward me as she adds, "Don't say a damn word."

I make the zipping my lips motion before gently taking hold of her wrist and guiding it toward me. She watches as I bring it up in front of my nose.

"Which finger?"

"Pointer."

I hum and pull the finger up, taking in the inflamed tip. The thick sliver is easy to spot, and I fight the urge to press my lips over it.

"Do you have tweezers?"

"Yes. And I know how to use them myself."

"I don't doubt you can. It'll be easier if I help, though. I've got incredible eyesight." My grin is wide as I wink at her and reluctantly release her hand.

She rolls her lips together, thinking. Probably contemplating whether or not I have a sliver fetish, which I do *not*, for the record. More like just an undying obsession with helping her with anything and everything.

"The guys get slivers all the time. I'm a pro at removing them at this point," I add, trying to sweeten up my offer.

Sighing, she nods behind me toward the house. "Fine. But you have to finish telling me about why you wanted to work on the ranch so young while you're performing surgery on my finger."

"I'll tell you anything you want to know, darlin'," I promise without a second thought.

She doesn't reply, and I don't push. Not even once we step inside and I'm led down a dark, stuffy hallway toward the bathroom. The wood panelling gives me the shivers, reminding me of the days I spent at my great-grandmother's house before she passed away. That place was truly haunted, and I really, really hope this one isn't.

With a flick of the light, the small—no, *tiny*—room grows bright enough to burn my eyes. Rory moves quickly through the space, grabbing the first aid kit from the shelf beside the standing sink, and sets it in the basin. I've never kept tweezers in a first aid kit, but when she pulls them out from within the mess of bandages and antiseptic sprays, I wonder if maybe I should.

Stepping behind her, I reach around her body and hold her wrist again. I need to pluck the tweezers from her grip, but I'm frozen. She sucks in an audible breath and darts her stare to the medicine cabinet above the sink. The mirror makes it hard to hide the brutal desire in my eyes as I stare at her, trailing my gaze over every inch of her beautiful face. From the few hairs on the arch of her left brow that stick up more than the others to the small white scar that cuts into her bottom lip.

I want to know how she got it and how it would feel beneath my finger as I trace the shape of her lips. Fuck, she's got me all tangled up inside. I just wish she would admit to herself that she feels the same way about me.

Her wrist is so small compared to the length of my fingers. They wrap around it with room to spare. The warmth seeping from her skin into mine is intoxicating. Addictive.

"Let me," I whisper, finally releasing her wrist and sliding the tweezers free of the death grip she has on them.

"I can do it myself, Johnny."

Her breathless tone has my cock straining in my jeans. She'll feel it if I don't take a step back, but fuck me, it feels like we've been tethered together, and pulling away will yank my heart right from my chest.

I swallow, grappling for my manners. "It'll be quicker if I do it."

Her lashes flutter as our stares hold in the mirror. "This doesn't feel quicker."

"No, I guess it doesn't."

The tweezers are cold between my fingers. So different from the blazing heat from her skin. I want to toss them in the trash and touch her again, but instead, I take that dreaded step back. When my heart stays rooted behind my rib cage, I take another step, giving us both room to breathe.

Her perfume lingers on my shirt, and that has my jeans growing even tighter.

"Let me see your finger," I coax.

She turns to face me, and the blue in her eyes is even more vibrant up close. You can almost see the rough waves crashing around her pupils as she looks up at me, her hand extended between us, fingers brushing my chest.

"Should I time how long it takes you?" she asks, the tease so obvious in her voice that I can't help but grin like a fool.

"Go for it, gorgeous. Maybe we should take bets."

She hums, pushing her fingers a bit harder into my sternum. I lean forward, encouraging her to keep going.

Shove them deep, Rory. Wrap them around my heart and feel how fast it beats in your company.

"Bets are dangerous," she muses.

"The best things are."

Her pupils flare, swallowing all that dark blue. Her palm makes contact with my chest, and I swallow a groan, dropping my gaze to stare at it. Five fingers splayed, she keeps it there, unmoving.

Suddenly, the last thing I want to do is talk about my history with the ranch. Fuck it all to hell, I just want to stay like this.

"Are you dangerous, Johnny?"

"Not when it comes to you."

Her lips part as she flicks her tongue along the bottom one, right over that small scar. "Liar."

"We were making a bet. I'll go first." I shift closer again, testing her. She doesn't drop her hand. Her elbow bends with the sudden lack of space between us. "It'll take me under a minute to get the sliver out."

"That's a confident bet."

I smirk. "Surprised?"

"Not at all," she says, finally drifting her eyes back up to mine. "Three minutes."

"So little faith in me, Rory," I tease, swaying even closer.

She rolls her eyes, and damn, I think her attitude turns me on even more. "What do I get when I win the bet?"

"When?" I blow out a long breath and reach behind her to grip the edge of the sink. The move brings us too close to pretend it's just my heart thumping like crazy. "No, darlin'. *If* you win."

"*If* I win, what do I get?" she corrects herself.

"Name it."

Her brow curves. "Anything?"

"Anything."

"Wanda's number." It's said so gently I wonder if she's scared of me hearing her properly. "I want Wanda's number. If you have it. If you don't, can you ask for it? I don't want anyone to know that I'm looking for it. For her."

My chest aches at her nervousness. At the pain that swells in her voice.

"Deal," I say.

Relief ripples across her expression. "What do you want if you win?"

I don't need to think about it. "A kiss."

"A kiss?" she echoes, eyes wide.

"That surprises you?"

"Well . . . no. I guess not. But you could have had anything."

"There's nothin' else I want."

Her cheeks flush a pretty shade of pink, and my heart thumps in answer. "Better get to it, then."

With a low laugh, I take a step back and take her hand in mine. Holding her finger up beneath the domed, yellow ceiling light, I find the nearly sliver in the pad of it and abandon the tweezers in the sink.

"Don't forget the timer," I remind her when I feel her eyes burying themselves into my face and bring her finger to press between my lips.

She shifts, slipping her phone out and setting a timer as her pink cheeks grow apple red. "Go."

It only takes me a handful of full breaths to slide her finger into my mouth and suck on the tip, my tongue swiping over the sliver once before it comes out. Far less than a minute. With the sliver on my tongue, I slide her finger free and wink at her.

"How did I do?"

Her glower and red cheeks are answer enough. "Is that how you get slivers out of all the ranch hands' fingers too?"

"Nah, just you, darlin'. You're the only one special enough for that treatment. The others get jabbed with tweezers because they don't know how to stand still and let me work. Stubborn mules, those guys."

"Are you saying that you aren't stubborn?"

"Depends," I say, flashing my best innocent smile, knowing my dimple's out.

"Right. Well, you won fair and square. I suppose you want to claim your prize?"

I shake my head, bringing her finger to my lips. Goosebumps grow over her skin. With a soft kiss to the red, inflamed skin, I declare, "Not quite yet. I've got plans for my prize, and they don't include claimin' it just yet."

18

Aurora

Despite winning our bet, Johnny left me Wanda's number last night.

On the back of an old gas station receipt resting on my kitchen counter, I found her phone number scribbled in nearly illegible writing.

780-555-1829. Call her Rory. She'll want to meet you.
Johnny, aka the pro sliver remover

It was too late to call her then and too early when I left the house this morning. I'll call her later today. That's what I tell myself, anyway. Every time I reached into my pocket and felt the paper there, I promised myself I'd call later. It's a pathetic excuse for stalling.

Staring out the bakery window, I rub the thin paper between my fingers. The girls are staring at me, each one of them wanting to ask why I'm gripping a piece of trash like it's a lifeline but holding themselves back.

They always do this.

Well, all except Bryce. Usually, she doesn't care about holding back when she's curious about something. It's in her nature to be blunt and precise, without a care. I respect her for it.

But today, she's quiet like Poppy and Anna are, choosing to dissect every slight change in my expression instead. That speaks to the magnitude of my inner struggles, I suppose. They're obvious to everyone around me.

"Everyone is so glum today," Poppy groans, obviously done with the silence but being the only one willing to do anything about it. She rips off a chunk of her chocolate croissant and brings it to her lips. "It's Sunday. And we didn't even get drunk last night, so nobody can claim to be hungover."

"Especially not you, Aurora," Bryce adds, continuing to sort through every emotion written on my face with her concentrated gaze.

I fist the receipt and drop my hand to my lap beneath the table. "What makes you think I wasn't drinking myself silly last night?"

"Were you?" she asks.

"No."

"I doubt Johnny would have wasted his first date with you getting drunk," Anna adds.

I tighten my hold on the receipt and ignore the heat crawling up my throat. "Does everyone know we were together last night?"

Bryce takes a swig of her steaming black coffee. "Why? Was it supposed to be a secret?"

"Well, no."

Anna tugs on the plastic straw in the lid of her iced coffee, creating a hair-raising screeching sound. "Then yes. We all know. It's not often he misses a Saturday night at Peakside."

"I told him to invite you out with us, but he was feeling selfish with your attention," Poppy says, fiddling with the shoulder strap of her pale purple sundress before plucking a piece of animal hair off Bryce's band tee.

All three women are dressed casually today, in a way that helps me feel even more comfortable around them. Blue jeans, T-shirts, the typical, flowy sundress that Poppy loves. There isn't any pressure to be done up all the time in Cherry Peak. No high standards that I feel like I have to hold every time I leave the house. It's comfortable, everyone non-judgmental for the most part. In my jean shorts and baggy tee, I feel accepted.

"Johnny wasn't out blabbing if that's what you're worried about. He only told us three and Garrison, and of course, we told everyone else," Poppy clarifies, looking at me now.

Anna reaches across the table for a napkin before starting to wipe her fingers free of the powdered sugar from her donut. "Would it be a bad thing if he had been out blabbing?"

The number of questions they're asking makes my hackles rise, but I know they mean well. I have to remind myself of that as I try to keep my answers from being so defensive.

They invited me out today, even after I've stopped working at Thistle and Thorn. Without my job forcing them to spend time with me from time to time, I half expected them to cut their efforts to spend time with me. It wouldn't have been surprising. I haven't given them any reason to keep trying.

But no. A week after starting a new job, and here we are, chatting like old friends.

"Johnny is . . ." I start, releasing some of the tension in my fingers. "I don't care if he talks about us. He'll be the one that will have to deal with the curiosity once I'm gone."

"If there's one thing Johnny doesn't care about, it's the opinion of others, Rory," Bryce says. "He's too unapologetically himself to give a shit about that."

"I've started to realize that," I reply softly.

Poppy scoots her chair closer to the table and offers me a smile that feels almost special, like only a certain number of people get to bear witness to it.

"He's smitten by you. Are you smitten by him?"

"Going right for the throat, Pops," Bryce mutters.

Anna laughs lightly, watching me. "You don't have to answer that question if you don't feel comfortable. I know we're all still getting to know each other."

And not for their lack of trying. It's been weeks of effort from them with little payoff.

My stomach tightens with guilt.

"He's rebuilding my porch; did you know that?" I ask, unclenching my fingers to press my sweaty palm flush to my thigh, the receipt paper crinkling beneath it.

It's Bryce who answers first. "I didn't."

"I was curious about the wood he dumped in the burn pile this morning, but I didn't piece together that it was from your porch," Anna says, and Poppy nods along with her.

"He insisted on doing these jobs around my house, saying it isn't safe enough for me. I didn't think he was going to start with something so big, but there was no stopping him once he pulled out a crowbar and got to work."

My smile is small as I recount last night, but Bryce doesn't miss it. She latches onto it with her icy-blue eyes until I can't help but say more, suddenly compelled to divulge far more to these girls right now than I ever have before.

It's a risk to open up, but maybe with these women, it'll be worth it.

"We made a stupid bet too. Like children. I used my chance to win something that would help me do what I came to Cherry Peak to do, but he only wanted something from me. Yet when he won, he didn't take his prize."

"What did he want?" Poppy asks.

I ignore the sparks of nerves in my belly. "A kiss."

Anna squeals and then slams a hand to her mouth as Bryce relaxes her features and leans back in her chair, laughing to herself.

"That's fucking adorable," Poppy says, a dreamy expression on her face.

Bryce glances at her best friend. "Adorable is for children, Pops."

"I don't care. Johnny's always been adorable. And it's really damn cute that that's what he wanted out of anything he could have asked for."

Anna cracks up, shaking her head at the both of them. "Did you think he was going to ask for something else? As if."

"Would you have kissed him if he had tried to claim his win? Or would it have been an obligation thing?" Poppy asks me.

My first instinct is to lie, but I have no doubt Bryce would call me out on it instantly. Besides, I've already opened up about this. I might as well go all the way.

"I would have kissed him. And not because of the bet. I wanted to kiss him before we even made it."

"That's good, Rory. Isn't it?" Anna asks gently, her lips curved into a small smile.

"I don't know," I answer honestly. "He's young and rambunctious. I'm neither of those things."

"Thirty isn't old, and twenty-two isn't that young either." Anna shrugs a shoulder, unbothered.

"Eight years is one of the better age gaps I've heard of. You could always be one of those women who dates an eighty-year-old billionaire on his deathbed," Poppy says.

Bryce snorts a laugh. "Clearly, Poppy has thought of taking that route before. She got lucky and found a thirty-year-old billionaire instead."

"Don't be jealous, you hag. And don't talk about me marrying anyone else around Garrison, or he'll get jealous and have me walking around bow-legged for the next week." Poppy cuts herself off and smirks. "Okay, on second thought, maybe do bring that up to him."

"You're disgusting," Bryce grunts, shoving Poppy by her arm.

Poppy pokes her elbow. "As if you're some saint. I've seen inside your nightstand."

"You're one to talk. I think you have an actual clinical dildo addiction. I know a therapist if you want their info."

"At least I haven't been pining after—"

Bryce cuts Poppy off with a hand to her mouth. Her glare is sharp like the tips of an iceberg. Poppy rolls her eyes, seemingly unbothered by her best friend's annoyance.

Is that because they have complete trust in one another? And if so, how did they open themselves up to the possibility of that? Maybe I should be taking advice from them.

Anna touches my forearm from the seat beside me, drawing my attention away from the two bickering friends. She's the newest one in the group outside of myself, and as such, I've always felt more of a pull to her. It's hard sticking your nose into a friendship that's been so solid for so long without feeling like a hang around. While none of these women have ever made me feel like that, Anna's the one I'm most comfortable with. It's like on some level, I trust her to be more accepting of me. I'm not as intimidated by her.

"Does Johnny being twenty-two actually bother you, or are you using it as an excuse not to give in to the feelings you clearly have for him?" she asks, keeping her voice low, the question only for me.

The bluntness of her question hits me square in the chest. "It's one of the many excuses I've been using."

"There are always a million excuses as to why we shouldn't do something. That doesn't mean that even a single one of them is worth using. I get why you're reluctant. Poppy does, too, when she's not bickering with Bryce. We've both experienced falling for someone when there are other forces at work that make it feel impossible. It's daunting not knowing what comes next, but I can tell you without a doubt that it's worth the risk, whether you stay or go."

She gives my arm a comforting squeeze. A reminder that she's here for me. "If I hadn't given Brody a chance because I knew that he was supposed to go back to Nashville, I wouldn't be as happy as I am right now, with a life that I could only hope for in my wildest dreams."

"I knew that Garrison was going back to Toronto, but I fell in love with him anyway. And it was the worst pain I've ever felt in my life to let him go, but he came back. Even if he hadn't, the heartbreak would have been worth it for the time we got together," Poppy adds, her eyes warm with understanding as they dart between Anna and me.

Bryce nods, but in the same way that she can seem to read me, I can read her. Maybe it's a shared talent we both have. Something that comes from being so guarded and defensive.

It's the stiffness in her shoulders and the twitch in the left side of her jaw that give her away. That make it obvious she isn't as believing as the other two are.

I let it go. "So, you're saying I should what? Demand he kiss me?"

"God no. He has to work for it still. Keep him on his toes, just don't close yourself off to the possibility of something happening between you yet," Anna says.

It's easier said than done, but something tells me every one of the women at this table has thought that and pushed past it. I just have to follow suit.

It's my turn to be brave.

19

Aurora

I've never believed in coincidences. Those once-in-a-lifetime occurrences spoken about on the news. Like the unbelievable tale of an old man winning the lottery after finding a five-dollar bill on the street and deciding to purchase a ticket for the first time in his life that I heard being told on the radio station Eliza had playing this morning.

It wasn't a coincidence that he found a five-dollar bill that day of all days or that he used it to buy a lottery ticket. It was simple chance. A spur-of-the-moment choice he made that paid off in the end.

Some days, I wish I believed in terms like fate and coincidences. It would make it easier to blame bad decisions on a sleight of hand from something bigger than ourselves instead of taking responsibility for our own choices. Hell, maybe it would make me hate Lee Rose less than I currently do.

If the universe called him away from my mother, then how could I possibly blame him for leaving?

Anger flushes my chest as I lean against the side of the house and heave an exhale. My phone weighs a thousand pounds in my hands. The number punched in and ready to dial mocks me. Doubts run rampant through my head until they're all I believe.

She'll tell me to get lost. That I don't matter and shouldn't have even attempted to come to Cherry Peak. That she couldn't ever want a sister like me.

My eyes burn at the thoughts, each one puncturing a pin-sized hole in my chest. The breeze is hot, simply blowing the muggy air into my face, even as I stand out of its full grasp, protected by the walls of the house. I'm hiding back here, behind the garden shed Eliza uses to store the tools for the flowers along the porch.

I didn't want anyone to hear me when I called Wanda. If Eliza knew, she'd offer me some sort of wisdom, and I can't deal with that right now. It isn't wisdom I need but a swift kick in the ass.

"It's not every day I see a woman hanging around back here. Don't tell me my brother has driven you into hiding."

The woman speaking to me is unfamiliar but gorgeous all the same, with round blue-grey eyes and hair the colour of ripe cherries. She smiles kindly at me, and the dimple on her left cheek has my eyes growing wide at how similar she looks to Johnny.

Swooped nose, strong cheekbones, and the same arch in their brows. Even their chins curve the same. Yet despite all that's similar, they're distinctly different. For one, I'd have attempted to count all of Johnny's freckles already if he had nearly the same number of them.

Clearing my throat, I collect myself. "You must be Daisy."

"So, he does talk about his sisters, then. I was beginning to worry we'd meet and you'd have no idea who I am," she says, approaching me to offer her hand. "And you're Aurora, right?"

I nod, something warm filling my belly at the knowledge that she knows who I am. "He talks about you guys a lot."

When I shake her hand, she swings her other arm awkwardly, as if she would have preferred to hug me instead of something so formal.

She beams at my words and takes a step back before rocking forward on her toes. "Everyone will be happy to hear that."

Times like this, I wish I was better with human interaction. This isn't the time for my mind to go blank, unable to come up with something to say. I could cry with relief when Daisy opens her mouth to speak, seemingly unbothered by my silence.

"So, what are you doing back here? Are you hiding from the guys? I wouldn't blame you if you were. They're like yapping hounds when women are around. You can treat them like it, by the way. A swift kick between the legs, and they'll be leaving you alone," she says, the pep in her voice as she speaks about kicking a guy in the balls a bit . . . interesting.

"I'm not hiding, per se."

"Just taking a minute?"

"Yeah," I say on a weighted exhale. "Yeah, a minute that's turned into quite a few."

"Is there anything I can do to help?" she offers.

I think about my answer twice before saying, "I need to make a phone call but can't get myself to press the button. Could you do it for me?"

Her nod is instant. She bounces a step toward me and holds out her hand. "You've got it, babe."

Giving my phone to her feels like a true test of my sanity. But thankfully, she doesn't hesitate to grab it from me, making the decision to give it willingly a lot easier.

"Count to three or something first—"

The sound of the dial tone has my muscles and joints locking up. Fear shackles me as ice water floods my veins, freezing me from the inside.

Daisy slides the phone back into my hand and rubs my shoulder in a soft, soothing motion. "Whatever this is about, you'll be fine. *It* will be fine."

I don't believe her and don't bother saying otherwise. Or anything, for that matter. Daisy gives me a squeeze and then shifts back, giving me room to breathe.

"You're beautiful, by the way. I knew you would be—Johnny said you were—but I definitely concur with him. I'm glad I got a minute with you without him hovering. Hopefully, we'll see each other again soon."

I jerk my head in a nod and watch her skip off, with my phone clutched so tight in my fist I'm shocked it hasn't crumbled to pieces by now. It continues to ring, even as I force my stiff arm to raise it to my ear. I gulp down a breath and wait.

It rings three more times before cutting off.

"Hello?"

I almost burst into tears at the first sound of her voice. My *sister's* voice. The half doesn't matter right now.

Clearing my throat, I lift a hand to my throat and say, "Hi. Is this Wanda?"

"That depends on who this is."

I flinch at the blunt tone but don't let it deter me. As the daughter of a famous public figure, I assume she deals with random people calling a lot.

"Are you sitting down somewhere? If not, you might want to."

"How about you just tell me what this is about."

"Alright," I mutter. Jumping right into it, then. "My name is Aurora Bennett and—"

My lips clamp shut when I feel a shift in the air. Whipping my head to the right, I feel that stupid fucking burn in my eyes again. Daisy went to him. That's why she left so quickly.

A coincidence, maybe. That Daisy found me in a moment I needed not only the company but unknowingly also someone to be my side through this conversation.

Johnny presses a finger to his lips and comes to stand right in front of me, close enough that when I drop my head forward, it rests against his shoulder. His arms wrap around me, anchoring me to his chest as I blink away the emotion in my eyes.

"And I'm your sister," I state into the phone.

A kiss on my head comes as I wait for a reply. The weight of a large hand on my back, rubbing up and down my spine, is a steady reminder that I'm not alone.

I'm not alone.

"I don't have a sister," Wanda says, her tone of voice hard and to the point.

I flinch again, but this time, Johnny's tightening his hold on me. "I didn't think I did either. But it's true. I can show you anything you want to see to prove it."

A weighted pause. "How'd you even get this number?"

"Does it really matter?"

"Of course it does. You're out to lunch if you think I'm going to take the word of some random woman who's somehow come across my number. Are you looking for money, is that it?"

I suck in a sharp breath, all of my fears coming back in full swing. Daisy's reassuring words get buried beneath them, never to be found again.

I'm so lost in my head that when a gentle set of fingers peel mine from my phone, I don't fight them. I keep my forehead pressed to Johnny's chest and inhale the smell of cologne and outdoors.

"Hey, Wanda."

"Johnny? What the shit is going on right now?"

I cringe at the fact the volume is loud enough he could hear every one of Wanda's comments before as I hear them all now.

"Listen, you've gotta come home. I know this is the last place you want to be right now, or ever, but Rory's telling the truth."

I count the seconds it takes her to reply. *Ten.*

"She's not. I don't have a sister, and she's tricked you into believing otherwise. What game are you playing? Is this some sort of dare?"

"It's not a dare."

"Is Anna there? Let me talk to someone else," she demands. "This isn't a funny prank."

Her adamant denial hurts. It's unfair to have expected her to be at all believing or accepting of this bomb I've dropped on her, but it still hurts regardless. Everything is unfair right now.

All but the man who's wrapped himself around me like a

shield. Who's still dressed in filthy jeans and boots to match. He keeps himself against me and his arms wrapped around my torso as if he's trying to tuck me inside of him.

I don't let myself think twice about my next move. Giving in to the desperate urge to touch him, I slide my arms over his hips and lock my fingers at the base of his back, hugging him right back.

"There isn't anyone else to talk to right now, Wanda. Just you, me, and Rory. And it's up to you now whether you buy what we're saying or not, but you've gotta drop that attitude before I tell your sister you aren't worth knowin'," he says.

I open my eyes to stare at our feet, his threat shocking me. The part of me that hates not taking care of myself and my own problems demands I grab the phone back and take care of the rest of this conversation myself, but the other part of me? It wants me to climb up this man's body and beg him to kiss me.

Hard. Preferably until I can't feel my lips any longer.

I haven't had anyone take care of me like this in a very, very long time, and despite everything, I want to let him.

"Give me your word, Johnny. Promise me this is serious, and I'll get on a flight as soon as I can," Wanda says, the biting edge in her voice dulled considerably.

His mouth brushes over my hair as he says, "I promise you that this is real. You've got a sister, Wanda, and you'll want to meet her. I can also promise you that."

20

Johnny

The moment Wanda hangs up with the promise of catching a flight out here this week, I'm fixing all my focus onto Aurora. She's tense in my arms, almost shaking with whatever it is going through her head. Disappointment or anger, maybe. I know I feel a lot of the latter.

Wanda grew up here in Cherry Peak with the rest of us. She's the same age as Brody, so I never had the chance to get to know her all that well. Although it wasn't necessary in a town this size where everyone knows everyone regardless of age.

It's public fact that she's accepting of strangers only when she wants to be, and if she does accept you, there isn't much of a chance to grow close before she's taking off on another one of her adventures. Nobody blames her for not wanting to stick around, considering the lack of tethers keeping her here. But that doesn't make me any less upset with the way she spoke to Aurora on the phone.

Shock can have a negative effect on just about anyone. There isn't a right or wrong way to handle something as heavy as learning you've had a sibling you never knew about. There is, however, a proper way to speak to someone, surprised or not.

Feel your emotions, but don't take them out on others. My

mom taught every one of my siblings that lesson when we were young. It's stayed with me since, and I try to live by that rule as often as I can.

"Are you okay?" I ask, my voice half-muffled by Rory's hair.

She breathes in and out and jerks her head in a nod. The fruity smell of her shampoo works its way up my nose as I press another kiss to her crown. Every minute that she stays in my arms, I grow calmer. More at peace. A sense of rightness settles deep in my subconscious, and I'm certain that this is exactly where I need to be.

Daisy wasn't supposed to be here until after lunch, and if she truly hadn't arrived until then, I wouldn't have gotten this chance with Rory. It was fate that brought my sister here early to say goodbye before heading back to Calgary, and I won't take a single fucking argument on that.

"Should I be okay after that?"

"You don't have to be. Not with me."

"What good will it do if I'm not? I wasn't expecting her to be happy."

The pain in her voice threatens to rock me back on my heels. It strikes deep, awakening instincts inside of me that I haven't felt before for anyone besides my family. The drive to protect and defend.

"Happy or not, she could have been nicer." *Should* have been.

I cup her hips and press us into the shadows, her back against the wall. She lets me move us, not letting so much as a peep escape her. It's worrisome, turning my protectiveness up a notch.

Flexing my fingers, I drop my head, bringing my nose to brush her cheek. My hat bumps her head, and I consider tossing the thing into the wind before she surprises me by ripping it off herself and hanging it at her side. I laugh softly at her eagerness, and she shivers in my grip.

"Don't laugh at me right now," she scolds, but there's no heat behind it.

"I'm not laughin' at you, darlin'."

"Right."

"I'm trying not to lose my shit right now, actually," I admit.

"Why?"

"Why am I trying not to lose my shit?"

"Yeah."

I almost laugh again. "Isn't it obvious?"

"Clearly not," she grumbles.

Pulling back enough to stare down at her, I curl a finger beneath her chin and lift it. With her red-rimmed eyes snaring mine, I struggle to breathe, let alone speak. It should be a crime for eyes this beautiful to be so sad.

"I don't like it when you're upset, Rory. Not one damn bit."

Her shoulder lifts. "It's not the end of the world."

"Feels like it to me."

She blinks, long lashes brushing the thin, still-wet skin beneath her eyes. I swipe at the wetness there with my thumb.

"You didn't have to come save me, Johnny. I can take care of myself," she murmurs.

"Do I look put out by comin'? Because I sure don't feel anything but grateful to have been here for you."

I hear her swallow before she tightens her arms around my waist and hugs me. *Hugs. Me.* With her cheek flat to my chest, I know she can hear the way my heart speeds to a dangerous tempo. I want her to hear it.

"Thank you," she breathes against my shirt, my hat brushing my back from where she still holds it.

I close my eyes and hug her just as tight. "Anytime, Aurora."

We stand here for minutes, hours, maybe. With my back to the world and her in my arms, I could have stayed here for a lifetime. Every noise around us is dulled, as if we've stepped inside a bubble meant just for us.

I never thought I could enjoy something so simple this much. And the guys would have my ass if they ever found out, but I'm almost inclined to make sure to tell them regardless. It's worth it for the chance to let them know she's my girl, even if she hasn't accepted that just yet.

We're getting there.

Slow and steady, I remind myself.

"Don't you have work?" she asks after a few more moments of silence.

I don't let her go just yet. "Nothing that can't wait a few minutes. I was planning on taking an early lunch, anyway."

It's not completely the truth. I was riding Joker back from checking on that damn bull fence again when I saw Daisy rounding the house. My to-do list flew away the moment she told me Aurora was "having a mild nervous breakdown" and skipped off to the stable.

"You're a shit liar, Johnny," she says before unwinding her arms and swaying back a step.

The loss of her against me is a shock to my system, but I try to hide the effect it has on me with an easy grin. "Do you have a busy afternoon? I've got somethin' to do that I think would help to take your mind off of Wanda."

Intrigue lights her eyes. "Like what?"

"I know you said you aren't the biggest fan of animals, but have you ever met a horse?"

AFTER HOOKING up the horse trailer to the hitch of the truck, I hop out of the cab and wave Rory over.

She comes over instantly, appearing almost excited. Seeing the appearance of her smile after what happened earlier is like looking up at the sun after a week-long rain.

In blue jeans and a baggy shirt that droops over her left shoulder, leaving it bare, the only way this woman could look any more like a natural rancher would be a hat on her head and boots on her feet. It's hard to want her to look anything other than herself, though. She's damn perfect the way she is.

"Hop in and we'll head out," I tell her.

"I don't know anything about horses," she warns.

"I know. I'm goin' to teach you. We've got a little over an hour on the road before we get there, so we've got the time for a rundown of the basics."

With a small dip of her chin, she rounds the hood of the truck and slips inside. I roll my shoulders to disperse some of my nervous jitters and join her.

The truck we're using today is not only big, but it's loud as fuck. One twist of the keys and it's roaring and puffing out plumes of black smoke. Aurora unrolls her window and watches the clouds of exhaust in the side mirror as I drive off the grass and onto the gravel road leading through the ranch.

Hanging my arm out my window, I ask, "Will you tell me more about your life in Calgary? Not including all the stuff with your mom, but everything else."

"Anything specific you want to know?"

"Hard to be specific when I want to know everything, darlin'."

She laughs, reaching out her window to run her fingers through the breeze. "Right. Well, I had a good job as a financial advisor for an auction company. It was boring, though."

"What did you do there?"

"The basic things. Kind of like what I'm doing for the Steeles. Budget planning, advise on large purchases."

I hum. "Did you enjoy it?"

"Enough that I worked there for six years."

"Would you have stayed there if you hadn't come here?"

"I don't know. Maybe."

Sensing that I'm approaching one of her walls, I switch topics. "Are you close with your mom?"

"Do I get to ask you any questions, or do you just get to ask me them?"

I flash her a smile. "You can ask me anything you want."

"What are your mothers' names? Eliza mentioned that you have two."

"Goin' right for my heart, I see," I tease while we pass the ranch house. "Jennifer and Rachel. They're two of the best people you'll ever meet."

"How do they feel about having so many daughters and only one son? You're a bit outnumbered," she says with a soft curl of her mouth.

"A bit outnumbered? Try a lot. I know more about periods and acrylic nails than I do cattle."

"So, does that mean you aren't one of those guys that gets sent to the store to buy tampons and has to send a thousand pictures of the different kinds for approval before finally grabbing one?"

I glance across the dash and wink at her. When I look ahead again, we're approaching the Steele Ranch gate. "Nah, gorgeous. You send me out, and I'll come back with all the top-of-the-line products, plus everything else you'll need. No picture sending necessary."

"That's a big promise," she muses.

"And one I can fulfill."

"We'll see."

My stomach tries to shoot up through my throat at her answer. It takes all my focus to turn out of the ranch onto the second gravel road leading to the highway.

"You say that as if I'll get a chance to prove it to you."

Her smirk is coy and makes my cock stiffen in my jeans. I shift in my seat and attempt to subtly adjust my hard-on.

"We've only been on one date," she points out.

"And your porch is nowhere near finished."

"Exactly."

I laugh, feeling it deep in my gut. "Let me take you out properly, Rory."

"I don't need to be taken out. I liked being at home."

"You deserve to be wined and dined."

She snorts, the noise drawing my attention. I cock a brow when she rolls her eyes at me. "I'm a homebody. In case you haven't noticed, people aren't really my specialty. It's easier to feel like myself at home."

"Okay, do you have anything in mind, then?"

"Surprise me."

Two words have never sounded so exciting. "That's a dangerous request to make of a guy like me."

"A guy like you?"

"Yeah, the type that wants nothing more than to impress a girl like you and is willing to do just about anything to accomplish it."

"I've never known a guy like you, Johnny," she admits softly, almost nervously.

I reach across the dash and drop my hand on her thigh. She glances down at it before looking over at me. I fucking love her pink cheeks.

"Seems we were both in for a surprise, then," I reply before giving her thigh a squeeze and keeping it there.

A claim staked for only us to see.

21

Aurora

We don't even make it fully out of the truck before a woman standing by a long stable shouts, "Johnny! I was hoping it would be you today!"

Johnny beams at her as he sets his hat on his head and slips from the truck. He swings the door shut with a grip on the half-rolled window as I sit in silence, my seat belt feeling like it's growing tighter by the second.

He strides toward the woman with a look I've grown used to seeing. Happiness, a steady calm. She tosses her arms around his neck and squeals while hugging him tight and for far too long. He hugs her back, and I inhale a sharp breath through my nose when something angry and very, very green flares in my mind. It's like I've tossed back a shot of poison as I work to keep my expression unbothered and climb out after him.

"It's been far too long since you've been out here. Wade's been gatekeeping you," she says as they part.

I wait for them to separate further, but she reaches out to hold his arms, keeping him close.

He doesn't move them out of her grip. His grin doesn't waver. Each step I take toward them feels like I'm wading through tar. After everything earlier today, this feels far worse than it probably is.

"Thomas knows more about these babies than I do, Jill. I missed this place, though. Especially the babies in there." He gestures to the stable.

Oh, he *missed* this place. *How nice.*

Jill, as he called her, smiles easily and freely. Some people have obvious vibes, like radioactive waves of personality that give you an insider view of how their minds work. She has too many waves. They're so thick they nearly choke me.

Maybe that's just my cattiness coming through.

Yeah, that's probably it.

She flips her long blonde braid over her shoulder and pushes the top of her hat back to expose more of her tan skin. My jealousy spikes again when I sweep my gaze over her features and find them near perfect. Smooth and pimple-free. I can't even find a single acne scar. How is that possible?

Probably because she's nearly ten years younger than you, Aurora.

"Well, it's nice to see you, anyway. I know the horses will be excited to see you," she says cheerfully.

"Wade gave y'all the rundown, yeah?" he asks, shifting his hips to face the stable.

I finally reach them, my arms hanging limp before I shove my hands into my pockets. He doesn't make a move to introduce me, and I deduce that to the fact he hasn't noticed me. Somehow, that's worse than any other reason.

The stable that holds his attention is more like a horse palace. It's tall and sleek, made of matte black and deep chestnut brown siding. The doors are bigger than the ones at Steele Ranch, and there are at least three more of them. It even has a second storey on the back half with a tall window that I'd bet even swings open.

Taking a look around the ranch, it's obvious that there's a reason for the extravagant stable. Horses are everywhere. In a back pasture and two huge circles with shining silver fencing and equipped with several wooden barrels.

This is a horse ranch. Maybe with the specific purpose of training them. Breeding too.

"I'm so sorry for my rudeness!" Jill shrieks, snagging my attention. "I'm Jill. This is my family's ranch."

I blink, refocusing to find her hand extended for me to shake. Taking it to avoid being seen as rude, I yank the corner of my mouth up into a smile that I hope doesn't look as much like a grimace as it feels.

Johnny's eyes are a brand on my face, but I ignore him. "I'm Aurora. This is a beautiful place."

"Thank you so much. It's been a long journey to get it to where it is now, but yeah, it's pretty great," she replies.

I pull my hand back and return it to my pocket with a nod. While it's always hard for me to make conversation in a normal situation, it's even harder with people I don't particularly want to converse with. It's not anything truly against Jill; it's just . . . me.

My ridiculous, misplaced jealousy and bitterness with how little I seem to exist to Johnny right now.

"Jill's family are the biggest horse breeders in Alberta. We've gotten all our horses from them," Johnny explains.

When he gets closer to me and slips a finger through one of my belt loops, I fight the instinct to shove him off. The pride in his voice as he speaks of her ranch bites even though it shouldn't.

Clearly, despite my best efforts, this man has weaselled his way into my heart and made a home for himself there. It's the only explanation I have for this desperate need to put on some cringy possessive act to scare Jill off like a wild beast marking her territory.

"How's Joker doing?" she asks him.

"Still full of attitude."

With a look of understanding, she turns to me. "Do you ride too?"

"No." I hate how stiff the word sounds.

"Rory's a new resident of Cherry Peak. A city girl from Calgary," Johnny says, the fingers not looped in my pants brushing the jean material at the top of my ass.

Jill jerks her head toward the stable. "Well, I hope you don't mind 'em! Ours are incredibly friendly."

I don't answer before she's leading the way. Instead, I keep my head on a swivel as we walk, busying myself with the sights around me so I don't have to speak with Johnny and wind up exposing myself.

I'd have preferred working with Eliza today instead of being driven out here just to be ignored for a woman who's clearly the opposite of me. If that's what he wants, he's been wasting his time.

"Have you had many coyotes out here recently?" Johnny asks her, keeping pace between the both of us.

One minuscule glance at the ground and I realize that his boots are nearly the same shade as hers. Fuck, even their hats are similar. Did they call each other to plan this outfit coordination this morning? Do they talk often? *Jesus Christ, this is not a rabbit hole I want to go down right now.*

I'm thirty, not thirteen. Grow up.

"No more than usual. You guys?"

"We did. But Eliza convinced Wade to get donkeys. Now, those fuckers kick the shit out of them when they get too close," Johnny says.

Jill's laugh rings through the ranch, carried on the breeze. I stiffen, and when Johnny tugs on my belt loop in an attempt to get my attention, I know he's noticed. He does it again, but this time, I step to the side, forcing him to let go of me.

We all stop in front of the first of the stable doors, and Johnny reaches for the handle before Jill can. She gazes up at him with a soft stare and thanks him. I swallow a scream.

He yanks the door open, and Jill steps inside first. I keep pace with her and move past Johnny without planning on saying a word. The hand on my arm when I step around him ruins my plans.

"What's wrong?" he asks quietly, those long fingers keeping a gentle hold on me. One jerk and I'd be free.

I stare straight ahead into the stable. "I'm fine."

"You're lying."

"We're here on behalf of Steele Ranch, Johnny. This is work."

"Oh, it is, is it? Shit, I almost forgot that you're the Steele's newest ranch hand."

I gnaw on my lip to stifle a laugh at his sarcasm. He hasn't used this particular trait of his often in my presence. It's hot, and now I'm even more pissed off.

"If you want someone to flirt with while we're here, I'm sure Jill is up to banter. You seem to be enjoying doing it already."

His thumb slips over the skin below my elbow, and something about the soft touch draws my eyes. The sight of him touching me is too much right now. My middle caves in as I ache to feel his hands all over me. Head to toe, I don't care. Anywhere would suffice. I'd take *anything* to stifle this want.

"Rory," he rasps. "Look at me."

I wet my dry lips and lie through my teeth. "I want you to let go of me."

He does immediately. I leave him there before I can tell him to hold me again. I'd never be able to scrape my pride off the ground after that.

"Over here, Johnny. This is Biscuit. Wade mentioned him first," Jill calls, waving at him from the end of the line of pens.

I ignore her and make my way to the other side of the stable. Most of the pens are empty, and if they run at all like Steele Ranch, then most of the horses kept in here are in use right now. Eliza explained that the horses belonging to the ranch hands and the family are kept inside. Special privilege exists in the animal world too, apparently.

"He looks good. Healthy," I hear Johnny say behind me.

"Just turned three this spring."

A soft patting sounds, and I can see Johnny giving the horse affection the way he does Joker without needing to turn around.

"Great. Yeah, he's a big guy for three. Should be a good workhorse."

A gate rattles as I move down the line of pens, peeking inside each one as if something's tugging me along. I nearly trip when a long blonde nose juts out over the gate one pen ahead and a snort fills the air. Leaning back on my heels, I keep still, waiting to see if the horse opens its massive jaw and tries to take a piece out of me.

"Um, hi," I mutter when a few seconds pass without teeth chomping.

Taking two steps forward, I keep a distance between myself and the mystery nose before peering inside the pen. My eyes go wide when I see the horse staring right at me, brown eyes curious.

With a coat so blonde it's almost white, the horse looks like it was dumped into a bucket of bleach when it was born. The single brown patch on the left side of its belly is almost comical.

"Do I stink or something?" I ask when it moves closer and sniffs loudly.

It sniffs again before jutting its entire head over the gate. The shiny white mane flowing over its neck looks like silk. I want to touch it but don't know if it'll have me for dinner quite yet.

"This is kind of rude," I mutter. "Demanding attention like this isn't sweet behaviour. How am I supposed to believe you won't bite me when you don't have any manners?"

It waves its head in front of me, as if telling me to pet it. I roll my lips before cautiously lifting my hand toward it, all too aware that I'm risking losing the damn thing.

I'm pleasantly surprised when the horse doesn't bite me but shoves that giant nose into my palm instead.

"Oh. You are nice, then."

"She likes you," Johnny says.

I keep my attention on the horse, moving forward and reaching to stroke my palm over its neck. The muscles there are thick and strong, while the hair is soft. When the silky mane blows over my knuckles, it tickles.

"Why did you come over here?" he asks, keeping his distance.

I think I hate that more than him being too close.

"I wanted to."

The horse releases a high-pitched noise and swings its head toward me again, bringing it so close I can see its short eyelashes.

"She really, really likes you, Rory."

"It's a girl?"

"You didn't check?" he asks, sounding like he's holding back a laugh.

I scowl. "No, I didn't check. I was busy doing other things."

"Yeah, darlin'. It's a she. A beautiful she too."

"She's gorgeous," I whisper, shifting my touch lower down her neck before scratching gently.

"Are you sure you've never even seen a horse before?"

"Never up close like this."

He makes a low sound in his throat before offering her his hand. The traitor seems to like him as much as she supposedly does me. One sniff and she's shoving her face toward him too.

"She likes you too, apparently," I say bitterly.

"Joker will be jealous when she smells her on me."

Seems Joker and I have a lot more in common than I thought.

"I can't say that I blame her for that."

"And why's that, Rory?" he asks, attempting to poke into my head.

I feign nonchalance. "No reason."

"Come on, talk to me—"

"Ripley's over here, Johnny," Jill says.

I straighten my spine. "Duty calls."

The heat of his body is what I feel first. His breath on my ear comes next. "This conversation isn't over."

I refuse the shiver that tries to ripple through me and keep my eyes trained on the horse. There's no doubt in my mind that he's right.

The moment we leave this place and he has me trapped back in that truck, I'm his to command, and we both know it.

22

Johnny

We spend the longest two hours of my life on the Kollers' ranch. Every minute that passes with Aurora giving me the cold shoulder feels like an eternity. She's completely closed herself off to me, and it upsets me nearly as much as it turns me all the way on. I've been walking around with a rock-solid cock from the moment I realized she was upset because of Jill.

Because she's jealous over me.

It's uncomfortable standing in front of Jill's father and one of Wade's closest friends with a boner, but for Rory, I suck it the hell up.

"Wade didn't mention wantin' that one," he grunts, his scarred hands set on his hips.

I keep my chin up, matching his intimidating stance with one of my own. "I know. I'm making the call to add her. You'll get paid whatever she's worth, along with the other two."

"She ain't from the same stock as the others. And hell, maybe I've already got another buyer lined up."

"I don't care about her stock. And you don't have another buyer lined up. Even if you did, you'd give us priority anyway. You know that as well as I do."

"I don't remember you having such a heavy set of balls on you the last time you were here," he mutters.

"Stop playing hardball, Dad. The Steeles will take good care of her," Jill says, standing close to me again, her hand on my arm.

A glance over my shoulder at where Aurora leans against the side of the horse trailer, her arms crossed and eyes shooting hell-fire at Jill's hand, has me nonchalantly leaning away.

I didn't want Rory here for this conversation, and I damn well know that asking her to stay by the trailer added fuel to her fire. It wasn't because I don't want her close but because I want to surprise her with something, and the only way I can do that is if she stays out of hearing distance.

"My girl likes her, Rich. That's all that matters to me."

Something pushed Aurora toward Frost, and I've been around horses long enough to recognize when an instant connection is born. I'd have been fucking blind to miss the one I saw between them.

"Let me load her up, and we'll get out of your hair," I add.

The grumpy old man stares at me, attempting to get me to break beneath the sharpness of his expression, but it's not going to happen. Not here, not ever.

Finally, he slices a hand through the air. "Fine. Fuckin' take 'er. But don't get used to coming here and callin' the shots, boy."

I'm already heading back to the stable when I call over my shoulder, "Got it."

Footsteps pound the ground behind me before Jill's falling into pace at my side. "I didn't know you had a girlfriend."

"I don't exactly." *Not yet.*

"Is that why she doesn't like me? If you had said something, I'd have kept my distance."

"You're fine, Jill. I've upset her myself."

"You didn't do anything besides be nice," she says.

Aurora tracks the two of us when we pass the trailer. I want to stop and plant a fat kiss on her pouty lips, but now isn't the time. I think I'd wind up with claw marks if I attempted that without a proper conversation first.

For now, I need to get this horse loaded up quickly. The sooner we're done here, the sooner I can confirm what I did wrong and fix it.

"I appreciate the talk, Jill, but I just really want to get this done," I tell her, softening my tone as much as possible.

Crossing into the stable, I head directly for Frost's pen before I'm tugged by the back of my shirt. I sigh and turn to face Jill. The spark in her eyes makes guilt creep in.

It's been a year since we went out for drinks that single time, and nothing came of it. I didn't feel anything besides friendship between us, and I've made that clear. She thought differently, and it's why I've avoided coming here since. Thomas loves horses and hasn't minded picking up the job. But today of all days, Wade put his foot down, and I knew better than to say no.

It's easy for me to be a nice, welcoming guy. Being a decent person is natural for me with how I was raised. But I'll only be pushed so far before even two fantastic role models aren't enough to stifle my annoyance. Having my words ignored and someone I care about hurt because of it has my patience thinning at an alarming rate.

"I missed you, Johnny. You've been avoiding coming here, and the time that you finally decide to come back, you bring a woman with you. Was that on purpose? To hurt me?" Jill asks, water filling her eyes.

My throat grows tight as she sets a hand on my chest and a tear drips down her cheek. "That's not what I was doing. Me taking Aurora here had nothing to do with you."

"It feels like it," she blubbers, letting more tears stream down her cheeks without attempting to wipe them away.

"I was honest with you after our date. I don't—"

"Are you almost done? I'm ready to leave." Aurora's voice is sheer ice.

I jerk backward, forcing Jill's hand to fall from my chest.

Alarm rattles me. Staring past her at Rory, I open my mouth to tell her . . . *fuck*, I don't even know what. Something. Anything. But she spins on her heel and leaves before I have the chance.

"She's nothing like you, Johnny," Jill declares.

"Good. I don't need her to be anything like me," I say stiffly. "If you're not going to help me load Frost up, then I don't have anything else to say, Jill."

And with that, I leave her standing there with her tears and judgmental attitude while I get my girl her fucking horse.

I FIND Aurora in the truck fifteen minutes later, her head tipped back and eyes closed. Her seat belt is already done up, and her arms are crossed over her chest. If she looked peaceful instead of tense and coolly calm, I'd have thought she was sleeping.

As opposed to the first time I started the truck, she doesn't flinch at the loud roar of the engine. I stare at her, wishing not for the first time in my life that I could read minds. She's completely closed off right now, betraying nothing as she continues to keep her eyes shut and mouth in a bored line.

I blow out a breath and double-check the hauling settings in the truck before driving us off the ranch. *None* of this went how I planned it to.

Not for a minute did I think that Jill would be as touchy as she was, nor that it would upset Aurora this much. I was hopeful that after a year of no contact, she'd have stopped caring.

This trip was supposed to be a chance to get Aurora out of town and away from the ranch for a while. Horses are an integral part of my life, and yeah, while I didn't want to go by myself today, I brought her here to introduce her to my world a bit more without the weight of everyone back home watching.

Instead, I wound up pissing her off and taking three steps back instead of forward.

I want to blame this all on Wanda and her shitty attitude toward Aurora this morning. It would be easier that way. But it isn't fair. I know better than that.

"We have an hour drive back. Talk to me, Rory," I say once we make it onto the main highway, darting my eyes across the dash.

"What do you want to talk about?"

"You know exactly what I want to talk about."

"Well, I don't want to talk about that."

"Why? Because you know if we do, you'll have to expose yourself? You'll have to admit what it is that's really bothering you and show what you think is what? Weakness?" I ask, choking the steering wheel with my hands.

She doesn't have even a slight visible reaction to my words, and with a snip of invisible sheers, my last string of patience is severed.

With a quick look in my tow mirrors, I find the closest turnout and pull the truck over. Only when I rip the keys from the ignition and hop out of the cab does she finally show some sort of reaction. Brows in her hairline, she watches me suspiciously. It's only been a few minutes since I've seen her beautiful blue eyes, but the sight of them now makes me weak-kneed.

"Get out of the truck, Aurora," I order, slamming the door shut.

I wring my hands together and walk to the back of the trailer. One of the horses whinnies, but other than that, they're calm and quiet. It's not too hot today—another blessing when it comes to this pause in driving.

"I don't like being ordered around, Johnny."

I huff a laugh. "Well, that's too bad, darlin'."

The first thing I notice when she rounds the back of the trailer is her glare. It snares me, promising to set me on fire. I almost surrender to the call of the flickering flames. Would they brand me with her initials or melt me from the inside out?

"I want to go home," she states bluntly.

"We will go home. After you *talk to me*."

"Why bother? You seem to know just about every thought in my head already."

"And that bothers you," I state.

She sucks in a breath, rolling her eyes up to the sky. "Yes, it bothers me. What gives you the right to read me so easily?"

"I don't know."

"It's unfair."

"You know what else is unfair?" I ask, nostrils flaring as I close some of the distance she's left between us.

She lifts her chin higher, that brave, angry gaze never drifting. "No, but I'm sure you're going to tell me."

"This attitude of yours is going to kill me, Aurora," I say softly, shaking my head. "We'll add it to the fucking list of things you do that drives me out of my goddamn mind."

"Are you expecting an apology from me for that?"

"Not in the slightest. But I do expect honesty in return for all of mine."

She breaks eye contact and spins around, facing an endless field of nothing. "What you want is for me to break myself open and spill every single thought I've ever had."

"When they involve me, fuckin' right I do."

"They all involve you!" she shouts, arms flying as she looks back at me. "From that first night, you've occupied my mind like a disease! It was curiosity at first. Confusion as to why you came for me that night and why I let you. I don't believe in fate or coincidences, yet every single day with you, the universe tries to change my mind.

"I shouldn't be drawn to you the way I am. It's trouble waiting to happen. You are heartbreak, Johnny. You're fucking *heartbreak*, and I've signed myself up for it anyway!"

My chest is pinched so tight every inhale is small, not enough air coming in to fill my lungs properly as I grow light-headed.

Aurora's shoulders droop for the first time in my presence. "You ruined my plans. Twisted me into a knot I can't untie, and for what? For fun? Something to fill the time while you're away from another woman?"

I blink, thinking I misheard her. "What do you mean 'while I'm away from another woman'? Do you think I'm the type of guy to have taken you to the home of a woman I've been wanting like that?"

"Don't play dumb with me. I saw the way you were with Jill."

"I know what you think you saw, Aurora. But it wasn't me wantin' another woman."

"Then what was it, then? Because I didn't see you shoving her off of you when she clung to you or touched you all day. You seemed to enjoy the attention she was giving."

I drag my thumb across my bottom lip, letting out a short, breathy laugh. "I knew you were jealous. Knew that's why you were so cold and closed off. I just hoped you had more faith in me than to believe I was enjoying anyone's company as much as I enjoy yours. Or that every time she spoke to me, I wasn't wishin' it was you instead. I was being polite instead of tossing her across the ranch the moment she touched me like I wanted to."

"How did you expect me to be thinking that? Do I really come off as the non-territorial type? Especially when I haven't given you any reason to be loyal to me."

"No reason to be loyal," I repeat, the weight of her admission hitting me full force. "What exactly should you have had to do to expect loyalty from me?"

"I don't know. Given you something, at least! We haven't even kissed, Johnny. I haven't done anything besides run—"

It only takes one step forward to be able to take her face in my hands. I drop my head and brush my lips over hers, testing the soft, plump feel of her mouth. Tasting her for the first time without taking our first real kiss. Swallowing the rest of her sentence and the wobbly exhale that follows.

"If you wanted me to kiss you, Rory, you should have just said so," I whisper, splaying my fingers to touch as much of her cheeks as possible before pressing our mouths together.

23

Aurora

I'M AWARE OF ALL OF THE FLAWS IN MY CHARACTER AND HAVE LONG since accepted them.

I know that I'm anti-social on most days, defensive without reason to be, and that I shut down when I'm upset. I'm picky when it comes to accomplishing daily tasks and would rather stay up all night finishing a project than risk falling a day behind. I've always been the girl who pulls away when she's hurt instead of confronting the one responsible and risking that pain growing.

I never feared abandonment before finding my mother's letters. Reading those broken-hearted words on tear-splotched paper damaged a part of me that was once perfectly functional. It broke me so terribly that I convinced myself carrying those letters around with me was normal. The worst of them sits in my nightstand. I force myself to read it every night, as if by going over it time and time again, I'll become numb to the pain it brings me. Exposure therapy, they call it.

Torture, more like.

The ache in my chest only grew once I learned Lee had a family. One created after abandoning mine. The feeling of being unworthy grew and grew until it started eating away at my soul.

Its feasting halted when I met Johnny.

For small moments in my every day, whenever he appeared with his crooked grin and dimpled cheek, that feeling of unworthiness fell prey to something else. Something warm and soft.

Affection. Care. Happiness.

And as he kisses me in this moment, it's like he's transported us somewhere entirely outside of time and space to somewhere my brain doesn't overthink and my chest doesn't ache for anything more than another dose of him.

I curl my fingers in the soft material of his shirt and moan at the soft pressure of his lips on mine. It's almost audible the way my chest cracks open at the patience he has with me as he waits, still not giving in completely to the kiss.

As if he's scared I'm going to turn and run.

With a tug on his shirt, I prove to him that that's the last thing I want right now. I'm the one to deepen the kiss and take my first real taste of him. The lingering flavour of the Twizzlers he ate on the drive out here and a longing so intense it's almost a living thing. He pushes back instantly, taking the opening I've laid out in front of him with vigour.

His scent wraps around me, and I moan again, completely past the point of caring whether he thinks I'm being too loud or too weird. It's not even the way he smells so damn sexy or how good it feels to kiss him that has me throbbing between my legs so fiercely, but the strength in which he holds me to him. With the confidence of a man who knows exactly what he wants and isn't afraid to do everything in his power to get it.

He releases my cheeks to cup the back of my head and my waist, his thumb stroking the underside of my rib cage. My body lights up at his touch, a million missiles self-destructing beneath my skin.

Guiding my head back further, he glides his tongue along my lips, tracing it once before I part them, allowing him entrance. My brain melts, turning to mush at the first stroke of his tongue inside my mouth. Another moan fills the air, but this time, it doesn't come from me.

"Do you believe me now, Rory?" he asks, the words slipping down my throat.

I swallow them before feeding him some of my own. "This counts as you claiming your betting win, by the way."

He laughs gruffly before tugging my lip between his teeth and sucking on it. My stomach tightens, heat blazing low in my belly.

"Tell me something," he starts while spinning us around and pressing me to the trailer. It's hot against my back, so I use that as an excuse to arch into him. His gaze drops to my chest, the desire within it so palpable I have to bite my tongue to hide the whimper that follows. "Do you have a habit of getting jealous, Aurora?"

The use of my full name angers me as much as it did the first thousand times he's said it today. "Don't call me that."

"Call you what?"

"Aurora. I'm not Aurora to you."

He leans close enough to kiss me but doesn't. "Why not?"

"Fuck you, Johnny," I hiss before curling my hand around the back of his neck and kissing him. He tightens his grip on my waist before slipping it down to my ass. "Don't call me what everyone else does. I'm not everyone else to you anymore."

I lay it out there, peeling back every protective layer I have just to give him a glance at what I hide underneath it all. And he grins in answer. A wicked, dirty grin that has me curling my toes and two seconds away from begging him to take me right here in the middle of nowhere Alberta.

Johnny squeezes my ass and pins my hips with his. The long, thick bulge he presses to my belly has my eyes rolling back in ecstasy without so much as being touched between my legs.

"Was that so hard, darlin'?" he teases, his smile obvious as he buries his face in my throat and sucks my pulse. "Telling the truth has its benefits."

"Benefits?" I ask on a weak breath.

"Mm," he hums. The stubble on his jaw scratches my throat in the best way. "If you told me I was just like everyone else, I wouldn't touch you like this. Wouldn't be hell-bent on bringing you pleasure as a reminder that you're the one I want. Not Jill. Not anyone else."

My head falls back against the trailer with a bang that echoes in my ears the moment he brings his fingers to the button of my jeans and then leaves them there, unmoving.

"What are you waiting for?"

"Something more."

It's hard to focus when he touches me. With a stroke of his fingernail along the waistband of my jeans, I shiver.

"Haven't I told you enough already?" I ask, too close to resorting to begging for him to slide his hand inside my underwear and feel the mess I've made because of him.

"Not even close."

"Touch me and I'll tell you more."

He pulls back, and our eyes meet again. I've never seen his so dark as they flick between mine, searching for the truth in the words I spoke.

I don't get an answer before he's popping open my jeans and working his hand inside of them. The first glide of his finger through my pussy has me crying out, my breath caught in my throat.

"Oh, fuck me," he groans, eyes flashing as he strokes me again. "You're soaked."

I jerk my head in a nod and grip his shoulder, gasping like a fish out of water. His finger is thick enough that I have to stretch around the first press of it inside of me. My jeans are too tight, stifling his movements as he stalls and glances down both sides of the highway.

"Take them off," I beg, already shoving the one side down my hip. "If you stop, I'm going to die, Johnny. I need—"

He cuts me off with a hard, possessive kiss. "I know what you need. You don't have to beg me for anything. *Ever.*"

As soon as he tugs my jeans down my thighs, he's pumping his finger the rest of the way inside my dripping pussy and sheltering me with his body. I want to spread my legs, but with the denim pooled at my knees, it isn't possible. He doesn't leave me wanting, though. One finger turns into two, and then he's hooking them deep inside, seeking out the spot that turns my vision white.

"You feel incredible. So goddamn wet you're making a mess of your thighs," he says lowly, his voice sounding rougher than I've ever heard it.

I bury my teeth in my lip and jerk my hips forward, my clit throbbing. With my hand still gripping his shoulder, I reach down my body and pinch it between my fingers before applying hard pressure.

Johnny watches my movements with laser focus, not missing a thing. His attentiveness only makes me want him more, but I swallow the words down despite everything said just minutes ago.

I gape at him when his fingers grow still inside of me. I increase the pressure on my clit and rub it in quick circles, continuing to chase the pleasure he built and then abandoned.

He slaps my hand away and glares down at me. "Don't turn into a liar, Rory. Tell me what it is you were just thinking about, and I'll keep going. You want to come, don't you?"

I could always make myself come. But is that what I want? Another mediocre orgasm brought on by myself?

"I like how attentive you are to me," I tell him.

He bends down and kisses me firmly, as a reward, I think. When he pulls back, I lean forward and chase his lips, not ready to be done yet.

"Yes," I whimper as he starts to slide his fingers inside me again. "It's so good. I'm close already."

"Tell me something else," he demands, his kisses growing

harder, like he's losing his control with every squeeze of my walls around his fingers.

I reach up to grab his other shoulder, needing to know he's not going to abandon me here once I speak.

"I wanted to throw mud at her head when she hugged you. It's not fair, but I want to be the only one who gets to hug you like that."

A deep noise rattles his chest as he drops his other hand between us and pinches my clit before rolling it in quick circles exactly how I was.

"Is that right, Rory? You want to have a claim on me, then?" he asks, his voice strained as he fucks his fingers into me harder.

Every curl of them has me jerking against him, my skin hot and sticky with sweat. I hold his shoulders and bite at his lips as we kiss, feral with the climax that's building and building inside of me.

He pinches my clit again, and I go off like a fucking firework. Colours fill my vision as I cry, "Yes! Yes, I want to have a claim on you!"

"Christ, that's it. You've already claimed me, gorgeous. Now it's fuckin' written in stone," he murmurs.

I crash hard from the high while he slowly works his fingers deep, every aftershock rippling around them. Blowing out a puff of air, I close my eyes and go still, letting my hands fall to rest against his chest.

"Look at me, Rory," he coaxes, slipping his fingers free from inside of me.

I'm too weak-willed not to deny him, and I'm glad about that once I see why he wanted me to look. My belly flutters at the sight of him sucking his fingers clean, my cum all over them.

It's primitive and dirty, yet I love it and want him to do it every single time we do this.

"Next time, I'm going to taste you right from the source," he promises.

And I believe him.

24

Johnny

A WEEK AFTER COMING HOME WITH THREE NEW HORSES INSTEAD OF two, Aurora still hasn't asked about Frost.

Her lack of questioning solidified my assumption that she hadn't noticed me loading her up. Too pissed off with me and Jill, she avoided looking back at us after stumbling upon our interaction in the stable.

I'm still a smug bastard about her jealousy. Her heavy admissions on that dirt road have replayed in my mind all week. There haven't been any new ones since, and I'm itching to pull more out. I know they're there, trapped deep in the well she keeps hidden inside of herself. Each smile and small tidbit about her life that she gifts me during lunch or glass of iced tea she hands me while I work on her porch every night has me sure of it.

My conversation with Wade that same night we got back comes tumbling into my mind for the millionth time since, attempting to plant seeds of doubt.

"Why the fuck is there a white horse in my stable?"

I come up behind him with my hands in my pockets. The stable is quiet, the horses tucked in and the other ranch hands done for the day.

"They were running a buy two, get one half off sale."

He spins to face me, a heavy scowl on his face. "The bill says otherwise."

"I'll take care of Frost, Wade. You've got my word."

"I thought you were happy with Joker. You've had 'er for years."

"I am. Frost isn't for me."

His brows dip, realization hitting him quickly. "What is it with you boys and your lavish gift buyin'? My wife's gettin' expectations."

"Eliza's been talking about a new fridge. One of those fancy ones with the ice makers built in," I tell him.

"Stop tryin' to change the subject. You bought Aurora a seven-thousand-dollar horse, boy. She's not even plannin' on stickin' around. I recognize that look in her eye. She's goin' to take off sooner rather than later."

"Not if I can help it."

"The horse a bribe, then?"

I laugh, giving my head a shake. "Rory wouldn't accept a bribe no matter how expensive it was. Nah, I'm planning on convincin' her to stay the old-fashioned way. Frost was a spur-of-the-moment gift. You'd have bought her, too, if you saw what I did."

Two lost souls finding each other in the dark.

Wade sets his hand on my shoulder in a sign of support. I don't know if that's a good or bad thing.

"You want my advice?" he asks.

"What do you know about convincing women to give you a shot? You tricked Eliza into marrying you two months after meetin' her. And she was from this life."

"You're right. I don't know shit about convincin' women to stay. But I do have some wisdom when it comes to tamin' wild animals."

"Aurora isn't a wild animal. And she'd have your ass if she heard you talk about taming her," I grunt, my tone harsher than I'd usually use with him.

His laugh is harsh from years of smoking. "Fair enough. She might not be wild, but she's got that same sense about her. That she may not be one to be convinced of anything. She's got her own path, and you best respect that."

"You're supposed to be on my side."

He squeezes my shoulder. "I am, boy. I fuckin' am."

Never in my entire time knowing Wade has he ever offered me advice. Let alone regarding a woman. If Brody was subjected to it growing up, it would make sense as to why he stayed single for so damn long after high school. I've never had a father to give me advice, so Wade's conversation with me meant more than I think he knows.

He may be right about Aurora having her own path, but if he thinks for even a second that I'm not going to try and make sure I play a part in her journey down it, he's lost his mind.

"You're frowning, baby," Mom says, sitting beside me on the couch. She strokes a soothing hand over my hair. "You've been quiet too."

"I haven't been quiet. Everyone else has just been loud."

"That's not a wrong observation," she says, laughing lightly.

Her laugh was one of my favourite sounds growing up. It's always been loud and clear and bright. I used to do the silliest shit as a kid just so I could make her laugh more.

As opposed to Mama's more subtle playfulness, Mom's a proud joker like me. We also look the most alike due to the fact it was her eggs they used during their IVF journey with me and Daisy.

Our hair is the same shade of midnight black, our eyes a cool blue, noses slim, and jaws strong. I also inherited her lightning-fast metabolism, which Mama *loves* to bring up after we tear through her meals and ask for seconds.

Daisy got more from the sperm than the egg. She fucking hates when I say it like that, but it's the truth. Our moms chose a sperm donor, and the rest is history. It still doesn't change the fact that while we share an eye colour and dark hair, she still looks our opposite. I think she likes being different, though. It makes her feel more like her own person instead of just my twin sister, and I like that too.

Dropping a hand to my bloated stomach, I try to change the subject by saying, "I missed Mama's cooking these two weeks."

Mom hums. "You're welcome to it every day, you know? Or have you forgotten with how busy you've been recently?"

"Let me guess. Daisy?" I ask, knowing the answer already.

It's a miracle I haven't had anyone show up at my house yet, demanding to know more about Rory. There's no doubt in my mind Daisy has been blabbing about her to everyone she sees, our family included.

Josette steps into the living room and flops onto the armchair in the corner. *Her chair*, she calls it. I should have sat there instead.

"Are we finally asking Johnny about his secret girlfriend?" she asks, picking at one of the tiny gems on her thumbnail.

"Hi, little brother, I missed you these past couple of weeks," Mama teases, appearing in the doorway before moving behind the chair to flick Jos's ear.

"I thought we weren't supposed to lie?" Jos asks.

I blow her a kiss. "You missed me. Don't even try to lie. You're terrible at it."

Mama tightens the elastic band in her long brown hair and comes to drop a kiss to my forehead. Her rounded glasses droop down her nose as she bends down before Mom's reaching across me to push them back up. My heart swells at the simple act of affection.

I grew up seeing those all the time. Small touches as they passed one another, Mama spoiling Mom with her favourite flowers for no reason. They've had consistent date nights every Friday for as long as I can remember. It's a tradition that I can see them still carrying on when they're too old to go out.

They're why I'm so open to finding my person. I've seen how *good* it can be. What a real family looks like.

"You've been gone for too long, Johnny," Mama says, the scolding light but apparent. She sits on my other side and grabs my hand.

"I've been busy. Wade's given me a shit ton more responsibility these last few months."

"Aaaaaand?" Jos sings.

"And you're a pain in my ass, Josie Cat."

She shoots fire at me. "I hate that nickname."

"I know."

"We ran into Eliza at the store the other day. She said you've been working longer hours?" Mom asks.

"That must be why you smell like that," Jos says, crinkling her nose.

I lift my arm and sniff. "I don't stink."

"If you have to smell your own armpit to make sure you don't stink, you have a problem."

"Why don't you come closer and you can smell my armpit yourself?" I ask, waving my arm in the air until Mom pushes it down.

"Why can't you just be sweet to one another like all the kids on TV?" she mutters.

"Because that's not real life. And we can be sweet when we want to," Jos says.

I lean my head back against the couch and shut my eyes. It's alarming how easy it would be to simply go to sleep right now.

"You'd be nicer to me if Daisy were here."

"That's not true," Jos says.

I open my eyes. "She knows too many of your secrets for you to be mean to me in front of her."

"You're trying to hint that you're her favourite, and you're not."

"What secrets do you have, Josette?" Mama asks.

Jos flips me off. "Look what you've done, Johnny."

"Me? You started it."

"You both started it. You're twenty-two and twenty-four. This bickering is tiring," Mom says.

I rest my arm over her thin shoulders. "Your lives would be

so boring if we didn't stress you out from time to time. Jos still loves me."

"Are you not going to say that you love me too?" Jos scoffs.

"'Course I love you, you pain."

She rolls her eyes, smiling softly. "Not as big of a pain as you."

"Was there a reason you finally stumbled over for a home-cooked meal tonight, my love?" Mom asks me.

"I missed you guys."

"We missed you more. But you know I'm not going to let it go, so out with it. Tell me the whole truth."

"Jen," Mama sighs.

Uh-oh, she's bringing out real names now. The big guns have arrived.

"What? You're curious too, *Rachel*. Don't play innocent now."

"You're right. But—" Mama stops herself and makes sure to tap my arm so I know she's talking to me. "—you don't have to share anything you don't feel comfortable sharing."

"Is this a new therapist technique you've learned?" Jos asks, looking like she's trying to hold in a laugh.

"Not every bit of my motherly wisdom comes from my work, Josette."

"Only most of it," my sister replies.

"I'm going to stop baking brownies for you every time you come home," Mama threatens.

Mom laughs at that. "As if."

"I've been working on rebuilding a porch after work every day. That's why I've been so busy. By the time I finish and get home, I'm ready to crash," I admit, breaking up the playful feud happening right now. "I don't have a girlfriend, Josette, but I want to."

My sister grins arrogantly. "That's what I thought."

"You're building her a porch? Oh, sweetheart," Mom sighs, clutching her heart like I just told her the most extravagant news.

"Aurora, right?" Mama asks.

Daisy and her loose lips. "She prefers Rory, actually."

Or darlin'. Personally, I think she prefers that over either version of her name. She'll never admit that, though.

Mom starts firing off questions instantly. "How is it going? Does it look good?"

"The porch?"

"Sure."

Josette snorts a laugh. "I think she meant with Rory, bro."

"Oh. I think it's going good? We have lunch together every day and meet up after work while I work on her porch. I got the new railing up yesterday."

"Are you going to ask her to be your girlfriend?" Mom asks.

"That isn't really a necessary thing anymore, Mom," Josette tells her.

"What? That's silly. How are you supposed to know if you're dating someone, then?"

Mama jumps in to save her wife. "I think it's more of a conversation that's had rather than a simple question. Like, both people saying they don't want to be with anyone else. Am I right?"

"You're right," Jos says.

Mom huffs. "Okay, in that case. Are you in a *relationship* with Rory? Have you had *the talk*? And if so, why haven't we met her?"

"No. She's not ready for any of that yet."

"What?" Mom squeals, sitting forward on the cushion and staring back at us. "She's not ready? Why not?"

"She's in town to find answers about her family. Her mind is there first and then on me and us. I'm trying to respect that. Taking things slow. But we're getting there, I think."

My chest flares hot at the images of just how *slow* we took things on the highway last week. The tight, slick feel of her pussy around my fingers keeps me up at night while I jerk off in bed. Christ, I could die just from kissing her. The taste of her tongue . . .

"Daisy mentioned she wasn't from here. I'd have known who she was if she were from Cherry Peak. So, where is she from, and how long is she here for?" Mama asks.

I gulp, blinking back into this conversation before I get a fucking boner in my parents' living room. "She's from Calgary. And she's here for a few more weeks at least."

"A few weeks is not enough time," Mom says, alarmed.

"I know," I mutter, ignoring the urge to rub at my chest. "I'm completely obsessed with her. All I want is to keep her here with me. I feel it, you know? The knowing that you told us about as kids, Mama."

Josette doesn't have a sly remark to throw at me this time. I look at her and watch as she stares at me with the same pouted frown that she has right before she cries. And it isn't even a beat later that Mom is throwing herself forward and wrapping me in her arms.

"Oh, my boy," she whispers, sniffling in my ear.

Mama's jasmine scent hits me before she joins the hug. Her words are spoken so softly I nearly miss them.

"Follow that feeling, Johnny. Grab it, and don't let it go."

25

Aurora

Mom: It's been three weeks since your last check in, Aura. I've lost track of the number of unanswered texts I've sent.

Mom: I'll call the police and report you missing if I have to.

Me: How would you know that it isn't my kidnapper texting you proof of life?

I SEND THE TEXT OFF BEFORE GRABBING MY COFFEE FROM THE BARISTA with a grimaced smile and sitting back at the table I chose when I walked in. It would have been ideal not to be dealing with my mother right now as I wait for Wanda to arrive, but what's a bit more stress when I'm already hanging by a thread?

After waiting nearly a full week for Wanda to get back to Cherry Peak, a text came through last night that nearly sent me into an early grave. It was only a time and a place with a sign-off of her name, but it was enough.

Tomorrow, five @ the bakery. -Wanda

Sleep didn't come easily after that. Or at all, if you don't count the seventeen minutes I got before my alarm went off. I feel like a zombie, and I look like one too. First impressions usually matter, but in this case, I hardly think less obvious under-eye circles or a power suit instead of jeans and a tee would do much for me.

My phone starts vibrating in my hand, and when I read the word "Mom" on the screen, I tense up tight. Nine weeks is the longest we've ever gone without seeing one another, and three is the longest we've gone without speaking, but the nausea I feel at the thought of talking about what happened before I left has kept me from reaching out. It's unfair, and I'm being stubborn, but I can't help it this time. This isn't a situation where I can just turn my feelings off and pretend like nothing's wrong.

Something is very, very wrong.

With a swallow, I send the call to voicemail. It makes me feel like a fucking child to do it, but when a woman suddenly appears at the edge of my table with slightly narrowed eyes, I drop the thought as if it were nothing.

"Aurora, right?" she asks, not waiting for my answer before yanking the chair opposite of me out from beneath the table and sitting. "You look exactly like you do in your Facebook profile photo. That doesn't happen often."

I blink, trying to catch up. "Thank you?"

"I don't know if it was a compliment just yet."

"Right. Well, you look like yours as well. I preferred the blonde hair, though," I return, snapping slightly.

It was an old photo that said it hadn't been updated in three years. I was expecting to meet a blonde woman today, not one with brown hair and a green money piece in the front. The brunette colour pales her a bit, but something tells me she doesn't give a shit about that.

She dumps her purse on the table and twirls the green chunk around her finger. "I recently learned that colouring my hair like this pisses off my father."

My father. I focus on not grating my teeth at the purposeful wording.

"Clearly, that's never been a problem for me. I had two-toned hair in college. One side teal, the other pink."

Running her gaze over my scalp and the lack of dark roots, she says, "And now you've gone back to natural blonde."

"Do blondes run in the family?" I can't help but ask.

"If you're wanting to know if Riley has natural blond hair, the answer is yes. But he hates it and dyes it as black as his heart every couple of months. Has for longer than I've been alive."

"Riley?"

Wanda huffs a breath, staring at me as though she truly has no idea why I'm here. "Lee Rose is truly Riley Rose. Lee is a ridiculous stage name he snagged years ago. That's something you should know."

I wrap my hands around my coffee cup and inhale, nodding to try and clear my head. *Wanda's guardedness was expected,* I remind myself. *I shouldn't take it personally.*

Unless I should. If it's me she has a problem with, then this just got a whole lot more fucking awkward.

"In my mother's letters, the ones that brought me here, she never called him by anything other than Lee. Everything was addressed to Lee Rose. But they were real. I have one with me if you want to see it for yourself."

"How do I know you didn't write it yourself?"

"You'll know when you read it."

It feels wrong to reach into my bag and pull out the neatly folded, yellowing letter from where I tucked it this morning. This letter is one of the most personal I read and downright heartbreaking. The tear marks are real, and the pain etched in every indent of my mother's pen only serves as further proof.

"How many of these letters were there?" Wanda asks, eyeing the letter I pull free from the interior pocket.

"Too many to count. Stacks of them, most still sealed and

stamped with a return-to-sender order. The few I opened were all I needed to see. That and the photos."

"And they were what led you here, then?"

"Yes."

After setting the letter on the table beside my coffee cup, I retrieve the small photo I brought along with it. I avoid glancing at the grainy image of my mom and Lee, hating the way the simple picture makes me want to scream and cry until my voice is gone and my eyes are dry.

Wanda doesn't have the same issue. She slaps a hand across the table and tugs them both toward her with no hesitation. Opening up the letter first, she starts to read.

One line after another, her gaze drags along the paper. Her hazel eyes darken, anger bleeding into them. I lift my cup to my lips and take a long swig, pretending my hands aren't shaking.

"Were they all like this?" she asks, her tone dropping some of its previous aggression.

"Like what?"

Her eyes dart above the paper, meeting mine. "Painful. Raw."

"To an extent, yes. Some were angry, some were tired. But more than anything, they were sad. She was scared and alone, and *Riley* was nowhere to be found. So, she stopped reaching out. She stopped trying to get a response from him and took to raising me on her own instead. I only remember asking about my father a couple of times when I was younger, but she told me she didn't know who he was. Eventually, I stopped caring."

She sets the letter back on the table and pinches the small photo between her fingers. Her throat jumps before she flips it over and reads the date scrawled on the back.

"This was years before I was born."

I nod. "Me too."

"I haven't seen him wear this jacket in years. He used to say he won it playing poker, but I never believed him," she whispers.

"Maybe he did."

"He hates poker."

I roll my lips, unsure what to say to that. Did my mom get him that jacket? If she did, why did he keep it for so long after they parted, as if he had any right to?

"I didn't mean to hurt you with this. It wasn't my plan to bring this up to everyone and cause problems. I just want answers," I admit, feeling that weight on my chest again, pressing down further and further despite how desperately I try to shove it off.

Wanda slides the photo and letter across the table, glaring at them like she's hoping to light them ablaze with her eyes. When she glances up again, some of that anger dies.

"And you thought I could give you them," she notes.

"I have so many blanks in the story. My mom doesn't want to talk about the details. It hurts her, and the last thing I want to do is make her pain worse. But I deserve answers, and I was hoping I could get them elsewhere first before tearing open her past with demands and my hurt in addition to hers. When she told me about you, I took that information and ran. It wasn't much either. Just your name and that you were from Cherry Peak.

"I'm not a spontaneous person, Wanda. Change scares me. Actually, it *terrifies* me. But I came here anyway, thinking you'd be where the internet told me you were. Except I didn't find you at the small-town hair salon I expected, and I didn't know what to do next until I met the Steeles. Eliza's helped me with a couple of my questions, and now so has Johnny by putting me in touch with you. Calling and asking you to come back here was never my plan, and I'm sorry if I've ruined whatever it is you've been doing. I just want to know my family history. I want to know why . . ."

I blink up at the ceiling, ashamed of the tears filling my eyes. They're not mine to shed. They're my mom's, and Wanda's, for driving her back to a place she clearly doesn't want to be. I'm inserting myself into this town, and I feel so completely out of place. An outsider digging around in history that shouldn't be mine to dig around in. But it is. I hate it, but it's mine more than anyone knows.

I widen my eyes at Wanda when she reaches across the table and takes my hands in hers. She doesn't smile at me, but it isn't necessary. The slight squeeze she gives me is enough.

"You have every right to know the answers to all of your questions, Aurora. I'm sorry for being so cold toward you. My family has never been . . . warm to each other, let alone outsiders that we're quite honestly scared of. I'll be honest and say that I expected you to be here for something entirely different. Maybe a chunk of the fame our father has built first and foremost. But also, if you were telling the truth, then you'd be just another roadblock between me and him. That was never fair of me. It came from a place of insecurity and hurt that I've never been able to grasp his attention."

"I don't blame you for being guarded. Even still, I haven't offered you much proof."

"I don't need more proof. I can see it in your eyes. The pain and desire for answers. Plus, you seem to have a good idea already of the man Riley is. If you truly were just here for the fame, you wouldn't care about that at all."

I laugh lightly, jerking my head in agreement. "It's that bad?"

Her features harden, tongue sweeping along the inside of her lip. "I spent a year trying to get his attention. I left Cherry Peak, flew to where I knew he was, and was met by the same shit that I'd always seen at home. He's busy, too busy for a family, let alone a daughter. And now that he's got two? I don't know what's going to happen, Aurora. I can't make you any promises that he'll even care to learn he's had a second daughter all this time.

"And I don't say that to hurt you. That's just me speaking from experience. I can count on one hand the number of my birthdays he's attended or Christmas mornings, for fuck's sake. He didn't show up to my high school graduation, and he's never paid any mind to a single one of the degrees I've gotten or businesses I've started from the ground up since in an attempt to make him proud of me. Riley Rose should never have been given the title of anyone's father. Thank fucking God there are only two of us to witness the disappointed he is."

"Fuck," I whisper.

Wanda sits back in her chair and meets my stare head-on. "Welcome to the family, Aurora. For your sake, I hope you're only here for a short while."

26

Johnny

"WAIT, SO WANDA, WHAT, GAVE YOU HER PERMISSION TO SEEK OUT Lee?" I ask, trying to get my head on track with the information Rory's just dumped on me.

She sets her sub sandwich down on her thigh and wipes her mouth with a napkin. "I guess so. Really, I think she was warning me against going to meet him. She gave me his address in Toronto before we left the bakery, but I don't think she wants me to use it."

"For her gain or yours?"

I've known Wanda for years, yeah, but Rory's my girl, and I won't have anyone trying to sweep the rug out from under her with this. She doesn't have enough people in her corner yet watching her back, and if Wanda isn't prepared to take on that task, then I'll make damn sure she is by the time I'm done with her.

"I think both of ours. I didn't feel anything malicious from her at all after we got talking. If anything, I think she was more concerned for me. Lee sounds like a shitty father, Johnny," she grumbles, her frown etched deep.

"I don't know him from Adam, but even I've picked up enough about his relationship with his family and all of Cherry

Peak. He'd win an award for most absentee parent. Still, that doesn't mean you don't deserve the chance to meet him to see for yourself."

She sighs, abandoning her food to wrap her arms around her knees. The new backyard lights I installed yesterday burn bright in the cover of night, illuminating her features. She continues to park her fine ass beside me on the porch instead of sitting in her camping chair. I've grown used to having her so close to me. During our lunch breaks at work, I tuck the spare rolling chair right up beside her and have focused on getting rid of any chewing noises I make during lunch just so she doesn't tell me to back off.

These moments are the ones that keep me content with taking things slow. I'd do just about anything to spend time with her like this, our thighs pressed together and my arm around her back. Comfortable, soft, *perfect*.

It's only been a few weeks, and with everything going on in her life, it feels wrong to push for more between us. Like I'm getting greedy or something. I'm content following her pace and hoping that one day she'll wake up and decide she's ready for the next step. I know I'm not going anywhere.

"What if he doesn't believe me? Or does and tells me that he wants me to leave?" she asks, the words reeking of vulnerability.

"He won't say that, darlin'."

"You can't be sure of that."

"You're right. I'm not sure of it. But I'm going to try and speak that shit into existence because you don't need any more doubt in your life." I lay my hand on her back and shift, my ass hanging half off the porch so I can get a full look at her. When she doesn't look away and instead fearlessly stares back, I think my heart doubles in size. "You're going to go meet him, and I'm goin' with you. Tell me when you want to leave, and I'll make it work."

She scoffs in disbelief, lightly pushing at my chest for me to sit back. "You're not coming, Johnny. Don't try and make me feel better by giving me false hope."

I fight against her push and inch closer toward her, taking her chin between my thumb and forefinger. Her breath grows tight, those pretty pink lips that I haven't stopped thinking about kissing for a week parting on nothing.

"I've never lied to you, Aurora. Don't plan on it either. Everything I've said to you has been the truth. I'm not the guy that's going to tell you what I think you want to hear if I don't believe it. I know you know that."

"I can't ask you to come with me," she murmurs.

"You didn't. I told you I was. But I would have dropped everything to come if you had asked."

"Will we finish the porch when we get back?"

I search her eyes for the meaning behind that question, the doubts in her mind, but get distracted by the beauty in them. The rough waters I've grown used to seeing have stilled, not a wave to be seen. They're inviting, the soft lapping of the tide nearly audible like a shell from the beach pressed to your ear.

"We'll finish it before we go," I promise her.

A crinkle forms between her brows as her lips close, expression closing off. "Oh, right. I guess it is almost done."

Reaching toward her, I wrap my palm around the back of her neck and bring her close. Forehead to forehead, a million words float in the space left between us. Some I have no fear of saying but would send her running for the hills if I did.

"Once the porch is done, I can focus on other projects. Like the state of the fireplace and lack of screens in the windows. I have a million things I want to do, Rory. But my priority is takin' care of you."

Her lashes flutter as her eyelids droop. The gap between our lips closes slowly, a millimetre at a time. I can almost taste her next words.

"How are you real?"

"The same way you are," I breathe against her mouth before taking it in a soft kiss.

It's gentle at first, tastes mingling. But then she's pressing harder, like she's searching for something. I'm happy to let her explore every inch of me for the answer. I'd offer her unlimited access to my mind without fear or hesitation.

I groan when she sets her hands on my shoulders and urges me back again. This time, I let her guide me, putty beneath her touch. There's nothing that could prepare me for her next move. I drop one hand behind me to balance myself when she sits herself in my lap, straddling me.

Gripping her waist with my other hand, I encourage her to drop her full weight onto my thighs, my skin burning with anticipation beneath my jeans. She lowers more, jean brushing jean.

"Is this okay?" she asks breathlessly, resting a palm along my jaw, stroking it.

"*So* fucking okay."

I kiss her like I'm scared she'll disappear. Like from that very first night, I've been hallucinating her. If she didn't feel so real beneath my fingertips, I'd think I was dreaming. How else could I get this lucky?

My plans for tonight linger in my head, an annoying buzz I can't shake. All I want is to keep her on my lap, in my arms, her hot breaths panted across my lips, swollen from the pressure of her kisses. But she needs what I have planned. More than she knows.

"Come with me somewhere," I pant, dragging my lips over her cheek to settle against her ear. "I plan to revisit this. Fuck, I could keep you here forever."

She blinks her eyes open, a gorgeous, dazed expression filling her face. "Where are we going?"

I tuck a piece of soft blonde hair behind her ear, tracing the shell of it. "Somewhere special."

"Did you miss work already?" she asks once we step out of my truck outside of the Steele Ranch stable.

The moonlight paints streaks through her hair, and I grin at the ethereal look of it. An angel in flesh and blood.

She cocks her head at me when she notices my staring, and I wink before inputting the code on the stable door. I lose my breath when she steps up behind me and rests her hand against my back, as if it's a casual move she's been doing for years.

"Does Wade know you're breaking into his stable?"

"It's not breaking in if I have the code, babe."

"Sometimes the best robbers are the ones we know."

"Fair enough. But I can't be robbing what I already own," I say with a glance back at her, my grin easy.

She rolls her eyes, and I steal a kiss before tugging open the door enough for us to slink inside. Flicking the light on, I watch as she glances around as if she's never seen the inside of the stable before.

Alarm skitters through me. "Has nobody brought you in here before?"

"I've never needed to see it before."

Again with that blunt honesty of hers. "You don't need to have a reason to see something. I'd have shown you around the ranch properly if I knew nobody else had before."

"Who says you still can't?"

"Yeah? Mission accepted, darlin'. After we finish in here."

I lead the way between the pens, knowing from memory where I'm going. Joker's already waiting in her pen when we stop in front of it. She whinnies and gives her head a shake before moving toward us.

"I haven't properly introduced you two yet, but this is Joker, Rory. She's my girl," I say, introducing them before cutting a look at Joker. "Be nice, yeah? Don't embarrass me."

"You'd embarrass yourself before she would," Rory teases, standing beside me, her hand finding my back again.

It takes everything in me not to tell her never to remove it again. Preferably to glue it in place. "You're not wrong."

"Did you miss her tonight?"

I slide my hand down Joker's mane and neck. "I always miss my Joker. But that's not why I brought you here."

With a final pat, I leave Joker and move to the next pen over. Aurora follows me, curiosity thick in her features. The horse lying on the pile of hay glances up at us and watches with her ears up and alert.

"Is that . . .?" Rory gasps.

"Her name is Frost. She's probably the best-behaved mare in here. Poor Joker has been made to look like a rowdy adolescent."

"Why is she here?" The awe in her voice hits me square in the chest, threatening to empty the air from my lungs.

"She's yours."

"Mine? I don't know a damn thing about horses!"

She's jumpy when I wrap my body around her from behind and grip the pen door, trapping her. Trying to twist in my arms, she huffs and winds up rubbing her cheek against mine.

"I'm going to teach you, darlin'. Every fucking thing that I know."

"Johnny," she protests, her ass grinding over my groin with every jerky movement of her body. "Let me look at you, dammit."

I drop a hand to her stomach and hold her against me, stilling her movements. "I've always believed that horses choose their owners. Joker chose me the first time I met her. It was like a string connected us down deep, right in my chest. The same thing happened with Brody and Sky, Wade and Kip. Hell, even Garrison and Kip. There's an animal out there for everyone. We're connected to them on a biological level."

"And you think me and this horse are the same? After one interaction?"

"It only takes once. You felt it too, told me yourself that you were drawn toward her pen. I took a chance on buyin' her, and if you don't want her, then I'll take her as my own. But I'm certain about this. Call me a dreaming idiot, but I won't apologize for believing what I do. She's yours, and you're hers. Kindred spirits."

She exhales a long breath, her muscles loosening slowly as she sinks back into my embrace. I splay my fingers over her stomach and rest my chin on her head, waiting for her next words.

They don't come for a long time. We spend the next few minutes in silence, nothing but the crunch of hay, horses breathing heavily, and the wind picking up outside to keep us company.

And just when I'm about to tell her that we can leave, thinking that I really did overstep here or that I read the signs wrong, she grabs my hand and spins in my arms before I realize what she's doing.

She tips her head back, gazing up at me while pressing my hand to her chest, between the generous swells of her breasts. The steady thump of her heart engrains itself inside of me.

"Can we go for a ride?"

27

Aurora

I SHOULD KNOW BETTER THAN TO EXPECT ANYTHING WHEN IT COMES to Johnny. Every time I think he can't possibly do something else to blow my mind, he goes and proves me wrong.

They certainly don't make men like him where I'm from. Every day I spend with him, I become surer that I'll never find one like him again.

"We're not taking Joker?" I ask when he lifts the matte-black saddle from the hook in front of Frost's pen.

Yeah, *Frost's pen*. Because she's *here*, on Steele Ranch, in a pen that looks tidy and cozy. With her own saddle.

"I am, but you're taking Frost. She's completely saddle broken. I've ridden her a few times this week to make sure for myself before I put you on her back. She's got the temperament of an angel, if not a stubborn one sometimes. Just don't let her get her teeth on any of the wild raspberry bushes out there, or she'll come back with a juice-splattered mouth. She's goddamn addicted to them."

I nod along with his words but continue to stare at him in wonder as he sets the saddle on her back and starts to fiddle with the straps and clips. Frost watches me, a sense of calmness radiating off her. She doesn't move an inch as he gets her ready to go.

"I don't blame her. I could eat cartons of raspberries at a time," I say.

Johnny grins over her back. "Oh yeah? Note taken, darlin'."

"Do you like them?"

"Yeah, but I prefer melons to berries."

My laugh comes out louder than I intended it to, far from ladylike. The suggestive wiggle of his eyebrows only makes me laugh harder as my stomach starts to cramp.

"What's so funny?" he asks, batting his lashes innocently.

I come up to Frost's side and gently place my hand on her side, feeling her strength. "Don't play innocent."

He swipes a hand through his hair. "Fuckin' love your laugh, Rory."

The admission sobers me as my laugh trickles off. My stomach fills with flapping wings. "Do I thank you now?"

"I also fuckin' love how you never know what to say when I tell you shit like that."

I shrug. "Nobody's complimented me so much before."

His expression tightens, growing serious as he reaches over Frost's back and strokes a knuckle down my cheek. "Good. You're mine to compliment. Now, let's get you up on this girl's back so we can go."

"Is it hard?" I blurt out.

His eyes snare mine, crinkling at the corners as he smirks. "Around you? Always."

"Johnny!" I ignore the heat flooding my cheeks and try to appear serious. "I meant riding."

He comes around Frost's front and gives her nose a gentle rub before stopping a step from me. My eyes are drawn up his body, over the wide expanse of a strong chest crafted from long, long hours on the ranch and shoulders that I've dug my nails into more than once and have fantasized about seeing above me, slick with sweat. Heat settles between my legs the longer I look at him, checking him out without a care in the world.

My fingers twitch with the desire to touch him and explore the body I can't look away from. He'd let me, I know he would. *I'd let him explore me too.* The realization of that isn't scary but relieving. I'm falling for Johnny more and more every day, and I've been holding myself back from taking a step further with him out of fear. But the more time we spend together, each day revealing something new about him that I can't help but love, the harder it is to keep up my façade.

I want him, and if he knew that . . . would he take me right now, as I am? No questions asked?

By the time I'm looking into his eyes, my skin has grown hot and sensitive. My clothes feel too tight over my body, and as the light blue of his eyes grows more intense, I debate asking him to take them off me.

"You'll give me a complex looking at me like that, darlin'," he murmurs, the thick lines of his throat working with a swallow.

"How am I looking at you?"

"Like you want me to work your tight fuckin' jeans down your thighs and bury my face between them. Just say the word, and I'll dive deep without giving a shit about coming up for air."

My entire body shivers at the promise in the gravelly words. "Do that, then."

"Not yet."

"Why?" I croak, a blast of cold ripping through the heat of the haze wrapped around my mind.

He takes my hand and tugs me closer to him before settling my palm over the large bulge in his jeans. I grip it on instinct and get rewarded by a tight-lipped hiss and slight thrust.

"You want to be taken in a stable, baby? I'll take you in a fuckin' stable so many times you'll feel the ghost of me buried deep the moment you walk inside of one. But not the first time. If you knew how many times I've dreamed of licking your pussy or sliding my cock inside of you, you'd never question how badly I want you. But I'm waitin', and I'm patient. I'm going to have you splayed out for me and your cum on my tongue tonight, but not yet. Not here. Okay?"

I drop a hand to Frost's side to keep myself upright as the weight of his words settles. The guttural promises that he's made and the way each one has cranked up the dial on the desire I feel.

Again, he touches my face, stroking my skin so delicately it's like he fears it'll crumble and blow away like ash if he's too rough.

"If not here, then where?" I ask, unashamed with how desperate I sound.

Fuck it all to hell, but I don't care.

"Do you trust me?" he asks, the words hardly more than a fan of breath across my face.

It should take me longer to answer him. To debate on whether or not I do. But there's no need for debate.

"Yes."

The joy that lights up his face right then is every reason as to why I do.

It's hard to concentrate as Frost and I trot alongside Johnny and Joker, the pace slow and steady. I should be grateful for that, considering how raw the inside of my thighs feel from the slap of them against Frost's sides and how every time I sway side to side, the pulse of pain in my lower back grows in intensity.

Yet, slow and steady is the last thing I want right now.

There's never been a time in my life where I've been as physically attracted to a man as I am right now, staring across the small space between Frost and Joker at Johnny.

Spine straight as an arrow, cowboy hat resting easy on his head, and those strong, veiny hands wrapped loosely around Joker's reins, he looks like a wet dream straight out of a cowboy movie. The ease and confidence with which he rides his horse, commanding her without force or sharp words, has the heat between my legs transforming into an inferno. I ache everywhere, and not from the riding.

The tension between us stretches, keeping us both trapped within it. I've kept silent as we rode off the ranch and into the ditch beside the highway, each clop of hooves sounding like a tick of a clock. Johnny knows exactly what I'm thinking about and hasn't stopped grinning since he helped me up on Frost and saddled up Joker.

I don't recognize where we are. Not because it's dark but because I've never ventured out this way. Unless I'm at the ranch, I don't leave town. I want to pay more attention to my surroundings, but I can't fucking focus on anything but Johnny.

"We're almost there," he says, as if sensing how close I am to losing my ever-loving mind. "How are you feeling?"

"Do you really want me to answer that?"

"Yeah, I think I do."

I scowl. "Too bad."

He laughs in answer, the deep, rumbling sound of it making my toes curl in my sneakers. I want to press my palm to his chest and feel that rumble work its way up my arm.

"Did you ever make wishes on shooting stars when you were a kid?" he asks.

I know he's looking at me without having to check. "I think every kid did that."

"What did you use to wish for?"

"Isn't the golden rule of wishing for something never telling anyone what you actually wished for?"

"Are you saying that your wishes never came true?"

"Not unless I've been walking around with a unicorn horn my entire life, no."

"You wished for a unicorn horn?"

"I was a kid. Were you making perfectly thought-out wishes back then?"

Reaching out with his foot to tap the side of mine, he says, "I was, actually. I've always known what I wanted more than anything. Even more than a unicorn horn."

I'm too chicken to pull my foot out of the stirrup to kick him back, so I shake my head at him instead.

"You're not allowed to tease me for that."

"But you like it when I tease you," he replies, nearly purring the words.

"Right now, I don't."

He makes a disbelieving noise in his throat before leading us out of the ditch and onto a dirt path formed between clusters of overhanging trees. Tiny twinkle lights have been strung in the branches of the trees closest to the road, lighting it up just enough that my eyes don't have to strain to see in front of us.

Frost follows Joker with ease, as if she's ridden this path a million times before. If I was nervous at all, her comfortability would have helped settle me.

"Have you ever watched *Cabin in the Woods*?" I ask him when a small house appears at the end of the dirt road.

Small may be an exaggeration. It's on the smaller side, but a good size with wide windows and a door with a stained-glass window. Its roof is peaked and adorned with two solar panels on both sides. The lawn is well-kept, the grass thick and green, not a weed in sight.

"Yeah, actually. I built my house based off the movies. Kept a few bodies inside for decoration as well. Hope you don't mind the smell of decaying flesh."

My mouth cracks open with a smile as I ask, "This is your house?"

"Yeah, darlin'. It was on Steele Ranch property when they first bought it God knows how long ago, and nobody made any use of it until I bought it from Wade two years back. A work in progress still, but she's home," he explains before swinging himself off Joker's back and leading her toward the long wooden post beside the house.

Clicking his tongue, he calls Frost over to join them.

"You bought it from Wade? He didn't want it?"

It's hard to understand why. It's secluded and private with the thick wooded area surrounding us. One glance up at the sky and I can see a thousand, maybe a million stars.

"It's too far out, and they've got all they need already close to the main house. Brody and Anna built their house up near the shop, and it's probably the closest place to here."

Once he's done tying Joker to the post, he moves to me next. "Hold on to the reins like you did when mounting, and put your weight in the stirrup. Pull your leg over her back and set it on the ground first," he coaxes, guiding me with a hand stabilizing my back.

It happens quickly, and before I know it, I've got two feet back on the ground. I rub Frost's neck a few times, hoping she can tell how much I enjoyed our first ride together, and walk beside her as Johnny ties her up.

"How big exactly is Steele Ranch?" I ask.

"Thirty thousand acres, last time I asked. It's a whole lot of empty fields, though. It gives us the room to rotate cattle when we need to. The horses like the space too."

"Is that why they're building another stable? For more horses?"

He gives our horses a final couple of scratches before turning, his back against the beam, eyes focused solely on me. "Me and a couple of the guys have been trying to convince Wade to take on more horses and expand into training. We've got a good couple of trainers that work with us to saddle break and whatnot, but taking it a step further than that would be good for the future of the ranch. Puts our foot in the door for opportunities outside of cattle."

I nod, enjoying learning more about this life that I've been sort of thrown into. There isn't much I know about ranching, and I feel almost embarrassed about that.

"Have you always loved horses?"

He extends an arm in front of him, calling me over, and I move without hesitation. His hand cups my waist and spins me so my back is to his chest before he's wrapping his arm around my front, tucking me against him.

"You're so curious, Rory," he hums, running his nose along the shell of my ear. My breathing picks up. "I want to tell you everything. About me, my family, my life on the ranch. My future."

"I wouldn't complain about that," I whisper.

"Ask me something first. Something you should have asked before I tied our horses up."

My brows knit together as I try to remember what I forgot to ask but come up short. His lips on my ear and cheek and jaw don't help me concentrate much either, damn him.

His laugh is low in my ear. "Ask me what I wished for when I was a kid, Rory."

"What did you wish for?"

I can hear the thump of my heart in the night. Or maybe that's his. Unable to help myself, I turn my head back to look at him. The affection in his eyes shifts the world beneath my feet as he speaks.

"You, Rory. I wished for you."

28

Johnny

I KNOW SHE HEARD ME BECAUSE SHE SWAYS IN MY GRASP, HER SMALL fingers burying themselves in my shirt. Her touch is hot, burning through my clothes. My blood rushes too close to the surface, making everything overly sensitive.

I'm one curl of her fingers away from tossing her over my shoulder and locking her inside my house for the next four to six business days. Shit, even that may not be enough time. Four to six months, then.

"How could you wish for someone you had never met?" she asks, sounding so damn dainty.

"I didn't know I was wishin' for you. Not yet. I was just a kid who was forced to sit on the ground in front of his sisters' beds and listen to the fairy tales my moms read them every night. They always got to my books after, but it was hard not to listen to their stories, even if I tried to pretend I wasn't. The princesses and Prince Charmings and their true loves' kisses.

"I pictured myself as a prince more often than I did a race car driver or MMA fighter like my friends at school. Of course, I never told them that. They'd have strung me up a flagpole by my underwear if I did. I only told my moms about it. They told me that I could be the prince or the princess or the fucking frog if

I wanted to. But I was adamant on which role I wanted, and everyone knew it."

I bump her nose with mine, desperate to touch her more but not ready to take her mouth just yet. If I do, there will be no more talking.

"I wanted to be the prince. The one with the sword and armour that weighed a million pounds. A prince that sought out a princess. Not a damsel in distress or a sleeping beauty. A princess made of steel and iron that could help carry the weight of his armour if it grew too heavy for him. One that loved jokes, *especially* his, and could laugh with him. A princess that knew how to stand up for herself but allowed him to do so on her behalf when things got too rough. Who could support him yet knock him down a few pegs if he was thinking out of his ass.

"That's what I wished for every night after I was tucked into bed, my moms leaving my curtains open so I could see the sky. See the stars as they shot across it."

I cup her cheek in my hand and simply hold it, feeling the weight of it and how right it feels to touch her this way. Because that's what it is. *Right.*

She tips her head back enough to look at the star-flecked sky, all so similar to the one from my memories. "I've never considered myself a princess before."

"What about a dream come true instead?"

"That's even less likely."

"Look at me," I murmur, guiding her chin down before brushing our mouths together. "That's what you are to me. It's why I was so drawn to you that first night and why I haven't been able to stay away from you since. I'm a believer in fate and every cliché, cheesy thing that's ever existed, and I'm not ashamed of it. It's who I am on a fundamental level."

"I love who you are, Johnny. But can you love who I am? Beyond everything you've just told me? Can you love my bitterness and social anxiety? My baggage?"

I glide my tongue along her bottom lip, taking a single taste. "What would you do if I said I already do?"

There's no verbal response. Only her mouth on mine and nails clawing at my clothes.

"Inside," I order absent-mindedly, too concerned with the sensation of her hands on me, tugging and pulling to stay out here.

The feel of her tearing open my shirt has a near savage sound escaping me. Her eyes are wide as she stares up at me, deep red blotches covering her cheeks. I puff out a breath and shake my head, having had enough of that embarrassment in her gaze.

In one quick move, I take both of her wrists and encourage her to tear the fucking shirt all the way in half. Her pupils blow as she focuses on my chest, inch after inch becoming exposed as we rip the fabric clean down the centre. The moment I release her, she's pressing her palms to my abs, her fingers tracing the dip between each one, counting them.

She doesn't so much as blink when I lead us back toward the house. There's no taking her attention off her task right now. Not yet. For now, she can explore.

There won't be much chance for her to do so in a few minutes.

"Step up." I breathe the demand when we stop in front of the single step to the front door. She does as she's told, blinking up at me in a daze. "Good girl."

Pleasure contorts her features, and I throb in my jeans, tucking that piece of information away for later.

I type in the code for the front door and kick it shut behind us before guiding us inside the dark house. Bypassing the lights, I take the same route I always do, down the hallway and to the right toward my bedroom.

"Need to make good on my promise," I tell her, leaning down to kiss her hard.

She sighs into my mouth, opening up for me to dive in. My ears fill with the sound of my blood pumping as I spin us inside my room and press her to the wall. It takes a moment for my vision to adjust to the dark, but finally, I can make out her features.

"You're the most beautiful thing I've ever seen," I whisper, grabbing her hands and threading our fingers before lifting them above her head, opening her up to me. "I want to touch you."

"Where?" she asks, her hips lifting in search of something between them. I grit my jaw and keep myself still.

"Everywhere. I want to strip you bare and trace every inch of your body with my tongue. I won't stop until I have you memorized. Until I know I'll be able to taste you in my dreams."

"You keep teasing me."

"I know, baby, I know. Let me make it up to you."

Her chin jerks in approval, and then I'm lifting her shirt over her head. My eyes nearly cross at the picture she makes in front of me. Chest heaving, big tits trapped within the cups of a bra. Her nipples are hard, stabbing through the lace. I drag my thumb across one, hearing the hitch in her breathing before doing it again, my touch feather light.

"Are they sensitive, Aurora?" I ask, the sound of my voice deep, a near grunt.

"Yes," she sighs.

Reaching around her back, I unclasp the bra, my thumb sweeping over her second nipple just once. She arches toward me, and the straps droop down her shoulders. Then I'm there guiding them the rest of the way, my attention focused on the slow fall of the cups as more and more of her breasts are exposed. A groan stalls in my throat once it falls to the ground, her chest bare.

I'm on my knees in an instant, falling hard enough they ache with the force. Grabbing her tit, I squeeze it slightly and guide it toward my mouth before wrapping my lips around her hard nipple and sucking. She gasps, hands swiping at my hat and sending it sailing through the room before finding my shoulders. I fill my hand with her other breast and squeeze it just a bit harder, feeling the hard jab of her nipple against my palm.

I become enamoured with tasting her chest, licking and sucking and even teasing her nipple with my teeth to see if she likes it. She cries out when I give it a small bite, and I grin like a fucking fool into her skin in response.

I'm harder than I've ever been in my life, my cock pulsing in my jeans. Every shift of my hips makes me shudder. I'm on a fucking hair trigger, and I refuse to come in my pants like a teenage boy.

Dropping a hand, I pop my jeans open and shove them down my hips just enough to alleviate some of the pressure. When I glance back up, Rory's eyes are trained on my crotch, those huge black pupils half-covered as her eyelids droop.

"I'm so fucking hard for you," I admit weakly, plucking at her jeans now, first the button and then the zipper. "I need to taste your pussy."

She watches, her head tipped forward to get a closer view as I start sliding her jeans down, the band of her panties becoming visible. I nearly blow right then and there at the first sight of her lace-clad slit. Leaning forward, I press my mouth between her thighs and drag a line up the centre of her panties with my tongue before sucking the fabric between my lips.

I groan at my first taste of her pussy, a switch in my brain flicking on as I tug on the panties, wanting them out of my fucking way.

"Take my jeans the rest of the way off, Johnny."

I only half hear the demand, but I follow it without a second thought. Her jeans go flying across the room once I've helped her step out of them, leaving her only in those panties I want to tear to shreds with my teeth.

"Please, Rory. Please, can I lick your pussy?" I beg, every breath I take burning without her on my tongue.

"Get on the bed first. You're not the only one of us who wants a taste."

"Fuck yes," I hiss before standing and taking her hand, bringing her to the edge of the bed.

Two hands pushing on my chest have me falling back, the mattress sinking beneath my weight. She takes my jeans off with more grace than I had with hers.

"Up. All the way to the headboard."

I move faster than I've ever moved before, shoving myself up the mattress. Only when I'm straining my neck to keep her in my sight does she follow me, straddling my lap, her centre finding a home over my boxer-covered cock.

One tiny grind down on me and I'm fisting my hands in her hair, dragging her mouth to mine. One kiss and I'm electrified, desperate for more, more, more. She parts my lips with her tongue before nipping at them, leaving them swollen.

"Is this the taste you wanted?" I ask.

Hands curled in the comforter on either side of my head, she lowers herself and presses down before dragging her pussy up my aching length. My briefs are wet and sticky, precum having seeped through the material. It's not enough, though. I want them goddamn soaked with her.

"No," she says on a shaking, pleasured exhale.

"Me either."

Sitting up, she slides her hands over my shoulders and pecs, those smooth nails leaving white lines on my skin as she touches me everywhere available to her. My stomach tenses when her nails move lower, trailing along the dark hair leading from my belly button to below the band of my briefs. They stall there, running back and forth instead of drifting lower.

She bends, pressing her lips to my abs and peppering kisses all over before her tongue darts out, swiping along each individual ridge. I moan, shuddering at the sensation.

"Please," I murmur, fighting back every impulse to thrust up against her, desperate for friction.

"Please what?" The question skitters along my wet, sensitive skin.

"Please, touch me. Take my cock out and wrap your hand around it. Then park that sweet pussy over my mouth and let me drown in it. Please, Aurora. I *need* it. Please."

My words make her shake and grind down hard on my thigh.

"Yeah, baby. You need it just as bad, don't you? Need me deep in your throat, my cum filling your mouth so full it drips down your chin. That's what I want. What I fucking need. *Please*, give it to me. To us—"

She moves so fucking quickly I'm missing my last chance to fill my lungs before her pussy hangs over my mouth, making it water. I tug her panties to the side before she has a chance to, freeing up her hands to tug my cock free instead.

"What a pretty pussy, baby," I whisper, staring at the sight before me. Every swollen, pink inch of her slit.

Her whine fills the room the moment I grip her ass in my hands and pull her onto my waiting tongue. I bury my moan inside of her as I lick from bottom to top, collecting every drop of arousal waiting for me.

I suck on her lips before drinking from the fucking source and finding her clit, circling it just once.

Hot breath fans over my cock, making my thighs tense. She teases me, keeping her mouth above the tip, so close yet too far to feel the wet warmth of it. I curl my toes, keeping from burying myself in her throat.

Turning my attention back to the clit beneath my tongue, I run a few testing strokes over it, grinning when she presses down in response, seeking out more of the sensation. Squeezing the soft flesh in my hands, I urge her forward an inch as I begin fucking her with my tongue.

"Oh, *fuck* yes," I spit at the first stroke of her tongue along my shaft.

She repeats the motion three times before slipping her tongue along the underside of the tip and then running it over the precum I know keeps leaking.

I wish I could see her right now as she slowly takes me into her mouth. Those pink lips must be straining to wrap around my thickness. She takes more into her mouth, her tongue flat on the downward glide before swirling around the tip on the way up. Wrapping a fist around the rest of my shaft, she uses her spit to lube it up before pumping in time with her mouth.

I adjust her so I can ask, "Can you take it farther?"

She hums, the vibrations travelling to my fucking balls before they're being gripped in a small hand. I lose control, thrusting up when she takes me deeper into her mouth. Her following gag pierces through the haze of pleasure as I try to sit up.

"Lay the fuck down, Johnny. Let me gag," she snaps before taking me deep again, this time gagging louder.

"Fucking shit, Rory. You want to gag? Then gag like a good girl," I demand.

With a thrust upward, I force almost the entire length of me into her mouth and down her throat. She tightens around my cock, taking me deep as my vision darkens at the corners, and I pull her clit into my mouth, sucking hard. I alternate between flicking and sucking, driven to near madness as her moans grow in volume, engraining themselves in my mind.

I want to make her come. Need to make her come. I'm far too close already to make her wait. I'll bring her there first, like I always will. Always her first, in the bedroom and out of it.

With a nip at her swollen clit, I get what I want. Thighs quivering, she collapses on my face, and I shove my tongue inside of her, taking my reward as it flows like honey. I moan, swatting at her ass before I can think better of it.

"Yes, Johnny, yes. *Oh . . .*" she whines, snapping her legs tight to my ears as she rides the waves of her orgasm.

She bucks against my tongue, her thighs relaxing before I let her move off my face. I tuck my arm behind my head and leave my other resting possessively on the curve of her ass as she sits beside my head, mouth still suctioned around my shaft.

"You have no idea how beautiful you are, Rory," I rasp,

straining my eyes to keep them from rolling back. "Not just like this. *Always*."

She's already collected her own hair, tossing it over her opposite shoulder so I can watch her work my cock, each downward glide sending me further down her tight throat.

"Ready to drink me down, Rory?" I ask, so out of my mind I don't care that I sound like a fucking beast right now.

She nods, moaning in answer. Her fist works in time with her mouth while the other plays with my balls as they draw up tight, my groin burning with the need to come. One more squeeze of her throat and I'm there, ropes of cum filling her mouth.

"Swallow it all," I hiss, arching my neck and thrusting up and deep. "Just like that. Good girl. So fucking good, Rory. *So good*."

When she pops up for air, she's gasping, and I'm waiting, collecting her in my arms and tugging her up my body until she's splayed over me. Burying her face in my neck, she sucks in lungfuls of air at the same pace I do. My legs quiver with aftershocks. My head is spacey, the only thing I see being the woman in my arms.

"Are you okay?" I ask, swiping damp hair off her forehead.

"Yes. Are you?"

I laugh, but it's a tired, blissed-out sound. "Very."

With a shaky hand, I reach over the edge of the bed for the discarded blanket and shake it out over her. She makes a quiet sound of appreciation while kissing my collarbone.

"You're mine now," I declare.

"That so?"

"That's fucking so."

She giggles. Yeah, *giggles*. "Is this an 'I lick it and it's mine' situation?"

"Among other things."

"Who am I to argue with that reasoning?"

She sounds so tired, and it makes me smile. I want to bottle up the blissful tone of her voice right now. It fits her, but not nearly as much as her usual stern, determined rasp. I love them both, and I'd be happy hearing them both for a long time to come.

"Close your eyes for a minute," I whisper, drawing lines up and down her back as my eyes close and her breath begins to even out.

She rubs her cheek on my chest. "Just for a minute."

"Mmhmm. Minute," I mumble.

Neither of us speaks after that.

29

Aurora

SOMETHING HARD PRODDING INTO MY ASS HAS ME BLINKING AWAKE, my mouth dry and crusty. The puddle of drool beneath my chin, pooling on the pillow, has me scrunching my nose and attempting to pull away. I sniff and grow more alert as the scent of cologne and aftershave registers, along with the crushing weight on my back.

Licking my lips, I attempt to shove the weight off, but it doesn't budge. That's when I notice the steady, hot breath in my hair and the hand cupping my belly.

I tense up momentarily before remembering where I am and who it is lying almost entirely on top of me. Johnny being such a clingy cuddler is no surprise. If anything, I expected it. And quite frankly, I like it. I've never been held like this before, so tightly it's like he's expecting me to be plucked out of his arms and hauled away at any given moment.

The opposite happens. I reach out with the only piece of me not trapped and touch his arm, feeling the warm skin and the way it makes my fingertips tingle. The same sensation happens every time we touch, like an omen or something. I've put it off, my stubbornness keeping me sure nothing like that exists, but

I'm beginning to get worn down. If there was another explanation for all of this, I'd think twice. But now?

I blow out a breath and shut my eyes. The dry space on the pillow is a welcome change to the wet spot, and I bury my face in it.

"I can almost hear you thinkin'," Johnny rasps, sleep deepening the tone of it and intensifying the slight drawl.

I throb between my legs and scowl at myself. "You're a pretty intense cuddler."

"Mm, can't say I've ever woken up to find myself wrapped around a woman like this before. Must just be you."

"You're incredibly hot."

He shoves his nose into my hair and chuckles. "Thank you."

"I meant you feel hot. You're a full-blown heater when you sleep. I prefer to sleep in the cold."

"I'm surprised you haven't ducked out and left yet, then."

"You trapped me beneath your body before I could."

"If I hadn't, would you have left, Rory?" he asks softly, the hint of a tease over the curiosity.

"No. You smell good."

He shifts back just enough that I can breathe properly before starting to play with my hair. "That's it, eh? I owe my sisters a thank you, then."

"Do they force you to shower or something?"

"Look on my dresser. I'm pretty sure they've bought me every single cologne known to man."

He's not wrong. Directly across from the bed, there's a grey wooden dresser with two rows of cologne that stretch from one end to the other.

"Have you ever asked them to maybe fixate on something else?" I ask.

"That's the problem with sisters. They assume they know what's best for you at all times. Oftentimes, they do, but not always. Clearly, I don't smell as bad as I did when I was a teen when they started this little tradition of theirs."

I shrug as much as I can with him still splayed over my back. "Maybe you do."

"Oh, is that so? Do I need to ask you to check for me? It isn't polite to shove a woman's face in your armpit, but I'll do it, darlin'. Don't antagonize me," he warns.

A blast of warmth hits me dead centre in my chest as I laugh, attempting to wiggle out from beneath him. He doesn't let me get far before he's sliding his arm around my front and rolling me beneath him. I don't stop laughing, my mouth cracked open in a wide grin that he stares at, a matching one brightening his soft expression.

He drops his head and kisses the tip of my nose. "Where do you think you're going?"

"If you put your armpit in my face, I'll pinch your nipples really hard," I threaten, poising my hands in front of his chest.

"Do it. It makes my dick hard."

I'm reminded then that we're both still completely naked. The hard length of him presses into my groin as he drops his head forward and covers my neck in the soft sound of his laugh.

"I don't think you need any help in that department," I croak.

He's hard, and I'm wet already. It would be so easy for him to part my legs and slide inside of me, but he makes no move to. I don't know if I'm relieved or disappointed when he flops onto the bed beside me, his arm falling over his face.

The bulge of bicep in this position is obscene. But it hides his eyes as I drag mine down the length of his naked body, shifting with aroused discomfort at the beauty of it. The sheer strength and muscle stretching beneath his skin. Even his thighs are thick with it, straining as he rotates his ankles, the bones cracking.

"Feel free to explore with your fingers rather than your eyes," he offers, the little shit.

"What time is it?"

"Late enough Wade's goin' to kick my ass when I get to work."

"Oh, shit." I jerk up in bed and throw myself off it before

hastily reaching for my clothes and slipping my shirt back on. "Get up, Mr. I Never Sleep In."

His smirk threatens to sweep my feet out from under me. "I knew you were paying attention to what I told you about me, even weeks ago."

I snag his jeans from the floor, ignoring the alarming gnaw of pain coming from my thighs and whipping them at him. "I've always paid attention to you. That's how I know that you're trying to get more responsibility at the ranch, and you won't get anywhere with that if you start slacking off."

My underwear is absolutely not going back on, so I leave them on the floor and start to tug my jeans up commando-style. It'll be a long day of having a scratchy ass, but it's better than the alternative.

Eliza's going to know exactly what I was up to last night the moment I walk into work. Not to mention the horses are still outside—shit! The pain that blooms on my inner thighs when my jeans rub along them tears a hiss from me.

Suddenly, a pair of hands are covering mine, guiding them away from my legs. Johnny crouches in front of me and presses his fingers softly into my thighs, avoiding the painful spots.

"Is it normal to hurt this bad after riding?" I ask with a wince when he brushes his thumbs along the edges of my sore spots.

"For beginners, yes. You've chaffed a bit, and you'll probably bruise up today. Don't finish putting these jeans back on. I'll get you something else to wear."

"I've got work," I protest as he goes off in search of these supposed clothes. "And I won't fit your clothes."

He doesn't reply. I huff and shake my jeans off again before moving toward the bed and lifting my leg to the edge of it, inspecting the bright red marks and splotches on the inner area. This is absolutely not what I had planned for my day, and as I slide my phone from the back pocket of my jeans, I get hit with a bolt of guilt.

Mom: No kidnapper would be able to match the sass of my daughter. I miss and love you, Aura.

"What's wrong?"

I lift my eyes to Johnny as he strides toward me, his stare brimming with concern and hands full of clothing. Feeling too exposed with my text conversation still open and half of my body still naked, I shrink back from the question and lock my phone.

Understanding my feelings without needing to hear me say it, he offers me the clothes and sits on the edge of the bed, not saying anything else. I look at the tag inside of the pair of black joggers and relax a bit at the size before tugging them on. They fit perfectly.

"They're Josette's. You're similar in size, and all of my sisters have clothes here in case. Daisy stays here a lot so she doesn't have to answer the line of questioning that always follows a surprise visit home. I think they all stay here for the same reasons," he explains.

"Thank you."

He smiles. "You're welcome, darlin'. Eliza's bringing ointment for your saddle chafe."

"What? You called her?"

"I did. She's bringing ointment. And another member of my family you haven't met yet."

I blink at him slowly, processing his words. "Eliza can't see me here like this. And neither can your family."

His smile drops. "Why can't Eliza see you? Because you're here with me?"

"No. Because I look like a mess. I haven't even brushed my teeth yet. I'm in no state for introductions."

"There's a handful of spare toothbrushes beneath the bathroom sink."

Alright.

When I head out in search of said bathroom, I have to waddle to avoid my thighs rubbing together. It's like a bad case of the sweat chafing I get when I wear shorts in the heat for a long period of time. In addition to that, the sharp pain that throbs from within my muscles makes me gasp every few steps.

"I can't possibly ride Frost back to the ranch," I say when I step into the hallway.

"You won't have to."

Johnny moves quickly, taking my arm and sliding it over his shoulder. He takes some of the weight off my legs as we slip into the bathroom.

"Sit on the toilet lid," he urges, guiding me down onto it.

I look around the room as he digs beneath the sink for a toothbrush. The first thing I notice is how modern it is.

A stand-up shower with soft brown tiles and two shower heads sits in one corner of the room, and a claw-foot tub that looks like I could sink my entire body beneath water and bubbles rests on the other. The vanity is long and has a matching-coloured countertop to match the tile in the shower. A mirror with LED lights around the edges hangs above it.

"Did you do all of this yourself?" I ask, finding myself staring at the tub with longing in my chest. I've never seen one so big.

He stands and starts cracking open the plastic packaging on the toothbrush. "Yes. Wade had me pay next to nothing for this place, so I put my money into renovating it. The bathroom is the first room I did. What else was I to spend my money on? There wasn't anyone else in my life yet, so I figured why not dump it all into my house."

"Well, it's beautiful."

When his smile returns, I'm relieved. He shouldn't have lost it in the first place.

"Thank you. There's more to it I want to show you."

He takes the tube of toothpaste from the cup on the counter and covers the bristles of the toothbrush with it before running it under the tap and handing it over.

I shove it into my mouth and start brushing as he grabs his toothbrush and does the same. It feels incredibly domestic to be brushing our teeth together in his bathroom. His eyes glitter as he watches me, our stares holding in a ridiculous way.

By the time we're done and he's rinsing both of our toothbrushes off, then sliding them both into the holder, there's a knock on the front door.

"Do you want to come or stay?"

"I don't think hiding in the bathroom would look any better than me waddling out like this."

"You're perfect regardless," he says, helping me up off the toilet and out of the room.

My cheeks flush. "Thank you."

I was too focused on being in pain and needing to get dressed earlier to take a good look at his bedroom, but I don't make the same mistake as we walk down the hallway and turn into the living room. In the light, when I'm not in a lust haze, the space looks completely different. I'm drawn in a million different directions. From the sleek brown hardwood floors, the neutral-coloured walls, and the black-rimmed, wide windows, the house feels open and inviting.

For a man, the furniture looks incredibly well chosen, all of it matching with colours and patterns. There's even a rug tucked beneath a rustic wooden coffee table.

"How old are you again?" I mutter.

"I've never paid much attention to my age, Rory. You shouldn't either."

"That's easy for you to say when you aren't the one robbing the cradle."

He chokes on a laugh, shifting in front of me and tucking a finger beneath my chin. "You haven't robbed any cradles. I'm older in maturity than age. And I'm not that young. You're not fuckin' old either."

I nod, trying to convince myself of that. I've never felt like I'm too old for him or that he's immature. Maybe that's why I forget sometimes that we're not the same age.

There's another knock on the door, and after stealing a quick kiss, Johnny moves to answer it.

"I was about to search for a spare key! Let me in, I've brought some goodies," Eliza demands, pushing her way past him.

She smiles immediately upon seeing me and rushes to close the space between us. An aluminum container covered with tin foil in her arms presses to my chest as she collects me in a tight hug.

"Come with me, my love. I've brought some cream for your thighs."

Before I can thank her, she's shoving the silver container toward the man now towering us in the hallway. Wade Steele takes it from his wife and offers me a half-smile.

"Mornin', Aurora," he says, voice low but not mean. His eyes drift to his wife once I've returned his smile and greeting. "You brought too much food for a man who didn't show up for work this mornin'."

She scoffs, offended. "Don't be such a grizzly. Bring that food to the kitchen before it gets cold. These kids need to eat."

The front door shuts a beat before the sound of nails clacking on the floor erupts through the hallway. I tense up a second too late.

"Oh Lord, here we go," Eliza mutters as a fluffy dog comes bounding for me.

It rams into my legs, and I jolt back a step before regaining my balance. A long, slobbery tongue reaches for my fingers, and I offer the thing my palm before petting it once on the top of its soft head.

"Tracker, where the fuck did your manners go?" Johnny asks, following behind it. "Be gentle with her. You aren't a linebacker."

"Tracker?" I bend to get a closer look at the dog without being able to squat. The dog's tail swats the air and thumps against the floor. With a quick look around the entrance, I ask, "Are you the family member I was supposed to meet today?"

"Don't tell me you had the poor girl stressed about meeting

family this morning, Jonathan," Eliza scolds, patting her thigh to call Tracker over.

He—I looked this time—abandons me just like that, and I straighten instantly, pulling in a breath.

Johnny smirks. "She never asked me to clarify."

"I didn't know you had a dog," I tell him.

"He spends most of his time at the ranch, keeping guard. Like he was last night."

"He's sweet."

It's an understatement. The brown, white, and black dog rolls over onto its back in front of Wade in a silent demand for belly rubs, its tongue flopping onto the floor. Wade rolls his eyes and leaves him lying there before Johnny drops to his haunches and rubs his belly.

Eliza turns to me, blocking everyone else out. "Cream?"

"Yes, please."

"Start dishing up breakfast, Johnny. You and Wade can chat while I take care of my girl." She doesn't wait for a response before giving me a gentle tug and helping me waddle back to the bathroom.

This time, not only do I know where I'm going, but I feel different. The feelings swimming inside of me are responsible for that. As are the two people that just arrived.

I feel comfortable. Taken care of. It's jarring, but as Eliza takes hold of my arm and steps with me into the bathroom, I accept it all without fear.

30

Johnny

Aurora's laugh fills my kitchen, and I feel like the luckiest man alive. She glances around the table with a soft, genuine smile and stabs the prongs of her fork through a piece of pancake before running it through a river of syrup.

Eliza sits on her opposite side, finally joining us at the table after ushering in and plating up for the two loiterers, Thomas and Loren, as they appeared at my door like hounds with the scent of food in their noses.

My four-seater table isn't enough room for everyone, so the two of them have made home on the couch, their boots lined up nice and neat in the entry. Four cowboy hats rest on the counter, Eliza having threatened us with a swift kick in the ass if we didn't take them off to eat.

"How come you make pancakes for Aurora and not us?" Thomas asks Eliza, his cheeks stuffed full. "They're damn good."

"Because you don't care what it is that goes into your mouth as long as you're fed. Now, don't complain, or you can eat with the horses from here on out. Be like Loren and eat in silence."

"Jesus, woman. You're goin' to scare off my employees. This is because of those women of yours," Wade mutters between bites of extra-crispy bacon.

"Don't speak about my friends in that tone, Wade. One of those women is your future granddaughter-in-law, in case you forgot."

"As if Brody'd ever let me," he grumbles.

Aurora reaches for the pitcher of orange juice, but I beat her to it and fill her glass. She blushes, and I have to clench my fingers around the pitcher's handle as I set it back down to keep from reaching out to feel her pink cheeks.

"Loren's only silent because he doesn't know how to make conversation with anyone. He's been stuck in the bull pen for too long," Thomas says.

I glance behind me at the two of them and catch Loren's eye roll. "You're an ass, Tommy. Watch your back, or he's going to be shoving you in with 'em instead."

"I'm too good-looking to risk winding up in there," Thomas says, food muffling his words.

"You saying I'm ugly?" Loren asks, the first words he's uttered since getting here.

It's not unusual for him to be so quiet. He's always been the silent, broody type. Women love it, from what I've seen at Peakside. I've yet to be able to crack him the way I've done everyone else.

"Your words, not mine."

"Thomas is just jealous, Loren," Aurora says, drawing everyone's attention, especially mine. Noticing that, she lifts a shoulder and swirls her final piece of pancake in syrup.

"What does that mean?" I ask her, some beastly, jealous part of me demanding to know exactly what she's thinking.

"You know what I meant."

"Nah, say it out loud, Rory," Thomas says, egging her on with a shit-eating grin on his fucking face.

I flip him off, and he howls a laugh.

Eliza tuts. "You're a bunch of asses. Leave her alone."

I rest my fork on my plate and drop my hand to my girl's thigh, leaning close as I whisper, "If you're trying to make me jealous, darlin', it's working."

"Hey! Don't whisper to one another. Share with the class!" Thomas shouts. "I've always wanted to see Johnny punch someone. Never expected it to be Loren, though."

Rory turns her head just enough to catch my gaze, her mouth twitching at the corner. "What are you talking about?"

I grin nice and wide, squeezing her thigh. I'd have planted a big, sloppy kiss on her lips right here, right now, if I felt like I needed to make a statement. But when she surprises me with one on my jaw, I can't think of much else besides the sudden cramped sensation in my chest, like my heart is too big to fit.

"She said you look like the rear end of a donkey, Lo. Sorry to break it to you," I say, not looking away from my favourite set of blue eyes.

Even Wade laughs then, the rare sound of it settling over everyone. Rory shakes her head at me, but sometimes, true happiness is impossible to hide. It's too bright. I feel the same sensation blazing in my gut and lean into it without hesitation.

"If we're at Johnny's, does that mean he has to clean up everyone's dishes?" Loren asks.

"Fuck no—"

"Yes," Eliza cuts me off.

Rory pinches her plate, lifting it. "I'll help."

"Not yet. I've got something to talk to Wade about first," I say, lowering her hand.

He stares at me with his typical blunt, unforgiving gaze. "About what?"

It doesn't intimidate me anymore. Hasn't since I was a teenager.

"I need a few days off." Aurora's thigh tenses beneath my palm, and I start massaging it. "I've got to go with Rory somewhere."

"You gonna tell me where?"

"You know where, Wade," Eliza says softly, glancing between Aurora and me.

"You don't want to go there, Rory," he grunts.

Eliza turns in her chair and speaks to the other two guys. "Go see if Frost and Joker need anything, yeah? We just need a minute here."

Loren doesn't hesitate to get up, not bothering to put his boots on before stepping outside. Thomas, though, he's always been curious. He's my friend, a good one at that, but it isn't my place to answer whatever questions he has.

"There's some dried apples in the cupboard for them," I tell him instead, pointing to the one closest to the fridge.

With a huff, he gets up and joins us in the kitchen to grab the bag of treats. When he spins to leave, he says, "This better not be about anything bad. For any of you."

"Everyone's fine, Tommy," Eliza promises.

A jerk of his head. "Fine. Alright."

Only after the front door snaps shut behind him does Eliza speak again.

"Wanda gave you your father's address? I haven't had a chance to ask you how your meeting with her went."

"It went . . . alright. She gave me his address, amongst other things. Most of which were warnings and examples of how shitty of a father he is," Rory replies, that blissful look in her eyes stomped out.

"Lee Rose is a selfish bastard. Leave him in the past, Aurora," Wade says, his tone as stern as the one he adorns before every breeding season.

Safety isn't an option; it's a necessity.

Eliza rests a hand over the one Aurora has clenching the edge of the table and scoots forward to peer up into her eyes. "I told him about Lee being your father. I was curious if he remembered much more about the Roses than I did. Your grandfather helped on the ranch from time to time, and they spoke often."

"And did you remember more?" I ask Wade when Aurora doesn't show any sign of being upset with Eliza. "Have you told them about her?"

He stares across the table at Rory. "No, I didn't tell them about her. And I didn't remember anythin' of use. They're good people, James and Bernice. If you want to meet them, I can make that happen. I guarantee they've got more of the answers you're lookin' for than we do. If you want my advice, I say talk to them instead of goin' to your father. This town, it's better for you."

"I need to meet him. Even just once. I should have that right," Rory says, back straightening. "I've spent the past thirty years of my life thinking my mother never knew who my father was because that's what I was told. I could have known who he was the entire time. Maybe that wouldn't have changed anything, but I'll never know now. If this is the only chance I have to see him face to face and ask why he left, then I'm taking it. I know the risks that come with that just as much as I appreciate your efforts to protect me from them.

"If he's as bad as everyone says, then that's for me to see. I just . . . I want this done with. I want to move on with my life without this hanging over me. Okay?"

Silence falls over the table. I look nowhere but at Aurora, my heart in my throat and stars in my eyes. A rush of adoration fills me from head to toe, and I lean closer to her without meaning to.

The determination in her expression has my dick trying to punch a hole through my jeans as I spread my legs to alleviate the pressure. This is my fucking dream girl, and I want nothing more than to take her back into my bedroom and keep her there for the rest of our lives.

I never could, though. She deserves room to run, and as long as I can be beside her while she does, I'll leave the door wide open.

"Okay, sweet girl. When are you leaving?" Eliza asks.

Aurora doesn't hesitate. "As soon as possible."

"And you're goin' with her?" Wade's focused on me now. "You'll take care of her? Beat that fucker's ass if he steps out of line?"

"I will," I declare. I've already gone over every outcome in my head five times over. Lee Rose already hates his hometown, but I'll make it my personal mission to make sure it hates him more if he hurts Aurora the way I fear he will.

He nods just once. "Then go. We'll make do without you for a few days. But sleep in again like you did today and we'll be havin' a very different conversation."

"Thank you," Rory says, blowing out a long breath.

Eliza pats her hand. "You're family. And we take care of our family out here. No matter what."

I can see the moment her words hit Rory. The visible shake of her features has me pulling my chair toward her until we're so close my knees jam into her thigh. I wrap my arms around her and pull her into my chest, kissing the side of her head while meeting Eliza's waiting stare. Her concern is evident, but so is the love she feels for the woman in my arms.

All I can do is nod, hoping she can tell that she isn't alone in that department. It's nice seeing someone else who cares this much about Aurora showing it. There are so many of us now, and it pains me that she doesn't have any idea.

In this moment, I decide to make it my mission to help her experience this feeling over and over again. I'm done allowing her to feel so alone when we could fill a football team's roster with the number of people who care about her and still have left-over players.

Cherry Peak was exactly where Aurora was supposed to be, and if I have anything to do with it, she'll be staying for as long as possible.

Not just for me either. But for her. For the family that she deserves.

31

Aurora

With tears dripping down my face, I launch the box of letters and memories down the attic hatch and listen to the box fall to the floor. I follow after it, too pissed off to care about the gasps my mom releases when she sees the lies spilled all over the floor.

"Aura," she whispers, squatting above a collection of torn-open letters.

"What the fuck is this, Mom?"

"It's . . ." She trails off.

I spin to face her, my hands shaking as I grip my hips and gulp down breaths. "It's what? Proof that you've been lying to me my entire life?"

"It's not that simple." She lifts a letter into her hands and stares down at it with a pain so sharp it makes me feel sick. "These letters are not important anymore. Either is the man they were addressed to."

My laugh is vile to my own ears. "That's not for you to decide. I deserved to know who my father was. I asked you! Over and over, I asked you, and you told me you didn't know. You lied to my face for thirty years!"

She looks up at me, devastation dimming the usual glow in her eyes. "You were better off without him."

"That wasn't for you to decide."

"Wasn't it? You're my daughter, and I've been the one here raising you. Lee Rose is nothing to you or me."

"It still wasn't right to keep this from me. Just because I was happy with you as my mom doesn't mean I shouldn't have been given a choice in the matter. It's different thinking you have no idea who he was. But now? You lied to my face."

She shoots to her feet, anger mixing with the sadness. "You had a good childhood, didn't you? I gave you everything I could. Was it not enough? Do you think it wouldn't have been easier to try to find him again once you grew old enough to understand?"

"Don't try to gaslight me right now, Mom. Of course I had a good childhood! This has nothing to do with that and all to do with the fact I could have had more. I could have—I could have experienced the same childhood as all of my friends," I admit, feeling that realization like a knife to my gut.

All of the afternoons I spent at my friends' houses, watching them joke around with their dads, or when I grew older and watched those same friends be walked down the aisle by them, knowing I'd never experience that. My stepdad is incredible, but it will never be the same. That soul-deep bond you're supposed to share with your father is missing. I've never felt it, and now that I know that chance was ripped from me, the hole where it should be is gaping and bleeding, and I have no idea how to fill it again.

"I'm sorry for lying to you, Aurora. But I won't apologize for keeping him a secret from you. Your father isn't the man you want him to be, no matter how much you try to convince yourself otherwise. From the letters you read, you know that I tried to get in contact with him. I wasn't going to keep you apart. He forced my hand by ignoring my every attempt at contact, and as I've grown older and smarter and have lived a good life, I know that him not replying to my letters was the best thing that could have happened to the both of us."

I shake my head, hurt creating a fog over my mind. "I want to know that for myself. I'm going to make that call on my own."

Her eyes widen, glossing over. "Please don't, Aura. You're going to get hurt. He's going to hurt you."

"Then he hurts me! You've done the same thing."

"I may have hurt you, but I also hurt myself."

I sniff, avoiding looking at her any longer. I'm hurt and pissed and sad. I've never liked secrets, and I've always hated lies. I'd rather the truth kill me than a lie give me false comfort.

Coughing to clear my throat, I ask, "Have you spoken to him since those letters?"

"No."

"I've never heard of Cherry Peak."

She nods, and I can see her pushing her hair back from the corner of my eye. "It's south of Calgary. A town nestled in the Rocky Mountains."

"I'll leave as soon as I can."

"Be sure you really want this before you ruin the life you've made here, Aurora. There's no going back after this."

"If I go to this town, is there anyone who I should know about? Any more surprises you've been keeping?"

The obvious shudder in her expression tells me her answer before she can speak. "Wanda Rose."

"His . . . wife?"

"No. His daughter."

"How do you know he has another daughter?" My words are wheezed, the air knocked clean from my lungs.

"He's a public figure. His life has been shoved down my throat for decades."

"She's publicly known as his daughter, then?"

"Yes."

I stare at the ceiling and blink back the tears I refuse to cry. If I thought knowing that he chose to ignore my existence hurt, finding out that he chose to have another daughter instead leaves me so devastated I grow numb.

The only thing on my mind as I turn and leave is that despite the pain in my chest, I know that I won't ever be content again without knowing every little bit of my family's past that's been kept from me my entire life.

Starting with Wanda Rose.

FOUR DAYS after our conversation with Eliza and Wade, Johnny waves off our Uber driver before meeting me on the curb. The weather is shit in Toronto today. Storm clouds rumble with thunder above us, and despite the umbrella I'm holding above our heads, the wind throws the rain in our faces.

"Is this one of your bad omens?" I ask him through my clacking teeth.

"It's just the weather, darlin'."

"Nothing is *just* something to you."

His hand finds my back, giving it an upward stroke. "I left all that in Cherry Peak. The only thing I know here is that you're going to be okay. Rainstorm or no. Okay?"

"I don't believe you."

He takes the umbrella from my hand and ushers us away from the curb. Traffic is crazy here, and for my first time in Toronto—Ontario in general—I would like to not get sprayed by muddy road water. Especially not when I put on my nicest pair of jeans and a soft pink blouse that I packed in my suitcase on a whim thinking I'd never wear but brought just in case. My appreciation for his small gestures of care grows before getting chomped on by the giant, fanged jaws of my fear.

The building behind us is massive. It has to be, considering Lee's staying on the thirty-fifth floor. The penthouse, Wanda said. Of fucking course it is.

For the hundredth time since boarding the plane here, I swallow the vomit that tries to come up and curl my hands into fists in the pockets of my burrowed jacket. My fidgeting expels a cloud of Johnny's cologne from the collar of it, and it's almost as good as it is straight from his body.

Johnny tucks my hair behind my ear and smooths a finger

along my jaw, staring down at me with an intensity that would have had me taking off in the opposite direction a month ago.

"We don't have to do this, Rory. Nobody is going to force you to walk inside this building and see him. I sure as fuck won't. But if you still want to, I'll be right here with you until you tell me to get lost. If you want to leave right now, we can find a bakery, and I'll order you as many cinnamon rolls as you want."

He wiggles his eyebrows at the last part, yanking a laugh from deep within my chest.

"I've only told you about my love of cinnamon rolls once."

It was a piece of information he learned two days ago when Eliza walked into the office during lunch with a tray full of warm, freshly baked ones with dripping cream cheese icing. I scarfed down two right then and there, and the both of them haven't let me live it down since.

"Doesn't matter. I listen to everything you say, especially when it comes to your favourite things. It was hard not to notice how much you love them when you had icing smeared all over your lips and were moaning up a storm."

I shut my eyes and lean against his body, burying my face in the collar of his jacket. He cups the back of my head and scratches my scalp, holding me there.

"I need to call my mom," I murmur before I can think better of it. The urge has been building for weeks but has grown worse over the past couple of days. Our lack of contact has been sitting on my conscience like a big fat reminder of how petty I can be when I'm upset. It's a terrible feeling. "I should have called her a million times by now. We've never gone this long without speaking. I was . . . I was punishing her for keeping this all from me with the silent treatment."

"Do you want to talk to her before we go in?"

I shake my head. "She'd tell me to turn around and go home. That I'm worth more than begging a man to care about me, father or not. I'd listen to her this time."

"She sounds like a smart woman," he says gently, his blunt nails continuing to work my scalp.

"Do you think I should leave? Am I making a mistake here?"

"I think that you've already come this far and that you know exactly what you want from this conversation already. That's going to keep you tough. You're not going to allow him to stomp all over you. That's not who you are, Rory. You don't take shit from anyone. Your tenacity is one of the things I love most about you."

Pressure builds behind my eyes as I nod, exhaling a month's worth of fear into his chest. "You're right. I've never begged anyone for anything in my life, let alone affection. I'm not going to start now."

"That's my girl."

Tipping my head back, I find him already looking down at me, the soft blue of his eyes making my heart beat a bit too fast. It's always like this when I'm around him. My skin prickles with his closeness, and my heartbeat takes off. It grows easier to smile and be myself. I feel like I can be proud of who I am, flaws and all, in a way that I could never accept before. It's not that I need him to believe in myself, but maybe it's that I want to more than I do without him.

Anti-social, nervous, blunt. They're all qualities that I used to worry made me unlikable to people. They made me wonder if the reason I never had many friends or romantic relationships was because of things that I say or do. But now? Now, I don't care if me being myself turns people off.

Johnny's never judged me for who I am. Not once.

People you love are supposed to make you want to be the best version of yourself, right? I think that's what this is.

I snap my eyes open. What the fuck? *Love?*

Blinking, I shove that to the back of my mind. The very, very, very back. Right now, that's the last thing I need to be thinking about. I'm too damn emotional to be contemplating things like that.

"Should we do this?" I ask, peeling myself away from him.

I don't go too far. I can't seem to take another step back, and it has nothing to do with staying beneath the umbrella.

His eyes drift across my face before he nods, grabbing my hand and intertwining our fingers. I glance down at the hold, finding that I love the sight of our hands like this.

"Say the word at any time, and I'll get you out of there," he promises.

"I know you will."

The apartment building is bougie enough to have its own set of security waiting beside a nose-in-the-air receptionist who scowls at the two of us when we walk in. I should have killed her with kindness, maybe a blindingly fake smile and wave, but Johnny swoops in before I have to.

With our hands still interlocked, he rests our umbrella against one of the main windows and tugs me along to the desk. Once we get close, he sweeps his eyes over the contents of the desk. "Good mornin'! Don't you look radiant today despite the terrible weather."

Radiant? I want to smack him upside the head for complimenting her but also laugh at how obviously he's trying to win her favour.

The receptionist blinks twice at him before smiling slightly and tucking a brown curl behind her ear. "Good morning. The storm came out of nowhere, but hopefully, it won't stay around for long."

"You didn't walk to work today, did you? We were going to walk, but after taking our new puppy out this morning and needing an emergency bath afterward, we chose against it this time," he replies, looking back at me quickly, just long enough for the woman's eyes to follow.

She takes me in with a frown, all of her previous pep washed away like the trash in the gutters outside.

Johnny pushes forward, undeterred. "You don't happen to know if there's a dog park nearby, do you? We're here to meet a friend today, but we've been contemplating buying in the building for a few months now. Our goldendoodle is just five months old but such a sweetie."

Goldendoodle? Dog park? I stifle my confusion behind a half-smile.

She looks at the picture on the desk before lifting her eyes back to him, and I take the opportunity to steal a glance at the two security guards watching us from beside the elevators. They're the second line of defense after this woman. If we get past her in the first place.

"You have a goldendoodle? So do I! Mine is six months, and holy, they're a handful. I don't live in the area, but there is a park about four blocks away that I've ventured to a handful of times. It's one of the less crowded ones and has a separate gated area for the smaller dogs," she gushes, eyes wide and nearly fucking sparkling as she stares up at him.

"Fantastic! We'll have to check it out," Johnny says, those damn dimples of his popping as he tries to sway her further.

With a squeeze of my hand, he reminds me that this is his attempt at gaining us access upstairs, not anything more than that. I already knew that, but I still appreciate the clarity. Even if I'm still feeling incredibly jealous that she's the recipient of his dimpled smile.

"Who are you here to see today? I'll buzz you up, and hopefully, by the time you're done, the rain will have stopped. A bit of sunshine would be nice today."

Johnny leans one arm on the desk and turns his grin up a notch, confidence damn near leaking from every pore in his skin.

"Riley Rose, apartment 3503. We were just out for dinner last night with his daughter, Wanda, but Riley couldn't make it and insisted we stop by today. It's been a long time since we got the chance to make a trip in from Mississauga."

The woman stops cold, eyes narrowing at the corners when they swing to me. Every second that she stares, I feel my neck grow hotter, sweat appearing at a too-quick pace. I can't keep up my fake smile, letting it drop under the weight of her disbelief. It's like every person in here knows who I am and wants to kick my ass out.

Johnny's grip on my hand grows tighter, and I'm not sure if it's out of support or if my palm is just so sweaty he can feel it slipping.

"I'll need to call upstairs and get approval before buzzing you in," she says, her tone flat. "What are your names?"

"Sure," Johnny agrees. "Johnny Mitchell and Aurora Bennett."

The two security guards have moved closer in the time we've been here, and one mutters something with a hand pressed to his ear. I'm prepared for the worst, my knowledge of how things work when it comes to celebrities lacking but not nothing. If these two men don't work directly for Lee and his team, then they're in contact with those who are. They've reported everything we've done and said since we've been down here to the people upstairs.

The receptionist lifts the landline on the desk and presses a series of numbers on the pad before lifting it to her ear. I turn away and tune out her words. With my back to everyone, I take a long inhale.

Johnny turns with me, ditching my hand to touch my back instead. He creates another barrier between me and them by shifting at my side. Despite how often I told myself that I was content on my own and only needed myself to be happy, it feels the complete opposite right now.

Johnny's my lifeline in this mess, and I don't think I could have done this—any of it—without him.

"Alright. You can go up," the woman says.

I spin back around, focusing on masking the sheer disbelief I'm feeling. "Thank you."

"Give your pup a belly rub from us," Johnny says, guiding us past her desk to the elevator doors.

The guards keep their eyes on us as we pass them, but unlike every horror thought running through my head, they don't yank us back and toss us on our asses in the rain.

Once we've stepped into the elevator and the doors close, Johnny presses the thirty-fifth floor and then moves right for me. He presses me against the mirrored wall and cups my cheeks in his strong hands, holding me. His eyes sear into mine, and a second later, I'm leaning up on my toes and kissing him. My eyes drift shut at the reassuring press of his lips. I let my worries go for this small moment, focusing only on him and me and the steady beat of my heart.

Reaching up, I run my fingers through his hair, completely unused to him not wearing his hat. The easy access is nice, but I've grown attached to the sight of it and his habit of flicking it up when he goes to kiss me. It's a piece of him that I wish he hadn't felt the need to forgo today.

"Never opt out of wearing your hat for me, Johnny," I whisper into the kiss.

"This isn't the place for it. You needed to be taken seriously."

I pull back, our lips parting slowly. "And I wouldn't have been if you wore your hat?"

"I doubt many ranchers own places in buildings like this."

"Lee wears a cowboy hat, doesn't he?"

He kisses my cheek before doing the same to the other. "I'm not like Lee, darlin'."

I scoff. "That's definitely not a bad thing."

"No, it's not. I'll wear my hat for you next time, Rory."

Dragging my fingers through his scalp one last time, I drop my hand. A giddy excitement blooms in my belly when I give his chest a shove.

"How else would I be able to place it on my head if you don't bring it with you?"

I watch in real time as his pupils flare, brows lifting. "You do that in an elevator and I'm pulling the emergency stop button."

"Mm, seems you missed a golden opportunity."

His chest heaves. "Did you ask one of the girls about what it means to put my hat on your head, baby?"

"Maybe." I shrug, keeping my lips flat and straight.

"Maybe," he repeats, his voice growing all deep and growly. "It's typically bad manners to meet your girlfriend's father with a hard-on."

Feeling the pulse between my legs, I can't help myself from palming said hard-on, drawing a groan from him.

"It's a good thing he's only a father in blood, then, isn't it?" I ask with a flutter of my lashes.

"You're goddamn trouble, Rory," he mutters before stealing another kiss and lingering afterward, as if he can't get himself to pull away.

Not until the elevator dings and the doors begin to slide open. Keeping his eyes on me, he turns to stand at my side, the promise of what's to come once we're finished here hanging heavy between us.

Once a long hallway with swirled carpet and sconces along the walls appears in front of us, I realize the next few minutes aren't going to be exactly what I expected. In every scenario I played out in my head, I thought the doors would open to the inside of a glamorous penthouse and I'd find Lee standing a few feet away.

But instead, we step out of the elevator and wander down the hallway in search of the door marked with 3503. The longer we walk, the more apparent it becomes that this apartment building doesn't have only one penthouse but three. And Lee's? It's the very last one.

The four guards standing in front of the door with their thick arms crossed and eyes tracking our every step make the gold-plated numbers on the door meaningless.

"Aurora Bennett?" one of them asks. Or demands, more like.

I nod. "Yes."

Another guard touches the small black device in his ear and

speaks in a low voice, not taking his eyes off us. My skin crawls with the distrust in their eyes.

"Wait there," the first guy snaps.

As if I'd try to waltz past them.

Johnny tucks one of his hands into the front pocket of his jeans and nods before leaning back against the wall. He's so nonchalant in front of these men while I stand frozen, focusing too hard on not puking.

Sensing that, he reaches a hand for me, and I stumble toward him. With a wince-like smile, I nod at the men.

It feels like hours that we wait there with not a single word spoken between any of the men or Johnny and me. I've contemplated ripping strands of my hair out by the time the guards move, clearing the way of the door.

When it opens, it isn't Lee that greets us but the ice-chip eyes of a woman I've never seen before and wouldn't mind never seeing again after this.

"I was wondering how long it would take for another Bennett woman to come sniffing around. Can't say I was expecting you, though. Was your mother too busy to come?"

32

Johnny

I BRISTLE AT THE TONE THE WOMAN USES WHEN SHE SPEAKS TO Aurora. The way she looks down her nose at her despite being shorter and purses her lips as she gives my girl an up-and-down glare tugs me forward half a step, making my presence known to everyone around us.

Whoever the woman is, she thinks she's above us. Above Rory, specifically. It becomes even more apparent when she folds her arms across her chest and nods, as if giving us permission to speak.

"Who are you? And how do you know my mother?" Rory asks stiffly.

"I know *of* your mother. I've never met her."

"Is that supposed to make a difference?"

"Yes, actually, it does. Now, I'll ask again. What are you doing here?"

Rory pauses, but her expression is too closed off for me to read her right now. I fucking hate that but don't let it clog my judgment.

I insert myself into the conversation without a care what this old woman thinks about it. "Where's Lee? And who exactly are you to him?"

She flicks me a disinterested look that lasts less than a second before glaring at Rory again. I huff a laugh, giving my head a shake.

"If you continue to glare at her like that, you'll need to ask those guards of yours to come a bit closer."

"Johnny," Rory whispers, letting her mask slip when she stares up at me, revealing a whirlpool of appreciation and nerves.

I let out a breath and settle my hand on her back again. Fuck, I love touching her like this.

"Lee is not here," the woman says, her glare lessening slightly. "Even if he were, he wouldn't want to see you. I would have turned you away in the lobby had I not wanted to tell you that directly. Don't come back—you'll only be hurting yourself with hearing the same answer again."

"When will he be back? I'm not leaving without at least seeing him," Rory pushes, standing her ground the way I knew she would.

We both know she's lying. There wouldn't be an entire team of security parked outside of his apartment if he weren't here.

"Not for a while." *Another lie.*

"Then we'll wait."

"That won't be happening. The building has a very stern no-loitering rule."

"I really, really don't want to make a scene. But I'm going to tell you again. We are not leaving without me speaking with my father," Aurora snaps.

A hush falls over the lot of us as she drops that bomb. The woman in front of us is the first to gather herself. She snorts, a phony smile appearing. The shake at the edges of it catches my attention, and I latch onto that nervous movement, my mind turning a million miles a minute.

"You aren't the first to claim such a thing, and you won't be the last. Leave. *Now.*"

Rory pushes forward, ignoring the order. "No. I know he's

inside, and I didn't come all the way here to be turned away. I've waited thirty years for this moment, and I'm taking it."

The door guardian's cheeks flare with red splotches as she glances at security, nodding quickly. They start in our direction on her demand, and I put myself in their path before they can get to the both of us.

Aurora levels the woman with an icy glare and steps toward her. "Tell him that I'm here."

"No."

"Please. Just tell him."

The devastation in her tone crushes me. I'm too fucking helpless in this situation. Short of kicking down the door and hauling Lee out myself, there isn't anything I can do to help her.

"No. Now, leave," the woman hisses.

Rory's shoulders rise and fall rapidly, her eyes trained on the door in front of her. I'm about to say fuck it to the consequences and kick that door down for her when it opens on its own.

If I hadn't seen him a handful of times around town when I was a boy, the gasp that escapes my girl would be enough to tell me exactly who it is that opened it.

"What's goin' on out here? You itchin' for a noise complaint, Beck?"

Beck. The woman at the door balks at his question and spins to scold him. "Go back inside, Lee. You're doing exactly what you're not supposed to right now. You have security for a reason."

He peers at me for a moment, sizing me up before doing the same to Aurora. I wait for the recognition to hit him. For some fatherly instinct to come alive inside of him that says this is his daughter, but when he dismisses her with a scowl, I can almost hear her heart crack.

"Why have they not been taken back downstairs?" he asks, but I'm not paying enough attention to him to know who he's speaking to.

I'm focused on Aurora instead. On the paleness of her skin

and slow rise and fall of her chest. Lips parted on silent words, she just stares at him. I move as close to her as I can without taking her strength.

There's no doubt that she's Lee Rose's daughter. Maybe I forgot what he looked like after all these years to not have pieced together their similarities. They're not as obvious as mine to my mom, but seeing them so close together . . . it's impossible to miss.

Rory's eyes have always drawn me to her, and now, they're the first thing I notice staring across the hall at Lee. It's hard not to see those same angry, rough waves that dare you to jump in without a life jacket. There's only one difference between them, and that's that Rory swept me up and out of those waves, and Lee would have ordered the captain of the ship to leave me there to drown.

I close off all other thoughts of their similarities because while they may share the natural wavy curls in their hair and the small upturn at the end of their noses, they couldn't be more opposite deep down.

"Do you know anyone with the last name Bennett?" Rory asks.

Lee visibly jumps at the sound of her voice, his cheeks blanching as if he's seen a ghost. Or heard one, more like.

"No."

Rory's next words are little more than an exhale. "You're lying."

Lee's face tightens when she speaks again. He looks at her, his eyes catching on hers before widening for the briefest of seconds, as if he's seeing for the first time how similar they are to his. "Where did you hear that name?"

"Go back inside, Lee. We'll have them taken back downstairs," Beck says, attempting to usher him through the door.

He lifts a hand and takes a step around her, repeating his question. "Where did you learn that name?"

"It's my last name," Rory states bluntly.

"A coincidence," he chuffs, turning his nose up at her.

"It isn't, and you know it."

Beck slips out from beside Lee, and I watch in slow motion as she rushes toward the security guards lingering nearby. They move toward us with predator-like stealth, following her direction without hesitation.

I've never had a reason to be violent in my life. Most of the time, I can solve my problems with a grin or an apology. But when the tallest of the guards rushes toward Rory, I act out on instinct. It's only a shove, but when he stumbles back into the chest of another guard and levels me with a dark glare, I know I'm in deep shit.

"Back off," I warn.

"I have questions for you, Lee. And I want you to answer them. I deserve the answers," Rory says, raising her voice to be heard over the commotion happening around us. "My mother deserves the answers."

Lee flinches, his eyes dimming at her last few words. It's everything I need to confirm that while he may not know Aurora, some part of him remembers her mother. Whether from the Bennett name or whatever he saw in Rory moments ago.

"You deserve nothing. I don't know who you are, but we're done here. Whatever outlet asked you to come here today can go fuck themselves. You tell your boss that my past is nobody's business," Lee mutters, the dismissal lacking the heat I expected.

"I don't work for anyone! Wanda told me where to find you. She—"

"I don't care what my daughter told you. She loves to get on my nerves, and this is only another example of that. Now, *leave,*" he demands.

Beck takes his words and uses them to have us removed. She waves at the guards, who crowd me, and one heads directly for Rory.

I can't do anything to stall that won't end with my guts getting plastered on the walls, but even that's a small price to pay to bring Rory peace. The devastation on her face as she stares at her father right now seals my fate.

Snapping a hand out at the security guard targeting her, I grip his shoulder and release a deep sigh. I tug on him, and when he snarls down at me, I wince, prepared to have my shit rocked.

"Let them go," Lee says, his back to us as he grips the door handle. You could bounce a penny off his back with how tense he is. "Make sure they leave, but don't touch them. The last thing we need is another damn scandal."

Beck scoffs, staring at him in disbelief. "Lee—"

"Let them go," he repeats. I release the guard. "I don't want to see them again. Either of them."

"Are you that much of a fucking coward?" Rory blurts, drawing my gaze. She clenches her hands into fists at her sides, but her expression is more hurt than angry, her mask nowhere to be found. "It makes sense now, at least. You never deserved my mother, and you sure as shit never deserved me. Maybe it was a blessing for all of us that you never had a place in my life. I wouldn't have known what to do with a pathetic excuse of a father like you anyway."

She spins on her heel and leaves, taking off down the hallway. I swallow, every instinct inside of me screaming to unglue my feet to the carpet and go after her before she gets too far. With a heavy step, I stare at Lee, finding him watching her leave. There's a heavy, deathly silence in the air as I leave, chasing after my girl.

I find her pacing in front of the closed elevator doors, her panted breaths too loud. The tears streaming down her face make my chest ache, a piece of it crumbling.

"Rory . . ." I start, approaching her slowly, my hand extended. It's shaking, but I ignore that.

She shakes her head, not looking at me. "I can't do this right now. I can't—I can't talk about it."

"We don't have to talk about it, sweetheart."

"Stop. Stop using that tone with me. I don't want it."

I clear my throat. "Alright. We don't have to talk at all if you don't want. Let's just get you back to the hotel."

"I'm not going to the hotel. I need fresh air. I want to be alone. Please." The plea nearly breaks me.

"You don't have to beg me for fucking anything, darlin'. Go and take your time. Just call me when you don't want to be alone anymore, and I'll come find you."

She sucks in a hitched breath, nodding her head, still not looking at me. The elevator dings, signalling its arrival, and I take two quick steps toward her. I cup the back of her head and drift a kiss over her cheek, feeling her tears on my lips.

"I'll see you later, baby," I whisper.

Sniffling, she tips her chin and rushes into the elevator the moment the doors open. It takes everything in me not to follow her, especially when she turns to face me and I see how deeply that man back there has hurt her.

I knew it was a possibility just as much as she did. But having it happen like that just now . . . suddenly, it's real. The pain is deep and scarring, and there isn't a damn thing I can do to fix it right now.

The second the doors shut, I'm tugging my hair at the root and leaning back against the wall. Toronto's a beast of a city, and neither of us knows a damn thing about it. She probably has as good of an idea as to where to go as I do. But if this is what she needs, then who am I to stop her? My only concern is her well-being, and that's what got me so fucking stressed.

The apartment floor is still empty, and as I look anxiously around the small sitting area across from the elevators, I freeze. Abandoning my place by the wall, I drop to my haunches in front of the small garbage and the folded paper hanging off the edge.

I know what it is the moment I pick it up. My breath catches at the small photo hidden beneath it amongst the trash.

The young Lee Rose is grinning, a woman perched in his arms that looks like a brunette-haired, brown-eyed version of her daughter. Rory may share Lee's eyes and nose, but her mother . . . she may as well be a carbon copy of her.

I tear my eyes from the photo to unfold the letter. The splotches on the pages warn me not to read the scrawled words, but I ignore them.

Hi,

That's as much of a greeting as I think I can give you right now. Is there even a point bothering now? This is my thirty-fifth letter, and I've accepted that this will go unanswered as the previous ones have. I've grown to expect to find them returned in my mail box. That's sad, isn't it? No. What's sad is that I've been so stupid in the fact I can't stop writing these letters in the first place. Yet here I am. Maybe I've always been stupid when it comes to you. Naive, too. But who cares? It's too late to try and change that.

Aurora threw her rice cereal at me today. The whole bowl splattered all over my face and hair. I left her in her highchair and went to the bathroom to scrub it off. By the time I got back, she'd thrown what was left on her table and coated the walls with it.

I cried when I saw the mess. Something so small broke me. My emotions boiled over. All of the sleepless nights and complaints from my neighbours about the crying because she still can't sleep for more than four hours at a time because of her colic.

I sat on the kitchen floor and cried until our daughter started laughing at the cat that always sits on the ledge outside the kitchen window. Simple as that, the beautiful sound of her laughter pulled me out of the pit I'd fallen into.

I was reminded then that you've never heard her laugh. Never heard her scream or cry, or felt the slap of rice cereal on your cheeks. I'm almost glad of that.

They played your song on the radio again. I threw it and it broke. Shattered, really. Now my boss is taking the cost of a new one out of my pay. It's a fair punishment, but I've had to cancel the trip to the zoo I promised my daughter because unlike you, I'm struggling with the pennies I have left-over at the end of every month. Oh, how grand it is to raise a baby girl on your own.

Do you remember that night in Blue River? It was our first time out of the province together, and we could hardly afford the gas to get there. We stopped at that small, blink-and-you'll-miss-it town, and you said it felt like home, so we found one of the few available camping stalls at the site just outside of town and put up our tent.

It took all of ten minutes to explore the entire town,

but then we found Eleanor Lake. God, it was beautiful there.

We sat on the edge of the dock and watched the families playing on the beach, and you promised me that that would be us one day.

I told you then that I feared being a single mother, and that if we were ever to start a family, I wanted a ring on my finger. A promise that I'd never be left to raise a child on my own.

You proposed then and there. I laughed and told you to try again in a year because I'd say yes then. If we could just get through the rocky start of your career, and you could get your foot in the right doors. Once we weren't struggling and stressed and fearful.

Well, it's been three years, Lee, and I'm still waiting.

I hope you're happy wherever you are,
Piper

My stomach turns at the smeared ink and tear stains all over the page. Every emotion written into that letter stabs at my chest.

I stand, gripping both the letter and picture in a tight fist. Warnings flare in my mind as I stride back down the way I came, to that penthouse at the end of the hall. I managed to avoid getting punched last time, but I don't know if I'll be getting away as easily this time.

Not if the anger pulsing beneath my skin has anything to do with it. I'm livid, every protective instinct I have demanding Lee

Rose pays for all the hurt he's caused. Not only to Rory but to her mother. Every doubt he's placed in my girl's head to make her feel like she's not good enough or important enough. That she doesn't deserve everything and more from those who care about her.

"Get me Riley Rose," I shout, staring the security guards down from halfway down the hall.

"Not happening," one replies coolly.

Another touches his ear and speaks again, and a moment later, the door is flinging open. I expect to see Beck, the woman who I undoubtedly know had some role in all of this mess, but it's not her that steps out.

"Look at you," I say, brushing off the warning looks from his security. "So brave. Where was this in front of your daughter?"

"Do you know how many people I've had claim to be my children over the years?" he asks, staring directly at the paper in my hand.

"How many of those women look like Piper Bennett? How many share your eyes? How fucking many would have access to letters like these?"

I close the gap between us enough I can shove the letter against his chest. He grunts at the impact and takes it from me. The photo falls to the ground, and he drops his eyes to it.

"Where did you get that?" he whispers, falling to his knees to pick it up. When I don't answer him, his gaze lifts and sharpens. "Tell me."

"You don't get to make demands of me after how you spoke to her. How you *treated* her. I get that this was sudden and confusing and probably terrifying. But you're a sorry excuse of a man to take it out on her. Believe it or not, all she wanted was a chance to speak to you just once. To have her questions answered. It would have taken one conversation with her to realize that she's your daughter. You're a fuckin' idiot not to have realized it the moment you looked at her."

He traces his finger along the edge of the photo and exhales a shuddered breath, not replying. I grind my teeth, not buying into the show he's putting on.

"Read that letter, Riley. Read it and fucking weep."

Shaking my head, I turn and leave, not sparing a single person another look.

They don't deserve one.

33

Aurora

Without an umbrella, the rain plasters my hair and face in seconds. I blink to clear my vision as droplets collect in my eyelashes and leave the building, my legs pumping and pumping until I'm not walking but running instead.

My sneakers pound the pavement, the erratic thump of my heartbeat in my ears. Most people don't so much as look up from their phones as I brush past them, and those who do dismiss me without much thought. Nobody knows who I am, and that makes it all that much easier to let my tears escape, falling down my cheeks alongside the rain.

A pain so hot it burns like pressing an iron to my chest pushes me to run faster. I want to scream from the lack of oxygen in my lungs and the fact I was such a fool to come here. My mom knew it the entire time.

Riley Rose isn't any more my father than he is a simple sperm sample. I wasn't expecting him to fill a role that isn't void in my life, but to be brushed off so easily, without a care . . . I clench my teeth to hide a sob.

This city is unfamiliar, and the further I venture inside of it, the more turned around I get. I don't stop running, though. Even as the warning grows louder in my pounding skull. What would be so bad about getting lost?

I stumble upon a park a few minutes later. It's empty, the rain apparently pissing all over everyone's plans for an afternoon walk. Slowing my pace, I pass through the gap in the fence. The grass is thick and green here, glistening with water beneath my feet. Everything is soaked, but I drop onto a wooden bench, anyway, not caring that my ass grows wet in an instant.

Only once I've sat and closed my eyes do I clue in to the way my body shakes and my lips are dry despite the rain. I lick them and press two fingers to the back of my hand. My skin is ice-cold. I let my shoulders fall forward and hunch over my knees before pulling my phone from my pocket and dialling the number I've avoided for a month.

She answers on the first ring. Just one single word, but one that forces every sob I've stomped down to come all the way up.

"Aura."

"Mom."

"What's wrong?"

I almost laugh. If I wasn't sobbing through my teeth, I would have. "What isn't wrong?"

"You went to see him," she says, certainty blaring from every word.

"You can say I told you so," I whisper.

"If there was ever something I wanted to be wrong about, it was this. I've never, ever wanted you to get hurt, baby girl."

"Why him, Mom? He's . . . he's horrible."

There's a pause, and I can hear the soft sound of background noise disappear completely, as if she's done everything to ensure I'm her main focus.

"He wasn't always horrible—"

"I don't want to hear all the good things about him," I interrupt.

"If you don't hear the good, how will you be able to understand why I made the choices I did? You deserved to hear these things before you left, but I didn't offer them to you because I was too hurt and full of regret. You need to hear them now, Aurora."

I lean back against the bench and shove my dripping hair back and out of my face. "Fine."

"I met Lee on my eighteenth birthday. There used to be a summer fair put on a few minutes outside of Cherry Peak that drew people in from all over the province, Calgary included, and my friends insisted we go to celebrate my birthday. I had on one of those silly birthday girl sashes and a tiara that we got at the dollar store, and because most of the rides had teenage boys controlling them, I got teased consistently for them. Their comments and jokes didn't matter because I was with my friends, but Lee was there with his own friends and overheard a few of them poking fun at me. He was nineteen at the time and already larger than life itself. I remember thinking it was a birthday miracle that this tall, handsome guy was there, threatening to shove one of the guys into one of the Ferris wheel seats and leave him at the top all night if he didn't leave me alone.

"Both my friends and his convinced him to let it go, and I think I was already in love with him by the time he asked me to grab an ice cream with him afterward. I hadn't dated before, not seriously, and Lee . . . he was funny and kind and protective. Being in his presence was like staring down at the world and finally seeing everything great about it. That night changed a lot for me, but it was the first time I ever felt seen. Your grandparents disapproved of him, only seeing a no-good, upcoming musician who wasn't worthy of their daughter because he had nothing to show for himself yet. I didn't care what they thought, and so the rift between us started. The one that lingered far longer than my relationship with him and now haunts you as well."

"Your parents were always arrogant assholes, Mom," I say on a breath, rubbing at my chest absent-mindedly.

"Yeah, baby. They were. But at one time, they did want what

was best for me. I often think about how if I had listened to their advice and left your father when they wanted me to, that I never would have had you, and you, Aurora? You're the most precious gift I've ever received. I'd go through a million broken hearts and painful memories if it meant I got you at the end of every story."

I sniffle, furiously wiping at my eyes and cheeks. It's hopeless. The tears don't stop falling, and neither does the rain.

Mom doesn't wait for me to reply before speaking again. "Lee and I were together nearly every day for three years. I was *happy*, sweetheart. He was everything I thought I could ever want, and he treated me very well. It might be hard to believe now, after everything you've seen and learned these past few weeks, but it's the truth. When we broke up, I thought I'd never be able to be that happy again. It wasn't until I found out I was pregnant three months after I saw him for the last time that I knew it was possible to feel that feeling again. With you."

"Did he know?" I blurt.

"About what?"

"About me, Mom. Did he know you were pregnant with me?"

"After we broke up, he moved to Toronto—"

I cut her off again, knowing that on a normal day, she'd have reamed me out for being so rude. "I don't care that he moved. I just want to know if he knew."

"No, he didn't. I tried a million times to tell him. You've seen the stack of letters, Aurora. Every single one was returned to me without being opened. They were my only way of reaching him, and he refused to read even one of them. I couldn't continue sending them once you hit the six-month-old mark. Every time I opened the mailbox and saw another returned, it broke that much more of me. I had to move on. And I did. I moved on, raised you by myself, and never paid Lee Rose another moment of thought. It was the best thing I could have ever done for myself. And for you. People change, even when we wish they wouldn't. And sometimes, it's for the worst."

"You kept the letters. And the photo. If you were so done with it, why not burn them all?"

"I could have. I almost did on multiple occasions, but those letters, while painful for me to read and see, hold memories of you. Of every battle we faced and every milestone that I bragged to him about. Everything I have ever done has been for you, Aura. Every single thing. I'm sorry I've failed you with this."

I've stopped trying to wipe my face dry. Every blink of my eyes forces more warm tears to mix with the freezing drops of rain. It feels like there's a hole in my stomach, and with every word I hear my mom speak, it doubles in size. Despite all the things I wish I had, I never *needed* a father growing up. How could I have when I had a mother who filled both roles the way she did? But when I met my stepfather, I didn't hesitate to let him in to take some of the weight from her shoulders. We formed a family made from love and care, not obligation and resentment. If Lee had opened those letters and come back into our lives, would I be able to say the same thing?

"He remembered you, Mom. I saw the look in his eyes when I mentioned you. For a second, I thought he recognized me too. Or at least that he saw something in me that made him believe the words I was saying. But I was wrong."

"You have his eyes," she says softly. "If nothing else, he would have recognized those pretty blues of yours."

"Well, if he did, he didn't care. He all but shoved me off his doorstep with a quick dismissal. I don't know what I was thinking leaving Calgary."

"Yes, you do. You wanted to learn about your history, and I've always known that one day, you may choose to do that very thing. It's your right. I should have brought it up to you earlier, on my own. I've had thirty years to tell you about the other half of your family history, and I'm sorry that I never did. I'm sorry that I lied to you instead."

I ignore her apologies for now, not trusting my emotions. "What are his parents like? I've been working with the Steele family in Cherry Peak, and they told me about them. Said I could meet them if I wanted to."

"Bernice and James are still in Cherry Peak? You're working with the Steeles? Who? Wade and Eliza?"

"Which question would you like me to answer first?" I ask, almost laughing at the rush of questions. "No, Bernice and James aren't still in Cherry Peak. They're up in Edmonton. Close enough I could go and meet them. And Wade and Eliza, I've been helping them with the ranch's finances. Do you know them?"

"I don't know them. Not really. But their names were on everyone's tongues in that town for the short time I was there. They're good people," she answers before sighing. "The Roses are your grandparents just as much as my parents are. If you met them, I have a feeling you'd have a much warmer response than you did from Lee."

"And if I don't? I can't take another rejection right now."

"Then you walk out and don't ever go back. I know it hurts right now, but you have to ask yourself if you'll regret not meeting them and closing this chapter of your life or if you'll be happy without knowing."

"I'll think about it."

"Okay, sweetheart."

I swallow, another wave of emotion swelling before drowning me in one fell swoop. "I'm sorry for not calling and for everything I sai—"

"Oh, it's okay," she soothes. "I just wanted to know you were okay. You're plenty old enough to take care of yourself, but you're still my daughter, and I'm still your mom. I'll always worry."

"I was so mad at you. It felt like you betrayed me and that I'd lost something I never knew I'd even had in the first place," I admit amongst the tears scalding my cheeks. "I don't like secrets. We've never had them between us before."

Her breath hitches, causing her reply to be wavered. "Your feelings are *valid*, Aurora. Anger is healthy, and so is pain. You just can't bottle it up, or you'll risk exploding from the pressure of ignoring it. I'm your mother, and I can take the hit always. I'm sorry I've hurt you so deeply."

"Tell me what to do now," I croak.

"I can't, baby girl. You have to do what you need to heal from this. Do you want to come home, or do you want to stay and learn more about your family?"

"They're not my family."

"But they could be."

Her words shake me. Suddenly, I'm smacked with the realization that I've already found family in Cherry Peak, and while I don't share blood with a single one of them, it doesn't matter. I'm sitting on this bench by myself, but I don't feel alone. I haven't for weeks now.

"I met someone, Mom." I whisper the words so softly it's like I'm afraid of speaking them out loud, even for my own ears. "He came with me to meet Lee."

"Tell me about him."

I inhale deeply, finally feeling some of the constriction around my throat loosen. With the sleeve of Johnny's coat, I wipe my eyes. They don't fill with tears immediately after this time.

"He's my opposite. An easygoing extrovert that could smile every minute of every day. I've grown distracted in Cherry Peak, and I'm glad I have because it meant I got to spend more time with him. You'd like him, I think. He's a believer in all things universe related."

"And you haven't gotten tired of his energy? Because I remember that one boy from middle school who you said wouldn't stop following you down the halls telling you those jokes from the book he carried everywhere. You told me you were going to shove the book into his mouth and make him eat it," she says with a soft laugh.

"That's the thing. I haven't grown tired of it at all. If anything, I think he's been pulling me out of my shell. I've met friends here, Mom. Good ones that don't care if I have resting bitch face or struggle to start conversations out of nothing. I don't have to fill awkward silence or feel bad about not wanting to go out after work. They accept me."

She sucks in a sharp breath before I hear her cry. It's hardly audible, but I catch it instantly. "So not all was lost, then. You're happy there."

"Yeah, I'm happy."

Really happy. Scarily happy. Somehow, everything I wasn't expecting to find in Cherry Peak, I did.

"I hope you know that you don't have to come back here. Not for me and your dad. Not for yourself. Not for anyone. Do you understand me, Aurora Bennett?"

I don't have the heart to tell her that it's not that simple. Not right now, when emotions are so high and I'm shaking like a leaf in the rain.

"I love you, Mom," I say instead.

"I love you more, Aura. Please don't take so long to talk to me next time. I missed your voice so much."

"I'll call you tomorrow."

"Thank you."

After a few more words, we hang up, and I tuck my phone away before it can get any more wet than it already is. Some of the pressure on my chest is gone. But there's still so much left. Questions and decisions and hard calls that I don't want to think about making right now.

Instead, I stand and start back the way I came. Only I don't get far before I'm halting and blinking profusely to make sure I'm not seeing things. Because leaning against the fence, his hair soaked and curling into his eyes, is Johnny.

34

Johnny

I LET AURORA GO, BUT THAT DOESN'T MEAN I WASN'T GOING TO still keep an eye on her. Being alone in a city as big and unfamiliar as Toronto, it would be far too easy to get lost or hurt or a million other terrifying things that I don't want to think about.

So, I let her run off, but like a level five stalker, I retraced her steps the moment I got off the elevator. The receptionist wanted nothing to do with me when I asked which way Rory had turned outside of the building, but she didn't hold off too long. Maybe I looked as concerned as I felt, or maybe she still had a soft spot for my imaginary goldendoodle. Either way, I took off without a second look at the building and its shitty residents.

Luck led me to the park, a tug in my subconscious that I followed blindly. It was easy to spot her on the bench, her blonde hair a shade darker wet. I wanted to run to her but forced myself to lean against the fence and watch her surroundings instead of her, not wanting to intrude on the conversation happening. Even when her sobs tore through the air and landed against my chest like heavy blows, I stayed with my back glued to the fence.

The conversation lasts minutes but feels like hours. I watch her shake and cry and turn damn near blue before tucking the phone back in her pocket and standing, her tears washed away in the rain.

Our eyes meet then. She blinks away her disbelief before smiling at me. It's a good thing she's the one to rush toward me because my knees wobble at the sight of those white teeth and crinkles at the corner of her mouth.

"What are you doing here?" she asks in awe, her hands finding purchase on my chest. They spread across the distance of it before smoothing over my shoulders and back again. "You're soaking wet."

I cup her cheeks and frown at the frozen skin. The rain stopped bothering me soon after I got to the park, but the thought of her getting sick from standing out in the cold doesn't sit right with me. "You're freezing."

Her smile melts into something soft and smooth. "Not anymore."

"Are you okay? Can we go back to the hotel?"

"What are you doing here, Johnny? Why are you standing in the rain when you could be somewhere warm and dry? I told you I wanted to be alone."

"And you thought I'd let you wander around in an unfamiliar place on your own when you're upset? Come on, darlin'. You know better than that."

"So, what is it, then? You're just a nice guy? You were looking out for me?"

I furrow my brows and drift my thumbs over her cheekbones in an attempt to bring some warmth to her skin.

"You tell me, Rory. Why do you think I came after you? Yes, I'm a nice guy, and yes, I was looking out for you. But we both know it's so much more—"

"I love you, Johnny."

My teeth clack from the force I use to shut my mouth. Surprise has me staring at her like an idiot rather than a man who just had a gift laid at his feet.

She laughs so softly I nearly miss it. "I love you. And I'd love if you took me back to our hotel room now."

I'm positive nothing has ever sounded as good—*as right*—as those words. They shift my entire world, making it brighter and warmer and complete. My next breath is the clearest I've ever taken.

I push my hand behind her head and tip it back while tangling my fingers in her wet hair. Her eyelids droop as I brush my lips over hers and bring our bodies flush. Rain drips down my nose and collects above her top lip, so I lick it off.

"Say it again," I murmur.

She moves her head side to side. "It's already two to none."

"I thought it was obvious," I say, teasing her just a bit. Fuck knows I can't help it when it comes to this woman.

Her eyes narrow as she leans up to nip at my mouth, a hand wandering up my neck to tug at the curled hairs there. "Say it."

"I love you, Aurora Bennett."

"Then kiss me in the rain, you helpless romantic," she demands, voice hoarse and breathless.

I don't have to be told twice. Dropping my mouth, I kiss her softly before slowly starting to press harder. I guide her forward, drawing her up further on her toes to chase me. The effect she has on me is electrifying. Once I get a taste of her, I can't stop, and once her small hands drop to my hips, I have to force myself off and away before we get a ticket for public indecency.

"Hotel," she whispers, rubbing her nose to mine.

"Yeah, let's go to the hotel."

"WE NEED to get you warmed up," I say once we step into our hotel room and shrug our dripping jackets off.

We should pick them up and wring them out properly before hanging them to dry, but I'm already trying really hard to focus on not rutting her up against the wall, so I'll focus on that instead.

"Shower?" she asks, flicking on the light inside the small room and peeking at me over her shoulder.

"Are you inviting me to join you?"

With a roll of her eyes, she pinches the hem of her shirt and peels the wet material from her torso before dropping it on the floor. I stretch, then curl my fingers, taking in the sight of her goosebump-covered skin and hard nipples, which strain inside her bra.

"Shower with me, Johnny. You need one just as bad as I do."

Permission granted, I'm stepping into the bathroom behind her and cranking the dial in the shower as hot as I think we'll be able to take. It's a nice bathroom, with white tile and a glass-doored shower with a separate bathtub. The quality of the space means shit to us right now, though. We could be in a sleazy pay-by-the-hour motel room, and it wouldn't matter.

"I love you," I tell her for the millionth time since we slid into the cab outside the park.

She smiles coyly, popping open the button of her jeans and beginning to shimmy them down her thighs. "I love you."

"You're not leaving this bathroom without having had my mouth all over you, Rory. I've tasted you before, but never when you were mine. *Truly* mine. I want to start from the beginning all over again."

Her jeans pool around her ankles before she steps out of them and reaches for me. I go to her without a second thought, her nails scratching my hip bones. When she starts to lift my shirt up, I work on my jeans at the same time. Her palm is so hot against my abs that I jerk at her touch. I'm cold on the outside but burning alive on the inside.

"You're stealing my thunder," she says, eyes dropped to watch as I push my briefs and jeans down in one movement. Her throat works with a swallow when my cock slaps against my abdomen, hard and wet with precum. "I was already planning on putting my mouth on you."

I take two steps backward into the shower and gasp when the scalding water hits my shoulders. Planting my hand on the slick tile wall, I groan, "Come taste, then, darlin'."

"Say please."

She sheds her bra and panties and follows me beneath the water, her eyes nearly rolling back at the heat against her frozen skin. I grip my cock in a tight fist and work it in slow movements, teasing myself. I'm harder than I've ever fucking been, and it's all because of the woman in front of me.

With a sigh, she presses me against the wall and licks up my throat. "I'm waiting."

"Please, sweetheart," I beg before my mind flashes white. She replaces my hand with hers and squeezes, learning how rock-solid I am. I speak without registering what I'm saying. "Please suck my cock. Take me in your throat and let me fill your belly with cum before I do the same to your pussy."

"Good boy," she whispers before lowering herself to the floor of the shower.

"Only yours. I'll be whatever you want me to be and do whatever you need me to, as long as you're the only one I do it for."

She doesn't answer with words.

Pressing her palm against the underside of my shaft, she holds it against my stomach and draws a hot line with her tongue from my balls all the way to the tip before sucking me deep, moaning loud. I fling my head back, letting it hit the wall as I reach down and smooth my hand over her head.

"How deep can you take me, Rory?"

Fire lights her eyes as she curls her fingers around my shaft and lowers her head, pulling me deeper and deeper before gagging when I hit the back of her throat. Spit drips over the length of me as she retreats and swipes her tongue over the tip.

"Try again, baby. One more time, like the good girl you are," I coax, so far out of my mind I can't make much sense out of anything but the pressure building in my groin.

I've never felt the need to come so quickly in my life, but the knowledge that she loves me while sucking my cock is driving me so far out of my goddamn mind I'm one breath away from exploding.

She nods, determination tugging at her features before I'm cursing and my balls are drawing up tight. Relaxing her throat, she slips me further than last time and inhales through her nose before pulling back.

"I'm gonna come in your mouth. Swallow it all, baby," I rasp, my fingers curling in her hair and tugging.

Pressing her thighs together, she nods and sticks out her tongue before jerking my cock into her mouth. She blinks up at me and watches as I come, my lungs pinched tight and thighs shaking.

Cum coats her tongue and slips from the corner of her mouth, but she doesn't stop stroking me until there's nothing left and I'm hauling her to her feet.

"Swallow," I demand.

She does, the elegant lines of her throat stretching with the motion before she parts her lips and shows me it's gone.

I shake my head, my thoughts scattered as I wrap her in my arms and hold her beneath the water. When my body stops shaking, I realize I was the entire time. From her, not the cold.

"It's my turn," I say a moment later, my mouth to her ear.

She shivers, nodding into my chest. "Not here."

"No. Not here. I want you laid out for me somewhere I can worship you properly."

I turn off the shower and ignore the towels before leading her out of the bathroom. We drip water onto the carpet as we bypass our suitcases and the small desk before she falls back onto the bed.

Once her head is nestled in the mountain of pillows, I climb on after her. She reaches up to hold my shoulders as I hover above her and trace the edge of her face with my knuckles. Her breath catches when I get to her lips and part them with my thumb.

"You're so beautiful, Aurora. I never thought I'd find someone like you."

"Someone like me?"

I hum in approval, kissing her nose while moving a hand down the length of her body. Lush curves and soft skin for miles.

"Someone who hears me and sees me for who I am beneath the humour and the grins. Yeah, that's who I am most of the time, but with you, I don't always have to be. You've given me the safe space to be myself, and I hope I've done that for you as well."

She jerks her chin, eyes flicking between mine. "You have."

I drop my head and press my lips to her collarbones, then the swell of both breasts. "You're strong and kind and brave. You don't let events from the past dictate who you'll be in the future. I love that about you. Fuck, I love everything about you."

Inching down her body, I drag my lips over her breast, laving at her nipple before shifting to the soft, warm skin of her stomach.

"I'd never seen a woman like you before that night in Peakside. You grabbed my attention with no effort. I remember thinking that I had never seen someone as gorgeous as you before. With your deep blue eyes and blonde hair, plump lips the colour of bubble-gum lollipops, and the curves I wanted to feel beneath my palms. I couldn't have dreamed you up this perfectly."

She wiggles beneath me, her touch growing harder, more fevered. I keep my gaze on her body as I drag my parted lips over her belly button and between her legs. Her thighs are soft beneath my mouth, and I give them my full attention, kissing and sucking and nipping at them one at a time until she tries to push them together.

"Johnny," she whispers, fingers scratching at my scalp.

"Yes, darlin'?"

When I look up at her, my breath disappears. I've never seen her eyes so bright. So clear. I hold her gaze as I set my mouth over her pussy and lick up her wetness.

"Oh fuck," she curses, hips jerking up against my face.

She's drenched, and my eyes roll back as I dip my tongue into her tight hole and feast on her. The panted breaths escaping her are telling enough, but the desperate way in which she touches me adds to my confidence. I could spend hours down here. Days or weeks, even.

Aurora turns me into a feral animal, and I think I could enjoy this feeling for eternity.

"Fuck me, Johnny. Please, I need to feel you inside of me," she pleads.

I pull my mouth from between her legs and lick my lips before nodding. I'm still rock-solid, not yet sated despite my earlier orgasm. "I'd give you anything you want. Tell me what you need, and you'll always get it."

Desperate to sink inside of her for the first time, I go to leap off the bed and grab a condom. Fingers wrap around my wrist, stopping me.

"I don't want anything between us. If you're okay with that too. I'm on the shot," she rambles, cheeks pink.

I settle back on top of her, cupping her hip, my thumb stroking the goosebumped flesh. "You're offering me the chance to feel you for the first time with nothing between us, Rory. That's real fuckin' okay with me."

Her lips tug at the corner. "Then what are you waiting for?"

I don't tease her back. My heart thrashes in my chest, my love for her spilling over. With a surprisingly steady hand, I hoist her leg around my hip and run my cock over her slit, smearing her wetness along it. She moans softly, covering the hand I have on her hip with hers.

"Are you ready?" I ask, needing to be sure.

"I'm more ready than I've ever been for anything."

I sink into her as gently as I can. The walls of her sex suck me in, so wet and warm I black out for a moment before blinking back awake to find her staring at me, mouth gaping.

"Jesus Christ," I mutter, pulling out to push back in, feeding her a couple more inches this time. "You can take more."

Her eyes are glazed as she nods, nails digging into the top of my hand. "You feel so good," she slurs.

Finally, I bottom out and suck in a long breath before slipping back until just the head remains tucked inside of her. When I thrust back in, she cries out, chest bouncing at the impact.

"Do that again," she orders, fingers dipping between her legs to tug at her clit.

I follow her orders, driving into her with fast, hard thrusts that make the orgasm I had in the shower pale in comparison to the one growing right now. Swatting her hand away from her clit, I replace her fingers with mine. She's so slick that every swirl of my finger around her clit is sloppy.

Shifting my position, I lower my body over hers and dig my elbow into the mattress so I can kiss her. She whines into my mouth, begging for more and twisting her hips beneath me in search of it.

"Take it, baby. Take this cock and come all over it like my good fucking girl," I groan, feeling my release climbing closer to the surface. She opens her eyes and nods, my praise feeding her in a way I haven't experienced before. "Need to feel you gripping me tight when I fill you full of my cum."

"Yes," she coos, gripping my shoulders as I fuck her hard, nails digging into my skin. "Almost there. So close."

"That's it. That's fucking it."

The force of my thrusts has her gasping in pleasure as I twirl her clit between my fingers. Her scream fills the room, and it sparks a flame within me that has me thirsty for the knowledge that everyone in this hotel will know that this woman is mine.

"Now, Rory. Come for me now, baby," I mutter, my spine tingling as I lose it and flood her walls with cum.

Her pussy quivers and tightens around me as she arches her back and screams again. "Yes! *Yes*. Oh my God, I'm coming."

Her words intensify my release. Up becomes down, and off is on as I work her through her orgasm and suck in lungfuls of air. It's minutes before we stop, both of us falling from the high and smacking back to earth. I bury my face in her neck and cover her sweat-flushed skin with kisses.

"I've never, *ever* had sex like that before," she admits, still sounding out of breath.

"Me either."

"You're the first man I've had sex with without a condom."

I pull my face from her throat and lift my brows in disbelief. "Yeah?"

"Yeah."

Dipping a hand between her legs, I drag my pointer finger through her lips and find the mess of cum leaking from inside of her. She's wet and puffy as I scoop it up and push it back inside.

Humming a moan deep in her throat, she asks, "That's very caveman of you."

"You make me feel very caveman. Like I should carry you over my shoulder to my lair and keep you there forever."

She fidgets beneath me and runs her hands up and down my back. "You could."

"I could, but you'd wind up hitting me over the back of the head with a club eventually. I'd tell one too many bad jokes, and you'd decide enough is enough," I tease.

"I don't think I'll ever think enough is enough with you."

My chest warms at the admission. "You've grown soft on me, darlin'."

"I don't hate it, though."

"No? Good." I pull my finger free from her pussy and wipe it on my thigh before saying, "We should shower again."

"In a minute."

"I've heard that before, and we ended up falling asleep."

"Would it be so bad if we did?"

I kiss her once more, lingering with my lips brushing hers. "No. But I need to take care of you first this time."

"Okay," she agrees on an exhale.

Pulling away from her feels impossible. The moment we're apart, I want to be right up against her again. She watches me with the same desperate gleam in her eyes, and I wink, loving how she rolls her eyes after.

When I lean back on my knees, she follows before slipping off the bed. I'm glued to her back the moment she steps toward the bathroom, and for the rest of the night, we don't stray further than an inch from one another.

We can't bring ourselves to.

35

Aurora

"Are you ready yet?" Bryce hollers from my living room.

I ignore her for the third time since she started asking and continue staring at myself in the mirror. Pinching the thin straps of my new sundress on both my shoulder, I tug them up and watch as my boobs lift to their proper height for a dress like this.

Going braless was Poppy's idea, but considering the heavy sag I'm seeing right now, I'm one bad thought away from putting one on, straps showing or not.

"Your tits look great," Poppy says. I look away from my reflection to find her peeking her head in the bedroom door. "Trust me, you don't want to be adjusting your bra straps all day trying to hide them. You have bigger things to focus on."

"Like meeting my boyfriend's moms for the first time or having to do that while also pretending I love big social events like these?"

It's been a week since Johnny and I got back from Toronto, and everything has been good. Really good. Fucking *incredible* enough that I haven't had much time alone to think about what happened with Lee.

Eliza took one look at me my first morning back on the ranch and decided not to ask about the trip. I didn't know how to tell her how much I appreciated that, so I said nothing, but she knew. Without hesitation, she began telling me about the upcoming barbeque Johnny's moms invited them to, my trip to Toronto becoming nothing but a bad memory.

That's how it's been every day since. Work hours full of conversation with Eliza and lunches full of shameless flirting and kissing with Johnny. My nights are a mix of all of the above with him, if we manage to stay out of the bedroom long enough to talk. That hasn't happened often.

The first time I got back on Frost after tearing my thighs up, we spent an hour exploring the ranch. Over the past few days, I think I've covered most of it. Johnny says I haven't, but I think he just wants an excuse to continue riding with me.

He doesn't need an excuse; I just haven't told him that yet.

Poppy sways into the room and flops down on the edge of my bed. A quick glance down proves that she doesn't seem to be experiencing the same sagging issue, even if her chest is undoubtedly bigger than mine. Somehow, she's able to wear a sundress like mine without a bra and not look like she could toss her boobs over her shoulders and tie them in a knot.

"Boob tape," she answers the question I didn't ask. "I've got some in my purse if you want. I'm not trying to come on to you here, but I can help you tape yours up if you want."

"I don't think it would be a shame to have a woman like you come onto me anyway," I mutter before looking back in the mirror. Cupping my boobs, I nod. "Get the tape."

She hops up and out of the room, returning a beat later with Bryce in tow. Bryce doesn't check out my chest the way Poppy did. Instead, she spreads herself out on the mattress with her eyes to the ceiling, in her own world.

Poppy ushers me into the bathroom, and I release a relieved sigh at the lack of other eyes on me for this. Bryce wouldn't judge me, but me and Poppy . . . we're more similar body-wise. There's something comforting about looking at someone and seeing the same thick thighs and protruding belly that you live with every day.

She shuts the door with a flick of her wrist. "Okay, just pull down the top, and I'll perk those titties right up."

I huff a laugh and do as she says. It's obvious that she's done this a few hundred times as she snips the exact amount of tape needed and peels the backing off before methodically sticking it to my skin in every which way. I watch her work, trying to memorize the spots she tapes and which way she pulls my boob to lift it properly. By the time she claps and steps back, I look like I've gotten a goddamn boob job.

"You should sell classes on that," I mutter while pulling my dress back up.

"If you knew how many sets of boobs I've touched while taping, you'd think I was the one in the group that was into women," she teases before opening the door.

I glance at my reflection in the vanity mirror and feel a swell of appreciation build in my chest. Refusing to overthink it, I turn and pull Poppy into a hug.

"Thank you."

She returns the embrace and squeezes me tight. "You're welcome. Having best friends means you'll always have someone to help lift your tits whenever you need. I'd have walked around behind you all day, lifting them with my hands if you needed me to. Any of us would have."

Leaning back against the sink, I meet her gaze and jump over the last hurdle between us. "I have some things to tell you. Both of you."

She nods slowly. "We're here to listen. Come on, Bryce is probably snooping through your things."

We leave the bathroom, and despite what Poppy expected, Bryce hasn't gone through any of my drawers. Poppy perches on the edge of the bed and tugs on Bryce's ankle to get her attention.

"Sit beside me," she orders her.

Brow lifted, Bryce scoots down to sit beside her. "Yes, ma'am."

The weight of their eyes on me makes my skin itch, but I ignore it. The kindness in the way they watch me is enough to settle me.

"Wanda is my sister," I blurt, ripping off the Band-Aid. "We share a father, and I came here to find them both. To learn about them."

"Oh, wow. I didn't see that coming," Bryce says, the first to recover from the news.

Poppy frowns, tapping at her knee. "Wanda Wanda? Like Wanda Rose?"

"Lee Rose is your father?" Bryce asks.

I nod at them both. "I should have told you sooner. And I know Anna isn't here, but I didn't want to wait any longer."

"You didn't need to tell us shit, Aurora," Bryce huffs, leaning forward slightly. "If you weren't comfortable sharing, then that's that. You're telling us now, so it doesn't matter what happened before."

"You three have been nothing but kind to me, and I was keeping this from you. I'm not the most open person. I don't make friends easily, *clearly*, and I was just freaked out to tell you so much and then leave once we grew close. It's a stupid thing to fear, but that's me. An overthinking grump," I admit.

Poppy reaches out and takes my hand. "We're human. We get afraid and worry, so we tell ourselves a million bad things just because we can. That doesn't make us bad people."

"You've been really good friends to me. Better than I've ever had."

"You deserve it," Poppy says.

Bryce's stare is intimidating, but not necessarily in a bad way. "Is there anything we can do to help? Does Wanda know?"

I exhale a laugh. "Yeah, she knows. We've only spoken a few times, but things are . . . tense, to say the least."

"It's an odd situation for both of you, I'd imagine. Have you spoken to Lee? Does *he* know?" Poppy asks.

"He knows," I answer tensely before dropping to sit on my ass in front of them and explaining everything that happened in Toronto. About every dismissive look and sharp, disbelieving comment.

By the time I'm done speaking, they look like they'd push the man in front of a moving car if given the chance. I smile at their protectiveness, knowing exactly how lucky I am to have them.

"I always knew he was a fucking prick not worth everything he's gotten in life," Bryce mutters.

I tuck my leg beneath my ass, humming in agreement. "I'm thirty years old and made it through the majority of those years without knowing him. I'll be fine once I get over the sting of rejection, but I just wanted to know all these random little things. Like if I have more family out there and if we have any genetic issues I should know about. What if I have aunts and cousins out there too? Maybe all of this is silly, but I still wanted to know."

"It's not silly at all. Whether or not you need him, it has to be impossible not to want to know him still. You share his DNA, Rory. That isn't nothing," Poppy says.

"Wanda could give you some of those answers. She's always said she isn't close with her family, but she'll still know some things," Bryce suggests.

I know they're right. But Wanda terrifies me. Maybe more so than Lee does. While he's a righteous asshole, she doesn't seem all that bad. Her acceptance is the one I want most, so what happens if I can't get it?

"Do you think she'll be at the barbeque?"

I don't know if she's even still in town. I've heard nothing from her since before I left, but I hope that she'd at least say something if she were leaving again.

"Johnny's moms invited nearly the entire town. If you were going to find Wanda anywhere, it would be there," Bryce says.

"Daisy will be there." Poppy smirks at Bryce.

Bryce glares at her, and maybe it's the lighting in here, but I swear her cheeks are pinking up. "Obviously. She's a Mitchell."

"Am I missing something?" I ask.

Poppy leans into Bryce. "Well, since we *are* in honesty hour right now, Bryce has had a crush on Daisy Mitchell for what . . . four years now?"

"I don't have a fucking crush. I'm not a teenager," Bryce snaps.

"An obsession, then." Poppy looks at me, that evil gleam still in her eyes. "Daisy's been gone for school, but she's got to be almost done by now. Have you met her yet?"

"I met her once. She helped me out when I needed it."

"Not surprising. Daisy and Johnny are like two halves of the same person."

Bryce stands and crosses her arms over her chest. She ignores Poppy and stares right at me. "That's exactly why you can't say anything to Johnny. God, with the mouth on him, everyone would be talking about this by tomorrow morning."

I straighten my spine. "In Johnny's defense, I don't think he'd tell your secrets to anyone. But yeah, this stays between us. I promise."

"Good. Because it would be rumours, anyway. I'm not obsessed with Daisy. Poppy's just trying to poke at me."

"I wouldn't need to use Daisy to poke at you, Ice, and you know it. The sooner you admit to yourself that you want that girl, the easier it'll be for all of us. I can only take watching you pine over her for so long."

Something passes over Bryce's face then. Longing, I think. It's so intense I nearly flinch.

She recovers quickly, steeling her expression in a way I'm familiar with. "We need to leave before we're the last to arrive and everyone stares at us when we walk in."

Poppy plants a big fat kiss on her cheek, whether because she just felt like it or as an apology, before standing and offering me a hand up. I touch Bryce's arm as we leave my bedroom, and she dips her chin at me in answer, a silent agreement coming to life between us.

One that promises we're in this together and that I'm here for her the same way she's here for me. I've never been happier to promise someone something before.

THE MITCHELLS' soft-blue-painted bungalow is adorable. The lawn is well-kept, with flowers in the beds beneath the windows and a stone walkway leading up to the front door with handprints sunken into every second stone. With the fence gate open, it's easy to see into the massive backyard and the crowds of people already there.

I shut Poppy's car door and step onto the curb. Bryce meets me first, and then Poppy joins us before we head up the stone path to the gate.

"What are his moms' names again?" I ask, starting to panic.

"Jennifer and Rachel. And his sisters are Giana, Josette, and Daisy. I don't think you'll meet Giana today. She hardly comes home anymore," Poppy says, rubbing my back.

"Right," I whisper.

Poppy pulls the gate the rest of the way open for us to slip through. "They're going to love you. This family is one of the best ones I know."

"There's my girl," Johnny drawls, striding toward us.

I hear Bryce snort beside me as I check him out in his Wrangler jeans, boots, and that deep brown cowboy hat. I've been trying to scoop it off his head and plant it on mine for the past week, but it's always the first thing he tosses off when he gets me in the bedroom. Maybe I can change that tonight.

His arms loop around my back as he tugs me into his chest and flicks his hat up before kissing me in front of everyone. My heart pounds at his proximity, and I kiss him back, throwing all my caution to the wind.

I've missed him, and I just saw him this morning. The ease with which I can admit that to myself goes to show how different I am from the person I was when I arrived in Cherry Peak. I think I like who I am now much more than I did then.

"Alright, Johnny. Save it for later. I'm literally right here," Bryce mutters.

He licks at my lips, and I let him in, letting him taste the shot of tequila I took before heading over here. Chuckling low in his throat, he pulls away and blows a kiss at Bryce.

"Stop turning down every single person who tries to take you out, Bryce, and you wouldn't have to be the only single one."

"You make a good point, but let's not forget about my brother," Poppy says.

"Darren's single because no woman can bear to be near him for longer than ten minutes at a time with his terrible romance skills," Bryce corrects her.

Johnny drapes his arm over my shoulders and tucks me into his side with a kiss to my temple. "You could always give him a shot. You wanna be a stepmommy, Brycie?"

Bryce's features twist into a look of pure disgust as she says, "Don't ever say that again. I'm perfectly fine with being an honorary aunt but never a stepmommy."

Poppy laughs beside us as we move along the side of the house toward the group of people blatantly staring at us. One face in the crowd has me a bit more alert. Wanda offers me a small smile before taking a swig of a beer.

"I've long since accepted that Bryce will never be my sister-in-law. We all know she'd eat Darren alive. I've made my peace with that," Poppy says.

"You make it sound like I've done you some great disservice by not being attracted to that ass."

"I love my brother, but he's not good enough for you, anyway. Besides, I always pictured you marrying a woman."

"I see that too," I add.

"Because I'm such a girl's girl?" Bryce asks with a laugh.

"Nah. It's just a vibe I get. You'd look beautiful beside a woman. Maybe one with red hair." Poppy pats her cheek and then swings out of the way as Bryce tries to swat at her. She laughs and starts to back away from us. "I'm going to find Garrison. I'm sure he's sitting alone sulking in a corner right now without me."

"Yeah, you run, Pops. Go hide behind your boyfriend before I kick you in the ass," Bryce threatens.

"You two are so fuckin' weird," Johnny says.

Bryce snorts before staring at the drink table and leaving us. "You've got no idea. I'll see you guys later."

"See you," I call.

Clouds of smoke drift our way, the smell of barbequed meat growing stronger. My stomach rumbles, making Johnny laugh.

"Did you eat today?"

"I was too busy having a wardrobe malfunction."

Tucking his face into my hair, he breathes over the back of my ears. "You look gorgeous. I've never seen you in a dress before."

"It was Poppy's idea," I murmur.

"Yeah, I bet it was. She's always wearing them to terrorize Garry. Now I know exactly why he's always complaining about them." He retreats enough to stare into my eyes, his grin toothy and pure. "What are you wearing beneath this dress, darlin'?"

"It's a secret."

"Fuckin' right, I bet it is."

"Behave and I'll let you see the moment we leave."

His smile drops into a smirk. "That right, baby? What if I reached beneath it right now and felt for myself?"

"I think you'd have to explain yourself to your moms," I whisper as I stare at the two women looking at me from over Johnny's shoulder. "I'm assuming that's them looking at us."

He moves slower than he should, keeping his arm slung over my shoulders. I make no move to wiggle out from beneath it. The heavy weight of it is comforting.

"How long have you been watching us like two creeps?" he asks the two older women, his grin returning.

The woman with the thick-rimmed glasses and deep brown eyes is the first to step in our direction, her pace hurried. The second woman follows after her, the similarities between her and Johnny taking me aback.

"Rory, this is my mama, Rachel," Johnny says, looking at the woman in the glasses before glancing at the second woman. "And this is my mom, Jennifer. Moms, this is Rory."

I thrust my hand out for them to shake, but Rachel swats it away and hugs me instead. The move is so similar to one Eliza would make that it drags a laugh up my throat.

"It's nice to meet both of you," I say.

"Oh, you as well. We were starting to think you were a figment of Johnny's imagination," she blubbers, rubbing my back in a soothing way.

Jennifer offers me a warm smile over Rachel's shoulder. "Are you a hugger, Aurora? We should have asked if you were okay with hugs first."

Rachel gasps and shoves herself away from me, guilt shining in her eyes. "I'm so sorry! I just got so excited and messed this all up already."

"You're fine. Hugs are fine," I say quickly, offering one to Jennifer in hopes my actions speak louder than my lack of words.

She sweeps me into her arms without another moment of hesitation. Lowering her voice, she tells me, "Thank you. My wife would have worried about this for weeks."

"I'm not sure I could be with your son without being okay with hugs." Stepping back and looking at Rachel, I add, "You've raised an incredible son."

She raises a hand to her chest. "Thank you. I'm very excited to get to know you. Johnny hasn't stopped singing your praises."

He comes back to my side and slides his arm along my back,

palming my hip. His wink makes my stomach flutter. "Don't try and freak her out, Mama. She's here to stay."

Here to stay. Is that what I am?

I'm still here, aren't I? There should be no reason as to why I haven't gone back home now that Lee is a lost cause. Wanda doesn't seem to want much to do with me. I haven't even attempted to approach her again to get a clear answer as to if she wants to get to know me. Instead, I've lingered, doing everything I can to keep myself from thinking about going back to Calgary.

That city isn't my home anymore. But the weight of that realization is too scary. I've been ignoring it out of fear. Once I admit it to myself, I have to make a decision far bigger than I was ever expecting to make on this trip.

Johnny's fingers stroke my hip, the heat from them warming me through my dress. I turn my head to stare up at him, wishing we were alone. He'd know what to say to help settle my mind. I need him to say a million things to me right now, and that desperation is sinking deeper and deeper as we stand here.

Feeling the weight of my gaze, he drops his to look at me, his expression growing tender as he takes me in. "I think it's time we get some food. You good with that, darlin'?"

I jerk my head in agreement. My smile is strained when I flash it at his moms and let him start guiding me away. My goodbye is weak. "We'll talk again today."

The two of them don't look put off by our quick retreat, and I release a heavy breath at that.

"They're going to hate me."

"Who? My moms?" Johnny asks, doing a visual sweep of the backyard.

"Yes. I'm so fucking awkward."

"They loved you, Rory. Trust me."

I do. That's the only reason I haven't ducked out and run off. "Do they really know all of these people?"

"This is a small turnout, believe it or not. If Brody weren't on tour right now, he'd be singing a couple of songs, and people from towns over would have come to see."

"And this happens how many times a summer?" I ask, my tone heavy with anxiety.

He laughs, kissing my temple. "Just this once, I promise."

"Alright. I can do once."

Tugging us beneath the draping willow tree in the corner of the yard, he takes my chin between his fingers and crowds my face, blocking out everyone around us.

"What happened back there? You looked upset. Like you were stuck in your head."

"I don't want to talk about it here."

"But we will talk about it, right?"

I focus on the soothing feeling of his fingers on my skin and let my eyes drift shut. "Yes."

He drifts his lips over my nose. "Eliza and Wade are here. There's a couple with them that I haven't seen before. They've been watching you since you got here," he murmurs.

My eyes snap open, immediately staring into his. "You don't think . . ."

"That they're Lee's parents? Yeah, sweetheart, I do. Tell me what you want to do here, and we'll do it."

"Eliza must have called them," I say on a breath.

"She saw how you were when you got back and made the call on her own. It's a very Eliza move."

"I want to talk to them."

"Then that's what you'll do."

I grip his belt buckle, feeling the bite of the cool metal. "Come with me. Please."

"I will. But I'm getting you food first. You need to eat."

"You're being demanding again," I tease lightly, unable to help myself.

"Just practicing for later. Now, come before your stomach growls loud enough for everyone around us to hear."

36

Johnny

Daisy steals a grape from Aurora's plate and continues to talk her ear off with information on our parents and sisters. Our moms are watching from the end of the patio table, speaking amongst themselves instead of joining our conversation. They've always been the gentle, relaxed types, and from the single interaction they've had with Rory, they read her nearly as well as I can.

It doesn't take a rocket scientist to tell my girl isn't a social butterfly, and in an environment like this, where everyone's loud and cheery and lacks the ability to give you personal space, it's obvious she's a bit uncomfortable.

I've been to a million of these barbeques in my lifetime, and I've never been as happy at one as I am with her beside me, socially awkward or not. I'm pretty sure I could sit with her in silence for the rest of my life if given the opportunity.

Daisy, however, doesn't share the same sentiment. She thrives off conversation with friends or strangers and can't stay silent for longer than a few minutes at a time before starting up again. It's why she excels in school settings, especially with children. They talk even more than she does.

"Giana hates this town. She hasn't been back since last Christmas," she tells Rory, not bothering to hush her words.

"She doesn't hate this town. Her work doesn't give her many days off," I correct her.

"That's just an excuse she tells us so the moms don't lecture her." Daisy takes another grape from Aurora's plate and tells her, "Gi's the social media manager for the Vancouver Warriors NHL team. I'm pretty sure that means she gets summers off."

"So she gets to take videos of them doing those stretches on the ice for a living?" Rory asks.

I lean my elbow on the table and gape at her. "Is that what you've been doing once I fall asleep at night? Watching those videos?"

She shrugs. "No. I watch them while you're awake."

Daisy laughs so loud she draws the attention of nearly every person standing around the yard. She doesn't pay a single one of them attention as she keeps focused on Aurora.

"I like you. You've got that blunt honour that I think is all too refreshing."

"Some people think it's rude," Rory says.

"That's because some people think just about everything is rude when they lack a sense of humour."

Rory stares at my sister with a soft look, an appreciative one. It makes my chest damn near explode with affection. I'll be thanking Daisy for this later.

"One of these fuckers here stole the turkey burger I had Mama get grilled for me," Josette grumbles, taking the empty seat beside Aurora. She drops her plate to the table and jabs her fork into the heaping pile of potato salad she gave herself before shoving it into her mouth. "I should have had someone brand it with my initials or something."

Rory stares at her in surprise, and I hide my laugh with a cough. Daisy rolls her eyes at our older sister.

"Are you going to introduce yourself to Johnny's girlfriend, Josie Cat?" she asks.

As if just realizing the woman she sat beside is Aurora, Jos swallows loudly and snatches Daisy's napkin to wipe her mouth.

The glare she gives me before attempting a smile in Rory's direction threatens pain. "I'm Josette. Jos is preferred. I'm sorry that you saw that."

"I'm Rory. And don't apologize. You were being genuine."

"Genuinely *rude*," Daisy says.

Jos levels her with a dull look. "I'm hangry. You can leave me alone."

"Girls, can you please not fight at the dinner table? We're not at home right now. There are special guests with us," Mama says.

I stroke a hand across Rory's shoulder blades as if to remind myself that yeah, she actually is here with us right now. *With me.*

"I actually like the fighting. There wasn't anything like this for me when I was growing up being an only child and all," Rory says, her cheeks and neck turning pink as everyone stares at her.

"Well, you'll find a lot of it at our house. There's never a dull moment," Mom pipes up. "These three used to cause quite the uproar when they were kids. What was it that Jos stole from you, Johnny?"

"Which time?" I snort a laugh. "The worst I remember from back then was when she stole my DS because she wanted to play Nintendogs, then ended up dropping the whole damn thing in a puddle and broke it."

"Oh, God. Not the DS. You didn't go anywhere without that thing. What was the game you played all the time? Indiana Jones?" Daisy asks.

"*LEGO* Indiana Jones," I answer.

Jos taps her fork to her plate, grinning wide. "Shit, you were obsessed with that game and the movie."

"He dressed up as him for like six Halloweens in a row," Daisy adds.

Aurora picks up the last grape on her plate before Daisy can get to it and lifts it in front of her smirk. "I was the same way with Lara Croft and Tomb Raider."

Fuck. Of course she was the female equivalent of Indiana Jones. And she still doesn't believe in fate? Not a goddamn chance.

"Maybe you two should dress up in matching costumes for Halloween. There's always a big party for it at Peakside to celebrate our birthday," Daisy says.

Rory turns to me, surprised. "Your birthday is on Halloween?"

"Yeah, darlin'."

"I hate sharing a birthday with a day like Halloween, but it could be worse. We could have been born on Christmas," Daisy says, scrunching her nose.

"I should have asked you this before, but when's *your* birthday?" I ask Rory, scooting my chair as close to hers as I can. When our knees touch, I stop moving.

"May."

"Jos's birthday is in May," Daisy butts in.

I'm grateful that Rory and I have finished eating already because I'm desperate to get her away from my family. I love them to death, but they can be a lot.

"I think I heard that Darren and his daughter just got here," I announce, standing and beginning to collect our empty plates. "It would be rude not to welcome them."

Daisy looks around the yard. "You did? I didn't hear anything."

"Oh, well, we'll go check it out anyway."

Staring up at me with a knowing glint in her eyes, Rory lets me pile her plate atop mine. She gets to her feet and walks with me to the garbage bin I hauled in from the street for my moms this morning.

"You could have made up a better excuse than that," she

says, holding open the lid for me to dump our plastic plates inside.

"I wanted to be alone with you so badly I wasn't thinking straight."

"You're a cheeseball."

"Yet you love me anyway," I tease.

She rolls her eyes and drops the lid. "Yeah, I do."

"I'm sorry for my family. They were just excited to meet you and have another woman to talk to, as if five weren't already enough."

"I like them. It's nice to be surrounded by so much family."

"Yeah?" I can't help but grin, tucking my finger into one of her belt loops. "Can you imagine yourself here often? Not with this many people around, of course. But with my parents and sisters?"

She keeps her eyes on mine, her gaze open and honest as she says, "Yes."

My lips part on words that never come when she lifts her hand and, in one steady movement, steals the hat from my head before dropping it on hers.

It's too fucking big for her, drooping low in the front to shade her eyes but not low enough to hide her beaming grin. I focus on that smile while flicking the hat back and gripping her nape, tipping her head back.

"You make a claim like this in public, and there's no coming back from it, darlin'."

Her pupils swell, melting into the dark blue surrounding them. "Good. Do we get to leave now?"

My chuckle kisses her lips before I chase after them myself. "Yeah, baby. Let's go home."

And fuck it, I don't care which home I'm talking about. Hers or mine, it doesn't matter. I'd consider any place with her home.

The sound of a throat clearing close by has me stiffening, an unusual blast of possessiveness following after. Maybe it's the setting or the fact I have my woman standing in front of me asking me to take her home wearing my hat on her head, but I don't want a single other person close to us right now. I want her all to myself.

Leaning past her, I take a look at the couple waiting a few feet away from us and rein in my frustration. Inhaling deeply, I press my lips to her forehead and release her neck.

"James and Bernice?" I ask, dropping my hand to hold Rory's shoulder as she tenses at the names.

The elderly woman nods, her gaze so intense it's almost painful. Her hair is silver throughout and tied in a bun at the base of her skull, but she reaches upward to fiddle with it as if it were loose. When Rory turns to face them, Bernice sucks in a sharp breath.

"I knew you were Lee's daughter from across the yard, but up close . . ." The man trails off, staring at Rory in disbelief, like he can't believe it's really her.

He's much taller than his wife, but they share the silver-hair thing they have going on. The crinkles beside his eyes tell of a life filled with happiness and laughter, but that doesn't mean much right now.

"Did Eliza invite you here?" Rory asks bluntly.

Bernice's smile is nothing more than a slight curl at the corner of her mouth. "Yes. But please don't be upset with her. I'm happy she did. We both are."

"We should go inside if you want to talk more," I suggest, jerking my chin in the direction of the back sliding door leading inside the house. The gossip mill has got to be turning already, but some privacy is better than none.

Rory nods, and her approval is all that matters to me.

"That would be great," Bernice agrees.

I link my fingers with Rory's, and we move inside. My moms don't like to let everyone in during events like this without supervision, and I'm grateful for that right now as I welcome them into the living room and wait for them to sit on the couch before claiming a spot on the love seat. Aurora joins me, and I sling my arm over the back of the couch behind her so I can play with the ends of her hair.

Bernice sets a wrinkled hand on James's thigh and straightens, focusing on her granddaughter. "We . . . we don't know where to begin. An apology feels insubstantial."

"What do you have to apologize for?" Rory asks.

"That's the question, isn't it? Everything is too broad. But apologizing on behalf of our son isn't enough," James says.

Rory shifts, her thigh pressing hard to mine. "My mom didn't write about you much in the letters I found. I know a lot about her family, enough about your son, but not anything about you. That's what I'm most interested in. I have questions about you, but also about the Roses in general. Would you answer them for me?"

"Yes, yes you can ask anything you want. I—I'm sorry. We're just having a hard time believing what we're seeing. You're our granddaughter, no doubt about it. But when Eliza called, I could hardly believe her. It didn't seem logical. How could we have not felt you out there somewhere? We should have," Bernice says, her voice tapering into a pained whisper. "But I feel it now just looking at you. Right in my heart."

"So do I," James agrees, eyes full of bewilderment.

Rory holds firm, so damn strong. "Your son didn't share the sentiment."

Bernice flinches like Rory had reached across the gap between us and slapped her. She sniffles, blinking a dozen times. "I'm sorry. I'm so sorry."

"It's okay."

"What happened with Riley? Was this recent?" James asks.

"He could barely love the daughter he knew. How could he have possibly wanted another?" Aurora's voice cracks midway through, and I shift her as close to me as possible without tugging her onto my lap. She grips my knee and continues. "My relationship with Riley is non-existent, and it will stay like that.

The only thing I care about now is having someone answer my questions."

"Then let us answer them. We'll tell you everything we know," Bernice says, nearly rambling in an attempt to speak as quickly as possible.

James stares at Aurora, reading something in her expression that I wish I could see. "It doesn't have to be today. We know you're busy, and we've just sprung up in the middle of the day with no warning. We'll be here for a few days, staying over with Eliza and Wade. You want to talk, just give them a ring. Anytime, Aurora."

"Okay. Another day, then."

"Another day," Bernice agrees.

Nobody moves, as if commanded by some higher power to stay where we are, until Rory suddenly jolts to her feet. I join her, and then the Roses follow. It's one of the most awkward situations I've ever been in as we all stand in silence, Bernice and James watching Rory like she's a gift from God while she reaches for my hand and grips me for dear life.

There are no friendly goodbyes or hugs shared between anyone. Rory mutters a quiet "See you later," and her grandparents return the sentiment before I spin us around and we head right for the front door, bypassing the rest of the party.

Rory doesn't question me or where I'm taking us as we head for my truck. There's only one place I know will help clear her mind, and as far as I'm concerned, that's all that matters right now.

37

Aurora

FROST SHIFTS BENEATH ME, HER THICK, POWERFUL MUSCLES contracting as we trot through the field back to the stable. I've grown far more comfortable in her saddle and am looking forward to not having to waddle around tomorrow morning.

We pass the raspberry bushes, and Frost makes one hell of an effort to grab a mouthful. I let her this time, not having it in me to deny her of the treat, and Johnny laughs, clicking his tongue to encourage Joker to join her.

"You give in too easy," he tells me.

"She's been good tonight."

"Yeah, she has. She can sense your mood."

"Is that a fact?"

"It is. They're used for therapy sometimes."

I rub Frost's neck, feeling the tickle of her mane on my knuckles. "Is that why you brought me out here? For horse therapy?"

"In a way. Frost's a good girl, but I also thought a ride might help. The fresh air helps clear my mind when I'm upset. I wanted to see if it did the same for you."

I nod. "Eliza shouldn't have called them without asking me first."

"She shouldn't have," he agrees.

"But I'm also glad she did. At least now, I can learn what I need to and move on."

"Is that what you want? To learn and move on? What if they turn out to be really good people and want to be in your life? They looked real happy to see you, darlin'."

"Then I'll think about letting them in."

His exhale is heavy, weighed down with emotion. "You're more incredible than you believe you are, Aurora. It fuckin' kills me inside that you don't know your own worth. They would be lucky to spend time with you."

I wish he wasn't so far from me. The brim of his hat droops into my eyes again as I watch him. I push it up with the back of my hand before tugging softly on Frost's reins.

"I've been wearing this hat for a lot longer than I thought I was going to," I state, changing the subject to something safer.

His brow jerks upward as he rakes his fingers through his loose waves. "Oh? I just figured you'd give it back when you wanted to."

"I don't want to give it back."

It's adorable how innocent he can be sometimes. Like he doesn't expect me to want him the way I do. It's a shame, really, because I don't just want him. I ache for him. I'm beginning to think that's all I do.

"Be careful what you say, Rory. I've been rock-solid from the moment you set that hat on your head, but I'm tryin' to be polite and respectful, given what happened today," he warns, his tone a deep rumble in the night.

"That's a shame. I want you to do very non-polite things to me right now."

I watch as he drops a hand to his groin and curses, eyes flashing. My nipples are hard as rocks against my dress, and I'm seriously considering how easy it would be to hop off Frost right now and have him bend me over against a tree.

"You ready for a run, darlin'? This won't be a slow trot back."

Digging my heels into Frost, I wink at Johnny. My heart pounds in my chest, excitement making my blood sing. "Race you."

My laugh is loud and free as we take off, the steady thump of Frost's hooves in the earth creating a beat that I feel deep inside of me. The wind flows through the ends of my hair, and I clap a hand down on Johnny's hat to keep it from flying away.

Frost knows the way back to the stable better than I do in the dark, and she takes us there without hesitation. Joker runs after us, a whinny sounding when I glance over my shoulder and see them catching up.

I can't tear my eyes away from Johnny, not once he gets close enough I can make him out in the dark. His body sways in the saddle, but he moves with the horse in a way that I'm still trying to replicate. It's like they've moulded together, and that connection must play a part in how quickly they catch up to us.

Frost returns the whinny, and Johnny comes up beside me, leaning over to swat at my thigh.

"Got you."

"You're a cheater."

"I'm not a cheater. You're just not as good as me."

I hum, shaking my head despite my smile. "Sure."

The solar lights spread throughout the ranch illuminate the gravel road as we grow closer to the stable. We pass the guest house with the lights on and Poppy's red car parked out front. The fact Garrison still lets her drive that shit box is hard to believe.

Johnny slows Joker to a trot, and Frost follows suit. Her training is extensive, far more than I can comprehend. Maybe one day, I'll understand how much goes into training a horse.

"We'll tie 'em up outside for now," he says, leading us around the back side of the stable instead of to the big sliding door in the front.

"Alright."

Crickets chirp in the fields, and the lack of other noise settles something in me. A final piece slotting itself into a puzzle I hadn't known was unfinished until I arrived in Cherry Peak.

Johnny slips off Joker's back and loops her reins around a post before taking Frost's from me and doing the same. Once he's finished, he offers me his hand, and I take it, dropping to the ground beside him. My dismount is still shaky, but I catch myself easily this time around, no longer swaying as I adjust to the sudden change.

"You have a habit of leaving these two outside together. They're going to think you don't like them anymore," I say.

He chuckles low in his throat. The sound makes me break out in goosebumps, the hairs lifting on my arms.

"They'll survive. I'll tuck 'em in after."

"After?"

He's in my space in an instant, the close proximity making it hard to breathe with the all-consuming attraction I feel for him. I'm already wet between my legs from earlier, somehow never having come down from that state of arousal, even as my head filled with too many other things.

I tip my head back and curse this damn hat for blocking my view of him again. He smirks at my frustration and reaches behind me to push the back down, lifting the front. Without it in the way, he snares my eyes, and my stomach tumbles at the blatant need in his stare. The overwhelming possession and desire. It's hard to suck in full breaths.

"Do I need to spell it out for you?" he asks, his drawl thickening.

"I wouldn't mind the clarification."

"Mm, right." Every step he takes toward me, I take one back. His smirk widens. "It would be easier to show you what I want."

My chest rises and falls rapidly in time with my breaths. "Show me, then."

We've wound up behind the stable, with nothing around us

but endless miles of grass and the stars above us. Johnny pins me beneath his gaze, and I go still. He sets a hot palm on my waist and turns me, pressing my back against the stable wall. The siding is rough against my arms, and I arch into his chest on instinct.

"I told myself I was going to wait. That I'd take us back to my place and have you ride me proper, my hat on your head and nothin' else. But fuck me, darlin'. I can't wait. I'm too goddamn hot for you," he rasps, shaking his head like he's angry.

If he's angry about wanting me this badly, then I'm furious.

"Poppy told me that men love sundress season," I whisper, tipping my head back to kiss the underside of his jaw. "Is that true?"

"I love every season when it comes to you."

I smile, curling my fingers around his bicep. "That's not what I asked."

His Adam's apple bobs as he drops his head and kisses me softly before pulling back. I chase his lips, leaning forward to taste him again. I'm buzzing beneath my skin and between my legs. If I hadn't worn panties tonight, I'm positive I'd be dripping down my legs at this point.

"I can't speak for all men, Rory. And right now, the thought of other men taking up space in that head of yours makes me want to fuck you like a beast, and I'm not a beast, darlin'. That's not me."

"You make me feel like one too," I admit softly, drifting my touch down the length of his arm and circling his wrist.

He drops his eyes to where I hold him, watching with strained focus as I guide his hand to my chest, between my breasts, where I know my heart thumps for him. His breaths are huffed, growing louder in the silence the further down my body I bring his hand. I shiver, unable to help it.

"Are you going to let me take you here, beautiful? Because if not, I need you to stop."

I don't think I've ever heard his voice so garbled and

strained. Not even our first time together. This is different, heavier. Something almost permanent about it.

Gathering the bottom hem of my dress with my opposite hand, I bring his to rest between my legs, answering him without words. I witness the moment he feels how wet my panties are. His pupils expand, jaw straining with tension. A hot, damp puff of air hits my lips a second before he's kissing me hard and dipping his tongue deep, stroking mine with it.

I lose grip on his wrist when he twists it and tugs my panties to the side, exposing my bare pussy to the evening air. The first stroke of his finger along my slit has me jerking against the wall.

"Wanted to slip my hand beneath your dress all day. But this . . . this is worth the wait. All of this is for me? Fuck, I'm a lucky man."

"I've ruined my panties."

"No," he mutters, moving his finger from where I want it. Suddenly, I feel a sharp sting on my hip before the sound of ripping fabric hits my ears and a cool breeze rushes over my entire mound. "Now they're ruined."

He lifts my pink panties between us, his eyes crossing slightly before he brings them to his mouth and sucks the gusset. My cheeks flare with heat as he pulls my arousal from the fabric and groans as he does it.

Pulling them from his mouth a beat later, he licks his lips. I watch as he tucks my panties into the back pocket of his jeans and lowers himself to his knees in front of me. My nails dig into the thick material of my dress, keeping it up so I'm bared to him.

"That was good, but you taste so much better like this," he mutters before parting my pussy with his thumb and forefinger and licking up the length of me. "Fuck yeah, that's it."

I gasp an inhale and release my dress, slapping my hand to the wall instead. The material falls over his head, draping over him as he feasts on me, knowing exactly what to do to drive me to the edge quicker and quicker each time.

Two fingers slide inside, stretching me as he flicks my clit with his tongue. Curling his fingers, he applies pressure to my G-spot and strokes it over and over until I'm crying out.

"Shh, you'll draw attention to us," he warns, teasing his teeth over my clit.

I shake, biting down on my tongue to stifle my moans. I've never done anything like this in public before, and even though we're hidden, it wouldn't be hard for someone to find us here. Why does that make me ache even more?

"I need you to come for me now, darlin'. I'm close to comin' in my pants, and I don't want to waste it in my briefs instead of buried deep in your cunt."

"Your mouth is fil—" I start before losing the words.

A third finger drives into me, and I lose my vision as my mind gets swept out from under me. I scream without sound, my throat bared to the sky. Johnny's moans vibrate over my clit as he sucks hard until I push him away, too sensitive.

He pulls his head from beneath my dress, expression feral with the desire for more. I'm a rag doll for him, allowing him to move me every which way when he gently grabs my arms and twists me to face the wall. With a hand to my spine, he encourages me to bend.

"Put your hands on the wall, baby."

The siding scrapes at my palms as I do as I'm told, too blissed-out to argue. There's no reason to, anyway. I'm too empty, ready and desperate for him to slide deep. To feel that connection that only him buried inside of me brings.

"You're a vision," he mumbles, almost to himself.

I moan mindlessly, closing my eyes. My dress is flipped up, my bare ass exposed before he's dipping his hand between my legs and stroking me again, spreading my wetness around.

The sound of his belt buckle clacking and his zipper lowering blows on the wind, and then he's there, the soft head of his cock spreading me and sliding between my lips. He nudges it inside of me, giving me a sliver of pleasure before taking it away and pulling back.

"Please, Johnny," I breathe out.

"I'm the one that begs. Not you. Not ever you."

"So beg. I need you now."

He pulls my hair to one side, baring my neck before bringing his lips to it and sucking on my frantic pulse. "Please let me fuck you. Please let me pleasure you the way you deserve. I want to fill you up with so much cum it drips down your thighs the entire way home."

"Yes. Yes, you can. Do it now," I order, the sharpness in my voice only seeming to turn him on more.

"Fuck," he spits before sliding in, every inch of him filling me to the point I wonder if he'll be imprinted there for days.

I drop my head forward, his hat slipping again. The feel of it brushing my forehead serves as another reminder of him, and I know I'm going to come soon, quicker than I ever have before.

"You're my paradise, Rory. The only place I ever want to be," he swears, slipping a hand around my front to tug at my clit while fucking into me harder and harder, not stopping once. "I've never felt like this. Not once."

"Me either," I whisper, his thrusts making my breasts swing beneath me. They're so heavy, so sensitive. "My safe place."

He drives harder while slowing the pace. Every forward glide steals my breath, the pleasure turning my vision spotty.

"Right there," I gasp.

Repeating the exact same motions, he asks, "Right here?"

Tears fill my eyes, the pressure on that perfect spot inside of me bringing me ecstasy. "I'm coming."

"I feel it. Squeeze me and take my cum, sweetheart," he grunts before I feel a blast of warmth deep inside of me.

His hand slides up my front and rests over my heart, slowing his thrusts until he stops completely. I don't bother pretending I'm not gasping for breath as he keeps his hand on my chest and feels the thrashing of my heart beneath it.

"You're my forever girl. My wish on a shooting star," he says, the words spoken like a prayer. "I've been waiting for you."

My tears aren't from pleasure this time. Just happiness. Love. They drip down my cheeks as I nod frantically.

"I was waiting for you too."

38

Aurora

"This damn stable has turned into a headache," Eliza gripes the next morning. With her reading glasses on, she glares at her computer monitor. "The costs keep adding up while the crew seems to be slowing down."

"How much longer is it supposed to take?"

"At least another three weeks. It'll take us right into the guts of fall now. We'll be lucky to have it completed before the first snowfall."

I pull up the invoice that came in this morning and scroll with my computer mouse, reading through the charges. Every sudden addition frustrates me, and it's not even my money. "Who's the foreman on the job?"

"Rick Thompson. He's also the owner of the company. We've used them several times, though, so I don't think it's all on him. Whichever employees he's swapped out in the past year have been an incredible downgrade."

"Has Wade spoken with him?"

"Oh, sweetie, if I'd let Wade speak with him, we'd have a half-completed stable and no crew left to finish it. Johnny's been taking care of it."

I frown. "He hasn't mentioned anything about this."

She glances at me, smiling reassuringly. "Don't take it personally. I'm sure he simply hasn't wanted to bore you with it. He's been given a lot more responsibility around here this year, and I think he's trying to prove he can handle it all himself."

"Has he?" I blurt. "Has he proved that?"

"This is an important test for him. With how this crew has been . . . *behaving*, I expect him to make a decision soon on what to do."

"I'd help if he asked me to."

"Oh, I'm sure he knows that, my dear. Men can be stubborn creatures, even ones as sweet as Johnny."

I nod, looking away from the computer screen to the window behind it. The original stable is directly across the road from where I sit, and as I stare at it, I feel a tug deep in my chest. My initial thought is that I miss Frost, even after being with her last night, but then I see my cowboy stroll out from inside, and suddenly, it makes sense.

He's so goddamn handsome it should be illegal. I check him out shamelessly, struggling to comprehend how I like seeing a grown man in a cropped shirt and filthy jeans so much. The hard cut of his abs showing beneath the hem of his shirt has my mouth watering, remembering exactly how they feel against my fingertips.

His boots are hidden beneath the denim, but I'd recognize that specific shade of brown anywhere. I burn from my toes to the tips of my ears when I focus on the hat on his head.

"Love looks good on you," Eliza notes.

Unable to look away from Johnny just yet as he lifts an arm to rub at his nape, exposing even more of that chest, I gulp, the lingering soreness between my legs more noticeable than it was when I woke this morning.

Shifting his hand from his nape to his forehead, he twists his torso and squints at the window. *My window.* His grin is dimpled on both cheeks when he spots me staring. I wave, and he blows a kiss back.

His attention shifts when Wade comes riding up beside him on Kip. My cheeks continue to feel warm as he plants his hands on his hips and nods along with whatever Wade's telling him.

"He's going to be looking in the windows for you all day now."

I turn my head, taking in Eliza's subtle smile. "I don't think that would be a bad thing."

"It certainly isn't a hardship to have a man that good-looking watching for you," she agrees, wiggling her brows.

"He is good-looking, right? Sometimes it's hard to think around him because of it."

"The first time I saw Wade, my jaw dropped, and I stared at him in complete silence for two minutes straight. He thought I was mute."

I release a startled laugh. "You're kidding."

"I wish I was. I'd also love to say it never happened again, but that man has made me speechless too many times over the years to keep track of."

"I'm sure you keep his ego from deflating too much."

She winks. "Amongst other things."

The innuendo is obvious. "Okay, none of that."

"None of what?" she asks, feigning innocence.

I roll my lips to hide a smile. "Get back to work, Eliza."

"Yes, boss," she sings.

It's hard to focus on sorting through the expenses from the past two weeks when my eyes keep straining up to the window every five seconds. I'm close to pulling the blinds and locking myself away when I attempt another peek for the millionth time.

Eliza doesn't pick on me for it, but from her little snickers every few minutes, I know she's begun to notice. I swear to God that woman notices everything.

I'm saved from my impending doom when my phone starts to ring. I swipe it up from the desk and answer it without looking at the name, too eager for something to distract me.

"Hey."

"Hi, Aurora," Wanda replies, her voice shocking me.

"Uh, hi."

"Is now an okay time?"

Eliza pretends not to be listening in, and I nearly laugh. "As good as any."

"Alright. Are you free this afternoon? Dad's in town, and he wants to meet with us."

The words make my stomach hurt and my chest feel like it's caving in. I grip the edge of my desk and squeeze, inhaling through my nose.

"Why?" It's a demand disguised as a question.

He shouldn't be here. Not in this town I've grown to love so much. Hasn't he taken enough?

"I don't know. I only got his text a few minutes ago. All he said was that he wanted to talk to the both of us. He mentioned you by name."

"I'm surprised he remembered it at all."

She pauses before asking, "What happened in Toronto?"

"He didn't believe I was who I claimed I was."

"Then why is he here?"

"I don't know."

But as a blazing fury slithers through my veins at the thought of him tearing through this place, I plan on finding out. He has no right to come back to the place everyone's told me he hasn't returned to in a decade. Not now.

It's mine.

Yet as I step inside the Rustic Ridge diner three hours later with my shaking hands hidden in the front pocket of my hoodie, I wonder if it wasn't truly his first.

The business is busier than I've ever seen it, with gawking customers who ignore the plates in front of them and stare at the table where he waits. Sitting alone, he scowls at the white porcelain mug in front of him before hearing my footsteps and glancing up at me.

"Where's Wanda?" I ask, grabbing the back of the chair opposite him. It's the only extra at the table.

"She won't be here for a bit."

"I just spoke with her earlier. I thought we—"

He waves a dismissive hand through the air. "I tweaked the time around a bit. It was you I hoped to speak with, but I didn't have your number."

"You don't have people who would have found that information for you?"

He ignores my question. "Sit, people are staring."

"They were already looking."

He exhales heavily, not hiding his frustration at my reluctance. "Just sit."

I pull the chair out and sit before he asks again. There are too many people watching to tell him off for demanding me like one of his employees.

"Why are you here?" I ask.

"I expected you to be happier to see me. Especially after how we left things."

"You mean when you all but told me to get lost?"

He jerks his chin. "I could have handled that better. I just wasn't expecting to see you."

"Because you didn't know I was alive. And whose fault is that?" I ask, folding my arms over my chest, my muscles so damn tight they burn.

There was a time for me to be kind and considerate, and he wasted it in Toronto.

"If all Pi—your mother, did was send letters, I never saw them. My record label took over all fan mail once I signed my first deal with them."

"Fan mail," I repeat, forcing myself to stay seated instead of storming off.

"That's what it would have appeared to be, Aurora. I wasn't making a dig."

"It doesn't matter if you knew or didn't know. That makes

little difference to me now. I'm thirty years old; the chance to go back and make it right has long passed."

"You're right."

"Wanda's only a year younger than me. How long exactly was it from the time you broke my mother's heart to the time you found someone else? A week? Two? Were you with her at the same time as you were my mother?"

My words hit their mark. He flinches and tugs at the collar of his fancy button-up as if that'll help him breathe easier. It won't, and I hope he chokes on his guilt long enough to feel half the amount of pain my mother did.

"I didn't cheat on your mother. I loved her, and if I had known she was pregnant with you, I wouldn't have left."

My laugh is cold. "Is that supposed to make me feel better? A relationship out of obligation is a one-way ticket to divorce down the road, and I wouldn't have wanted that. My mom found a good man who took us in and raised me without that obligation. He chose us because he wanted us."

"If these are the questions you want to ask me, then what I came to Cherry Peak to offer you is even more important. These aren't answers I want to give here."

"In public, you mean? Where everyone can listen? Or maybe where they can take pictures of us and post them so the world knows about me. That would be terrible for you, wouldn't it?"

I hate the way my voice cracks as I speak, decades' worth of pain and hurt and anger that I hadn't ever felt before now alive and burning through me. But none of those emotions come close to the raging curiosity that still lives inside of me, never calming, even as I remind myself that nothing he could tell me would matter.

It's a lie. It *would* matter. Every single answer would mean something to me. Whether good or bad. I hate that I'm so desperate to learn about him. There has to be something wrong with me to still crave that knowledge. That connection and bond with a man who I don't even know.

He leans forward in his chair, pushing his mug to the side to fold his hands on the table. "Come back to Toronto with me, Aurora. Learn everything you need to there. You can stay with me, and I'll tell you everything about the Roses and my life from the moment I went to Toronto until now."

My phone buzzes in my pocket. I ignore it.

It buzzes again, and I know then who's trying to reach me. I was supposed to have dinner with Johnny tonight, the way we do every night. Just the two of us on my back porch beneath the stars. But I've stood him up, deciding not to tell him about this meeting out of fear he would tell me that I didn't have to come.

I should have gone home and listened to him.

"I'm going to ask Wanda to come as well. I didn't give her the proper attention when she came to see me, and, well, I've had a bit of a wake-up call here with you. We can all get to know each other. You want that, don't you? Surely you don't hate me deeply enough to turn down the chance to get to know me and your sister," he adds, exposing every single one of my soft spots.

"You make it sound as though you're doing me a favour, Riley. I don't want any favours from the man who's supposed to be my father."

His jaw ticks, at which part of my statement, I'm not sure. "I want to know you, as well. You share my DNA."

"I spoke to my mother after I left your place. She told me how you met and about how happy you made her. Did she make you happy too?"

"Your mother was an amazing woman."

"I suppose if I ask why you left her despite that, you'll say I can find out in Toronto."

"She deserved better than me and what I could have given her at the time. That's the answer I'll tell you now, in this place."

I suck in a shaky breath, sweeping my eyes over the busy diner. Dread drips slowly into my belly. "I have to think about it. I'm . . . I'm happy here right now."

"You can come back afterward. Cherry Peak doesn't change regardless of how long you're gone for."

"I don't think that's true," I disagree, looking back at him and wishing he wasn't so hard to read. "I think you're just too hell-bent on hating where you came from to see that it has changed. You just weren't here to witness it."

"Maybe that's something we can uncover together."

My gut tells me to tell him to go fuck himself. His twisted opinion on this place doesn't matter to me, and his past shouldn't either. But my head and heart say the opposite. They tell me to give it a chance, an opportunity to learn what it is I so desperately want to.

"I'll think about it," I repeat.

Because there's someone I need to talk to first.

39

Johnny

I'M PACING RORY'S BACK PORCH WHEN I HEAR HER PULL UP OUT front. She was supposed to be here an hour ago, and while I'm perfectly aware she's found a life here with people outside of me, it isn't like her to leave me without an update on her whereabouts. Especially not when we had plans.

Every potential reason for her absence—the bad and outright terrible—played over and over in my mind until I'd driven myself half-crazy and called Daisy, asking if it was acceptable for me to get in my truck and drive around Cherry Peak in search of her. She said fuck no, so I listened and collapsed on the camping chair that I'm pretty sure I ripped with my ass to wait it out a bit longer.

I only made it ten more minutes before I resumed pacing.

Swinging myself off the edge of the porch, I rein in my frustration. She's here now, and that relief is far more important than anything else.

Her car door slams shut before the beep of her doors locking echoes through the cooling evening air. I'm already halfway around the house by the time she steps onto the curb, her purse nearly dragging on the ground beside her with how slouched her shoulders are.

"Where were you?" I ask before wincing at how aggressive that sounded and correcting myself. "Are you okay? I was worried."

The need to pull her into my arms chomps at me. She's here in front of me, and with how distraught she looks, that has to be enough for now.

"Can we sit? In the backyard?" The heaviness in her voice makes my heart crack.

"Yeah, darlin', of course we can."

I keep my eyes on her, watching closely as she passes me with little more than a brush of her fingers against my chest. With my stomach bunched into a knot, I follow her to the porch. She drops her bag before joining it on the edge, her legs swinging as she runs an antsy hand through her hair.

"You're freakin' me out a bit, sweetheart," I say, sitting beside her.

Our thighs brush, and I press mine right up against hers, needing the small contact to soothe me just a bit. When she doesn't pull away, I take that as a good sign. I can almost hear her mind running as she stares blankly at the tiny wooden shed beneath the crabapple tree across the yard. The ground used to be covered in its apples, but once we brought baskets of them to Eliza, she turned them into jam. I never thought I'd enjoy picking apples off the ground as much as I did then. With Rory, I think I'd enjoy just about everything.

"I'm sorry for ghosting you," she apologizes.

"Don't be sorry. I just want to know what's wrong. Do I need to kick someone's ass?"

There's no sign of humour in her expression. "I should have called you earlier so you weren't wasting your time here waiting for me."

"It's okay, Rory. I was worried, not upset because I was wasting my time. There's no such thing, 'kay?"

She tips her shin and swallows. "Did you eat?"

"No. I was planning on making you something. If I have to

eat another burger from the diner, I might actually turn into one."

"They've started to taste like sawdust."

I laugh softly at the blunt reply. "Come inside with me, and I'll cook you something with substance. I'm not the best, but let me try."

"Not yet. Just . . . Just sit here with me first. I want to talk out here and watch the sun set."

It'll be any minute now. The stars will be out before we know it. "Okay. We'll stay here."

She inhales deeply before speaking. "I was late because I was meeting Lee."

"He's here? Why? What does he want?

"He claims to want to get to know me. And Wanda. Both of us. He'll answer all of my questions."

I choke on an immediate refusal. It isn't my decision whether she agrees or not. But fuck, my gut screams that this is a terrible idea.

"He flew all the way here to tell you that?" I ask stiffly.

"He said he didn't have my number, so he couldn't call."

"Un-fucking-likely."

"I know, but it doesn't matter now. He's here, and I haven't given him an answer."

"Are you going to say no?"

She has to, right? He's a piece of shit who doesn't deserve a minute of her time, let alone as many as it would take to settle her curiosity.

Her pause in answer has my throat constricting. Staring at her, I search her face for anything that'll give away her decision, but she's a steel wall. The sight of her mask after weeks without it is enough to make me want to vomit.

"I don't know if I'm going to say no," she admits, her voice almost too quiet to hear, even in the silence.

"Why not? Did he do something worthy of your forgiveness?"

"No. But he's offering me what I wanted in the first place. The answers he has for me is why I left my life in Calgary and came to Cherry Peak. I'd be an idiot to turn away this chance."

I try to understand where she's coming from, nodding along with her words. She'd be okay here in Cherry Peak, with all of us at her back in case he stepped out of line. I'll tie him to the back leg of a bull and let it take him for a ride through the field if he hurts her.

"Okay, so how long is he planning on staying?"

She doesn't reply right away. Seconds tick by as I wait, my pulse thundering in my ears.

"He isn't staying here. He flies back to Toronto in two days, and he wants me to go with him."

I stop breathing. "Go with him?"

"Yes. Both me and Wanda. We'd stay for a couple of weeks."

With a weak inhale, I turn my head straight forward, unable to keep staring at her. "You want to leave?"

"No. I want to stay. But it isn't that simple. Not for me."

"Why not?" I ask, jolting to my feet. Rejection throttles me, hurt following close behind. Maybe it's selfish of me to be upset, but that doesn't make it easier not to be. "You don't need this guy. Are you really going to leave this place and everyone here for him?"

Are you going to leave me for him?

She twists to stare up at me, the first crack appearing in her armour when she frowns. "I'm not going forever."

"So you can guarantee that once you know everything you need to and have that closure, that you're going to come back for good? You said you came here for answers, so what happens once you have them? Will you leave again?"

She pushes to her feet and takes a step toward me before stopping herself from coming closer. "You have to think about this from my perspective. I just met the other half of my DNA after thirty years of not knowing him. It's not as simple as just accepting he's an asshole and moving on with a fuck you to my curiosity. I can't help but want to know him. He's supposed to be my family."

"Then just tell me you'll leave Toronto after you're finished there and come back to me. If you come back, then I'll wait for you. I'll hate it while you're gone—we both know I'm too goddamn needy when it comes to you to be happy with you gone—but I'll suck it up. If you choose this place and you choose me, then nothing else matters."

She looks away from me. "So if I decide to stay in Toronto, then what?"

I reel backward, a fist lodging itself in my chest. "Stay in Toronto?"

"I grew to love this place. What if I grow to love it there? I don't know if I'll want to live there forever, but maybe I'll want to stay for a few months."

Licking my lips, I shake my head angrily and take a single step toward her. "You're trying to push me away so you can make this decision easier for yourself, but I won't let you. We both know you won't stay in Toronto. You grew to love Cherry Peak, yes. But you falling in love with me had something to do with that. Admit it."

"He's my family, Johnny," she says, her eyes stormy, scared.

"I'm your family!" I shout, my chest huffing. "Eliza and Wade and Anna and Poppy and Bryce are your family. James and Bernice are your family. Your mom is your family. Riley Rose is just a man who was in love with your mother decades ago and who treated you like you were nothing when you went to him. We would never do that to you. I could never toss you away like you were nothing."

I take my hat off and tap it against my thigh while running my fingers through my hair. That air feels hotter than it is, my skin damp. "Blood and DNA aren't everything. Sometimes it isn't enough. You've found another family here full of people who chose to be in your life without obligation. Isn't that worth more?"

She flinches, the remnants of her mask crumbling. The devastation and helplessness that fill her eyes nearly strikes me down at the knees.

"You're right. But I need this. I can't explain why, but I do, and I hate it! I don't understand why I'm feeling like this, but all I know is that there's something inside of me that's unsettled. It's like a piece is missing. It could be Riley or a million other things, but I don't know!"

"I want you to find that piece, Aurora," I tell her, defeat dripping from every word.

I could continue to push her toward the outcome I want, but this has to be her choice. This isn't a decision I can make for her, even if the choice she wants to make is killing me inside. She's my fucking person, but I can't force her to stay with me. I've always known that Aurora was a woman who made her own decisions and followed her own path. I just never thought those two qualities about her would be the ones that hurt me the most.

She blinks, and tears leak from the corners of her eyes before she angrily swipes them away. Sniffling, she stares at my hat, then my boots, anywhere but my face.

"This is why I didn't want to fall in love here."

"Don't do that. You're not allowed to regret us. I sure fuckin' don't. I'd have rather had you for these few weeks than not at all."

"I didn't want—this wasn't my plan. It should be easy to leave. A clean break."

I close the gap between us and hold her cheek, letting my eyes drop at the comfort touching her brings me despite everything. She rubs her cheek against my palm, breathing fast as her eyes finally lock onto mine.

"I love you. Your happiness is the most important thing to me. If this will make you happy, then go. You deserve to have everything you've ever wanted. I'm not going to stop you." Each word carves out a bit more of me, but I force myself to continue. To drop my heart at her feet and offer her everything I can at the risk of her kicking it across her yard. "The one thing I won't give you is a clean break, Rory. You don't get to leave and not come back. So, I'll be here waiting for you. You go, and you learn what you need to, but *when* you come back, it'll be my arms you run into. So take your time, darlin'. Get your answers and your peace because once I get you again, I'm not lettin' you go again. Not ever."

More tears fall down her cheeks, but I'm there wiping them away before she can.

"I can't ask you to wait. If I take too long—"

With a single shake of my head, I stop her. "You're not asking. I'm telling you it's what I'm doing. I've already waited for you for twenty-two years; what are a few more months?"

She tries to drop her head forward to hide her pain, but I keep it right where it is, not letting her pull away from me. Squeezing her eyes shut instead, she bites down on her lip and cries, her chest shaking with the force of it.

"I love you," she declares between sobs.

I tuck her into my body and stroke the back of her head. "I know. I'll keep loving you even while you're gone. There's no other option for me."

"I don't deserve you."

"Yes, you do. We deserve each other."

I've never been surer of anything in my life. And I'll spend every moment I can making sure that one day, she believes it too. Whether she's here beside me or across the country, my heart is in her back pocket.

40

Aurora

I feel hollow. It's a sensation I haven't felt for weeks. The space in my heart that was empty filled so quickly with love that I never had a chance to miss it. But now . . . now it's cold and silent.

My head is lost in thought when Eliza looks up from her rocking chair and spots me lingering at the bottom of the porch stairs. I'm too early to be here for work, and one up-and-down look at my appearance has her beckoning me to her.

"Sit beside me," she says soothingly, placing her yarn and crochet sticks in the basket beside her chair.

I sit beside her in silence. The chair rocks beneath me, and I grip the armrests tight for stability.

"You're here early, my sweets."

"I couldn't sleep."

Even after Johnny insisted on cooking for me despite everything that happened and I went to bed alone with a full belly, I tossed and turned all night. It was my first night alone in weeks, and the sheets still smelled like him. That made it all the worse.

"Does this have anything to do with why we were woken before dawn by Johnny on a tractor spearing bales?"

"He's here already?"

She eyes me curiously. "Were you hoping he wouldn't be?"

"Yes."

Humming, she drapes a hand over my wrist. "Would you like to tell me what's goin' on?"

"I'm leaving tomorrow. Just for a little while. I know I'll be leaving you in a tight spot again after the chance you offered me, so I'll be doing everything I can to work remotely on all the tasks I can do. You won't be abandoned again," I promise, having used some of the long hours this morning to plan out how I'll work in Toronto. "I can do ninety-nine percent of the same work there. But I do understand if you want to replace me with someone else because of this."

"Slow down. Tell me why you're leaving first," she says, rubbing my wrist soothingly.

I'm almost embarrassed to tell her why, and that's all wrong. "Lee's in town. He asked me and Wanda to go back to Toronto with him. It's supposed to be a bonding experience."

"Oh," Eliza says, rolling her lips and blinking in surprise. "That's a sudden development."

"I know."

"And you chose to go? He didn't force you to say yes? Because I have no problem sending the boys after him."

"No, he didn't force me. I want to go. It's a good chance to get what I've been wanting."

"It's certainly a change of heart. Did he explain why that happened?"

"No. I'd assume it's guilt, though."

She nods. "There's nothing like the lingering weight of a heavy conscience to change a man's mind."

"If this is my only chance, then the reasons behind his actions don't matter. I just want closure. I need it."

"And is the only way you can get closure through leaving, Rory? Or is there another way? I don't want you to leave, honey. And that's me being both honest and selfish. I'm too old not to be both."

I wring my hands in my lap and look around the house for any sign of Johnny. If I see him now, I don't trust what I'd do. He can't be anywhere near me right now.

I almost changed my mind once last night, with his hands on my face and his honest declarations swirling around my soul. I'm not strong enough to do it again.

"If there was another way, I wouldn't contemplate this one," I say.

She hums again, rocking her chair. "What is it you want more than anything, Aurora?"

"Right now?"

"No, not just now. What do you want for your future? What is it that you want from life?"

My mind goes blank. Tugging in my brows, I part my lips before closing them again.

"I asked myself that question a million times before I had an answer. But once I had it, it made every decision easier. There will always be hard choices in this life with more than one route to take, and I find that it's important to make sure we don't jump at one before investigating the others," she adds.

"What if I can only see two routes?"

"You came here for answers, Rory. But you got a lot more than you bargained for in the process. I love you like family, and regardless of where your life journey takes you, you will always have a place here with us. That's my promise to you. A love like the one you have here, with not only the Steeles but with Johnny and your girls, can create a beautiful life.

"I can't tell you what to do or which path to take. I understand why you feel like taking the one that leads to Lee, and I respect you for your loyalty. My only advice is to remember that home isn't always a place but a person or a group of people. And family is made from love, support, and respect. If anything, please just remember that. Carry it with you wherever your journey takes you, even if it doesn't lead you back to us."

"I love you too, Eliza," I whisper, feeling that familiar burn climbing up my throat that I've been battling since yesterday. "Thank you."

She gives my wrist a squeeze, her smile soft and warm. "You're welcome. And as far as work, I will not be replacing you. You take whatever you need with you, and once you're back, you can get back to normal."

"Both you and Johnny seem certain I'll be coming back to stay."

"Should we think differently?"

I almost laugh because no, they shouldn't. The decision was made for me the moment I started falling in love with this place and the people here. There's nothing waiting for me back in Calgary. My mom is happy with her husband, and we're not worlds apart with me here and them there.

"No you shouldn't," I say.

"What are you going to do about James and Bernice? Would you like me to tell them?"

I hunch my shoulders and lean over my lap, sighing. "No. I'll do it. They're staying here, right?"

"I'm damn sure Bernice has been watching us from the living room window from the moment you pulled up."

Glancing at the window, I catch the blinds smacking against the glass and stifle a laugh. "You don't mind if I speak with them now?"

"Go ahead. Investigate every route."

I dip my chin at her before standing and leaving her to continue crocheting. The inside of the house smells like cinnamon and bacon, and suddenly, I'm wishing I came earlier to catch breakfast. But then again, maybe it's better I have an empty stomach. Just in case.

Bernice is perched on the edge of one of the two armchairs in the living room, while James stands beside the fireplace with Wade. It's been a few days since I've seen all three of them, but the last time I saw Wade, he didn't look as bothered as he does now.

I don't know if that hard expression is pointed at me or if he just naturally looks like that under normal circumstances. There must be a reason why all the ranch hands always straighten up when he's near. Maybe who I'm seeing now is the Wade Steele the world knows and not the one who melts around his wife. The brutal rancher who has the respect of every single person in Cherry Peak and those hundreds of kilometres outside of it.

Bernice perks up when I step into the room and clasps her hands in her lap. "Aurora! Good morning."

"It's Rory to everyone but Johnny," Wade corrects her gruffly. I didn't know that he had picked up on Johnny's nickname for me or that he realized I loved it. *Darlin'* of all things shouldn't make me as happy as it does. "She prefers Rory, just like I already told you both."

Blushing at the mention of Johnny, I stare at him questioningly. He simply lifts his shoulder. Appreciation flutters in my stomach, a sense of acceptance following.

"Rory," James echoes. "I think I like that even more."

"Did your mother choose that name for you for a certain reason, or did it just call to her?" Bernice asks.

"I've never asked her that."

The corner of her mouth lifts. "Maybe I will, then. If I get the chance one day."

The statement is simple, but it has a much weightier effect than I think she was intending. The insinuation that she's planning on being in my life long enough to see my mom again has me dreading telling them what I need to all that much more.

I look at James and gesture to the second armchair. "Do you want to sit so we can talk?"

He takes a seat quickly, whether he wants to or just doesn't want to risk telling me no. I wouldn't have cared either way.

"What do you want to talk about?"

"I'm gonna head out," Wade announces, stepping my way. Stopping shoulder to shoulder with me, he lowers his voice and meets my stare head-on. "Already told 'em to answer all your questions. So grill 'em, Rory. If you need Eliza or myself, just shout. I'll be wranglin' that man of yours back into shape before he runs over my cattle with a fuckin' tractor."

"Thank you," I blurt, a lump building in my throat.

"Don't thank me. I take care of my family" is all he says before leaving.

My eyes burn as I focus on my grandparents, my next words sounding dead wrong. "I know you came all the way down here to meet me, but I'm leaving tomorrow. Lee asked me and Wanda to go back to Toronto with him."

"He what?" James asks, that soft tone of voice hardening. "Why?"

"Bonding, I guess. You came all this way, so I just wanted to apologize."

Bernice raises a dainty, wrinkled hand to her chest. "You have nothing to apologize for."

I don't believe her, but I push forward anyway. "I had things I still wanted to ask. Is that okay?"

"You leaving changes nothing," Bernice declares.

Seeking confirmation from James, I look his way. He nods quickly. "Sit first. If you pace, I'll start pacing, and I already went for my walk this morning."

"Don't act like your doctor hasn't told you multiple times to take more than one walk a day," his wife chides as I sit on the love seat. Then she tells me, "High blood pressure. Too many bags of ketchup chips in his younger days."

"You can never have too many bags of ketchup chips."

James claps and points at me. "That's exactly it! See, Bernie?"

"Don't tell me you prefer salty to sweet too?" she asks, humour colouring her words.

"Guilty."

"That's what I like to hear. But back to the ketchup chips. What brand do you prefer? And know there's only one right answer." James grins.

I don't hesitate with my answer. "Old Dutch. Hands down."

He claps again, grin spreading wider. "That's right."

"We're not supposed to be fixating on chips, James," Bernice says.

Sobering at her tone, he sucks in his laugh. "Right. Ask your questions, please, Rory."

"Okay. How well did you know my mom?"

Bernice is the one who answers. "Not well enough. We met her a handful of times, but once they left Cherry Peak, Lee didn't like coming back."

"You're the second person to hint at him hating it here. Why didn't he like it?"

"Because here, nobody cares who you are. Sure, there's a shock factor to coming back, like I'm sure he's experiencing walking around town now, but it isn't because of his fame or success. It's because he abandoned this town and his family for a taste of the good life. Cherry Peak wasn't big enough for him. He wanted more, and he burned every relationship he had in this town to get it. The one he had with your mother especially," James explains coolly.

Nothing he's said surprises me. I believe every word. "You truly didn't know my mom was pregnant then."

"No! If we had, we would have been there. She would have been taken care of. You both would have been," Bernice says, voice shaking as she lifts her shirt sleeve to the corner of her eyes. "Thirty years, Eliza said. We lost out on thirty years with you."

"It's not your fault."

"Maybe not. But pain doesn't care who's at fault," she says with that same soft, motherly tone that Eliza has. "You're so beautiful, Rory. You've got Rose eyes. That deep blue that draws attention everywhere you go."

"It was the first thing I noticed when I saw Lee."

"I'm not surprised. They're usually the first thing everyone notices about us," James adds. His eyes are just like mine and his son's.

Bernice releases a breath. "What else do you want to know, sweetheart?"

And so starts a two-hour conversation about anything and everything from what my great-grandparents' names were, what James and Bernice did for work before retiring, to if Lee is their only child.

He is, but Bernice has three sisters, all of whom had three children of their own. That was only the tip of the iceberg. Turns out that I have more cousins and second cousins than most people have members in their entire extended family times three. I lost count after the second set of names.

It's an information dump in the best way. I ingest the information with greedy nods and even more questions. The two of them don't hide anything from me or ignore any part of my curiosity.

I slowly let them in, and by the time we finish, I grow to hate my decision to leave that little bit more.

41

Johnny

My feet hit the ground hard enough for my ankles to hurt when I jump from the tractor. With a slap of my hand, I shut the door and leave it parked between two others. It's been at least six months since I was behind the wheel of a tractor, let alone to do something as time-consuming and boring as moving bales, but it was therapeutic.

I hate how quiet it is around here today, like everyone's made themselves scarce around me. I'm antsy, so full of nervous energy that I feel like an over-shaken bottle of Coke with the lid starting to loosen.

"You need somethin' to do, boy?" Wade shouts, appearing with his hands on his hips in a power stance.

"Please."

"That fence you seem so damn set on? I ordered the materials last week, and they just showed up. Load 'em up and get started."

"Wait, you ordered them? I thought you wanted to talk about it more still."

"Do you want me to return 'em instead?" he grunts.

I rush toward him, my head shaking furiously. "No, sir. I'll load them up as soon as I get back."

"Good. Loren can meet you out there with the welding gear. Do you need anyone else?"

"Thomas is always a good bull distractor. Could send him runnin' around the field with a red flag."

His straight-lined lips tug into a tiny smile. "I don't need a death on my shoulders along with all this fuckin' other work. I'll send him over with the first trailer. Get the bulls tucked up and out of the field before startin' to tear the old fence down. Two in the trailer at a time, and get Zeus out of there first. Take 'em to the empty pasture on the east side."

Zeus is the meanest fucking bull I've ever met, and while he's kept in a paddock all his own, if he sneaks out amongst the others, we'll be breaking up bull fights all day.

"The one with the runoff?"

He jerks his head in a nod. "Take a radio and keep me updated."

"Will do." My chest hums with pride. "Thank you."

"Don't thank me yet. If this doesn't fix the problem, it'll be your ass chasing the bulls down the highway when they break out," he threatens.

"I thought you were positive they wouldn't break out?" I smirk, feeling ballsy with the built-up energy pulsing through me.

"You know, I was plannin' to give you love advice, but now you can continue sufferin'."

I stop smirking. "Hold on, hold on. I want your love advice."

"Yeah, I bet you fuckin' do. All that attitude in you, you're no better than my wife when it comes to convincin' me to watch those damn reality shows with her."

I think he secretly loves them, but I keep that to myself. "Consider it dropped. I don't think I've ever needed advice more than I do now. I'm already going out of my head, and it's been less than twenty-four hours."

"Since what? Somethin' to do with why Aurora's already here and looked like she was fightin' off tears?"

My heart thumps hard. "She's here?"

"She came to talk to Eliza. Last I knew, she was in with her grandparents."

"Oh, right."

"Stop poutin', Johnny. You're workin', and I swear to God I've been dealin' with you boys and your love problems more in the past two years than I have in my entire life." He huffs, glancing around the field. The giant metal-sided shop is up ahead, surrounded by trucks and tractors and every kind of attachment for them known to man. "She's leavin', yeah? Goin' to spend time with her daddy up in Toronto?"

"You're an eavesdropper, Wade," I note.

"Eh, they were chattin' in my house. It's my right to listen. But that doesn't fuckin' matter. Are you plannin' on respectin' her decision to go?"

I frown, trying to figure out why he's asking me such a pointless question. "Yes."

"Then you're as good of a man as I thought you were. Forcin' a woman to stay in this town when she wants to stretch her legs and explore would make you both a coward and a man undeservin' of her. I can't say that I expected you to find a woman this summer or that, if you did, she'd be eight years older than you in both age and life experience, but there's no one I would have chosen that would have been more fitted for you than her.

"She keeps you grounded, your head level instead of in the clouds. I admit I don't know her all that well. Hell, I doubted whether she'd fit here at first, but I plan on changin' that when she comes back. She's just right for you, and I think you do the exact opposite to her that she does to you. You make her feel young and alive. Opposites attract for a reason. This is exactly why."

I swallow the sticky feeling in my throat and say, "You said when she comes back. You really think she will?"

"I'd bet the entire ranch on it."

My eyes bulge. "Fuck. Really?"

He looks at me like I'm a goddamn idiot, and while sometimes I am, now I just feel desperate. Desperate for confirmation that I'm not being a hopeless fool by anticipating her return only to be left fucking crushed months down the road when she's living a new life in Toronto without me.

Slapping a hand on my shoulder, he leans close, a no-bullshit expression on his rugged features. "Yeah, Johnny. She's goin' to come back. I was wrong to think she was goin' to take off on you the way I did, but now, I know it deep in my bones that she's meant to be here. Right now, you just have to let 'er go so she can learn what it is she really needs."

"And that's me?"

"A family. She needs a real family. And you can give her one."

"CRAZY FUCKER!" Thomas shouts, jumping back after he locks the back of the trailer.

Zeus grunts and snorts, and the trailer shakes as he throws himself around it. The three of us stand around rigid and huffing, the past few minutes a lot more than we expected.

Loren takes his hat off and bends at the knees to shake his hair out, sweat flying. "I'm not touching another one of those again. It nearly bit my goddamn hand off."

"Pain in the ass he's such a good breeder," Thomas grumbles. "Wade won't give him up. He actually reminds me of you when we first met, Lo. Fucking everything that breathed your way and taking bites out of anyone who tried to get to know you. But hey, you've softened right up for us, eh?"

"Do you ever get tired of hearing yourself speak?" Lo throws back.

I chuckle. "No, he doesn't."

"Don't even get me started on you, Jonathon," Thomas snaps, a long finger jabbing my chest.

"What the fuck did I do?"

"You took my tractor out this morning without permission."

I roll my eyes. "Your tractor? Be for real."

"Is it true that Rory's leaving with Wanda?" Lo asks, the level of curiosity in his expression making me glare.

"It's Aurora to you, fuck boy."

Thomas holds his hands in front of him before spreading them out in a rainbow shape. "Lo, the emotionally available fuck boy. That's a good one. Has a ring to it."

Loren flips him off but repeats his question for me. "Is it true?"

"Yeah. It's true. They're goin' to Toronto with Lee."

"When?"

Panic flares in his eyes, and I tug my brows together while trying to piece together why. "Tomorrow. What does it matter to you?"

"If you're going to admit to wanting Johnny's woman, Lo, I'm going to have to encourage you not to. I'd have to hand you over to Zeus," Thomas says.

Whatever it was running through Lo's mind clears enough for him to snap back into the conversation long enough to frown. "What? Fuck off with that. I don't want Aurora."

I believe him. "So? What was it, then?"

"Wanda?" Thomas asks, a smirk slowly spreading his lips. "Ah, shit. You're into Wanda? You're fuckin' with us."

Loren reaches out and shoves Thomas in the chest, but the instigator just laughs. "I'm not talking about this with you."

Thomas covers Loren's hands and keeps them on his chest, encouraging him to shove him again, the fucking masochist. "So you admit it, then?"

Loren doesn't answer him. He rips his hands away and starts toward the truck hooked up to Zeus's trailer. I chase after him, leaving Tommy behind to collect himself.

"Hey, don't fuck off yet," I say when he reaches for the

driver's door. He stalls, huffing. "He's just trying to get a rise out of you. Ignore him."

"I know. He's a shithead."

"It's more than Tommy, then, I take it?"

He nods once. "Yeah."

"If you ever want to talk, you find me. Okay?"

"Alright. And for what it's worth, Rory's obsessed with you. You guys will be fine," he says, surprising me.

"Thanks, man."

Opening the door, he hops inside before tipping his chin at me. "Yeah."

"You coming back after dropping Zeus off?"

He's the only one of us who knows how to weld, so we'd be screwed without him once we get the current fence down.

"I'll be back."

I shut the door for him and slap it once before he starts the engine and pulls away. Thomas is waiting when I spin and head back. He looks like a naughty child after being scolded and sent to the corner.

"One of these days, you're going to get your ass beat, you know?" I ask.

"Yeah, yeah. I'll apologize when he gets back."

"If he is interested in Wanda, that's his business unless he makes it ours too."

"You're a giant softy, Johnny," he teases, but it's true, and we both know it.

"Yeah, well, my girl likes it, so I'm pretty content."

"Should I start calling you Mom and Dad now?"

I bust out a laugh, and it feels really damn good.

"Yeah, might as well. We'll save you a seat at our dinner table when she gets back."

Aurora

BRYCE FROWNS at me as I lean forward on the top of my suitcase and try to yank the zipper closed. It hasn't been long enough since the last time I struggled to fit all of my things in a suitcase.

"What's wrong with you?" I ask, staring over my suitcase at her, my brows lifted.

"It's a sign that your suitcase won't close."

"Ice," Poppy warns.

She holds her phone in front of her, Anna's face on the screen as we FaceTime. She's only been gone on tour with Brody for a couple of weeks now, but even already, I've grown to hate FaceTime.

Bryce keeps her eyes on me. "You shouldn't be leaving."

I huff and abandon the zipper, planting my palms on the hard shell of the suitcase instead. "Why not? Because you don't think I should?"

"Yes. But also because you're not going to feel any better after getting to know Lee than you do now. You just think you need to get to know him because of blood obligation, so you've convinced yourself this will somehow make everything better. It won't."

"And you have experience with situations like these? You've suddenly learned about a father you never knew and were given the chance to get to know him the way I have?"

"No. But I do know what it feels like to know both of your parents and still not be important to them. Have you thought about how you'll feel if your father tells you everything you want to know but doesn't want to know anything about you? Are you ready for that pain?"

Anna gasps over the speaker, and Poppy's quick to insert herself between Bryce and me. It's silly. Neither one of us is going to beat the other up. But I appreciate the sentiment either way.

I extend my hand to Bryce, and with a reluctant sigh, she takes it. "It'll fucking suck, Bryce. I'll feel like shit if that happens. But at least then I can move on. I'll know without a doubt that he's a terrible man, so I can stop wasting my time thinking about him. This is the choice I've made, and I need you to act like you support me, even if you really don't."

"He's a piece of shit for how he treated you, and I'd knock his teeth out if you let me," she declares like an angry guard dog.

"I know. I love you for it." I glance at Poppy and then Anna. "I love you all for it. You took me in and showed me true friendship when I didn't know that's what I needed. Thank you."

Bryce yanks on my hand and brings me into a hug. She smells like spiced oranges, and I never thought I'd find comfort in that smell until now. Poppy curls around my back, her cheek on my shoulder and arms covering Bryce's. Tears prick my eyes, and I swallow down a cry, not wanting to ruin the moment.

"I'm going to need you to come back, Rory. It isn't fair I can't join in on this hug," Anna sighs through the phone.

"I'm coming back, and we'll have a thousand more hugs," I promise.

The women around me agree and hug me that bit tighter, as if they're afraid to let me go. Truth is, I'm afraid to let go too.

42

Aurora

Leaving Cherry Peak hurts worse than leaving Calgary ever did.

Every kilometre that ticks by intensifies the gnawing sensation in my gut that feels a lot like homesickness. The kind I used to get when I was young and slept over at a friend's house. I used to spend those nights wishing I had stayed home with my mom and wishing that I had her to tuck me in instead of a stranger I only faintly knew.

It's a sign as obvious as any I've ever known. Even if I was still adamant about not believing in them, I'd have second-guessed this one.

Wanda hasn't spoken much the entire drive. She's busied herself with her phone and the paperback book she brought with her. Usually, I enjoy silence, but not when it's the awkward type. And this? This is awkward.

Is she regretting leaving the way I am?

"Does awkward silence not bother you?" I ask, too nervous to look across the car to see her reaction.

"It does. It *really* does. But I don't know what to say."

"There should be a million things for us to talk about. We just have to find one."

She tucks her phone beneath her thigh and twists to face me as much as she can with her seat belt on. "When's your birthday?"

"May thirteenth. Yours?"

"June seventh."

The closeness of those two months makes me cringe as I check the rear-view mirror and see nothing but dust kicking up behind our tires. Dirt roads are always a pain, but with the constant tinging of rocks jumping around the wheel wells and the inability to see behind you, they drive me nuts.

Tightening my hold on the steering wheel, I glance at the GPS instructions on the dash and ask, "You're a traveller, right? Where's your favourite place you've travelled?"

"Scotland. You?"

"I've never been out of North America."

"What?" she shrieks, causing me to jerk on the wheel in surprise before straightening. "You've never left North America? How is that possible?"

"I don't like planes. The longest flight I've ever been on is five hours."

"We'll have to change that. You can't be thirty and not have experienced another country outside of Canada and America. Trust me, those are the two least impressive places ever."

"Why Scotland?"

She whistles softly. "Why not Scotland? You've got the Highlands, the castles, the wildlife. It's beautiful and scenic and just . . . a breath of fresh air after being trapped in cities like Toronto or Calgary for so long. I'm at peace there. Before I went to Toronto, I spent three months in Edinburgh. I had to force myself to leave."

"It sounds incredible."

"It is."

The GPS tells me to turn in a kilometre, and I carry on with the random and personal questions while starting to brake. "Are you seeing anyone?"

"Like dating?"

"Yeah."

"God no. I haven't been in a relationship in three years. It's hard to date when your dad is famous." She winces, adding, "Boohoo, I know. I just mean finding someone who isn't just interested in getting to know Lee isn't ideal."

"I know what you meant. That hasn't been much of a problem for me, so I can't say I understand, but I can imagine."

"Speaking of dating, you and Johnny, right? He's a nice guy. How is he doing with this?"

"With what? Lee or the fact I'm leaving to go pretty much beg him to love me?" I ask, hearing how bitter and angry I sound and hating it.

"Shit. I guess both?"

"I haven't seen him since I told him I was leaving. Goodbye in person would have been too hard, so we spoke on the phone before I left to get you."

"Can I be frank with you, Rory?" she asks, and my stomach twists with discomfort.

"I'd prefer that."

"Dad . . . he's not the guy you're hoping he is. Yeah, he's our father, but that doesn't excuse his behaviour and the way he treats people. Take it from someone who grew up with him in her life when I say that he's not doing this out of the kindness of his heart. He feels guilty for both of us, and if there's one thing I know about him, it's that he doesn't like feeling bad about anything. Once he gets what he wants from us, we'll be invisible to him again."

My throat grows tight. "Why are you coming with me, then? You shouldn't be giving him the satisfaction of spending time with you if he doesn't deserve it."

"Because I want to get to know you, Rory. This seemed like as good a chance as any. If you're going to Toronto, then so am I."

I don't realize I've pulled over onto the side of the road until a truck whizzes by, spitting rocks at the hood of my car. Once I've shifted into park, I pull my foot off the brake and look at Wanda. She's already watching me softly, patiently.

"I don't want to go," I admit out loud for the first time.

She isn't surprised by that. If anything, she looks relieved.

"I know."

"Should I call him?"

"Lee or Johnny?"

I almost laugh at how obvious I have to be for her to ask me that. "Lee."

She hands me her phone, and I take it with shaky fingers. His contact name isn't dad or father; it's Riley.

The line rings three times before he answers, sounding annoyed. "What is it, Wanda?"

"It's Aurora."

"Oh. Well, what is it? Is there something wrong?"

I bristle at his tone. "I can't go with you. I don't want to leave Cherry Peak. It isn't right."

"Leaving Cherry Peak is always right. Don't go back on your decision now."

"I still want the chance to get to know you."

"So, you are coming, then?"

I shake my head even though he can't see. "Can you stay here for a couple of weeks instead? Even for a few days? Just long enough to talk—"

"No. If that were an option, I would have already offered it. Come to Toronto if you want to talk," he snaps, sounding completely done with this conversation.

"Why?"

"Toronto, Aurora."

Wanda rubs my arm, watching my every reaction. I offer her a weak, appreciative smile.

"No."

He pauses. "No? What do you mean, no?"

"I'm not going to Toronto. Maybe if I knew that this was for both of us and not just for me, then I would. Can you honestly say that you want to get to know me as much as I want to get to know you?"

"Look, Rory, I can't stay."

"It's Aurora to you," I correct sharply. "And can't or won't? Because you're avoiding my questions, and that's answer enough. I want to know you, but I also imagined that you'd want to get to know me as well. Even slightly."

"Don't waste this chance because of ties you've made in Cherry Peak like Wanda and her mother have. Let me show you what life could look like outside of that place."

I swallow the fury climbing up my throat. "I've seen what life is like outside of Cherry Peak, Riley, and it pales in comparison. Do you even want to get to know me, or do you just want to be able to know you took me out of the one place you seem to feel is unworthy of Roses?"

"If you make memories in that town, they'll only hurt you in a few years. You'll walk down the street and hate every storefront and set of porch steps. Trust me, Aurora, you'll want to leave and not come back."

Suddenly, it all makes sense. Hurt shackles me before contempt replaces it. A throttling anger that tints my vision.

"This is about my mom, isn't it? Maybe you did hate Cherry Peak because it wasn't good enough for you, but now you're too scared to stay because it reminds you of her. The woman you lost because your desire to be adored by others became more important than her. And now? Now you think you owe it to her to spend some pitiful, allocated time with her daughter as if that will earn you forgiveness."

I laugh humourlessly, the sound cold in the car. "You won't get it. There's a reason my mom never mentioned you once in the past three decades. You're nothing more than a ghost of her past. I'm glad you turned out to be the man everyone else told me you were because now I can move on. Thank God I realized before stepping onto that plane."

Wanda watches me with tears in her eyes, smiling proudly at me as she nods. I exhale a breath heavier than I've ever released, returning the smile.

"Goodbye, Lee. You'll be leaving Cherry Peak alone."

"Put Wanda on the phone," he demands, but I pull the phone from my ear and end the call without bothering to tell him no.

Wanda collects both my hands in hers and holds them tight. I squeeze her fingers, letting this moment sink in. Not just my final words with Lee but the sisterly support and love that swirls between Wanda and me. It's a feeling I've never experienced and one I didn't think I'd ever get to. I could have used it a thousand times growing up, but I don't want to live in the past anymore.

Right now, I have everything I could ever want.

Well, almost.

After leaving Wanda at the house she keeps in town, I head straight for Johnny's place. My gut tells me he's there, and I refuse to ignore that instinct again the way I did with Lee.

I struggle to find the proper road to take to his house, especially because I stayed with Wanda longer than I anticipated, and now it's dark out. I can't see for shit when I'm driving at night. I'm so concentrated on not hitting a deer or coyote that I nearly miss the road I remember riding down on Frost's back.

Slamming on the brakes, I press a hand to my clammy forehead and turn onto the twinkle-lit road. It's as pretty as I remember. Something out of a fairy tale.

I'm positive that was the reasoning behind why he strung them.

I bring my car to a jerking stop in the middle of the road when I see him standing in front of the house, watching me. My breath stalls in my throat as I take him in. The purity in his lazy grin and wonder in his eyes.

He's got his hair hidden beneath a backward cap tonight and

another one of those damn cropped shirts on with his usual jeans and boots. I've never seen him without his boots outside, and I don't want to.

I'm out of my car in a blink, the door left open in my rush to get to him. He stands patiently and waits for me, his hands patting at his thighs.

"You're back," he whispers when I get close enough to hear him.

I fly into his chest, my face buried in his throat and arms around his neck. He tugs me the rest of the way against him, hips to hips, toes to toes.

"I'm sorry," I cry, slickening his throat with tears. He shooshes me, but it's no use.

Jerking back, I meet his eyes and blink to try and clear my vision. The strong lines of his face slowly become visible, and I lift a hand to trace his jaw.

"I don't want to find another family. *You* are my family. Everyone in this town is. You were right about everything. I was desperate to get to know Lee out of some fucked-up sense of blood loyalty, but that's gone. Leaving to get to know him was not worth the risk of losing what I have here. The family I've found in Cherry Peak is the best one I could have ever asked for.

"I'm sorry that I made you feel unimportant to me or that I wasn't head over heels in love with you. I was a fool, and I'm begging you to forgive me because I don't know what I'll do without you. You're engrained in every molecule of my being, and I—"

He shuts me up by lowering his head and kissing me. It's gentle, a soft brush of our mouths, but it doesn't matter. He steals another piece of my soul with it, anyway.

I sigh into his mouth and thread my fingers through the hair at his nape, loving how long it is now as it curls around my knuckle.

"There's nothing to forgive," he murmurs, gliding his nose up the length of mine. "I will never be the man who makes you choose. But I will be the one that helps you learn what it is you need or waits while you figure it out on your own. I love you, and I'm just happy you're here. You chose me this time."

"I'll choose you every time," I promise.

"I like the sound of that."

Pulse thumping at a natural pace now, I tip my head back and push onto my toes to kiss him. His large palms frame my face as he meets my enthusiasm with a passion that makes my toes curl. I shiver, inhaling a lungful of his scent.

The addition of sawdust to his regular smell makes my brows scrunch as I look at him curiously.

"Why do you smell like sawdust?"

With a smirk, he tucks my hair behind my ears and then turns me to the right. In my rush to get to him, I completely bypassed the wooden lawn chair and long table with a giant saw built in standing beside it on the grass.

The chair is a light brown colour with a high back that grows shorter on either side as it gets further to the edge and thick armrests that round at the ends. I take a slow step toward it, my eyes focused on the words burned into the first arm before swinging my head to the second.

Once upon a time . . .

I wished upon a star . . .

"I wanted you to have something of your own for when you got back," he says softly, stepping up behind me. "You're renting that damn haunted house, and I was plannin' on continuing to fix it up just like I promised I would. The owners don't deserve all the work we've done to it, but I like to think it'll be yours for however long you want it to be. So, if that means I need to work on it every damn night for the rest of my life until I believe it's good enough for you, then that's what I'm going to do. At least now, you can sit and watch me work on a real chair."

Reaching down, I trail my fingers over the burned words. He joins me, his touch steady as his palm covers the back of my hand. Lips press against my cheek, holding there.

"If I could, I'd go back and change all of my wishes," I say, my voice hardly more than a puff of air. "Maybe we'd have met earlier."

He removes his lips and tucks a finger beneath my chin before turning it until I face him, our eyes clashing, emotions bared. "I think everything happened exactly the way it was supposed to. Couldn't have asked for anything more than what I have right now."

Flicking his eyes upward, he laughs in disbelief and snags my waist. I follow his stare and gasp as a star shoots across the dark sky.

"I haven't seen one in years."

"Take the wish, Rory."

I stare up at the star-flecked sky and shake my head. I've never been as happy and content as I am in this moment. As at peace.

"Let someone else make a wish. I have everything I need right here."

She just shrugs, unbothered. "It won't be happening. I don't get jealous."

Poppy bursts into laughter, the latest gulp of her cocktail spilling out from between her lips. Garrison's there with a napkin, patting her lips dry in the blink of an eye.

Aurora drops a hand to my thigh, her fingers spread wide before she strokes her thumb over the denim and looks at Bryce. "Everyone gets jealous."

"Not me."

"I'd love to test that theory," Poppy says, recovered from her laughter.

Bryce brushes her off. "I wouldn't hold my breath."

"So, no to the male strippers for the bachelorette party?" Anna asks, grinning.

Her fiancé—shit, that's new—palms the back of her head. "Anythin' else, Buttercup. Choose anythin' else. I'm beggin'."

"You guys are so lame, but fine. I'd claw someone's eyes out if they tried stripping in front of Garrison, so I guess it's fair," Poppy says, glancing over at her boyfriend with a look that has me immediately looking away, feeling like I'm interrupting.

It's always like that between them. I'm happy for them, especially now knowing how it feels to be in love with someone who turns your entire world upside right.

Those two will be the next to get engaged, and I'm hoping Rory and I will follow. It's only been two months, but I've never been surer of anything in my life than I am about her. We're not rushing, though, and I like that. I'm loving getting to know every single little thing about her as we spend every day together.

She's found a life here, and I'm content giving her all the time she needs to live it to the fullest before taking that next step.

"Yeah, I would have to agree. It's hard enough watching Brody get pawed at when he's onstage, and those women have their clothes on," Anna says.

Brody's grin grows at her statement. "I've only got eyes for you, Buttercup."

"Yeah, you better."

"Or what?"

Bryce makes a gagging noise in her throat before starting to shove the two of them out of the booth. "I'm never sitting here again if you can't keep it in your fucking pants. Ew. Let me out."

Brody laughs and steps out of the booth before helping Anna. Bryce scurries along the bench and jumps down before beelining it for the bar. We watch her go with knowing smiles while Brody and Anna stay standing beside the table.

"Anyone up for dancing?" Anna asks us.

"Yes, please!" Poppy's eyes light up at the mention of dancing, and it's only a second before she's tugging Garrison out of his chair.

He doesn't argue with her, instead taking her hand and leading her onto the dance floor. Although he's still stiff and hard-shelled to most, the guy's so different from how he was when he showed up here the first time.

"Do you want to dance?" Rory asks once we're alone, the only two at the table.

"Fuck yeah, I do."

I help her up and immediately drape my arm over her shoulders before leading us away from the table to where everyone else has gathered. Both couples are smiling and spinning, but the moment Rory moves from beneath my arm to flat against my chest, I don't give them another thought.

"I'd dance with you anywhere," I say, holding her around the waist while taking her hand and starting to lead her in a simple two-step.

"Even between tables again?"

"I think that'll always be my favourite spot for dancing."

She holds my gaze, her eyes soft and light. "I prefer where we are right now."

"Why?"

Her smile is timid but oh so fucking happy. I know I look the exact same because I feel it.

"Because here, everyone knows you're mine. And I've never wanted to make a statement so publicly in my entire life."

The only thing I can think to do is kiss her, creating another statement that no number of words could beat. One of many, many to come in our life together.

EXTENDED EPILOGUE

Aurora

HALLOWEEN

With a final tug at my thigh holster, I glance at my reflection in the mirror and grin at my costume. It took some online shopping to collect all the pieces necessary, but with the grey shorts, tight white tank top, and holsters galore, I've pulled off Lara Croft pretty well. The push-up bra I'm wearing has my boobs nearly beneath my chin, and I cup them for a second to test the hold before nodding in approval.

"I wish you didn't make us get ready in different rooms, because this? This is a damn good fuckin' costume," Johnny boasts as he comes into the bedroom.

I whip my head to look at him, and he freezes, brashly checking me out. He insisted we dress as Lara Croft and Indiana Jones this year, and I agreed instantly. Now, I'm glad I did.

He grins lazily at me, and it only intensifies the attraction sparking low in my belly. His long-sleeve button-down has been torn open to expose his entire chest, and he's ripped the one arm, leaving his bicep bare, farmer's tan obvious. I've never seen him in a pair of khaki pants before, but I think I have a fetish for it.

Facing him, I take another inspection of his outfit. "The ripped shirt was a good touch. You look ridiculously good."

"Only the best for my baby."

"We need to go," I say, resting my hand on his bare arm. "Anna and Brody are back."

He hums, tucking my hair behind my ears. "They are. And all of my siblings are back in town."

"And Eliza's been baking all week in preparation."

I still love going into work every day with her, and even during this week, where her attention has been spread through a thousand different things, she's been the most helpful person ever. She still refuses to take more time off, but it works for us. I've grown to think of her as the grandmother I never had, and between her and Bernice, I've been showered with the kind of love that can only come from a grandparent.

My mom has come down to meet both of them, and while there were a lot of tears and apologies, there's a sense of peace between everyone that can't be measured. It's overwhelming in the best way, and I'm glad my mom is experiencing this now, even if it is a few decades overdue.

"She's somehow kept it hidden from all of us. Tommy's been sniffing around like a hound," Johnny jokes.

"We should go before he finds it and eats it all without us."

Twenty minutes later, we're walking through the fake spiderwebs hanging from the doorframe and stepping inside the ranch house. It's loud already, with the soundtrack to *Ghostbusters* playing over the chatter.

I choke on a laugh at the sight of Poppy and Garrison dressed in matching *Star Wars* costumes. Poppy looks like a goddess in her Princess Leia outfit, but her boyfriend scowls at everyone in his head-to-toe Darth Vader costume. With the helmet gripped in his hand instead of on his head, he can't even hide from everyone's ogling. Poor guy.

Bryce is dressed like a devil, with her legs showing in tight red shorts and lower stomach exposed beneath her tiny matching red top. She looks hot, and I'm not the only one who thinks so. Flipping off Thomas when he waggles his brows at her, she downs whatever's in her plastic cup before staring at someone across the room. At Daisy and her angel costume.

My eyes bulge as I take in the obvious moment between them. I've never seen them in the same vicinity like this, but from the heat in Bryce's stare as she focuses on Johnny's twin, I can imagine why. Bryce gives herself away so easily, her façade of indifference non-existent.

Did she know Daisy was going to dress like an angel? Considering I thought Bryce was being a *Ghostbuster* again...

"Eliza and Wade throw quite the rager," I say in an attempt to keep Johnny from noticing the way Daisy glances back at Bryce, something secret passing between them.

"The birthday boy!" Eliza calls, and we both turn in the direction of her voice.

Incredible timing. I blow out a slow breath.

She's wearing a long, flowy dress and has her hair tied in an elegant updo that I'd bet Anna styled for her. "I hope you forgive me for not dressing up. I've run out of ideas at my age."

"You don't need a costume. You're beautiful just like this," Johnny tells her, hugging her tight. "Thank you for tonight."

She sniffles into his chest as Wade appears beside her, eyes sharpening when he hears the sound. He lifts a brow at me, and I nod to show everything's okay.

"No costume for you either?" I ask him.

"I don't remember the last time I wore a costume."

"Oh, I'd say four years ago," Eliza says, stepping into her husband's chest and staring up into his heavy gaze. "You were the scarecrow, and I was Dorothy from *Wizard Of Oz*."

"I don't remember this," Johnny says, sounding offended to have missed the chance.

Eliza pats Wade's chest. "That's because I couldn't get him out of the house with the costume on."

"Alright, that's enough walkin' down memory lane, woman," he grunts.

I stifle my laugh with the back of my hand as he tugs her away from us. He glances over his shoulder and wishes Johnny a quick happy birthday before they're leaving the room.

"Is it weird to consider them cute? Wade'd have my balls for considering him cute, but damn. Only Eliza would be able to get that man into a costume," Johnny says.

I wink. "I'll keep your secret. We don't want him to demote you."

Johnny doesn't have any actual title for Wade to demote, but after the stable construction was finished and marked as a success due to his handling of the crew, Wade's been piling more and more responsibility onto him. Nothing too heavy for him to handle, but just enough to make it obvious that my man's really important to the smooth running of this place.

One day, I could see him and Wade speaking about even more responsibility, maybe the drastic kind that would have Johnny taking over for him once the time comes.

There's no one that would do as good of a job as him if that day did come. I know that for a fact.

Taking his hand in mine, I lace our fingers and step in front of him. Like it would pain him to look away from me for even a second, his eyes follow me, the corner of his mouth tipping up.

"Have I told you lately how proud I am of you?" I ask softly.

"Yeah, but I'm always up to hear you say it again."

"I'm proud of you, Johnny. You're the best man I've ever known."

He cups my cheek, bringing his head down to kiss me just once. It's enough to make my toes curl and heart rate jump.

"It's you and me forever, darlin', my wish come true."

"Forever," I whisper.

All of the chasing I've done led me here. To him and a family —*a home* that I never knew was out there waiting for me.

THE END

Thank you for reading Chasing Home! If you enjoyed it, please leave a review on Amazon and Goodreads.

The fourth book in the Cherry Peak series is coming next with Bryce and Daisy. Get ready for pining and sapphic grumpyxsunshine deliciousness.

While you're waiting for more of these characters, jump into my backlist!

Cherry Peak:

Strung Along — Anna and Brody (Text pals, annoyance to lovers romance)
Catching Sparks — Poppy and Garrison (Friends with benefits, one night stand billionaire romance)

Want to learn a bit more about Garrison before he met Poppy? Or meet Anna before she came to Cherry Peak? Jump into my Greatest Love series or start from the beginning in Cherry Peak!

The Greatest Love series:

His Greatest Mistake – Maddox and Braxton (Hockey romance)
Her Greatest Adventure – Adalyn and Cooper (Brothers bff, age gap romance)
His Greatest Muse – Noah and Tinsley (Rockstar x boxer romance)
Book 4 — Releasing Sept/Oct 2024

To be kept up to date on all my releases, check out my website! www.hannahcowanauthor.com

And subscribe to my newsletter!

And to my readers, thank you for everything.

About The Author

Hannah is a twenty-something-year-old indie author from Canada. Obsessed with swoon-worthy romance, she decided to take a leap and try her hand at creating stories that will have you fanning your face and giggling in the most embarrassing way possible. Hopefully, that's exactly what her stories have done!

Hannah loves to hear from her readers, and can be reached on any of her social media accounts.

Facebook Group : Hannah's Hotties
Website : www.hannahcowanauthor.com

Printed in Great Britain
by Amazon

45324280R00219